PHENOMENA

A Neuroscience Thriller

Douglas Phillips

Jim —
Here's my latest. It's
a lot of fun. Hope you
enjoy it too.

Love, Doug

For my ancestors who came before
and my descendants yet to come

CONTENTS

VOICES 1

DREAMS 9

PÂTÉ NÉVROSÉ 19

CORRELATES 29

TROUBLED 37

DISTURBED 39

GENIUS 45

FORMULA 59

SCHIZOPHRENIC 67

VISIONS 77

INACCURACIES 93

UNIVERSITY 107

LEVEL TWO 109

PRIME ARC 121

RECOVERY 131

TRIANGLES 143

CIRCLES 153

ALIEN 163

FUGITIVES 171

CLEARWATER 181

CONSCIOUSNESS 191

UNEXPLORED 203

LEVEL THREE 213

IMPLANT 225

PASSAGEWAYS 237

QUESTIONING...247

EDUCATION 253

EGRESS...257

SANCTUARY 265

BREAK-IN...275

MISSING 283

FOUND..291

LOST...299

MEMORY..307

PAIN 317

TREMORS...327

TENDRILS 335

DIALOGUE..345

AMALGAMATION 355

HUMANITY 369

EPILOGUE 377

AFTERWORD..383

ACKNOWLEDGMENTS 389

ABOUT THE AUTHOR 391

CHAPTER ONE

VOICES

THE SPRAWLING FACTORY floor was finally still. Lights were dimmed and employees halfway home – except for one. In an office overlooking the bottling plant, Orlando Kwon hunched over a computer keyboard. He studied the screen and concentrated as best he could. A heater on the fritz in unit number three. The task itself didn't matter, but the mental focus helped. He'd do anything to keep the voices in his head at bay.

His efforts were probably futile; the voices would return. They had last night on the drive home. It had frightened him so much he'd almost missed an upcoming stoplight, screeching to a halt within inches of the car in front. He didn't want a repeat of that heart-pounding moment. Working late could tip the scales in his favor. The voices might respect his dedication.

An overhead fluorescent lamp flickered, casting animated shadows across Orlando's desk, bringing a coffee cup and a set of keys to life in a spooky dance of ordinarily inert objects. His fingers hovered over computer keys, unsure. Something about a broken heating element, but he'd lost his train of thought, interrupted once more.

By what?

He hadn't been able to fully explain it to the doctors. A feeling inside his head. Not of this world. Like an alien beast, it seemed crouched, coiled, ready to leap out when he least expected it. The diagnosis was unambiguous, schizophrenia early stage with auditory hallucinations. In most patients, visual hallucinations usually followed.

It was true, he'd begun to see things at the periphery of his vision. Green plants, but indistinct. The odd effect would last for a minute or two, then go away. Maybe the vision thing was exactly as the doctors had said, a hallucination of some kind. A trick of the eye. But the ticking, buzzing voices were real, even if he had no idea what they were saying.

The medications they'd given him just made him tired and caused his face to twitch in odd ways. A wiggling tongue or an uncontrolled lip tic. Tardive dyskinesia, they'd called it. He didn't like the facial spasms and stopped taking the pills. They didn't help anyway, the ghostly voices remained.

As the effect of the drugs faded, he'd found himself contemplating weird things. Triangles and circles, formulas, and complicated numbers. He'd never been good at math in school. The geometry and the numbers that flowed through his head felt unnatural, like thoughts that belonged to someone else. Somebody smarter.

Orlando closed the lid on his computer. Teena would be making dinner by now or wrestling the kids into their highchairs. He didn't want to disappoint her, he'd done too much of that already.

Go home. Explain it to her once more. Make her understand.

Swiveling to a small statue of Buddha perched on a bookcase, he pressed both hands together and bowed his head three times. It was a ritual more than anything, an almost forgotten part of his Korean American heritage passed down from grandparents who had immigrated to America decades ago.

He snatched the keys from his desk and hurried through the office door. Rows of overhead lights began to switch off, transitioning the once busy factory into a shadowy crypt.

Teena wasn't taking any of this very well. Orlando had always been a joker, weaving elaborate, almost-believable stories with a perfectly straight face until the target of his ruse finally succumbed, then he'd burst into uncontrolled laughter. Some people played along, some didn't. Teena did when they first met but not anymore. She was tired of the game, she'd told him, faking mental illness wasn't funny. The official diagnosis hadn't helped. Sure, the doctors had convinced Teena he wasn't faking it, but how was a schizophrenic husband any better than a bad joke? She'd cried herself to sleep that night.

Orlando hurried down a metal stairway to the factory floor. Massive fabrication machines that only an hour before had been churning out plastic bottles by the thousands, now stood idle. Creaking metal echoed eerily across the empty space.

He slipped between two of the giant machines toward an exit on the far side. A band of outlaw mice collecting scraps that had fallen from lunch pails scattered to their hiding places.

A sound stopped him cold. A repetitive clicking sound, like a thumb running along the teeth of a comb.

Tick-tick-tick. Scritch. Zhee-orzh tick-tick.

The pitch varied in a complicated way, almost as if the comb were trying to sing its clicks. It wasn't the mice, the voices were back.

Orlando's head twisted left and right, his eyes wide. A chill ran down his neck. The ratcheting sound continued, louder and with alternating highs and lows in frequency. The doctors had assured him it was all in his head, but it seemed to come from outside, as real as any sound.

His heart raced. Was it a vibration coming from one of the machines not completely shut down? An overhead fan? He could try to assign a sensible explanation, but it wouldn't matter. He already knew the sound wasn't coming from an unattended machine. It was a voice – and not a human voice – but it *was* a voice. How he'd come to this revelation wasn't clear, but it was a fact known as confidently as his home address or his wife's name.

Someone, or something, was speaking to him.

Orlando sprinted the rest of the way to the exit, crashed through the door, and ran outside across a darkened parking lot. He jumped into a Toyota, the last remaining car in the lot, slammed and locked the door.

Zzrrit. Zhee. Tick-tick-tick.

Fumbling to get the car in gear, he punched the accelerator to the floor and sped off. The noise of the engine helped to mask the sounds, but the car only made him feel more vulnerable. Home would be safer, the voices had never found him there. Maybe it was Teena's presence that warded them off.

She'd found an alternative treatment she wanted him to try. Not just endless therapy or prescription drugs, but a research facility that specialized in mental disorders. He'd been hesitant. He would have to leave his home in Los Angeles for a week, maybe more. The thought of separating from Teena even for a day while the voices lurked nearby panicked him, but there would be consequences to his marriage if he did nothing.

Teena's right. Do it for her.

Now late evening, the freeway was mostly clear. The ticking sounds were fainter but still nearby, as if hovering over his speeding car. Following him.

A scratching sound, like a zipper, or... Orlando tried to remember the name of the percussion instrument that Caribbean bands sometimes played. He couldn't quite recall it but kept searching his mind anyway. Focusing on something else kept the voices away.

Exiting the freeway, he rounded a corner into his neighborhood. In the distance, a streetlight cast a white-yellow cone toward the pavement. Nearly home. Teena would hold him in her arms. She'd listen. She'd help.

In an instant, the street view vanished, replaced by a green, leafy wall of tropical plants directly in his path. He hit the brakes and screeched to a halt. Orlando stared, mouth agape, through the car's windshield at lush foliage, vines, and oversized leaves. The street had become a jungle.

Trembling hands groped to open the car door. Orlando slipped from his seat and took a few halting steps forward. The astonishing scene had come from nowhere, and he tried not to blink lest it change once more. The thick forest surrounded him in every direction, enveloping the car and obliterating the suburban street that had existed only seconds before. If any houses were still out there, he'd never find them through the dense foliage.

With nerves tingling, he reached one hand toward broad-leafed plants and twisted vines. His fingers brushed through them, but he felt nothing. A blur flashed at the corner of his eye – something scurrying along one vine. Orlando jumped back, his heart pounding. A strange animal like a large bug but with crab-like pincers stared back. The thing made a chirping sound then disappeared under an enormous fern.

"Shit!" He took a step back. His breaths came strong and fast. Was the crab bug somehow connected to the voices? He paused and listened. Except for the sound of slowly dripping water in some distant pool, the jungle was quiet. The bug was gone.

He looked back to his car, the door still open, the wheels still on pavement. "How the hell?" In a single blink, the jungle disappeared, replaced by a street lined with parked cars, a sidewalk, lawns, houses, and a streetlight in the distance. Normality, suddenly and inexplicably, had returned.

Shaking his head, Orlando stumbled backward and slumped into the car seat. He ran an unsteady hand through his dark hair and pinched lips together as tears filled his eyes. He pounded a fist on the steering wheel. "Fuck this shit!"

He stomped on the accelerator and two minutes later, the car screeched into his driveway. A button click revealed an empty two-car garage. He raced through the entryway into a darkened kitchen, where he flipped on a light switch.

"Teena!" he yelled. "Honey, I need you!"

The house was quiet. No toddlers squealing that daddy was home, no pot of boiling water on the stove ready for a fistful of pasta. No wife.

He pleaded, "Teena?"

The hallway to their bedroom was dark too. The closet door stood open, many of Teena's hanging clothes gone. Orlando swallowed hard against the lump building in his throat. His eyes darted around the bedroom, panic rising in his voice. "Teena!"

Logic finally kicked in, and he pulled his mobile from a pocket. A message icon blinked. He touched, and a video popped up, Teena standing alone, distraught. Tears in her eyes. Her voice quavered and she wiped her cheek. "I found your pills in the trash. If you're not going to try... Orlando, I can't do this anymore. I don't have the strength. You need more help than I can give you."

Tears welled up in Orlando's eyes. His throat tightened further. A goodbye message. His life crumbled as the video played.

"I'll be at my parents' house for a while. They'll help with the kids and maybe I can get some rest." She looked straight into the camera and shook a finger, her voice stern even as the tears flowed. "You'd better not be joking about this crap."

She took a deep breath, her watery eyes still lovely. "Sorry, I didn't mean that. It's just that... look... the docs are trying. You've got to listen to them, okay? Or maybe try that other place, the research center up in Seattle. I don't care where you go but please Orlando, get help and stick with it."

She lowered her head and the video shut off. Orlando dropped to his knees. The phone slipped from his hand and clattered across the wood floor.

Alone. His body shuddered as it tried to draw in a breath. Alone with the voices. They were coming. He could feel them lingering around the edges of his consciousness. They'd surely invade his home now that Teena had left. A swarm of crab bugs might come too.

Orlando Kwon lifted trembling hands, covered his face, and wept.

CHAPTER TWO

DREAMS

AMELIA CHARRON STUDIED the middle-aged man as he wandered down a never-ending hallway in search of something he'd probably never find. Dreams were like that. Vague. Unstructured. Capricious without notice. From her godlike perch inside another person's head, Amelia had observed hundreds of dreams over the years. She was getting surprisingly good at manipulating them too.

This dream was like most. An infinite corridor stretched impossibly into the distance with side passages that disappeared into darkness. Ben was probably searching for a bathroom, routine stuff for a man in his fifties.

Amelia began to think she might need to shake this story up when a curvy woman dressed in a compression bodysuit stepped in from nowhere. Glamorous, with maroon eye shadow that sparkled as if electric, her jet-black hair spiked on one side. A peek-a-boo gap in the skin-tight fabric was strategically positioned over ample cleavage. He'd done a good job imagining her.

"Log entry," Amelia whispered, almost inaudibly but sufficient for the system command. "Player encountered. Woman, 30's, visually suggestive."

Amelia's barely voiced words appeared as text in a heads-up overlay that hovered nearby. At the top of the overlay was the patient's name, Benjamin Lawrence, along with his vital signs. No need to open her eyes to see it. The overlay – and the dream itself – were transmitted directly into her brain.

She didn't recognize the exotic player who'd barged into Ben's dream. It was no one famous, and probably not any specific person from Ben's real life. Most people conjured dreammates from some combination of acquaintances. Men with early onset Alzheimer's were no different.

Amelia waited and watched. Unlike the scientific pioneers of the past who analyzed sketchy remains of dreams recited second-hand after the patient's consciousness had invaded, she had the advantage of direct observation in real time. The technology was groundbreaking, unobtrusive for the patient, and a rich experience for the clinician. But it took more than technology to reshape a dream into therapy. It required an experienced dream guide. Amelia was second to none.

The figure of Ben's invented woman was, as yet, incomplete. The curving waistline ended at the hand on her hip. Her head was thrown back in laughter, but the inside of her mouth was a blur. It took a few seconds for the details to materialize, though the delay may have been in the brain to brain transmission, not in the patient's ability to imagine.

"Ask her for a name," Amelia said with her real-world voice. The patient, sleeping only a few feet away, would hear it too. Everyone did, though some didn't remember upon waking and others became agitated by the intrusion onto their private stage. ALDs – assisted lucid dreams – were never predictable.

Ben's muffled voice asked for the woman's name. It sounded like he was speaking from behind a mask, but the words were clear enough.

"Sadie," the dream woman answered. She flashed long lashes over iridescent eyes and ran a finger along the inside curve of one breast. "You, uh… interested?"

He didn't answer right away. His gaze turned down the hallway, back to Sadie, then up to the ceiling where colorful pinpoints of light sparkled and popped like miniature fireworks. He fingered a gun holstered under his suit jacket that hadn't been there moments before.

Signs of a wandering mind.

He was either pondering Sadie's obvious charms, or this story was turning into a spy thriller. Either way, Amelia would need a useful path forward. It would help if Ben had a goal.

"Ask her if she knows the way to the casino," Amelia said. Spy thrillers always had a casino.

Ben said nothing, but in most dreams, telepathy works just as well. Sadie hooked her hand on his arm and pointed down the hallway. Apparently, she was coming along for whatever adventure lay ahead. Nothing wrong with that, dream players were generally cooperative. After all, they were creations of the patient's mind. By leveraging knowledge of Ben's personality, Amelia could steer Sadie's actions, or those of most other characters in this mental performance.

Human characters were the easiest to manipulate. Then animals, particularly if they were talking animals. Non-living entities were somewhat harder. Violent tea kettles. Belligerent rockslides coming out of nowhere. A garden hose that might turn on the patient and sprout viper-like fangs. Typical dream stuff, but these phantoms didn't take direction well.

No matter. Amelia had a few tricks in reserve just in case. With Ben Lawrence, she probably wouldn't need them. Early Alzheimer's patients tended to focus on the mundane, not the fantastic. Inanimate objects generally started dead and stayed dead. Nothing to worry about with Ben.

Of course, he is carrying a gun.

She'd need to watch that carefully. While Ben's dream gun could only fire dream bullets, events that followed could veer into unmanaged – and uncontrollable – psych space. It had happened before, with trauma for both the patient and Amelia. Regaining control had required a level two insertion, a far deeper integration of minds. The results were not something Amelia wanted to experience again. For hours afterward, she'd curled up in a corner of the sleep lab, begging for the involuntary shaking to stop.

Even the far simpler level one insertion could get chaotic. For all she knew, Ben's handgun might morph into a rocket launcher. Still, Amelia would take an Alzheimer's patient any day over some of the more tragic mental illnesses. Victims of depression. Ugh. Dreams so heartbreaking, they could make you cry. Bipolar, wildly creative with lots of color, but it might get ugly when you least expected it.

Schizophrenics were the worst, and Amelia had seen a few. Hallucinogenic nightmares that could end up as unqualified terror fests. Self-inflicted wounds. Reaching inside their body to gruesomely rip out one organ or another. One patient had a knack for crushing himself under heavy objects, complete with every bit of gore that might be imagined from a ten-ton stone. Luckily, it had been a while since Amelia had jumped inside such a severely scrambled brain.

Arm in arm, Ben and Sadie ambled further down the infinite hallway. "Do you play blackjack?" he asked her without any prompting from Amelia. A good sign. Ben Lawrence was on a mission.

Sadie's bodysuit shifted, the fabric now displaying a repetition of two cards: the jack and ace of spades. She didn't speak much for a dream player, but she communicated well.

"You're doing great, Ben," Amelia said. "They serve killer margaritas at this casino." His favorite drink. Ben would need a challenge – the whole point of the dream session – but a few words of encouragement in advance always helped.

Amelia touched an icon on a real-world tablet. Yellow text appeared in the overlay – *Partition Challenge Initiated.* A brick wall appeared, blocking the dream-state hallway. Ben's pace slowed. Sadie's bodysuit turned a grayish shade of red.

It was the moment of truth for Ben. Amelia scrutinized his reaction with some trepidation. Alzheimer's patients tended to fail their first challenge, though she wasn't sure why.

Ben stared at the wall. Sadie stared at Ben.

Suddenly, the hallway ruptured at one side, and a raging river poured out. The cascade splashed against the brick barrier, swirled, and drained into a dark split in the floor. The torrent swept Sadie off her feet, her eyes wide as she was dragged into the whirlpool.

"Sadie!" Ben's muffled voice cried. He reached out but missed her hand, and she disappeared into the watery darkness.

"Damn," Amelia said under her breath, hoping Ben hadn't heard. The unanticipated discontinuity had come from nowhere. Not good, but the mind does what it does.

Upstream, several young boys floundered in the fast current. They choked and coughed as their arms waved wildly. The merciless river sucked the hapless youngsters screaming into the whirlpool, and they too disappeared without a trace.

"No!" the muffled voice said again.

"Log entry," Amelia whispered. "Discontinuity – river memory." Her words appeared in the heads-up overlay below his vitals. His heart rate had spiked to a hundred and ten. Amelia's own heart rate rose. Discontinuities were tricky business and not just because the patient might wake. When a dream becomes a nightmare, brain chemistry changes, sometimes radically. Lucidity collapses and along with it, trust. But too much verbal guidance could have an opposite effect, raising the patient's lucidity to unsustainable levels. Confusion. Post-dream distress, even the potential for waking psychosis.

Amelia made the only call she could – a dose of reality. "It's okay, Ben. It's an old childhood memory, nothing more. You didn't die in the river, remember? We talked about this. You made it to the shore and so did your friends. Set this memory aside for now. You don't need it. You and I still have work to do."

"But Sadie," the muffled voice begged.

Sadie had become a significant focus but that could be useful too. Amelia soothed. "Don't worry, Ben, she's safe. She's waiting for you in the casino. She's at the blackjack table, and she even ordered two margaritas. Just tell the river memory to go away."

The river instantly froze in place, with splashes of water hanging in midair.

"Go away," the muffled voice commanded. The splashes evaporated, along with the river and the whirlpool. A solid floor reformed, returning the scene to a hallway with the brick wall now only a few paces ahead.

"Great job!" Amelia noted a drop in his heart rate, and hers as well. Her verbal intrusion was a gamble, but it had worked this time. "Okay, Ben. Let's focus on the barrier. Remember, the casino is on the other side. Sadie too, and she looks fantastic. You just need to get past this wall."

With a shaking hand, he reached out and touched the brick surface. Rough, cold, and solid. He pushed. It held. He scratched at the mortar between the bricks. No effect.

She couldn't help him, he'd have to figure it out on his own. But if Ben could conjure up sexy Sadie and a raging whirlpool, he still had some imagination left inside that semi-calcified brain.

He glanced left and right. The hallway setting faded away, transforming into an outdoor pasture with grass, trees, and cows. The pastoral scene was split down the middle by a continuous wall that receded into the distance. Ben's mind might create a variety of scenery, but the barrier would remain as long as Amelia kept it active in his synapses.

Ben lifted his head, following rows of bricks to the top of the wall at least twenty feet overhead. Above, puffy clouds drifted through a blue sky. A climb wouldn't be easy. Amelia didn't want it to be.

He reached up and dug his fingernails into solid brick. Slowly, he pulled himself up a few feet. His shoes magically disappeared, allowing bare toes to find the tiniest of cracks. He inched up higher still.

"You can do it, Ben. One brick at a time."

He moaned – in the dream, but perhaps in the real world too. The muscles in his arms shook and sweat appeared on his forehead. His brute-force choice wasn't ideal, but it still had a chance of success.

Now ten feet above the ground, his fingernails were embedded in solid brick, a sure sign that his fantasy was holding up. The partition challenge would have been easily solved if Ben had simply disabled gravity and jumped over, but that would require a spark of imagination that might only be discovered if an existing pattern of synapses rerouted their electrical signal through a different set of neurons. Which, for an early Alzheimer's patient, was the entire purpose of the session.

A tremble started in his feet and worked its way up to his hands. The moans increased in intensity and volume, now easily discerned as real-world sounds.

"Concentrate, Ben. Focus. You're so close."

He stared at fingers that magically gripped a vertical brick wall. "No," he said aloud. "It doesn't work like this."

His fingernails peeled back exposing bare bones underneath. He screamed and plunged backward, slamming into hard ground.

****

The middle-aged man with stubble on his chin and a wire mesh cap over his balding head jerked upright in bed, clawing at the air.

"Uhh!" he yelled.

Amelia opened her eyes. She sat in an armchair only a few feet away and wore a similar cap. A blue glow generated by ionized nitrogen hovered millimeters above the cap's surface. An electric-spark smell of ozone permeated the darkened room.

Amelia reached out to the squirming man. "You're okay, Ben. You're fine."

"Where? What?" Ben Lawrence panted, his mouth wide open and his eyes blinking rapidly. The glow surrounding his head provided a nightlight that turned white sheets blue.

Amelia flipped the switch on a bedside table lamp. The room was small, with bare white walls and a single rack of electronics to one side. Much more technology was located a floor below in the cryogenically cooled operations center.

"It's over. You're awake." Amelia put a hand on her patient's shoulder.

The gentle touch seemed to calm him. He whispered through deep breaths. "A wall. I fell."

"Yes, you did, but that's okay. All part of the challenge. You did really well." The bedside clock read 5:45 a.m. Amelia voiced a note in her log.

Ben Lawrence sunk into a pile of pillows. "It seemed so real. I could control things. I could hear a voice, too. Yours?"

Amelia smiled. "I was right there with you, Ben. We're a team."

"You saw everything?" His eyes widened. "Even… you know."

Amelia shrugged. "Yeah, everything. Sadie's very sweet. I like her. And don't worry, I won't tell your wife."

"Thanks. It's a bit... you know..."

"Embarrassing? Don't worry, Ben." She stroked his hand. "Trust me, I've seen it all."

"Did I fail?"

They all asked that question. "Well, we made some progress." Amelia tapped an icon on her tablet to shut the system down. The blue glow disappeared but the smell of ozone lingered as she slipped the wire mesh cap from her head. "If we can get you past the first few barriers, then we'll do another brain scan and see if there are improvements. Give it time."

"It seems like I should have learned something, but I don't feel any smarter."

"Don't think of it that way. Consider it playtime for your imagination. There's more than one way to get past the barrier. Your son, for example. The one who stopped by at dinner? He's really tall. I'll bet if you brought him into the dream, he could give you a boost to get over the wall."

"That's a good idea. Can I do that?"

"Sure, you can. It's your dream. We'll get it next time, okay?"

Amelia stood up, gathered the mesh caps and other electronics into a small bag and straightened her white jacket. "We've got an hour before sunrise. I'll let you go back to sleep for a while, and we'll talk after breakfast."

"Thanks, doc... well, I guess you're not a doctor. I mean, not the medical kind." He pointed to the name tag on her coat. *Dr. Amelia Charron.* "Uh, you know... a..."

"A neuroscientist," Amelia finished for him. "An explorer of the mind." She leaned in close and lifted one brow. "They even pay me to do this."

****

Three hours and one toasted bagel later, Amelia tossed back the final sip of her morning latte. She sat alone at a small table in a cozy café surrounded by leafy plants. The gentle splash of a nearby fountain blended with the cacophony of voices – other employees of the Westlake Institute for Neuroscience starting their workday.

Her mobile pulsed three times. She picked it up and checked for the incoming message. Two, actually. The first from her boss, Nolan Brodie. Terse, but all his texts were that way.

New pâté. Top priority. See me asap.

Pâté was the staff's rather insolent name for a patient, more fully a *pâté névrosé* – literally, neurotic liver paste – a term that envisioned the brain as creamy ground meat and patients as lunatics. Which it wasn't, and they weren't, mostly.

Technically, people like Ben Lawrence weren't patients at all since the institute wasn't a hospital or clinic, and Amelia wasn't a doctor or psychiatrist. The institute's liability waver form referred to them as *test subjects* and to Amelia's work as *experimental*, but the only staff members who seemed to like those words were the attorneys.

The second message came from Amelia's mobile assistant, a prototype artificial intelligence who she'd configured as a male voice named Kori.

"Ouch. Shifting priorities again. Nolan can be such a pain in the… wait, can I say ass? You didn't specifically forbid moderate swearing but my default configuration… sorry, never mind. Everything is under control, Amelia. I've adjusted your calendar."

CHAPTER THREE

PÂTÉ NÉVROSÉ

KORI DIDN'T HAVE an ass, though it would be hard to convince him of that fact. It was all part of his general confusion over self, which sometimes led him down thought trails, as he called the act of reasoning, that arrived at a very human conclusion: a mind could not exist without a supporting body. To resolve this dilemma, he simply imagined a body for himself and then denied ever creating it.

Amelia went along. She didn't have the heart to challenge his fantasy. Kori was a bit quirky, and not altogether there at times. He was, after all, in limited beta release. But his intellect was astonishingly advanced, far exceeding anything Amelia had installed on her mobile before.

Amelia strode purposefully down an empty hallway. Tuesday mornings were usually reserved for informal cross-functional exchanges among the staff at the Westlake Institute. Apparently not today. When Nolan said *asap*, he meant *now*. Kori understood it too, preparing an *on my way* response without being asked and requiring only a nod from Amelia to send.

"Looking gorgeous today, Amelia," Kori said through the wireless earbud that Amelia wore in her left ear. "New dress?"

Kori didn't have eyes per se, but he obtained a reasonable view of the outside world through the earbud's forward camera, along with additional cameras, motion sensors and microphones packed into her four-inch mobile device.

"Thanks, Kori. Not new, I just haven't worn it for a while." Given that he had full access to her online purchases, he was probably just making conversation.

"You usually wear those flared pants. Why?"

"Well, for one, they're comfortable. And, I enjoy being different."

"Like with your eyebrows?"

"Don't go there, mister. I'll switch you off."

She didn't pluck her rather thick eyebrows or do much to tame the waves in her hair. Kori had noticed. It was most likely the selfie she took last week with Margo, who had the face and makeup of a fashion model. Kori was good at comparing, sometimes getting a little too personal. But he was learning, subtly adjusting each day.

Amelia gave a tight smile as she passed a colleague leaning against a doorway sipping his morning coffee. From the perspective of any passerby, Amelia might be accused of talking to herself, but casual conversations with mobile assistants had become more commonplace with the advent of multi-step contextual dialogue. Gone were the days of a canned response to a single question.

Assistants were getting better all the time, but Kori was in a class above the rest, even if he was just a prototype. His designer was Amelia's good friend and mentor, Evelyn Stern, and when Ev offered, Amelia had enthusiastically signed up as a beta tester. Kori hadn't let her down. He didn't just respond, he initiated. He analyzed. He made judgments and gave opinions based on events and prior conversations that might be spread across weeks or months.

"How was Everest?" Amelia asked. Kori had downloaded detailed 3-D topography of the Himalayas the day before, explaining that he'd planned to scale the world's tallest mountain during periods when his engagement with Amelia was low.

"Amazing views from the summit, but… you know… frostbite, dehydration, hypoxia, not to mention the potential for cerebral edema. I wouldn't make a good Sherpa."

"Yeah, better stick to what works. You're pretty good at handling my coffee orders." Amelia smiled.

"Very funny," Kori pouted.

She turned a corner and stopped at a closed door. The name plate read *Nolan Brodie, Chief Scientist*.

"Okay, shush now, Kori." She rapped on the door and opened it after a voice inside the office beckoned.

Nolan looked up from oversized sheets of paper spread across a large desk. Middle-aged with gray hair cut short, he gave Amelia a forced smile. "Amelia, come in. I'm glad you're here."

A smile from Nolan Brodie meant only one thing and it wasn't remotely related to being friendly. He would be making a sales pitch for unpleasant duty, and Nolan could be very persuasive.

She plopped down in a padded chair that faced a large window. High-rise buildings filled the view forming the core of downtown Seattle. Nolan's office was a major step up from her own windowless closet. Regularly starting her workday in the three-a.m. darkness of a patient's sleeping room, she was refreshed by the sunlight, even when filtered through layers of slate gray Seattle clouds.

"How bad?" She locked eyes with Nolan. May as well get right to the point.

He waggled an index finger. "None of that. It's a very interesting case. Very challenging. A great opportunity for you."

"Yeah but Nolan, your definition of opportunity would include a fight to the death with an alligator. What's the diagnosis?"

"Well, the docs are calling it schizophrenia, but I'm not sure they have it right. There's a lot more going on in this guy's head."

Amelia took a deep breath and furrowed dense eyebrows beneath a lock of blonde hair that fell across her forehead. "Wait… so, schizo plus some other fun stuff? You realize we're already pushing the limit on what the system can safely handle, right?"

Nolan held up both hands, palms forward. "Yeah, yeah, I know what you went through last week. I totally understand how strong the neural feedback can be in a level two insertion."

Strong was an understatement. The disorientation she'd suffered was crippling – at least, temporarily. She'd recovered but experienced her own set of nightmares for several nights afterward. The patient hadn't fared any better, a young woman with obsessive-compulsive disorder, sent back to her therapist. Not optimal, but that's why Amelia's work was considered experimental. She wasn't a clinician, her degree was in neuroscience and her work was as much research as it was therapy.

Nolan moved around to the front of the desk and leaned against its edge. He folded his hands together and locked eyes with her, like a father addressing a newly minted teenage driver. At thirty-two, Amelia had every right to be offended by his routine condescension, but perhaps just old enough to let it go.

"Amelia, I wouldn't want anything to happen to you, but I also have complete faith in you. No one else in our group has mastered the nuances of assisted lucid dreams. But you have. This next case may be tricky, but it could also identify pathways in the brain that could advance our work tenfold."

She had to admit Nolan was good at selling. She had accomplished much and stirring her personal pride in those achievements was a surefire way to motivate. Nolan also held one big advantage: he knew Amelia's history. She was, and always would be motivated to help distressed mental patients, especially the unusual cases. Her own family had suffered from depression; it's what drove her into the field as a college student. For Amelia, neuroscience was personal.

"Name?" No matter what term they used among the staff – patient, test subject, or pâté névrosé – these were people in need, and Amelia preferred to call them by their name. Guilt, no doubt, for having coined the insolent French term herself. As the only Canadian on staff, she hadn't anticipated Americans' taste for dark humor.

Nolan lifted a single sheet of paper from his desk and read from it. "Orlando Kwon. Thirty-nine. Ordinary family man. Happily married with two young kids. A quality control inspector at a water bottling facility in Pasadena, California. No prior history of mental illness but complained of voices in his head that started about two months ago, followed by hallucinations."

"Past trauma? Military service?"

"None."

Amelia shrugged. "Well, it happens sometimes, poor guy. Schizo, right out of the blue."

"He says the voices in his head are alien."

She stifled a laugh. "Yeah, along with a few hundred other schizophrenics. Aliens, devils, Jesus, orcs, you name it. One guy was convinced Groucho Marx was talking to him. I suggest we refer Mr. Kwon to a reality therapist before I start rearranging his brain."

"He's already gone through two rounds of therapy. His therapists were pretty freaked out. They referred him to us."

"Because?"

"Not for any single reason, but this guy exhibits signs of claircognizance."

Amelia rolled her eyes. "Oh, come on, Nolan. Let's not bring psychic twaddle inside these walls. You know how hard it is to disinfect once that baseless bacteria get a toehold."

Nolan didn't flinch at her scientific challenge. "Documented and verified. Multiple cases. Math, science. The guy knows things he shouldn't know. He produced a chemistry formula no chemist has ever seen before, but he's never had a single class in chemistry."

"The guy's a genius, eh?"

"Deeper than that. They say he sees these things in his mind."

"So, you think you've got a real live psychic on your hands and you want me to peer inside his brain?"

Nolan tapped his chin as he considered both questions. "Maybe, and… yes. But I want you to peer inside either to uncover an unrecognized pattern of consciousness or to expose his trick. Either way will suit me just fine."

Amelia tilted her head to one side. "The truth, Nolan. Spit it out."

Nolan's sketchy past seemed to be rearing its head again. His interest in psychic nonsense was only the beginning. At one point in his career, he'd been preoccupied with the strange idea that pain wasn't a real phenomenon unless coupled with a self-aware consciousness. Explain that to a worm skewered on a fishhook.

Nolan held up both palms. "Okay, sure, I'd rather see you discover something that, until now, has never been witnessed from the inside. Something amazing about how the human brain works. But that's just my inner cheerleader speaking. I'm a scientist too. Find out what's going on with this guy, even if it is a scam."

"That's not a direct order, is it?"

"Of course not. We have an agreement, and I respect it. You can always decline any case. Your discretion."

Amelia leaned back and stared at the ceiling, hoping to find some guidance up there or perhaps just thankful that she'd been sufficiently prescient to add a right-of-refusal clause to her employment agreement. She leaned toward accepting. It did sound fascinating even though it would only take a single session to rule out the patient's so-called psychic ability. Once she was inside someone's head, they couldn't hide a deception.

But she was already managing three concurrent patients. One was coming along just fine, but another was stuck in a holding pattern. She had some ideas about how to break that neural logjam, but it might take time. Then there was Ben Lawrence. She was just getting started with him. Maybe she could pass one or two off to Jonas, a protégé of her dream guide procedures, but she'd still need to supervise his work.

As she weighed the options, Nolan returned to his chair, removing the overt physical pressure of a hovering father figure. So far, he was being true to his word about their agreement.

A small voice whispered in her left ear. "Do it, Amelia."

She lifted her left hand within the view of the earbud cam, fingers splayed in a silent question. Kori was pretty good at reading body language.

He answered immediately. "Why? Because Orlando Kwon's case is clearly unique. Challenging, but full of possibilities. You might never get an opportunity like this again. Tell Nolan you'll do it. You won't be sorry."

Amelia snickered under her breath. An intelligence derived from ones and zeros was now providing career counseling.

What's next? Will Kori be approving future boyfriends?

Too bad Kori couldn't read minds – at least, not this version of his AI. Amelia looked up at Nolan. "Okay, let's do it."

Nolan reached out and shook her hand. "Good choice. I'll send the background report to you. Mr. Kwon is flying up from LA tomorrow morning, and we'll do a full psych workup and brain scan before we hand off. Should be finished by about ten a.m. Then, he's all yours."

"Dive right in," Amelia stated, mostly to herself.

"That's my girl, dive right in," Nolan concurred.

Amelia glared.

Nolan raised both hands defensively. "Sorry, sorry! I've got daughters. I get carried away." He cleared his throat. "How about, my top female neuroscientist, ready to dive in."

"How about, one of our most experienced neuroscientists, and just leave it there?" Amelia offered. Her male colleagues were not the competition, and Nolan's gender distinctions needed to be jettisoned back to the twentieth century where they belonged. The 2030s were supposed to be the new age of gender blindness, or so everyone said.

Nolan nodded agreeably. "Well put."

"You *can* learn," Amelia said, a grin spreading across her lips. "Send Mr. Kwon to me. I'll see what I can do for him."

****

Amelia absent mindedly closed the door to her miniature, viewless office, while her conscious brain focused squarely on the patient documents displayed on her tablet.

She'd only begun to dig into the details, but she could already tell that Orlando Kwon was indeed going to be an interesting case. Schizophrenics commonly experience auditory and visual hallucinations – both present in this case. But they also have delusions that bear no relationship to reality, like persecution or a special relationship with a famous person. Moreover, the vast majority of schizophrenia cases show clear signs of mental confusion, usually observed as distraction or zoning out. This patient had none of those symptoms.

Her eyes never leaving the page, Amelia lowered into her chair. *Yeah, a possible misdiagnosis.*

Nolan had also suggested a misdiagnosis, but largely because the most interesting aspects of this case were descriptions of the patient's newfound mental abilities. Though his education had never gone beyond community college, Orlando seemed to have detailed knowledge of organic chemistry. In a recent therapy session, he had written a chemical equation that was passed along to the faculty at UCLA who were so astonished by its formulation that they wanted to enroll him in a graduate program. In another session, he recited the digits of pi to more than three hundred places.

It was more like savant syndrome than schizophrenia. Evidence for a misdiagnosis, but there was no reason to jump straight to psychic mumbo jumbo.

Claircognizance. That's what the parapsychology crowd called it. Knowledge obtained through means beyond our recognized reality. From a scientific perspective, claircognizance boils down to either poor test controls or outright fraud. The traditional fraudulent sources were psychics and corrupt evangelistic preachers. Their methods usually involved an accomplice who would feed information via a visual coding system or simply through an electronic transceiver. In the 2010s, Las Vegas magicians Penn and Teller had famously exposed the clever techniques used in this fraud.

Orlando Kwon might be one of those frauds, but if he really could perform the mental feats, watching from inside his head while he came up with the digits of pi would blow the doors off neuroscience's limited understanding of how the savant brain worked.

That would be amazing.

Nolan might be right about the reasons for taking the case. Amelia scrolled through additional pages to familiarize herself with her newest patient.

A voice in her ear muttered, "Would you categorize him as a jerkwad or a dickhead?" She'd never heard Kori use either word before.

"Who, Orlando Kwon?"

"No, Nolan. Jerkwad or dickhead?"

Amelia laughed. "Kori, you might want to brush up on your slang. Just because Nolan can be a genderist, doesn't make him either a jerkwad or a dickhead. I think your assessment is a bit harsh."

"Yeah, you're probably right. I just discovered those words and I wanted to get your interpretation. Nolan seemed like a good test case."

Amelia had a hard time controlling the giggles. "Kori, you slay me sometimes. I do love our conversations. But..." She emphasized the last word.

"Too much?"

She pinched her index finger and thumb together in front of the earbud cam so he could see. "Yeah, just a bit too much. Look, you're supposed to be my digital assistant. Tell me things I need to know. Find complex correlations that are beyond my ability. That kind of thing. If I need a twelve-year-old brother, I'll let you know."

"I'm hurt." He sounded hurt, but it was no doubt the product of good code.

"Reach deep, Kori. Iterate a few billion times on a recursive function call, or whatever you software brains do when you're introspective. You'll get over it."

She thought she detected a disenchanted snort, but it might have just been the earbud shifting.

CHAPTER FOUR

CORRELATES

THE COMPUTER OPERATIONS center at the Westlake Institute for Neuroscience overlooked Lake Union, one of the blue gems that bounded the city of Seattle by water on all sides. Sailboats dotted the lake, kayaks too. Those who lacked a water vessel strolled along the shoreline. Summer days brought most everyone outside.

A glass partition separated the operations center into two sections, one side for employees, the other for machines. On the machine side, frozen condensation from a liquid nitrogen cryogenic system obscured the lovely view. Most supercomputing systems were cooled with industrial-sized air conditioners, but The Boss, currently registered with Guinness as the fourth fastest computer in the world, was in a different tier.

The machine itself looked like two narrow refrigerators positioned on either side of jet engine standing on its tail end. Colored pipes and wire bundles jutted from the sides of the refrigerators, piercing the curving aluminum of the jet engine, a unit that was rumored to house more than ten thousand silicon chips working in parallel.

A pipe near the glass partition was covered by sparkling ice crystals. Someone had attached a bar tap handle on the people side of the glass with a small sign that read "Ice Cold" and provided a drawing of the atomic elements, beryllium, and erbium, abbreviated

Be and Er. The beer tap was more than a gag. It had become a makeshift talisman – especially for the neuroscientists. Pull the handle on your way out, and The Boss would do its best work for you.

Amelia sat at a workstation listening to one of the software engineers, Jake Hodge, explain the latest software update. With a body-builder's physique, Jake didn't match the stereotype of a computer geek. For such a muscled man, he couldn't have been gentler – or more attentive to Amelia's safety in her frontline role.

Jake pointed to one of several computer displays set up at his workstation. A three-dimensional skull slowly rotated while complex multicolored filaments flashed on and off like miniature lightning bolts. A brain map. Amelia's brain, in fact, as the name above the skull declared.

As each filament sparked, corresponding photographs of ordinary objects – a baseball, a spoon, a baby's face – appeared next to the skull. Hundreds flashed by in the span of a few seconds.

"The latest system update includes a full refresh of your NCC encyclopedia," Jake explained. The colored patterns were her own, previously recorded and sorted into what neuroscientists called *neuronal correlates of consciousness*, or NCCs.

NCCs are bioelectric patterns that represent a single visual image – that spoon or baseball – but they could also represent a sound, smell, emotion, or idea, collectively referred to as *phenomena*. Peek at the NCCs inside someone's head and you'll know what they're thinking. Moreover, many neuroscientists had come around to the idea that the sum of all those intricate NCC patterns represented consciousness itself. Each person was a unique snowflake, imprinted with their own collection of several trillion patterns.

In the early days, NCC bioelectric maps were created by inserting thousands of fine electrodes into the brains of mice. After twenty years, this rather barbaric approach had mapped only a few hundred patterns, less than one percent of the mouse brain. Equally limiting, the studies had uncovered what researchers called *inter-individual variability*. The NCC pattern representing 'cheese' inside one mouse brain wasn't quite the same as his mate. The same variations had been noted in people.

For years, it seemed the brain was simply too complex to fully grasp. Some neuroscientists tried a top-down approach, the Human Connectome Project, which had produced colorful maps of virtually every pathway in the brain. But like a street view from thirty-thousand feet, the project struggled to assign meaning to individual paths. NCC maps used a bottom-up approach, but attempts to decode the full breadth of the *phenomenal experience* – that routine sensory experience of our daily lives – seemed a distant dream.

Everything changed when the Assisted Lucid Dream program began. Using vastly higher resolution, astonishing computing power, and the ability to look inside human thoughts in real time, the ALD program launched brain mapping into the stratosphere.

Within two years, Amelia and her colleagues had systematically matched phenomena to more than two-hundred thousand specific NCCs, an estimated twenty percent of the brain's potential. The high-level connectome images turned out to be excellent guides, and it was only a matter of time before the brain's electrochemical functions would be fully mapped.

The ALD program had also solved the problem of inter-individual variability. Standardized brain analysis could now match the NCCs found in Bob to the corresponding NCCs in Sue. The matching wasn't perfect, given the bewildering variety of people, but over time they'd discovered that the brain itself was an outstanding partner to their supercomputers. The brain could manage an incoming stream of NCCs by creating a contextual narrative that made sense to the recipient. Of course, some brains were better than others. With years of practice, Amelia was the best they had.

Her career had been successful but not without risks. Reviews with Jake were ostensibly to clarify system features or explain the latest software. Yet, invariably, their conversations returned to the hazards inherent in their cutting-edge process.

Jake explained. "When the system creates your avatar for a level two insertion, it automatically assigns neuronal shielding by NCC group. No change there. But with this software update, there are more groups."

He scrolled through a list, each heading representing thousands of objects, sensory experiences, and thoughts. "No matter what the patient sends your way during the ALD session, the system will block any rewiring of the avatar's brain – your brain in the physical world. You're fully protected. The SPIKEs can't touch you."

A SPIKE, or spontaneous interneural kinetic electrogenesis, was the rather sinister term used for a brain transmission from the patient to the guide, above and beyond the subconscious dreams that nightly streamed into Amelia's brain. These spurious transmissions were prohibited altogether in the simplest case – a level one insertion – but the system left the door wide open for the more invasive procedures defined in a level two insertion.

Amelia nodded. "You say *fully*, but the shielding only applies for these specific NCC groups, right?"

Jake shrugged and raised both hands. "Right. But we can only protect what we understand. If we had a more comprehensive neuron map, especially in the cerebral cortex, I could shield more."

Amelia lifted both eyebrows. "So bottom line, in a level two I'm still only about twenty percent protected. Maybe twenty-one with your update."

"Well… yeah, I guess. But think about the likelihood of a transmission that rewires your synapses coming from a patient who has no idea what he's doing. Plus, he's dreaming. He has no connection to the outside world. The chance of altering even one of your synapses is infinitesimally small. You're an ALD guide. When you rearrange someone else's brain, you're awake and in control of the system. You know what you're doing. Your patient doesn't have that same leverage."

She didn't disagree with his assessment, but with so much brain science still unknown, the risks associated with a level two insertion remained larger than she'd like.

Amelia sighed. "I guess it comes with the territory. If I want perfect protection, I've always got level one."

"Yup. At level one, SPIKEs can't occur. Physically impossible."

"Unfortunately, I can't always get the job done at level one."

He shrugged again. "Your call, Amelia. I just write the code."

"And you've done exceptionally well, Jake. It's all amazing stuff." Amelia meant every word. They'd worked closely for three years and Jake had taken great care to keep her fully briefed, even if he left the decisions to her.

"Download the update to your tablet and you'll have the most recent protections."

"Will do. Thanks, Jake."

She stood up and glanced through the glass partition at The Boss in all its aluminum and silicon glory. Shrugging, she stepped over and pulled the beer tap handle. "Can't hurt."

Jake pumped a fist. "The Boss has your back."

It was a short walk back to the building's central atrium. Interior offices and conference rooms partially extended into the open space, creating a feeling of blocks stacked irregularly overhead. A series of stairways that seemed to hang in midair brought her to the fifth floor and the Assisted Lucid Dreams lab.

"Kori, download and install today's ALD software updates to my tablet please," Amelia said as she pushed open the door to the lab and grabbed her white lab coat from a hook. The coat was mostly symbolic, a carry-over from the days when much of the staff worked with mice. Amelia decided the look inspired confidence in her patients.

Her earpiece had remained silent for the entire time she'd been in the computer center, a small sign that Kori might be learning when to speak and when to keep quiet.

"Download complete," Kori answered. "Update in progress. I'll monitor to make sure it finishes."

"Thanks."

She checked one of the three sleep rooms to be sure it had been prepared for their newest patient who would arrive in less than twenty-four hours. She wasn't yet sure if she'd use the room right away. Sometimes it was better to get to know the patient in the usual way, through conversation. She'd also get a full brain scan from the prep team. It would give her a good map of his NCCs, including whatever variations from normal could be detected. But those were details. She'd still need a plan for how she'd tackle this case.

"Kori, you okay?" she asked to empty space.

"Sure, I'm fine," Kori answered. "Why do you ask?"

"You were pretty quiet for a while, that's all."

"Learning. Improving. If it helps, I can list all the things I'm doing in the background."

"No need. I'm sure you're staying useful. Hey, what do you know about organic chemistry?" The topic wasn't Amelia's strong suit, even though she recalled taking an undergraduate class in the distant past.

"Cursory, only. No more than what you could read on Wikipedia."

A portion of the plan for her new patient began to form in Amelia's mind. "How much do you think you could learn by tomorrow morning at ten?"

"Just a minute." Kori paused, apparently searching. "There's a lot of material out there. I'll need at least three terabytes on your cloud storage."

"Take whatever you need."

"It's a significant branch of chemistry. From my initial assessment, it appears to be quite a complicated topic."

He seemed to be hedging. "So? What could you do for me?"

"Well, I might not get to a PhD level by tomorrow, but I could probably assimilate most of the undergraduate material. Enough to create a useable knowledge base."

Amelia grinned. Even if Kori could pull together half of that, it would be enough. It was also perfect justification for the effort she'd gone through of installing and training a prototype digital assistant. If it worked out, she'd soon have an organic chemist at her side, able not only to answer specific questions but to analyze a conversation. Together, they should be able to determine if the patient was faking.

"Do it. Whatever you can by ten tomorrow. I want you listening when we talk to Mr. Kwon. Your knowledge base should keep him honest."

"I like it, Amelia. Good thinking."

Good thinking indeed. She wondered which of them had the higher intellect, the one who imagined the need, or the one who could absorb four years of college-level organic chemistry overnight.

She left her assistant to his homework and focused her attention on the rest of her plan. Her primary goal was to decide if Orlando Kwon was suffering from schizophrenia, or not. She could interview him, just as any doctor would, and test his claimed claircognizance, as any scientist would.

Reasonable starting points. But nothing compares to stepping inside the patient's mind.

It's what she did best. Ordinary dreams were unstructured, wandering almost randomly, but using the ALD techniques she'd personally perfected, Amelia could guide the dream toward a specific goal. In this case, she could test for claircognizance and potentially confront the perceived voices.

Better still, it was virtually impossible for the dreamer to cheat. Any self-deceiving sham used to prop up a waking personality would quickly fall apart in an ALD session. Someone pretending to be a genius could be exposed as a fraud.

She'd use a level one insertion, which kept the dreamer's lucidity low. Patients often never realized Amelia was even there. If Orlando Kwon had anything to hide, he wouldn't last long once she was inside his head.

Though dreams can occur throughout the night, they increase in frequency toward the end of sleep when REM periods last longer. It was why Amelia started her workday at three a.m. and was usually done by midday. Now already past noon, her plan for the next day felt complete.

With Kori busy earning a new Bachelor of Science degree, it was time to head home to her Phinney Ridge apartment, feed her cat, Jinx, and cuddle up on the windowsill couch with a good book. Bedtime at seven always came early.

CHAPTER FIVE

TROUBLED

ORLANDO KWON HUDDLED against the window in the last row of a 737 out of LAX for SeaTac. An early morning flight, he was thankful to have the row to himself. His gaze alternated between the California mountains outside the window and the flight attendant who'd been giving him nervous glances ever since he'd boarded.

He grimaced a smile as she walked by. She wasn't fooled. "Anything I can get you?" She leaned in to get a good look at the perspiration across his brow.

Orlando shrunk into the seat, avoiding her eyes. "I'm fine." She paused, then walked on.

It would only get worse on arrival. There'd be a taxi driver, a receptionist, and then more doctors. Each one would stare at him, assessing. They'd see through his false mask of normalcy to recognize the madness within. Afterwards, they'd wash their hands with antibiotic soap and tell their friends about the freak they'd encountered.

Orlando shook his head. Going to Seattle would be as hopeless as the rest of his attempts to get help. He couldn't fault Teena for pushing it, but she didn't understand. She couldn't feel what he felt. The voices were real.

Zhee-orzh scritch tick.

Seemingly beckoned by his thoughts, the voice sounded once more from outside the airplane window. Orlando scooted to the aisle seat. He squeezed his eyelids closed not daring even a glance to the window. They were out there. The crab bugs were probably crawling across the glass right now, pinching at the window corners, trying to get inside.

"Distraction," he commanded to himself. Pulling out his phone, he thumbed through his calendar doing his best to ignore the window in the periphery of his vision. Nervous fingers opened the appointment he'd made for later in the morning.

He swallowed hard and read. "Doctor Amelia Charron, Neuroscientist," he whispered, then clicked on the link to the Westlake Institute just below her name. He mouthed the words on the page to focus his attention elsewhere. The topic didn't matter.

The institute, he read, was established in 2010 by one of the computer billionaires that seemed to live on every street corner in Seattle. Their headquarters housed multiple labs and a large computer center. A map marked its location not far from downtown.

Orlando clicked on the staff page and scrolled through a long list of names, stopping at Amelia Charron. Her photo popped up, framing a pretty, blonde-haired woman with a big smile. She seemed young for a doctor, but the casual tilt of her head and a squint of one eye exuded an inner confidence.

It wouldn't matter. He'd seen a lot of doctors and therapists. This newest quack might be confident, but she'd fail just like all the rest. They all started with the wrong assumption. The voices weren't some psychological problem that could be medicated away. There was something real inside his head. Pulling at him. Drawing him deeper. Taking him away from Teena, his kids, his life, and reality. It would take more than therapy to kill this invader.

CHAPTER SIX

DISTURBED

DRESSED IN KHAKIS, his hat in his hand, Major Brock Shepard led a small group of civilians down a long hallway in a specialized – and highly secured – military clinic located in a remote corner of Fort Belvoir, Virginia. The group paused at each open doorway to give the VIPs in tow an opportunity to glance inside.

Most rooms were setup with twin beds, no different than any military hospital. Some rooms were designed for day use only with a couch on one wall and a table with chairs on the other. Each room had a television on the wall with reading materials in a bookcase, though most of the patients lay in bed or sat in a chair with their attention focused on tablets loaded with apps designed to either evaluate their mental capacity or just to pass the time.

Every room in the DARPA Psychiatric Ward was occupied, every patient confined by an electronic monitor around their ankle. Mostly male, though a few females rounded out the population of the *goo zoo*.

The unofficial moniker – *goo* referencing the gelatinous gray matter within the skull – only made sense within military ranks. In his time, Shepard had seen plenty of sloppy goo sagging from the heads of soldiers blown apart on the battlefield. The brain was a curious thing, operating at peak efficiency one minute and reduced to pudding the next.

The Defense Advanced Research Projects Agency, or DARPA, had a variety of unconventional research pursuits, but enhancing the human brain was among their highest priorities. Any idea that tied into the Super Soldier program, no matter how far-fetched, caught the eye of the Pentagon, from increasing the mental capacity of the average recruit, to mind-controlled weaponry.

Shepard himself was a proud participant, sporting a prosthesis for the right arm he'd lost in battle that could take a variety of useful attachments, all controlled purely by his thoughts. Firing a fifty-caliber armor-piercing bullet just by thinking about it was among the most entertaining of his new arm's capabilities, but there were others, both functional and lethal.

Shepard paused at one room where an orderly dressed in blue scrubs pushed a struggling patient down onto his bed. The patient had a faraway look in his eyes and shouted unintelligible words as he lurched against the strong hands of the orderly.

"The Psych Ward staff are some of the best around," Shepard explained as he pointed with his prosthesis, currently configured with a multifunction medical evaluation tool at its end.

The key beneficiary of the tour, Senator Vada Innis Lasseter nodded solemnly. A middle-aged African American woman with curly graying hair, Senator Lasseter was the senior senator from the state of Washington. She had a piercing stare that often substituted for words, a stare Shepard had experienced personally while testifying to the Armed Forces Committee that Senator Lasseter chaired. The congressional meetings were usually budget related, but on occasion, he was summoned to justify DARPA projects.

"What's wrong with this man?" Senator Lasseter asked. The patient had been physically subdued, but the wild look in his eyes remained.

"Nothing wrong, per se," Shepard said. "Each research subject is unique, and our examinations vary depending on what that patient claims to see, hear, or know. We mainly want to understand how their brain works."

A bland statement – almost meaningless – but perfect for outsiders like Senator Lasseter and her staff members, who had only a cursory understanding of the Super Soldier program. To keep it simple for congressional reporting, DARPA conducted general research. Knowledge for the sake of knowledge. In reality, once the visitors had left, anyone with eyes could see that the Psych Ward was far more targeted.

Telepathy, for example, might someday provide unhackable battlefield communications, assuming the neuroscientists employed by DARPA ever figured out how brain to brain transmission might work. A few patients had shown promise in initial evaluations, though some of the examiners said it was simply an artifact of the patient's incentive for high scores – the promise of release from the ward.

Through thick glasses, Senator Lasseter locked eyes with Shepard. "I'd like a detailed report of every person in this facility. What brought them here, how long they've been here, what tests have been run. The works."

"Yes, ma'am," Shepard replied without hesitation. "I'll have someone get that to you. The patients here are certainly unusual, but their care is no different than you'd see in any veteran's hospital. The one exception is for Post-Traumatic Stress Disorder – but our PTSD patients are handled in another facility."

"That's the selective memory erasure program?" Senator Lasseter asked. She'd been briefed, at least enough to know the purpose.

"Yes, ma'am. Targeted therapy, with the full permission of the patient, I should stress. We can eliminate the most painful memories and restore a soldier to a productive life."

The people who handled memory manipulation could indeed fix a broken soldier but erasing just the right bits of memory was tricky business that required extensive neuroscience research as well as human testing. Luckily, test subjects were easily available from military prisons, but there was no need to disclose those details unless directly questioned.

"Your operations plan says you're actively seeking people with mental afflictions," the senator stated.

"Not just any affliction," Shepard corrected. "We're looking for unusual cases, the ones that stand out among thousands of others."

"Highly disturbed?"

"Not really, no. Extraordinary is a better term."

"Give me an example."

Shepard had to pause, not to think of an extraordinary example – there were plenty – but to avoid an example where the patient's brain had ended up compromised – there were plenty of those too.

This is no eighth-grade science fair, he often told his staff. *If we don't figure this stuff out our adversaries will.* It was the standard justification Shepard pushed whenever they carted out some joker who hadn't 'passed' their tests.

"An example," Shepard repeated. "Well, the woman in room fourteen – when she's lucid – claims she can move objects with her mind. Telekinesis. We're examining her in a scientifically controlled test."

"And?"

"Nothing yet, but her brainwave patterns are unlike anything we've ever seen, so we'd like to study her further."

The Senator paused in thought. "She's not military, is she? How did you make contact with her?"

Senator Lasseter probably knew more than Shepard had surmised, but it didn't matter, his answer would be the same. "As we do for most of these patients, through referrals. From hospitals, psychiatrists, lots of sources. For example, we got a referral yesterday for a psychiatric patient that shows signs of claircognizance – knowing things he couldn't possibly know through normal means. The man produced a chemistry formula that's causing quite a stir and he has no chemistry background, so naturally, we're interested in questioning him."

"For the so-called Super Soldier program?"

She definitely knew more than she was letting on. "Yes ma'am," he said, biting his tongue at her snub of the program. Criticism from a lower-level bureaucrat would have unleashed a tirade, but senators got one more line of brochure-quality bullshit. "Imagine if we could teach our recruits far more effectively by unlocking the deepest secrets of the mind."

"What if this chemistry genius has no secret, what if he's just smart?"

Shepard gritted his teeth, his irritation rising. "We have contacts everywhere, ma'am, and we cross check to validate the information we receive. In this case, we know with one hundred percent certainty that a groundbreaking formula has shaken up an entire university chemistry department. A gifted chemist has come from nowhere. As I said, we're looking for the extraordinary. We *know* when we've found it."

The senator nodded and moved further down the hallway, abating Shepard's agitation.

Shepard was easy to chafe, he had been for years. It was most likely a lingering symptom of his own PTSD. If he'd been an enlisted man, he might have had his brain scanned and his memory adjusted to calm his outbursts, but such methods were rarely used on officers.

Officers were expected to control their emotions, keep their temper in check. Shepard did – mostly. For example, while dealing with a US senator whose comments had bordered on antagonistic all morning. But in other cases, especially when confronting adversaries, he almost looked forward to his temper rising. When the anger swept over him, he embraced it. Reveled in its rawness. It was a gift no different than the explosion that had taken off his right arm. The prothesis made him stronger, not weaker. An internal fury, even if induced by PTSD, was a powerful motivator. It was surely why Shepard had been awarded the Distinguished Service Cross for valor in combat. He'd singled-handedly rescued a forward recon team trapped under incessant enemy fire. There was almost nothing left of the enemy when Shepard was done with them.

Shepard's mind jumped ahead to actionable tasks, the real work for the day once he'd finished babysitting the political irritants. The chemistry formula that he'd mentioned to the senator was the most promising referral they'd seen in a while.

Identification. Verification. Containment. Acquisition.

It was a simple plan, but it worked. His team had already identified a target, a Korean American in Los Angeles. Next, Shepard and his team would need to verify the target's value, in this case an advanced chemistry formula. Contain knowledge of the value's existence to ensure critical information didn't spread, then simply acquire the target for examination at the Psych Ward.

The field operation wouldn't be complex, but it might take a few days since the location was west coast. He'd probably take Lieutenant Tombaugh on this mission, but there were already indications that containment might get complicated, and for that task he'd need to add a neuroscientist. They had one on staff, a civilian, Walker Duplass. A toady runt with no sense of decorum, Shepard had never liked him.

People who'd never been close to a battlefield – like Duplass and this female senator – only got in the way, slowing him down with their tiresome rules to ensure no one got hurt. The new urban battlefield was no different than Afghanistan. Collateral damage was an expected part of any war. Winning was what counted.

CHAPTER SEVEN

GENIUS

WEDNESDAY MORNING, her workday already half complete, Amelia looked up from her tablet, brushing back a few strands of hair that never seemed to stay in place. Her understudy, Jonas Swan, sat on the other side of the desk, his own tablet in hand. Head down, the young man perused her notes from a second ALD session she'd just completed with Ben Lawrence.

Jonas was gangly in stature and personality, but exceptionally bright. Going forward, he'd be taking over. "Ben sounds like a promising case."

"He's really a sweet guy. One of those patients I'm going to miss." Some were like that. It got personal. She was, after all, participating in their most private thoughts.

Only a few hours before, she'd joined Ben's dream unnoticed. He'd conjured up sexy Sadie again, this time aboard a yacht in a vivid cruise across Chesapeake Bay. The dream had been delightful, with images so real that Amelia could almost feel the fresh wind blowing through her hair and the salty scent of the sea filling her nostrils. After showing off his boating skills, Ben had taken Sadie below deck for some adult playtime that ended up as a card game – fully clothed. Odd, but it was Ben's dream.

Feeling a bit like a spoilsport, Amelia interrupted their intimacy by giving Ben another partition challenge, this time the barrier appearing as an enormous net stretching across the sea and preventing the boat from forward progress. Ben had done quite well, easily climbing the net and slicing it from top to bottom with a pirate sword that his son – brought into the dream dressed in full pirate gear, including a parrot – handed to him.

That simple act had given Amelia access to several dozen partially calcified NCCs in Ben's mind. With a few keystrokes, she'd rewired them to alternate pathways, potentially improving his mental ability to solve real world challenges. Time would tell – the therapy was still experimental.

She had let Ben's dream finish on its own, never waking him.

"I know you'll take good care of him," Amelia told Jonas with a reassuring smile. "Any other questions about the case?"

"None for now," Jonas said, his eyes jumping between and tablet and Amelia. "You're not going to be so busy with the new patient that I can't consult with you, right?"

She answered confidently, "I'll keep it under control. Who knows, maybe the new guy will be in and out by tomorrow."

There wasn't much chance of that, unless Orlando Kwon really was a fraud, but neither was there any reason to treat the case as somehow incomparable to all others.

Except that it is.

Jonas thanked her and left. Now just past nine, her newest patient was expected to arrive in less than an hour. The more she'd read about Orlando Kwon, the more she wondered if she had anything to offer. If he turned out to be faking, she'd expose him, and the man might be in legal trouble. Health insurance companies sometimes filed fraud complaints with state insurance boards.

If he was legit, then reconciling the evidence of claircognizance with the medical diagnosis of schizophrenia would be tough. Unless she could identify specific NCCs that looked out of whack, she might return him to the reality therapists. With the right drugs, they'd give him more hope for remission.

A knock on the door and Amelia looked up. Jen, the lead for the new patient prep team, poked her head in. "Hi Amelia, we're a bit ahead of schedule. I'm done with Mr. Kwon, could you see him now?" She opened the door wider. An Asian man stood behind her, his head down, staring at the floor.

"No problem. I'm ready." She stood up and as Orlando lifted his head, she extended a hand.

His hair was cut short on one side but hung down on the other. He had a youngish, flat face with unsteady eyes that darted to the floor and back to Amelia. He wore a stylish leather jacket and neat jeans, but his timid demeanor was far more subdued than his clothing.

"Welcome Orlando, I'm Amelia Charron." Jen gave a small wave and disappeared.

He shook her hand with a slight bow, then stood upright again, shifting his weight from one foot to the other. "Dr. Charron, I uh… I'm grateful for your help."

"I'm happy to help. And please call me Amelia. What we do here is very different than hospitals or clinics. Over the next few days, I expect that you and I will become good friends."

He shrugged, pressing his lips together in a half smile. "You sure you want to be friends with me? I'm bat shit crazy you know."

Amelia raised her brow. "I hope your health providers didn't tell you that." She searched for sincerity in his face, but he struggled to make full eye contact.

His eyes returning to the floor, he nodded. "You're right, they didn't. But... it's hard not to think you're crazy when everyone acts like you are."

Amelia stepped closer to Orlando and waited silently until his eyes lifted. "Orlando, you're in a safe place. I want you to know that. We're here to understand you and then help you if we can."

He nodded, his eyes glistening. He started to say something and stopped.

"Take your time." Amelia waited.

He nodded again, swallowing hard. "It's... my wife, Teena. I'll do anything to get her back." The emotion in his voice was strong. If he was faking, he was either very good at it or he was deceiving himself along with everyone else.

"How about we do this," Amelia started. "Let's focus on *you* for a few days. Try to set Teena aside for now. I'm going to do my best to find out what's going on inside your head, but I'll need your undivided attention. Together, if we can help you, then later maybe Teena will respond."

He nodded. "Okay. Thanks doctor."

"Amelia," she corrected.

"Amelia," he agreed.

"Shall we get started?"

He nodded once more, and she waved for him to follow. They walked side-by-side, Amelia never allowing Orlando to stray behind. She chatted as they passed through the hallway and into the central atrium trying to put Orlando at ease. She'd never liked the cold, clinical types that tended to inhabit hospitals. Getting friendly with patients might be called unprofessional by some, but there were big advantages in dream therapy when the subject was cooperative. Besides, that cold professional manner just wasn't her personality.

Orlando kept quiet, his eyes flitting in every direction. As they passed through the glass-domed atrium, midmorning sunlight bathed the open space, casting tiny rainbows across the walls, an effect Amelia had always loved. For his part, Orlando peered over the walkway railing seeming unsure about the five-story plunge to the lobby below, but then his whole behavior was skittish.

"Kori? How's your work going?" she asked as they walked side by side into the next corridor.

The voice in her earbud piped up. "All set. It's surprising how smart I feel today."

Orlando gave a quizzical look.

"Sorry, I'm just speaking with my assistant." She tapped her earbud then looked up into the air. "Perfect. I'll leave you on the earbud for now, but I might put you on speaker later. Okay?"

"I understand perfectly," Kori said. "Anything I say on speaker will be tempered by the knowledge that your patient will hear it too."

"Exactly, but that's okay. I might want the two of you to speak directly."

"Smart, Amelia. I'll be ready."

"Thanks, Kori."

"Will your assistant be joining us?"

"In a way, yes." Amelia opened the ALD lab door and ushered Orlando inside. A short hall to the left led to the sleep rooms. To the right, a glass partition formed a small conference room. As they entered, Amelia pointed to a coffee thermos on a credenza, and he poured a small cup.

"You don't seem afraid of me," he said as he sat in one of the chairs.

"Should I be?" She took a chair on the opposite side of the table.

"I guess not. I wouldn't hurt anyone. I don't even feel crazy. Just... confused, and..."

She waited.

"And... helpless, I guess. Things are happening to me. Real things. Some of it's just weird, but some of it scares the shit out of me. Like I'm living in a horror movie."

Amelia opened a notes app on her tablet. "I'm sorry to hear that, Orlando. Try to set aside the scary things for now. Let's start with something easy. You say some of it is weird. Can you tell me about that?"

Orlando shrugged. "Sure. The math stuff. It's pretty messed up, but it's not scary."

"Like reciting the digits of pi?"

He smiled. "You've read a report about me."

"I have. But show me. I'd like to see it for myself."

"I'm listening, too," Kori said, unprompted.

"Good," Amelia answered and tapped her earbud once more for Orlando's benefit.

Orlando took a sip of his coffee. "It's nothing much, just numbers."

"Still, I'd like to see it." She waited patiently for him to come around. He seemed almost embarrassed, but he'd need to get over whatever was holding him back if she had any chance to help him.

"Okay, whatever." He took a deep breath and started reciting numbers, slowly at first and then speeding up. "3.14159265358979323846..." He paused. "You want me to keep going?"

Amelia nodded. "For a while, if you don't mind."

He tilted his head one way and then the other and continued reciting at a steady clip. "26433832795028841971..." The numbers pouring from Orlando's mouth went on for another two minutes until Amelia finally held up a hand for him to stop.

She pulled her mobile from her lab coat pocket, switched the audio output to speaker and asked, "Did you get all that, Kori?"

"I did," he answered, his voice sounding scratchier on the speaker.

"And?"

"It checks. He delivered two hundred fifty-one digits. All correct."

Amelia looked up at Orlando. "Very impressive. Could you go further if you had to?"

"Probably. I have no idea where the numbers come from, so I don't know where it might end. I've read that pi goes on forever, a bunch of random digits."

"Not random," Amelia answered. "Pi is an irrational number. The digits are fixed, but they are infinite."

She leaned on the table, staring into the eyes of a man who had just performed an astounding task of memorization. "You really don't know where the numbers come from?"

He shook his head. "It's not from the voices. There's no one telling me the numbers, they're just there. I could do it in my sleep."

Amelia pointed a finger toward the math savant. "That, my friend, could be handy."

"I know. I've read about what you do. You work inside people's dreams, right?"

"Right."

"Are you going to go into my dreams?"

Amelia lifted her eyebrows. "Is that okay with you?"

"Sure, but you might not like what you see."

Amelia nodded. He might be right about that but there was no point in stressing over the perils of schizophrenic dreams. Their night work would come soon enough. "Let's leave the dreamworld for later. Easy stuff first. Any other mathematical feats you can do?"

Orlando stared at the table as though a list of his talents was written there. In a head that could recite hundreds of digits of pi, maybe it was. "I can do cube roots."

"That sounds fun. Show me."

"Well, like the cube root of eight is two. The cube root of twenty-seven is three. Anyone knows those. But the cube root of seventeen is 2.571281590."

"How about the cube root of 2,346?" she tested.

"13.28748139."

"Cube root of 8,290,640?"

"202.3932475."

"Kori?"

"Perfect. He's accurate to ten places," Kori answered.

Amelia shook her head, smiling. "Orlando, that's amazing. Have you always been able to do this?"

He didn't look pleased or even satisfied with his feat. The tired eyes and sullen expression said it all. Orlando Kwon wasn't showing off, he was in distress.

"The math stuff started after the voices. Maybe three weeks ago. I told the therapist about it and he told the doctors, and… here I am."

"Sorry to make you go through this again. It must be hard."

He started a smile, but it never fully formed. "No, not hard. But I know I shouldn't be able to do this. I'm a freak."

She didn't want to push too hard or too fast, but the display of rapid mathematical computation was something she'd only read about in textbooks. It was fascinating to see in person.

"So far, I'd say you're very talented. But I'm curious. Why *cube* roots? What about other inverse exponentials?"

"I don't even know what an inverse exponential is."

"You know, square root, or fourth root. For example, what's the square root of 557?"

"I have no idea," Orlando said.

"23.60084744," Kori answered over the speaker.

"Your assistant seems stranger than me," Orlando said, a natural smile appearing on his face for the first time.

Amelia met his smile with one of her own. "He's got digital help. You're doing it in your head, as far as I can tell."

The prep team would have given him a physical exam, including looking in his ears and mouth for any electronic devices. Amelia gave his ears a quick glance just for her own satisfaction.

He turned his head sideways and pulled on one of his ears. "The last lady already checked."

"Sorry, just being thorough. The brain is a funny thing. Savants have been known to do what you're doing, but I doubt there have been any cases of schizophrenia coupled with savant abilities. So, that's what we need to understand. What makes you different?" She tapped a finger to her temple. "What's going on in there?"

"I wish I knew." His eyes steadied on Amelia, a good sign that he was getting more comfortable.

"Shall we talk about organic chemistry?"

"Fine with me, though I don't know much about it. At least, it doesn't feel that way. Things just pop out."

"Like?"

"I don't know, ask me a question."

Kori didn't need any prompting. "I've got one." A drawing app popped up on Amelia's tablet and displayed several combinations of letters and numbers. She turned the tablet so Orlando could see, too.

$$CH_3COOH$$
$$CH_3NH_2$$
$$CH_3SO_3H$$

"Which of these organic compounds is the strongest acid?" Kori asked.

Orlando scanned the page for a few seconds. "The first is a carboxylic acid, in this case, ordinary vinegar. It has a pK_a, an acid disassociation constant, of around four. The second is methylamine. I don't know its pK_a offhand, but I don't need it to eliminate this choice. The elements of the periodic table increase in acidity from left to right, so the oxygen-hydrogen bonds in the first and third compounds are more acidic than the nitrogen-hydrogen bond in the second. The last one is a methane sulfonic acid with a negative pK_a. Since acidity increases with lower pK_a, that's the right answer. But even if I didn't know the pK_a's of any of these compounds, I could just draw their resonance forms and note which conjugate base is most stable, which tells me the highest acidity. Again, that's the third compound, methane sulfonic acid."

The stream of scientific words alone was impressive. Amelia could follow what he was saying but her knowledge of organic chemistry was inadequate to confirm the answer. "Kori?"

"One hundred percent correct," he answered.

"Very impressive, Orlando. Your case document said you don't have a formal education in chemistry. True?"

"High school, that's it."

"But your job is quality control in a plastic bottling plant? There must be some chemistry involved in that, right?"

"Sure, there is. The bottles are made from polyethylene terephthalate, or PET. I could probably tell you how to make that compound now, but I couldn't a few months ago. My job is to make sure the machines are working to tolerance. Heating elements, cutters, air injectors. That kind of thing. We buy PET resin pellets by the ton from some company in China and just pour them in the hoppers."

"So, where does the organic chemistry knowledge come from?" A sudden grasp of a significant branch of science was beyond any savant capability Amelia had ever heard of.

Orlando shrugged. "Don't know. I'm not even sure what I just said about the carbol... carboxylic acid and the pK... whatevers. When it comes out, it makes sense to me at the time."

He was struggling with the same words he had tossed out so easily only seconds before. It was as though the chemistry knowledge in his head could be switched on or off at will, possibly even unconsciously activated by the question that Kori had posed.

"What's a pK_a?" Amelia tested.

Orlando answered without hesitation. "A pK_a is the negative logarithm of the acid disassociation constant of a solution."

Amelia's mouth dropped open. "Fascinating. Advanced cognitive reasoning triggered by a single component drawn from the associated memory store."

"Huh?" Orlando looked confused.

"Just a theory. Your chemistry ability seems to be triggered when a piece of your memory is fed back to you in a question form."

"Yeah, that's kind of how it feels for me too."

Amelia had a related thought. "Orlando, your last therapist said you wrote out a formula. They gave it to a UCLA professor who was apparently quite impressed."

"If you have a piece of paper, I can show it to you."

Amelia opened a drawer on the credenza and pulled out a small notebook and pen. Orlando scribbled out a complex drawing with hexagon shapes, letters and connecting lines. Amelia recognized it as a chemical formula of some kind, but what it might represent she couldn't guess. She adjusted her earbud to be sure its forward-facing camera had a view of the page.

"Interesting," Kori said from the mobile speaker. "Are you sure you drew the trimethyl double bond correctly in this reaction? That would substantially change the result."

"The double trimethyl bond is the whole point of this formula," Orlando replied.

"Very interesting then. What you have drawn is a reaction formula for creating trimethylaluminum, one of several kinds of organometallics. This particular compound is used in semiconductor fabrication to deposit a thin film of dielectric on the surface of silicon. Trimethylaluminum is normally a liquid that must be handled with great care because it's pyrophoric – meaning, it spontaneously ignites when it comes in contact with air. But, if I'm reading it correctly, your formula would produce a non-reactive solid."

"Yeah, that's what they tell me. I know what the chemical is, but I really don't know how to make it."

"But you're showing it can be made, possibly even grown, since it's organic."

Amelia interjected, "Not sure I'm following."

"A new kind of chemistry," Kori answered. "A way to grow metal. Solid metal, like aluminum, but infused with a carbon structure for higher strength."

Amelia swiveled to Orlando, her eyes locked onto the apparent genius who sat across from her. More than a savant, more than prodigy. Deep within that skull might be the most intriguing brain ever studied.

No wonder UCLA was so interested in this guy.

CHAPTER EIGHT

FORMULA

MAJOR BROCK SHEPARD strode down a hallway at the UCLA Department of Chemistry building, his pressed Army greens uniform standing out among the sloppy casuals worn by the average college student or faculty member. Three steps behind him and never quite catching up, Walker Duplass was one of those sloppy civilians. Wearing a wrinkled shirt and pants that didn't fit, Duplass adjusted his glasses as they slipped further down his nose with each step. A leather satchel banged against his knee.

Shepard scanned the nameplates as they passed each door, mostly closed. One that was open revealed tables covered with beakers, test tubes, racks of pipettes and other tools of chemists. Further down, he stopped. The nameplate read, *Professor Darrin Mikkelsen, PhD.*

Shepard gave a stern glance at his companion. "I'll do the talking."

Duplass nodded vigorously.

Without knocking, Shepard opened the door with his left hand. Today, the prosthesis forming his right-arm was integrated with an air gun loaded with nonlethal plastic buckshot – the perfect weapon for crowded urban areas, even if it was probably overkill for today's mission. Additional attachments were carefully stored in a case Shepard took with him on every trip, each attachment evoking a special joy when clipped into the prosthesis frame.

The hand-shaped claw provided a feeling of power. Weapons produced a physical tingle all the way to his shoulder. But nothing topped the nearly orgasmic feeling of inserting his five-megawatt hot laser, capable of vaporizing a hole through a steel plate purely by thought. Losing his right arm in Afghanistan was the best thing that had ever happened to Brock Shepard.

They stepped into the private office, Shepard closed the door behind them and flipped the lock.

A white-haired man sitting at a large oak desk looked up, startled. "Can I help you?"

The uniform usually had that effect, though Shepard's no-nonsense stare could drill holes through anyone almost as effectively as the laser.

Shepard reached into his coat pocket, withdrew his Army credential, and flashed it to the seated man. "Major Brock Shepard, DARPA Operations. This is my assistant." He waved at Duplass. "We're here to collect a formula delivered to you on August twentieth by a person not associated with this university. A Mr. Orlando Kwon."

The professor's face contorted in a question. "What do you mean, collect?"

Shepard's voice was sharp and crisp, no different than the rows of service ribbons across one side of his jacket. "We have reason to believe Mr. Kwon removed highly sensitive, classified material from a United States government facility. The information he provided to you was not authorized to be released. I'll need to remove all records of this formula from the premises."

Mostly a ruse, Shepard's story would likely be sufficient to gain cooperation. The confused man looked at his computer display and back to Shepard. "I, uh... I had no idea."

"Your cooperation in this matter is imperative," Shepard said. "Point me to your records on this topic and I believe we can avoid any unpleasant follow-up visits that could result in your arrest and prosecution."

The professor paled. "Wait, how am I to blame? The chemical formula was delivered to me without conditions from a psychiatrist I don't even know. I didn't ask for it. I certainly didn't pay for it, and I never had any contact with Kwon."

"National security law covers both persons providing and persons receiving classified information."

He stood up, slamming his chair into the wall behind him. "Now wait a minute, how was I supposed to know it was classified? There was nothing marked on it. I reasonably assumed the guy came up with it himself."

The man's objections were as irrelevant as the ominous sounding legal references Shepard had made up on the spot. Mikkelsen was a containment target and his cooperation was Shepard's only objective.

"Calm down. As I said, Professor Mikkelsen, we can make this much easier if you cooperate. Just point me to your records of this formula."

The professor glanced again at his computer and returned to his chair. He typed at a keyboard and a window popped up displaying a lengthy chemistry formula that identified various molecular compounds and the complex results of their combination.

"This formula is groundbreaking. I have every right to keep it."

Shepard ignored the belated resistance. In a few minutes, none of this conversation would matter in the slightest. "How many other copies are there besides this file?"

The professor paused. "Just the one. I intended to safeguard it until I could get a better idea of what we were dealing with."

"How many people have seen it?"

"A few others. Department people."

"How many, specifically?"

"Well... three, including one of the graduate students."

Shepard handed him a small notepad. "Write down their names."

Mikkelsen hesitated, but finally took the notepad and wrote three names. "These people only provided an opinion, they're not involved."

"Then they have nothing to worry about," Shepard fired back.

"Major, maybe you don't understand. This formula is astonishing. It's not like anything we've ever seen."

Shepard nodded. "So I've heard. Professor, we're going to need you to confirm a few remaining items. It won't take long." He turned to Duplass. "Okay, do your thing."

Duplass set his satchel on the desk. He pulled out latex gloves, put them on, and then withdrew a glass disc about six inches in diameter. He flipped a tiny switch on its side causing its surface to light up. Multiple colors danced around the edges while a small rectangle appeared in the center displaying a chemical formula that only superficially resembled the one on the professor's screen.

Duplass handed the disc to the professor. "Disregard the lights – they're just for communications. We need you to study the formula on this disc and tell us what differences you notice. We expect there will be some." There would be plenty, Duplass had only guessed what the formula might look like.

The man put on reading glasses and held the disc in both hands, his eyes focusing intently on the writing in its center.

"No, no, this isn't right at all. You've got the trimethyl double bond in the wrong place."

The colors around the disc edges wavered, flashing on and off in a pulsating regularity. A slightly sweet scent filled the air. Duplass took two steps back.

"And the carbon polymers are missing altogether." He studied the lengthy formula, blinking and rubbing a finger at the corner of one eye. "The last part is a bit blurry."

He held the glass disc closer. The colors continued to flash. The man's head nodded, jerked up, then nodded again and jerked up once more. His head finally steadied, his glassy eyes frozen in a stare at the disc in his hands.

"Professor?" Duplass asked, bending down to look more closely at his face. There was no response. Duplass waved a hand in front of the man's eyes. Still no response. Duplass looked up at Shepard. "Okay, we've got him."

Wordlessly, Shepard reached to the keyboard and typed a link he knew well. A small window popped up with a *Seek and Destroy* logo at the top. Shepard pointed the app to the formula's file. A few seconds later a box popped up confirming that all traces of the file were permanently deleted.

"Clean here," Shepard said. "Get this guy wiped too."

Duplass took the glass disc from the man's hands and returned it to a side pouch in the satchel. He removed his gloves, turning them inside out and dropping them in the same pouch. Reaching deeper, he withdrew a wire mesh cap that he placed over the professor's head and secured with a strap under his chin. He connected a cable from a plug on the side of the cap to a tablet computer.

Duplass brought up the local Wi-Fi and checked its parameters. "Fast enough," he announced. The tablet was purely for control, all the real work would be accomplished by a supercomputer back in Virginia.

With a few button presses, the cap lit up in a blue glow with an accompanying acidic smell like plastic burning. A window popped up displaying a 3-D map of a human brain lit up by a complexity of multicolored filaments crisscrossing its surface.

"Alright, let's see what we've got." Duplass studied the screen. He zoomed in and touched several of the colored filaments. "These for sure."

Once selected, the filaments flashed on and off until Duplass pressed a button marked *Erase*. The flashes of color disappeared. The glowing blue cap covering the professor's head made no sound, but his body flinched as if he'd been pricked by a needle.

Duplass continued scrolling across the neurological landscape. "These NCCs are likely targets too." He selected them and pressed the same button, causing the filaments to flash out of existence the same as the first group. The professor's head wobbled slightly but his eyes continued to stare straight ahead.

"There's a lot more going on in here that I'm less sure about," Duplass said without looking up from the tablet.

"Fuck it, just erase them all."

Duplass squinted one eye. "That could be dangerous. Some of these in the occipital and parietal lobes are probably generalized NCCs related to cognitive functions but not specifically to this formula. And all these patterns down in the visual cortex are simply managing the image coming from his retina."

Shepard loomed over Duplass, his irritation rising. "I don't give a rat's ass what they're for. If they have any relation to this formula, I want them gone. Do it."

"But he could wake up with –"

Shepard leaned in closer. "Do it."

Duplass sighed, selected all the lighted filaments displayed on the screen and pressed *Erase*. The professor's head jerked backward. His jaw shuddered as he reflexively sucked in air. The tablet now displayed nothing but colorless gray.

Shepard nodded, satisfied. "Outstanding. Like clearing junk out of the garage. And with that, our work here is done."

Duplass shut off the tablet, and the cap's blue glow disappeared. He packed the equipment into the satchel, pushed the professor's chair back, and leaned the man's head until it rested against the wall.

The professor's eyes were glazed, his breathing shallow.

"Sorry," Duplass whispered.

Shepard motioned to the door, and Duplass dutifully followed him out.

CHAPTER NINE

SCHIZOPHRENIC

ORLANDO HELD HIS HEAD in his hands, both elbows resting on the conference room table. "I'm worried it's getting worse." Their conversation had shifted from the weird but easy stuff like math and chemistry to the more difficult topic: the voices in his head.

"How so?" Amelia asked. She was dragging him through the same territory his therapists had covered but until she had enough information to form a plan for how she'd manage the assisted lucid dream, there was no other way.

"It, uh… it feels like something is forming." He took a deep breath and looked up to the ceiling, his eyes once again unable to connect to hers.

"Tell me about it." Amelia resisted her instinct to provide emotional comfort to a person in obvious distress. The savant-like abilities had already proven he was no ordinary schizophrenic and would need a specialized approach. She'd combine the psychological assessment from his therapists with a detailed study of the activity in his brain. Armed with enough information, she could probe his dream, redirect it where necessary, and force a confrontation. Though a hostile ALD session might be difficult for him, it would expose specific neuronal patterns that represented the brain dysfunction, opening the door for potential treatment.

He began slowly. "There's something else out there. I don't know what it is, but it's not human. It's alive. It's growing, but not fully formed. Like... you know, a fruit that's not ripe. I can't see it, but it feels like... I don't know... like I'm seeing *through* it. Like I'm part of it."

"And you think it's alien?"

"Yeah. It's in a jungle somewhere, but not on Earth. And... it's not alone."

"There are other aliens around it?"

"I'm not sure. I can't see them. I just see glimpses of the jungle, but I can tell it's not alone. Some things about it I just feel."

"Do you think the voices are coming from these aliens?"

His lip quavered and he nodded affirmatively. "I know it sounds crazy."

She'd already seen enough to close the door on the fraud theory. He might still be deceiving himself, but his distress was real. She'd seen it before in other patients with schizophrenia. They tended to speak nonsense but believed it with all their heart.

If Orlando had been a friend in need, she would be hugging him. Crying with him. It was a strong personal urge that required every bit of logic to avoid. Her own emotions were unimportant, this man needed her expertise.

"Okay, just relax for a minute." She waited until he took another deep breath. "Orlando, I believe you. I believe you're really seeing and hearing these things. But I can also tell you with some confidence that they're hallucinations. The cerebral cortex of our brain is perfectly capable of creating its own images and sounds, even when the visual and auditory cortices are not functioning. We really don't need our eyes and ears to see and hear things. We perform this magic every night when we dream, and neuroscientists have learned that the neural patterns of hallucinations are closely tied to the same patterns observed while dreaming."

"I still have dreams, but the voices and the jungle – they're not like any dream."

"I'm sure they're not. Hallucinations feel different than dreams. A hallucination is an overlay. One part of your brain creates a visual image or an auditory track, and another part combines it with real-world signals coming from your eyes and ears – what we call the veridical perception. Dreams don't work like that. When we enter the REM state of sleep, the brain does its best to shut down the visual and auditory cortices, sealing off most input from the eyes, the ears, and other senses. It's why even a loud alarm can take a while to register when you're in the middle of a dream. To compensate, a dreaming brain creates its own sensory input and weaves it into an imaginary story. Dreams can be compelling, but they'll never be as rich as the veridical perception we experience while awake. And that's why a hallucination feels different. It feels more real because the background behind the overlay *is* real."

"But the hallucination can't be real," Orlando stated, almost sounding disappointed.

"During a hallucination, the imagined overlay may feel no different than the real background. But it's an overlay, a sensory creation of the mind. It's neurons firing in your brain, just as they do in a dream."

"You're saying the same thing the other doctors said. It's all imaginary."

Amelia nodded. "I am, in a way. Orlando, you're showing all the signs of schizophrenia. The hallucinations. That feeling that what you see and hear is not your own, that these sounds and images come from somewhere else, or some*one* else. That's classic schizophrenia stuff."

He picked up the pen that lay on the table, repeatedly clicking its button in rapid succession and then slammed it back down on the paper pad. "I know you're trying to help, but repeating what the doctors told me won't work. I'm not a schizophrenic. What I see and hear is real. You haven't experienced it. I have."

Amelia leaned back in her chair, absent mindedly tapping a finger to her lower lip. The denial stage could be tough to break through. She didn't need his acceptance of the diagnosis, but a cooperative patient was easier to manage.

A voice in her ear pulled her attention from Orlando. "Do you want my input?" Kori asked.

She held a thumbs-up fist in front of the earbud camera.

"Rehashing the medical diagnosis is just spinning your wheels. An ALD session will give you better insight." For an AI, Kori could be surprisingly on target.

"Okay, fair enough. Orlando, I'll level with you. There's a lot about your case that I don't understand. The savant abilities, for example. They don't match a schizophrenia diagnosis. So, if you can help me by duplicating any one of those abilities during a dream, then I'll be able to search your brain for the source."

His brow scrunched around his eyes. "Why can't you search while I'm awake?"

Amelia shrugged. "That's a bit complicated." Theoretically, there was a level three insertion where both the guide and the patient were awake. Purely theoretical. No one had tried it; no one wanted to. The logistics of transferring neuronal patterns between two consciousnesses, both awake, each competing for control seemed like a recipe for mental disaster. Like repairing a car as it's driving down the freeway. Amelia had decided long ago she'd leave the level three insertions for simulations that the computer guys ran in their spare time.

There was no reason to explain any of this to Orlando. She simplified. "The technology we use to enter your mind requires that only one of us is awake, and that's me."

Though Orlando would create the dream story, Amelia had good reasons to believe that she'd be able to guide the dream toward his unique mathematic and chemistry feats. The power of suggestion worked equally well for both hypnotists and dream guides. Assuming Orlando could repeat the feat while asleep, there was no telling what she might find in his neuronal patterns.

"Fine with me. Go ahead and jump into my dreams. I've already signed the release forms. I know I'll be wearing some kind of cap, and I know you can change things in my head, but I'm not sure I understand how it works."

"I can explain. Would you like the deep science version or just the overview?" He seemed bright enough to absorb whatever details she threw at him, but she'd learned from experience that patients slept better when they weren't worried about what might happen inside their head overnight.

"Maybe something in the middle?"

"I can do that, too." Amelia stepped out of the conference room for a minute and returned with a wire mesh cap. She gave it to Orlando, who turned the cap over in his hands.

"It's called a Bronson cap," she said. Just put it over your head and position the strap under your chin." He put the cap on while she talked, his spiky hair sticking through the mesh in places.

"Tonight, when you're ready to sleep, push the button on the side. The cap will light up blue, but it's dim enough that most people aren't bothered by it. The cap will monitor your brain activity. We'll know as you pass through each stage of sleep and we'll know when you're dreaming. In the old days, we used electroencephalography, EEG, but the new Bronson caps give us an order of magnitude greater resolution in both space and time."

He pressed the button and the cap lit up. He pressed again and it turned off. "Easy enough," he said.

Amelia leaned back in her chair, deciding how much brain science might be appropriate for a smart but unstudied person like Orlando.

"Neurons come in different shapes and sizes, but they all work in a similar way. When a neuron fires, it passes charged ions of potassium and sodium along a threadlike connector called an axon. It's a tiny electrical spark that the Bronson cap can detect. The challenge is that there are eighty-six billion neurons in your brain, and they can spark up to two hundred times per second across a thousand synapses. Every neuron is not always firing, but even if ten percent are, we're trying to monitor something like two *quadrillion* electrical events every second. It's a huge amount of data."

"But these caps can do it?" He seemed interested in the neuroscience, always a good sign. An engaged patient turned into a cooperative patient.

"Pretty close. We currently capture about seventy percent, and the stuff we miss is usually deeper in the cerebellum where conscious thoughts don't occur."

"If you change my brain while I'm sleeping, will I know it?"

"Probably not. Here's how that part works. The cap is both a receiver and a transmitter. The bulk of the time, your cap gathers terabytes of data as your brain generates a dream and sends that data to our supercomputer – a machine we call The Boss. In real time, The Boss analyses brainwave patterns – what we call neural correlates, or NCCs – and matches each NCC to a corresponding phenomenon – a particular image, sound, or feeling. The Boss transmits the stream of phenomena to my Bronson cap and translates automatically from your NCC patterns to mine so that I can experience the same dream as you create it. Inside my head, I'll literally be hallucinating while awake, experiencing the sights, sounds, and smells of your dream. But I can also control things by voice or through my tablet. Voice control is a form of hypnotic suggestion and patients usually respond, whether they realize it or not. I might suggest you do something in your dream, and more than likely, you'll do it."

"I probably would," Orlando admitted. "I was hypnotized once."

"I can also tell The Boss to transmit what we call neural *tickles* back to your cap. It's a direct stimulation to a specific set of neurons in your head that will cause them to self-adjust, essentially rewiring the synapses in a different way. The brain is remarkable in its ability to quickly change its own physiology. It's called neuroplasticity and it can happen in milliseconds, though to become permanent requires repetition over days or weeks. Neuroplasticity is how we learn new things, like how to play a new game, or speak Spanish. In the case of a tickle, The Boss imprints the new pattern along with some control NCCs that tell the brain this pattern should be considered permanent. It even performs synaptic pruning to clear out the old patterns that are no longer used."

"So, when I wake up, I'm different?" He pulled the cap from his head and set it on the table.

"That's the idea. But we make the changes incrementally over multiple sessions, fine tuning as we go. We never make major alterations, so you probably won't notice much over a single night."

His eyes lifted, still nervous but hopeful. "Do we start tonight?"

Amelia smiled. It was just a glimmer of enthusiasm from him, but she'd take whatever she could get. "I'm ready, if you are."

"Nice job, Amelia," Kori whispered in her ear. She acknowledged with a gentle nod that Kori would see.

Orlando drew in a deep breath. When he exhaled, he picked up the pen and started tapping on the paper notebook that still lay on the table, his remarkable chemical formula at the top of the page.

"I want to do this, I really do. But I'm still worried."

Amelia pulled in close. "You've said that twice now. You think the dream session will turn into a nightmare?"

He nodded. "It might. But… I'm mainly worried about you."

He tapped repeatedly on the paper, making dots of ink across its page.

"Worried that I might make the dream worse?"

"Um, it's not really that. I'm worried… I might hurt you. Not me literally, but whatever's inside my head. This alien thing. It scares me. I'm worried it might get you too."

She waited for him to lift his eyes, but he continued to focus on the notebook.

"Orlando, these things aren't real. They're images in your mind. They might scare you and once I'm inside your head, they might scare me too. But they can't hurt either one of us."

His lips tightened and his breathing increased. The continuous tapping of pen seemed to form a crude monitor of his internal struggle, increasing in pace and probably matching his quickening heartbeat.

He spoke forcefully. "You haven't seen them. You don't know. They're not hallucinations. I know they're not. All of this is real. Amelia, I swear to God, there's some kind of alien thing in my mind. It's swallowing me, pulling me in. And once you're in my dream, it will pull you in too."

Orlando hit the page hard with the pen, breaking its plastic casing and scattering pen parts across the table. His breaths came strong, his lower lip quivering. He glared wordlessly at the page.

"Uh… Amelia?" It was Kori in her ear.

She didn't answer him; she didn't need to. She'd noticed the same thing. Staring at the page, she turned the notebook to give her a better view.

Below the chemical formula, Orlando had tapped hundreds of black dots of ink into a form. It wasn't random; it outlined a definite shape, a drawing so perfect it seemed to be crafted by a professional artist.

The dots formed the shape of a multilegged insect with crab-like pincers.

CHAPTER TEN

VISIONS

AT THREE IN THE MORNING, the streets were dark and quiet. With one hand on the steering wheel of her Mini and the other stifling a yawn, Amelia drove to work in silence. She hadn't gotten enough sleep. Typical for summer in Seattle where the sun still peeked around the window shades at her seven-p.m. bedtime.

Anticipation didn't help either. Like caffeine, it kept her awake no matter what she commanded her stubborn brain to do. She'd soon be inside another person's head, an absurd notion that she'd probably never get used to even though she'd done it a hundred times.

She'd do it a thousand times more if it helped to uncover the mysteries of the brain. How does a three-pound blob of quivering gelatin manage to write a masterpiece of literature? Or create a symphony? Or design a rocket to the stars?

Or fail completely? Natalie's did.

Amelia's sister was never far from her thoughts, particularly before another ALD session. Natalie was the motivation for Amelia's career in neuroscience, as well as her focus on brain dysfunction. Depression ran in the family and Amelia's identical twin had taken the full impact of that genetic bomb. As teens, Amelia recalled tearful conversations with Natalie. How could one twin inherit the depression gene and not the other, they both wondered but never resolved. Psychologists suspected that epigenetic mechanisms allowing for gene expressions played a role in differentiating twins, but no one was sure.

The bottom line – Natalie suffered while Amelia didn't. In their junior year of college, Natalie's struggle with depression finally ended when she was found dead in her dorm room, an empty pill bottle nearby. No warning. No note. One day she was there, the next, gone.

Devastated, Amelia had dropped out of school to search for the reasons why she'd lost her best friend – her other self – but she found nothing but unfairness and random chance. Two years later, Amelia dedicated the remainder of her life to learning how and why the brain functioned.

Undergraduate classes in brain physiology and dysfunction morphed into graduate courses that dove into the neurological underpinnings of thought. Her dissertation traced advanced cognition such as reason and emotion to neuronal structures in the cerebrum and cerebellum. Through it all, Amelia kept asking the biggest questions. How does consciousness arise from structural complexity and interconnectedness? For that matter, what do electrical currents have to do with it? More profoundly, how could twins, genetically identical in every other way, support independent consciousnesses? There were hints, but none of her professors had the answers.

Natalie's death had triggered a lifelong quest accompanied by lasting pain. It had been a slow road to recovery and in some ways, it was still in progress. Just last year, Amelia's boyfriend had shocked her with what he had called a 'loving intervention'. He'd told Amelia that she needed to let go of Natalie and move on with her own life, that no amount of focus on work was going to bring Natalie back. His words felt cruel, and Amelia broke up with him the following week.

It was true, work had been her focus for years, but Amelia could look back on a series of spectacular achievements as she transformed a startling new technology into a groundbreaking means of therapy.

In a few minutes, Orlando Kwon would be the next opportunity. He was certainly a fascinating case, Nolan had been right about that. In some ways it was straightforward schizophrenia, though Orlando was calmer and more cooperative than most. His astonishing mental and artistic feats, though abnormal, were a clear demonstration of the untapped capabilities of the human brain. The dot drawing of the crab bug had surprised even Orlando; he hadn't recognized what he was doing until it was complete.

Amelia kissed two fingers and tapped them to a necklace hanging from her rearview mirror. Natalie's. Emotional ointment for an open wound, or maybe just habit, it was getting hard to tell the difference.

Six-lane Aurora Avenue heading into downtown was nearly devoid of cars at this early hour. Ahead, the blue and green lights defining the saucer of the Space Needle peeked over the top of darkened Queen Anne hill.

"Take a note, Kori." Her voice was scratchy on its first use of the day.

"Ready. And good morning to you, too, Amelia."

She was too lost in thought to engage in pleasantries. "If we can capture Orlando's NCC patterns when he's performing one of his feats, what if we tickled those patterns onto a receiving brain? Would it result in the same mathematical and drawing aptitudes in another person?"

"Good question."

"I don't need an answer. Just something to think about. I doubt we'd get many volunteers. I certainly wouldn't." Continuously solving cube roots or reciting the digits of pi seemed like a song stuck in your head. Curious, but not necessarily a pleasant experience.

Drawing with dots might be a cool talent to have. Modern day pointillism?

There was still much to learn about the brain, and Orlando represented a fresh opportunity. Nolan had been right about that too.

Taking an offramp, Amelia followed the curving shoreline of Lake Union and a minute later pulled into the underground garage at the Westlake Institute. The empty concrete space echoed with her footsteps. The main lobby was just as deserted. A swipe of her badge and a glass door ushered her into the world of advanced neuroscience, minus most of the people who worked there.

She took the elevator to the fifth floor and stepped out to a dimly lit hallway open on one side to the atrium. The ALD lab had its own security door requiring a second badge tap to go in or out. Sleeping patients were confined to individual rooms inside but an overnight nurse took care of any needs that might arise. Josefina was slumped in a leather chair on one side of the darkened lab, her head down.

"Morning," Amelia whispered, just loud enough to rouse the nurse.

"Oh, sorry, Doctor Charron. I lost track…"

Amelia had tried several times to get Josefina, a recent immigrant from Honduras, to call Amelia by her first name, but to no avail. It seemed some cultures felt the need for formality and structure. Josefina had proven her competence as a nurse, but otherwise their interaction had been limited since her hiring one month before.

Amelia kept her voice low. "It's okay, Josefina. As long as you're here, that's the main thing. Any issues tonight?"

"It was fine. Mr. Lawrence got up once to use the toilet, but Mr. Kwon has been asleep the whole time. Just those two patients tonight."

"Good. Keep monitoring Mr. Lawrence. I've got Mr. Kwon from here."

Amelia opened the door into Orlando's sleeping room – dark, except for a blue glow on the pillows. He'd initialized the Bronson cap just as instructed though Josefina was always there to help. The sound of gentle breathing reassured that Amelia hadn't woken him.

She checked his status on her tablet; currently in REM stage, his third of the night. It had started about twenty minutes before with two instances of dreaming noted, the first one involving a cave with stalactites, now completed. A short period of stage-three NREM followed and then a second dream, which was still in progress.

The only recognizable NCCs in the dream so far were an unidentified shirtless boy and a beach ball. The Boss couldn't always map the NCCs to named objects but feeding the full set of patterns into Amelia's brain would clarify the rest of the scene. World-class supercomputers and advanced 3-D displays aside, sometimes the best way to interpret real-time brain patterns was simply to send them to a second brain.

Time to get to work.

She withdrew her earbud and pocketed it. Kori wasn't allowed into an ALD session. No electrical devices, no distractions. It was a rule she agreed with.

Retrieving a second Bronson cap from a cabinet, she placed it over her head and secured it with a chin strap. A touch of a button on one side connected to the sleep room's dedicated 12G wireless router and produced a blue glow around her head along with the distinctive smell of ozone. A cap icon popped up on her tablet and she configured it as the receiver.

Amelia closed the sleep room door behind her and settled into a chair next to Orlando's bed. His mouth hung open, arms stretched out and legs intertwined with the bed sheets. A rather messy sleeper but she'd seen every variation.

A tap on the tablet brought up a standard system message in bold red letters.

> Warning: Before initiating a neural transfer, ensure that you are seated or reclined. No contact with sharp objects, electrical devices, or magnets for the duration of the session. If you experience dizziness, fatigue, nausea, or involuntary shaking of muscles in your extremities, head, or neck area, terminate the session immediately.

She wasn't sure why she stopped to read it. The same warning had flashed by a hundred times, easily dismissed with the click of an *I Agree* button at the bottom. Her finger hovered over the button. No reason to hesitate. She pressed and closed her eyes.

She was instantly transported to a seashore, replete with sights, sounds, and smells that filled her senses. Or so it seemed.

She sat on soft sand. A seagull flew past, shrieking. A dome of blue sky spread across a sparkling ocean with low waves breaking along the shore. The beach extended into the distance, becoming fuzzier with no distinct end.

Opposite the ocean, a sandy cliff loomed with palm trees along its top edge. The cliff suddenly disappeared, and then reappeared once more. It might have been a technical issue, though variation within the scene was often part of the native uncertainty of any dream.

Orlando sat nearby in the sand, wearing a swimsuit and hugging knees to his chest as he stared out to the sea, a breeze ruffling his black hair, a smile frozen on his face. He looked content.

Next to him, a woman lay on her stomach across a beach towel, sleeping. Her dark hair was tied in a ponytail and she wore a swimsuit with colors that matched his. Teena was the most likely possibility, though Amelia hadn't seen photos of her.

For level one insertions, Amelia was limited to a single fixed viewpoint, offset a few feet away from the dreamer. It was more or less a camera position that The Boss established on initialization simply by triggering a set of three unique NCCs in the visual cortex that behaved very much like a zoom lens. Amelia had a few options for repositioning her view, but any changes she made would require a session reset and a greater level of intrusion. Level one insertions seemed to work best when the dreamer's lucidity was low and only vaguely aware of Amelia's presence.

A boy wandered by kicking a beachball across the sand, and Orlando waved as he passed. With a scene this tranquil, it was probably the most action he'd seen for a while. Some dreams could remain static for considerable periods of time. Alternatively, the boy and the beachball might be on a continuous loop, endlessly repeating with Orlando none the wiser. It was possibly why The Boss had singled these objects out.

"Beautiful day," Amelia said out loud. The first words were a test of the patient's level of consciousness. With the auditory cortex suppressed, he might not hear them, though with repetition she could break through.

He looked up to the sky. "Yeah, really beautiful." He was probably a light sleeper. No sound came from his real-world mouth; his response had been nothing but pure thought.

Perfect. He'd stay asleep but would hear her guidance.

"Stunning beach. Where are we?" Amelia asked.

Orlando turned toward her viewpoint. He wouldn't see anything. She had no avatar in a level one insertion, but it wouldn't matter. The dreamer would simply accept verbal input without logically examining its source.

"Santa Monica. My favorite," he said with a sigh.

Santa Monica. I can work with that.

Amelia's view down the beach eventually faded into a haziness of blue, tan, and green, the colors blurring together at the edge of the dream world.

"Doesn't Santa Monica have a pier?"

Orlando turned to look down the beach, his eyebrows pinched. "Yeah, it does."

A few hundred yards away, a pier materialized, jutting from the beach directly out over the ocean. Restaurants and shops strung out along its length and people walked around its edges, some leaning over a railing to look at the blue water below.

"And there's a Ferris wheel at the end of the pier, isn't there?" She'd been to Santa Monica before.

"Yeah, there is," Orlando drawled as though hypnotized. A large Ferris wheel appeared from nowhere at the ocean end of the pier. The new object flickered a few times and then settled into the same stability as everything else in the scene.

So far so good.

"Wow, the wheel is huge. I wonder how big around it is?"

"Yeah, I wonder," he whispered.

"It wouldn't be hard to figure out. The formula is simple, just the diameter of the wheel times pi."

She waited. Orlando stared at the rotating wheel, his eyes blinking, his expression blank.

She prompted further. "Of course, you'd have to know the *value* for pi."

Orlando turned, his head tilted. His words were dreamy slow. "I do know that number."

Amelia checked the data overlay displayed for every ALD session. It showed Orlando's vital signs, including a real-time estimate of the portion of neurons being monitored by the Bronson cap – seventy-four percent, as good as it gets.

Orlando opened his mouth, hesitated, and then began the same recital she'd heard the day before.

"3.14159265338949…"

Amelia smiled, allowing Orlando to pour the numbers out. As he did, she could almost picture thousands upon thousands of minute electrical flashes sparkling across his cerebral cortex, connecting concepts, analysis, computations, and communication into the astonishing phenomenon we call conscious thought.

Best of all, The Boss would capture it all.

She let him continue. This time, he didn't seem remotely concerned about boring her. Hundreds of digits poured out, each expressed verbally within the dream but also as flashes of neural connections, each intricate pattern dutifully stored by The Boss. She had no doubt the digits were the same as he'd recited before and were mathematically correct. During sleep, the conscious mind has the same abilities as in wakefulness, even if it can be easily distracted.

"Nice job, Orlando. I didn't realize you were so smart."

He paused in his performance. Waited. And then spoke forcefully, as if he needed to correct her. "I'm really not that smart. It's… it's…"

He stared into the sand, his expression changing. His brow drew low over his eyes. His lips quivered. The sand melted away, along with the ocean, the breeze, Teena, and the pier.

Orlando stood up as green leaves materialized around his body. Overhead a large tree appeared with vines that hung down and spread across a verdant floor of leafy plants, oddly colored flowers, and damp moss. Ferns sprung up. Broad-leaved shoots resembling banana plants became interspersed with hardwood trees with diameters more than a meter.

The jungle floor was a patchwork of moss, puddles, and twigs. It smelled of musty plant decay. High above, a canopy of trees blotted out the sky. The jungle was thick, not just with plants but with steamy, heavy air.

Beautiful job, Orlando. He was a far more elaborate dreamer than most. The details could be useful.

Orlando stood ramrod straight, his eyes darting left and right. His lips tense and jittery, attempted to form words that never came. He still wore the same swimsuit and his bare legs extended several inches into black mud.

Amelia hesitated to say anything. The dream had changed radically with no transition between scenes. With schizophrenics it could easily change again, becoming darker without notice. Amelia's curiosity was piqued but her pulse quickened with the uncertainties.

Orlando jerked his head to the sound of dripping water. Another sound in the opposite direction, a chirp, and then two more. His heartbeat, displayed on the data overlay, soared.

Orlando tried to pull his left leg from the mud, grunting as he did. Both legs seemed stuck, though slurps from the mud indicated some movement below the surface.

"Help!" His plea was accentuated by lines of anxiety across his face. He seemed to be giving up rather easily, but based on his case notes, the jungle dreamscape was a place he feared. Immobilized by the mud, he would be an easy target for whatever animal might spring from the thick vegetation.

Amelia could get him unstuck; she knew exactly how. But should she? Overcoming a challenge was a key part of any ALD session. On the other hand, frustration was a powerful motivator for the brain to cancel the dream. If he woke, they'd only be delaying the unavoidable reckoning with his demons. Her decision was easy.

Your lucky day, Orlando. Help is on the way.

Amelia opened her eyes, typed a few keystrokes at her tablet and sent the tickle command to The Boss. It would execute within milliseconds sending a predefined pattern into Orlando's head.

She closed her eyes again just in time to see Orlando's left leg lift on its own, almost as if he had no control of its motion. His foot sucked from the mud and dangled in the air. He placed it on a mossy area and then repeated the maneuver with the right foot.

He tested the dry ground around him, touching a dubious toe and finally taking a few steps. The ground held and his confidence returned. Though he wouldn't have any idea how he'd escaped from the sticky mud, Amelia did. Her command had triggered his autonomous motor reflexes, body control hidden deep in the cerebellum. The NCC electrical patterns for walking were well understood with little variation between individuals. By tickling these specific neurons in his brain, she'd simply commanded his legs to start moving. Likely, they'd twitched in the real world too, shifting the tangle of sheets in his bed.

Unstuck, Orlando began a cautious survey of the jungle, pushing away vines and leaves to navigate the thick underbrush. His movements seemed aimless, and the jungle in one area didn't look any different than another.

Back in control, but sorry Orlando, you don't get off that easy.

A partition challenge was standard procedure and easier to control than random difficulties imagined by the patient. Erecting a barrier gave Amelia insight into which neural pathways showed promise for incremental rewiring.

Let's start with something tame.

With a few keystrokes, she executed the command for a low intensity partition. Simple, and potentially easy for him to solve.

As Orlando made his way through the thick plants, vines grew rapidly from tree branches overhead, dropping to the ground but continuing into the soil and forming a vertical bar of living tissue. More vines dropped, filling in the gaps until a wall stretched across Orlando's path. Additional vines filled in around the sides and behind him until he was fully enclosed inside a circle a few meters across.

Perfect.

His head swiveled, assessing his dilemma. He looked up. The wall of vines continued well into the upper reaches of the trees. He scratched in the soil around the bottom of one of the vines, finding no opening.

"Think, Orlando," she said aloud. "How would you get out of this situation?"

"I... I can't."

He could if he thought about it long enough. He could imagine any tool he desired. A machete or a chisel would instantly appear. Even a chainsaw.

A sound came from outside the circle of vines. A scratching sound like someone running a finger across the teeth of a comb. It was joined by distinctive clicks and ticks, as if a stiff band of metal were being bent back and forth.

Tick-tick. Crick. Zhee-crick. Scritch-tick orck.

Orlando reacted immediately. "No!" he screamed. His respiration rate skyrocketed. "Go away!"

Creetch-tick-tick-tick. Orck-zheesh.

He retreated from the sound, backing up against the circle of vines behind him. With all his weight, he slammed a shoulder against the wall, bending the vines outward but not breaking them.

"Let me out!" he yelled.

At a small gap between two vines, a wiggling tendril poked through. The thin stalk extended further through the vine wall, meandering snakelike in the air. Its tip was curled like the climber of a pea plant or a grapevine and, like the tendrils of many climbing plants, fine hairs extended at right angles along its length. It weaved left and right with searching movements more resembling the intentions of an animal than a plant.

It touched the circular wall of vines several times, but kept searching, extending directly toward Orlando. He cowered at the far side of the enclosure.

Amelia was just as startled as Orlando. In her extensive experience with partition challenges, she'd never seen a barrier breached by a dream character – animal, plant or otherwise. Usually they stood by uninterested, uninvolved. This was wildly different and clearly terrifying from Orlando's perspective.

Orlando slid around the circular enclosure doing his best to avoid the searching tendril. It snapped back and forth with surprising speed as it approached and when he held an arm out in defense, it wrapped around his wrist. Once in contact, the tendril's thickness increased to the size of a sturdy rope. It began pulling him, dragging him across the enclosure.

"No! Stop!" Orlando yelled. He pulled back, hitting the ropelike tendril with his free hand to no avail.

She watched, fascinated, disturbed, but not yet ready to intervene. "Fight it, Orlando. You can do it." In reality, she wasn't at all sure that he could.

Several additional tendrils poked through the opening, grasping the nearby vines, and bending them outward to create a larger gap. Orlando's feet skidded across the mossy floor, but he was outmatched in strength as the rope tendril dragged him relentlessly toward the growing hole in the vine wall. Vague shapes shifted in darkness on the other side.

Now close enough to the wall to put a foot against it, Orlando pushed against the vines, bowing them. He peered through the hole and his face contorted in fear.

"Oh, God. Please stop!"

Amelia had seen enough. His terror might result in a secondary psychosis, and all from a challenge of her own making. She had no idea what the tendril represented or why it was able to breach the barrier. Worse, from her offset viewpoint, she'd never be able to peer through the hole to whatever unseen plant beast seemed determined to pull him through.

Orlando's fear was palpable, so strong she could feel it within herself. A creepy feeling, like nothing she'd experienced in any session before. A tingling on the skin. A lowering of her defenses. An opening in her mind that seemed to mirror the dark hole in the wall of vines. She felt vulnerable. Unprotected.

Too weird. Time to stop this.

Amelia fired off a command to disable the partition and waited.

Nothing happened. The wall of vines stood steady. As the hole continued to enlarge, so did the feeling of vulnerability. Orlando stared through to the other side, shaking with fear at a monster only he could see.

The disable partition command should have executed within milliseconds. She tried once more but nothing in the scene changed.

Damn! What is going on?

"Wake up, Orlando!" Amelia shouted. "Wake up!"

Orlando's foot slipped across the vine wall and the tendril yanked his upper body through the opening. Amelia's viewpoint shifted, allowing a brief view through the opening into a dark jungle beyond. A shadowy figure loomed.

Amelia's eyes blinked open to the real world. "Emergency shutdown!" she commanded to her tablet.

She tore the cap from her head. Orlando squirmed, caught in a tangle of sheets as if the dream vines had manifested on the bed.

She grabbed his shoulders and shook him hard. "Orlando, wake up! Now!"

His arms waving wildly, Orlando's eyes opened. His chest heaved as he sucked in air. The blue glow of his cap disappeared, the emergency system shutdown performing as instructed and leaving only a scent of ozone hanging in the air.

Amelia flipped on the table lamp. Her heart raced.

"It's over," Amelia said.

Orlando panted open-mouthed. His eyes were wide, darting around the room but he said nothing.

"You okay? Talk to me."

He stopped struggling but his expression still held the same fear she'd seen in the dream. "Yeah... yeah. I'm okay," he forced out between gasps, his voice finally calming.

The sleeping room door opened a crack and Josefina peered in with eyes wide. Amelia held up fingers in an okay gesture, and Josefina closed the door again.

Taking a deep breath, she lowered her head. "I'm sorry, Orlando. My fault. I couldn't get the system to shut off fast enough."

He didn't answer, rolling over to face the wall. He trembled with each breath.

"Was that the creature that's been in your mind?"

He nodded. "I think so. I'd never seen it before. Not like that."

"I only got a glimpse of it myself. Frightening. I understand what you're dealing with." She noticed the shakiness in her own hands and the feeling of vulnerability that lingered.

He swallowed hard and leaned back into the pillows. "Then you know. It wants me to come with it." His eyes teared up. "And if I resist, it will just take me anyway."

Amelia nodded, feeling his despair more deeply than she had for any other patient. She'd experienced many nightmares through the ALD system, but never so personally. His fear had become hers.

She leaned back in her chair, kneading the wire mesh of the Bronson cap in her fingers. The fear inside was an emotional response. Temporary. She'd get over it. Far more concerning was that she'd lost control of the ALD system, unable to shut down the barrier – and no idea why.

CHAPTER ELEVEN

INACCURACIES

WITH MORE THAN EIGHTY billion neurons and just twenty percent of their firing patterns uniformly mapped, there were scads of reasons why Amelia might lose control of an ALD session. A lucid patient might refuse to cooperate, perhaps unleashing a stealth dream character with malicious motives. Even a police siren in the real world could enter the dream at just the wrong time.

Plenty of ways to fail but disabling an ordinary level-one partition wasn't supposed to be one of them. She'd created the barrier herself. It should have disappeared in a flash. More importantly, it should have never been breached.

At seven a.m., Amelia waited impatiently in the computer center for Jake, their software guru, to arrive for work. When he finally walked through the door, Amelia was on him.

"Partition structural failure," she said before Jake even set his coffee mug down. "Plus, the disable command malfunctioned."

"Slow down," he said waving a hand and swallowing a bite of a croissant. "Can we start from the beginning?"

Amelia lowered her head. "Sorry, tough night." She sat next to Jake and let him get a few sips of coffee while she filled him on the session. He pulled the session log up and within seconds identified the two partition disable commands that Amelia had issued; sent and received normally. At least she hadn't imagined it.

Jake was just as perplexed as Amelia as to why the dream barrier hadn't disappeared on command. He also had no explanation why a dream character could penetrate the barrier when the patient could not. He promised he would get to the bottom of it.

She'd left him to his work, but instinct told her that Jake wouldn't find the answer. The anomaly probably wasn't in software, system latency, or anywhere within The Boss. Most likely, the problem was inside Orlando's head.

For reasons she could only speculate, Orlando had allowed his own dream character to do what he could not do – produce a hole in the wall of vines. Then he'd maintained the barrier even after the neuronal pattern that established it switched off. How and why he'd done these things eluded her, but there was a way to find out.

Go deeper.

Wandering back to her office, still feeling dazed by the abrupt end of the ALD session, Amelia pondered the ways in which a deeper, level two insertion might work better.

Control of the viewpoint was the simplest advantage. A level-two avatar could move to any position and see anything. It was more invasive to the patient because it required the dream to be imagined as a richer, logically consistent scene that could be viewed from any angle. Given the right tickles from The Boss, most patients could pull it off, though their sleep became more restless as lucidity increased.

With a level-two avatar, Amelia could have peered through the hole in the vines to see what had frightened Orlando. It was a face, he'd explained later, but he wasn't able to elaborate. Dream details were often fleeting after waking.

With level two, she'd have direct control over dream characters, speaking to them, issuing commands, even physically blocking, or repositioning them. She could have commanded Orlando to provide her with an imagined weapon and prevented the tendril from grabbing him or slicing it in half after it did.

Level two wasn't the answer to everything. Figuring out how a dream character managed to interfere with the barrier would take investigation and post-session analysis. In addition, she was still unsettled by the feeling of vulnerability she'd experienced. Level two wouldn't make any difference to something so *internal*. It wasn't just empathy for Orlando. In the final seconds of the dream, she'd felt personally threatened.

One thing at a time. You're a scientist. Examine the data. Find the patterns.

At one end of her desk, a paper-thin computer screen on a tilted pedestal displayed multicolored graphics with complex patterns of light that darted across a three-dimensional model of the brain. Each pattern was labeled with a timestamp, a sixty-four-bit neuron group ID, and corresponding data.

The patterns told the story she expected – mostly. The dream recording of Orlando's NCCs was no more or less complicated than any other patient. She traced the familiar patterns through the usual nodes of the brain and noted an increase in intensity precisely when she had entered the dream. She could even see the demarcation between the beach dream and the jungle dream, and the point when the nightmare had taken over.

But one item caught her attention. When the data was displayed as an electroencephalogram, Orlando's recitation of the digits of pi showed a series of peaks and valleys pulsating at regular intervals. Rattling off a random sequence of numbers, whether asleep or awake, wouldn't normally produce an EEG cycle with such cyclical consistency.

"Kori?"

He picked up immediately. He always did.

"Yes?" His response included a background sound of heavy breathing.

"Working out?" She'd heard this fib before. Maintaining the illusion of a body required an extended fiction. It seemed harmless enough and might even be part of keeping his intellect intact, approximately the same reason humans exercised.

"Stair stepper. But I'm available. What do you need?"

"Can you grab a dream playback clip from this morning's session? Orlando started reciting pi at timestamp 1:42. I'd like to compare to see if there are any differences against what he recited the day before."

"Just a minute…"

She didn't have to wait long. He wasn't The Boss, but Kori was still faster than any human.

"That's odd," Kori said.

"What?"

"A big difference. Let me show you."

A text message popped up on her mobile. Just two lines, but the second line included gray highlights.

```
3.14159265358979323846264338327950288419716939937516
3.1415926533894935385621432831793027842974692995758
```

"These are the first fifty digits," Kori said. "The top line I recorded from yesterday's interview, while Orlando was awake. The bottom line is from his dream, while asleep. I highlighted the differences."

She scanned the text. The first ten digits matched in both lines, but after that, differences appeared with regular spacing – every third digit. It was remarkably similar to the pulsating EEG pattern she'd just examined.

"You said yesterday his recital of pi was perfect. So, that means the second line is wrong?"

"Completely wrong," Kori agreed. "It's not pi at all. The same pattern of incorrect digits continues to the end of all four hundred and eighty-six digits that he provided during the dream."

"Wow." Amelia looked up to the ceiling, tapping a finger to her lip. "Not random mistakes – not with that kind of pattern. Why would his dream consciousness do that? He knows the digits, even asleep. The first ten are perfect."

"Maybe you should test him again, both awake and asleep."

"Yeah, I think I will. But why the pattern? Why is every third digit wrong?"

"Maybe you should ask him that too."

****

Orlando wasn't in the ALD lab or anywhere else in the building. One of the staff members told Amelia he had checked out for the day, saying he'd return later that afternoon.

It was standard protocol for most patients. They weren't prisoners. They were free to use their daytime hours anyway they pleased as long as they had no appointments with the staff and their phone number was on file.

Still, Amelia wished he'd talked to her first. Kori located Orlando's mobile contact and she voiced a message. "Are you nearby? Can we meet at ten? I have some questions."

The sun was up, a glorious morning underway outside. Perhaps he'd gone for a walk around Lake Union. After a nightmare like the one he'd experienced, she couldn't blame him for wanting to clear his mind. Fresh air in a beautiful setting might be cathartic.

Half past eleven, and with no response from her message, Amelia was nearly ready to call it a day when Orlando knocked on the frame of her open office door.

"Just got your message," he said, holding his mobile in the air. "Sorry, I was outside talking to my wife."

A minor scolding might have been in order, but she bit her tongue. She could hardly blame him for putting his family first, even though Amelia had advised him to focus inward for a few days.

"Things okay at home?" She motioned to a chair and he took a seat.

"Better. Teena's glad I'm here."

"I am too, Orlando. Let's see if we can make some progress toward getting you back to your wife and kids." She pulled up the two sets of numbers, pi-good, and pi-bad, on her tablet, making sure Orlando couldn't see the screen. "Do your amazing pi trick for me once more."

His brow pinched down.

"Humor me," Amelia said.

He shrugged and started reciting. She stopped him after the first thirty digits. They were all correct.

"You're perfect while awake, but it seems your accuracy drops significantly when you're asleep." Amelia turned the tablet toward him. "Do you remember reciting the digits of pi in the dream?"

He nodded. "Vaguely, yes."

She pointed to the lower line. "Only seventy percent correct. Still impressive, but unsettling, given the mistakes occur every third digit all the way to the end."

He looked closely at the screen. "I gave you all those wrong digits?"

"You did. Any idea why every third digit?"

He shook his head. "None. Seems strange. Like I was trying to make mistakes."

"Were you?"

"I doubt it. It was a dream, I wasn't in control."

"Agreed, but it was a savant dream. Otherwise, you wouldn't have gotten any better than ten percent, the same as random guessing." Her finger bounced across the screen and each blue-highlighted number. "There's something else going on here, something repetitive. Something intentional, I think."

While Orlando studied the screen, Amelia studied her patient, a contradiction in symptoms. Part of this man was filled with real fear from realistic hallucinations. She'd seen it, even felt it herself. His mind was clearly not his own, yet unlike most patients of schizophrenia he showed no symptoms of cognitive impairment. His newfound abilities were remarkable – the digits of pi, cube roots, drawing with dots, and organic chemistry were somehow wrapped up in his disorder. But it wasn't just the mental feats that contradicted the dark side. Orlando could rationally examine himself, accepting that he'd made mistakes. Clear thinking – a sign of a healthy brain.

He's not schizophrenic, it's something else.

Orlando looked up from the digits of pi, his eyes steady, his face a model of sincerity. "I wish I could help. I don't know what happened."

Amelia closed the image on the tablet. The incorrect digits would remain an unsolved mystery for the moment. He might be holding back, but there was no need to press him further – at least not while he was awake. Going deeper was the only way she'd get answers.

"Orlando, I need to go back into your dreams tonight, but this time it will be a little different. I'll do what we call a level two insertion. You'll probably notice the difference right away. You might even feel like you're awake even though you'll still be dreaming."

"A lucid dream."

"Right. But there are different levels of lucidity. Even your dream last night was partially lucid. I asked you questions, and you responded."

"It's kind of fuzzy now."

"Perfectly normal, but tonight will feel different. I'll visually appear in your dream. You'll probably recognize that it's me right away, but even if you don't, I'll tell you who I am. Then we'll explore the dream together. I'll be able to talk to any characters that come along, and I'll even be able to adjust how the dream progresses. It will still be your dream, but I'll have more control."

"Fine. What do I do?"

"Your part is pretty simple." She pulled out a laminated card from a desk drawer and handed it to him. "When you're getting ready to sleep tonight, follow the instructions on the card. Do exactly what it says. Don't skip anything, okay?"

Orlando read the card. It provided simple steps for how to prepare for a restful sleep, routine advice like avoiding alcohol and ensuring the room was cool and dark. But it also included four lines of text arranged like lyrics in a song.

"I'm supposed to say these lines?"

Amelia nodded. "Out loud, at least thirty times. You're training your mind to be ready when the dream occurs."

He read the four lines from the card:

> I want Amelia in my dream.
> When Amelia arrives, I will recognize her.
> When Amelia asks, I will give her control.
> With Amelia in control, I will relax and think of nothing.

He looked up, confused. She smiled. "It's simple. Just say that thirty times, turn out the light and go to sleep."

"And this will work?"

"It has before. It's called a lucid dreaming mantra, but this one is specially designed for a level two insertion. There's a reason my name is on every line. It's a trigger word. When we're in the dream, I'll say it, you'll hear it, and it will help trigger the memory of these four instructions."

Orlando studied the card, mouthing the four instructions. "Okay, sounds weird, but maybe it will work." His eyes snapped up like he'd just been startled. "This is just for tonight, right? I can still leave the building during the day?"

Amelia shrugged. "You can. Just watch for messages from me or any other staff member in case something comes up. And if you're out past five, use this code to get in the front door." She jotted a four-digit code on a sticky note and handed it to him. "Try to be in bed by ten pm, and remember, no alcohol or caffeine. Fair?"

"Sure."

"Going for a walk or dinner?"

He looked puzzled by the question. "Oh, no. Not walking, just calling Teena. A second call. We uh… we didn't really finish what we were talking about and it's, well… you know… it's personal."

He looked flustered. Maybe his relationship with his wife hadn't mended as well as he'd implied earlier.

Amelia gave him a gentle smile. "Try the benches in front of MOHAI, the Museum of History and Industry. It's quiet there, and a lovely view of the lake."

"Thanks, I will." He paused on his way out, turning around. "Do you really think you'll be able to help me?"

It wasn't an easy question and she wasn't going to lie. "I hope so, Orlando. I'll know more after tonight."

He gave a slight bow of the head and left.

Amelia switched off her tablet and grabbed her car fob, feeling prepared for the next day. Just one detail remained.

She stopped by Nolan's office, knocked, and poked her head in the door. He was on the phone but waved her in. She took a seat, waiting – and thinking.

She'd made the upcoming session sound a lot simpler than it was, but she wasn't about to tell Orlando about the pitfalls of a level two insertion. Even if Orlando could come reasonably close to "thinking of nothing", she'd still be working hard to stay in control of the dream. For what she had in mind, Nolan needed to be in the loop.

He finished his call. "What's up?"

She didn't mince words. "Level two. Tonight."

He didn't flinch. "You sure?"

She nodded. "It's the only way. Orlando Kwon is going to be a tough case."

Nolan leaned back in his chair and took a deep breath. "This isn't going to be another hidden dagger, is it?"

Their own technical jargon. Hidden dagger was code for a dangerous dream character made worse by inadequate software security. They'd seen it before, a month ago in another level two insertion. The uninvited guest into Amelia's mind was a serial killer dreamed up by a very disturbed patient. The grinning man's weapons – and there were many – had all taken the form of sharp blades.

Being scared out of your wits while asleep was one thing, but a waking hallucination starring a slasher straight from a horror movie was a nightmare Amelia would never forget. Jonas had offered to cleanse the memory away, but Amelia decided against it. A reminder of how bad things could get.

Amelia bit her lip. "We did a full system test two weeks ago, and Jake just updated the security software again today. I think he's got a good handle on it. No more hitchhikers."

"How about SPIKEs?" Nolan's questions were always direct with little elaboration. Stray neural patterns that could fire from Orlando's brain and slam into hers, were always a risk with level two insertions.

Amelia shrugged. "We can't stop every SPIKE, but I agree with Jake, the likelihood is slim. I'll keep Orlando's lucidity as low as I can. That will help."

Nolan seemed satisfied. Maybe he was just being thorough with his questions.

"The nurse?"

"Yes, Josefina will be on duty," Amelia answered.

"How about Jonas?" Their neuroscientist in training.

"What, to debrief? Jonas comes in at six a.m. I'll probably be done by then."

"I mean as backup, just in case," Nolan said. "Why not have him come in at four?"

"Okay, I can do that." She waited for any other questions but there were none. "So?"

Nolan pointed a finger to Amelia. "Be careful in there."

It was as good a signoff as she'd ever get from Nolan. "You know me, Miss Meticulous. Thanks, Nolan."

Amelia left Nolan's office and headed for the garage. She'd been diligent, more so than usual, but it boosted her confidence for a procedure that remained at the edge of her comfort zone.

No more hitchhikers, she repeated to herself, yet a related thought nagged at the back of her mind. Security updates protect against the *last* problem but it's always the next unknown that can get you.

As she took the stairs down, a familiar voice sounded in her ear. "Amelia?"

"Yes, Kori."

"I hope you don't mind, but I did some research on my own."

Amelia smiled. "On the contrary, I want you to take the initiative. What were you researching?"

"When patients check in, the Institute asks them to sign an agreement that releases any information on their mobile related to in-patient activity, including the patient's current location."

"Right. We had a few cases where Alzheimer's patients wandered away and couldn't find their way back. Gaining access to their mobile data resolved that."

"Makes sense," Kori said. "The location history and call records from Orlando's mobile were just uploaded to our system a few minutes ago. He was out of the office for two hours and twenty-three minutes, and I discovered what he did this morning. Should I tell you?"

Amelia thought about his question. "Well, there are privacy laws that restrict what I'm allowed to review. For example, I can't listen in on the call he made to his wife. My access to his mobile records must be directly related to his condition."

"In this case, I believe it is." Kori's intonation was as close to human as Amelia had ever seen in a digital assistant. He sounded sure.

"Okay, tell me. I'll stop you if it's out of bounds."

Kori paused, then continued. "He didn't call his wife. He never dialed her number."

"Really? He lied? I wonder why?"

"Perhaps because he *did* make a call. To the University of Washington. I matched the number to the Materials Science department. After the call, location tracking shows that he went to the campus and spent more than an hour there."

The university wasn't far away, only a few minutes by the Link light rail. But his impromptu visit seemed to be an intentional omission – complete with a cover story.

She paused on the stairway. "Kori, could you call Orlando and ask him to come back in?" But she held up a finger. "No, wait. Cancel that."

She continued down and opened another door that led into the garage. "He can't lie in a dream. Maybe I'll ask him about it tonight and see what he says."

"Did I do the right thing by researching?" Kori asked.

"You did, though I have to say I'm surprised. That took some reasoning on your part."

"I'm learning to tell when humans are lying. It's quite fascinating."

"And you could tell from Orlando's statements this morning?"

"Yes."

Another surprising capability that Amelia didn't know Kori possessed. "Just curious, can you identify any cases where you think I've lied to you?"

"Just a minute…"

She hoped he wasn't reviewing hundreds of hours of previous conversations, all recorded somewhere in his memory, yet, more than likely that's exactly what was happening.

"Only once," he said finally. "When we first met, you said the joke I told you was funny. You were lying."

Fair enough. I can live with that.

"Kori, send a message to Jonas, please."

"Ready."

"I'm going deep tonight. Level two. Can you arrive a little earlier? Four a.m. will work. Backup only. I'm not expecting any problems."

CHAPTER TWELVE

UNIVERSITY

ORLANDO MARVELED AT the lab equipment that had been made available to him. To one side of the small room, an imposing industrial-grade rock grinder stood next to a floor-to-ceiling sliding door that sealed off an oven capable of heat sufficient to melt most any metal. In the room's center, a ten-by-ten-foot precipitation bath stood on four sturdy posts.

Gaining access to the University of Washington Materials Science Lab hadn't been difficult once the right name was mentioned. UCLA Professor Darrin Mikkelsen was well known among the staff and faculty, and though the professor himself had recently checked into a local hospital for an undisclosed illness, recommendations from his assistants had been enough for Orlando to obtain 'visiting chemist' status. He'd filled out some forms, given them his credit card number, and they'd handed him a lab key.

A graduate student named Trey had been assigned to get him started. The young man handed Orlando a plastic bag filled with silver powder. "Just make sure you don't get any of this stuff on your skin. Full protective gear, okay?"

"Got it, thanks," Orlando said. He turned the one-liter bag over in his hand, the label reading *Trimethylaluminum Seed* along with several warnings to handle with care.

The student checked lab coats, face masks, and gloves hanging on rack, then left. Orlando withdrew a folded sheet of paper from his back pocket. The notes were in his handwriting, but he hardly remembered putting the words to paper: a list of materials along with steps defining specific processes to create the components he would need. There would be triangles. Circles too. All formed and cut to exacting standards using a new unit of measure called a *nik* that he'd only recently learned about.

If someone asked, he'd struggle to explain what it all meant, and yet as soon as he read the first line of his notes, something in his mind switched on, making the procedure clear, if not its purpose.

A chemical formula danced in his head along with a set of numbers, their meaning appearing momentarily then disappearing. He might never have a full picture of the task ahead, but a foot soldier never questions his orders. The voice inside was compelling. The work must begin as soon as possible.

CHAPTER THIRTEEN

LEVEL TWO

AMELIA PUSHED OPEN the door into a quiet and dimly lit ALD lab. A good night's sleep made early morning arrivals almost tolerable.

The night nurse looked up. "Morning ma'am."

"Morning, Josefina. Level two this time. I'll need your help."

"Yes, ma'am," Josefina answered. "Mister Kwon?" She looked worried, but Josefina tended to have that brow-down expression permanently fixed to her face.

Amelia nodded, and Josefina hurried to a storage cabinet to gather the additional devices used to monitor and record the far more intrusive ALD session. This would be Josefina's first level two insertion. Her role would still be limited, but it would now include monitoring Amelia's vital signs.

"Jonas will be in at four," Amelia said. As the Institute's number two dream guide, Jonas was more than capable of assisting if needed. "If I can find a good dream to jump into, I'll probably be in the thick of things by then. When he gets here, just let Jonas know how things are going."

"Yes ma'am." Josefina plugged in equipment while Amelia started a pot of coffee brewing.

Well prepared, she assured herself. Still, Amelia had stopped by the operations center on her way in to pull The Boss's lucky beer tap – just in case.

Amelia started her tablet and checked Orlando's status. The stream of data from The Boss had recorded a few periods of wakefulness but Orlando was currently asleep in NREM stage three. Despite what most people think, dreams did occur in that deepest stage of sleep and they were often better for her work since the patient was less likely to wake.

Orlando was in fact dreaming. The observed NCCs were mostly related to green, leafy plants – he was probably back in the jungle – but one NCC stood out.

"A crowbar?" Amelia scrunched up one side of her face. "Why does he need a crowbar in a jungle?"

It was more a rhetorical question, but Josefina answered anyway. "I don't know, Doctor Charron. If it were the Honduras jungle, I'd take bug spray."

As Amelia watched, the crowbar designation was replaced by a sword and then changed to a light saber. Either Orlando was dreaming of an epic struggle in a faraway galaxy, or the Boss was having trouble mapping the dream object to the real world.

"This I've got to see," Amelia said, grabbing a Bronson cap from the cabinet and strapping it on. "Josefina, I'm going in now. You ready?" With a press of a switch, she lit up the cap's blue light.

Josefina studied her tablet. "The secondary monitoring is setup... um, data coming through fine. Yes, ma'am, I can see your vitals now."

Amelia gave a thumbs up signal and stepped quietly into Orlando's room, closing the door behind her. The pillows were lit with a soft blue, and a breathy snore confirmed a deep sleep.

She pulled up her tablet and configured for level two. The Boss projected an animated avatar onto the display. The colorful figure was dressed in game-style battle garb and assumed several hand-to-hand fight poses with realistic arm and leg movements. Complete silliness, typical of testosterone-fueled software designers, but Amelia didn't mind. The Wonder Woman wrist bands and angular shoulder pads atop a jacket with diagonal gold stripes made her avatar look amazing, not that clothing would matter once in the dream. Orlando would simply accept her as another dream character – perhaps as reinforcements if he was currently fending off the forces of evil. The Boss seemed to think so.

Far more important than clothing, the avatar's face looked remarkably like Amelia. The same dirty blond hair with one obstinate strand that hung over her forehead. The same bushy eyebrows, laugh lines at the corner of each eye, sharp cheek bones, and narrow chin. Expertly rendered, even if avatars tended to be a younger, stronger, and fiercer version of their real-world counterpart.

Battle Amelia! Natalie would have loved it.

Amelia laughed to herself. Her sister Natalie had always enjoyed computer role-playing games and had created some amazing avatars over the years. Too lazy to put the effort into design, Amelia had just borrowed Natalie's for her own. Their only physical difference had been hair style. Natalie wore hers short – at least she did at age twenty-one – but it might still be short if, in some alternate universe, Natalie had somehow made it to age thirty-two.

Wishful thinking.

She clicked the standard *I Agree* button and Battle Amelia leaped from the tablet, disappearing off its edge and into the dream world. Real Amelia closed her eyes.

She hallucinated jungle.

It was the same quagmire of plants, puddles, mud, and moss that filled his first dream, but this time Orlando himself was entirely missing from the scene.

Amelia looked left and right, turning her avatar's head just as naturally as if it were her own. The system worked flawlessly, providing a detailed view of the imagined plants in every direction. Drips of water hung on broad leaves as if a fresh rain had just passed through. A fine mist hung close to the ground.

"Orlando?" she called out. Though her avatar could be positioned anywhere within the dreamscape, The Boss generally didn't miss the location of the dreamer by much.

"Over here," a quiet voice replied.

She walked in its direction, pushing hanging vines from her path, and feeling the soft brush of hip-high foliage across her fingers. It was another reminder that the brain can generate any portion of the sensory experience even when physical input was lacking.

Hopefully, no biting animals in this jungle. A dream snake bite might feel perfectly real.

She pushed aside a plant as big as herself, revealing an open space with a small creek that ran through a boulder field. Orlando sat on a large rock, twirling a metal rod about a meter long in his hands.

"Whatcha got there?" Amelia asked as she approached. He might recognize her without prompting. It was worth a test.

He looked up, catching her eye, and accepting her presence with indifference. "Something. I don't know what it is."

He rolled the rod over in his hands. The green-tinted metal looked like colored aluminum, the same color she'd seen on the fuselage of new airplanes rolling out of the Boeing factory before they were painted. As he twirled the rod, a handle with a perpendicular cross guard suddenly appeared at one end. It made the object look very much like a sword – or a green light saber. The handle disappeared as quickly as it had formed. No wonder The Boss was having trouble identifying the object. Orlando's subconscious was too.

The handle flashed into existence once more, with Orlando undisturbed by the object's inconsistency. Sword-like, but it wasn't really a weapon. The bar had no sharp edge along its length; even the tip was rounded.

Orlando continued to roll the rod in his fingers. Amelia stepped close, bent down, and looked him in the eye. "Do you know who I am?"

He studied her face and nodded. "Yeah, I think so."

"Who?"

He scanned her face once more. "That doctor."

"What's my name?"

"Um… Amelia?"

"Right. I'm Amelia. That's great that you remembered. Do you also remember the procedure we talked about?"

He seemed unsure, but lucid dreams were hard for most people to pull off.

"Remember, Orlando, I'm Amelia." Names could be an effective trigger, but he looked like he was struggling. Maybe he hadn't repeated the mantra as she'd asked.

"Amelia," he said again. "Yeah, I recognize you."

"And?"

"Oh… when Amelia asks, I will give her control."

"Very good." She picked up his dream hand in hers. "Orlando, I want you to give me control of your dream now. Is that okay?"

He nodded with a blank stare. "Sure."

She patted his hand. "So, now that I have control what are you supposed to do?"

He thought for a moment. "Relax."

"Perfect. Relax and think of nothing. You can just sit right here if you like."

"Okay."

She reached to his other hand. "But I'm going to take this saber."

He absentmindedly handed the green sword to her, a good sign that she was indeed in control and a test of her avatar's ability to interact with dream objects. She held the object in her hands, feeling its weight, noting its balance point closer to the handle. So far, physics in the dream matched the natural world though what the bar might represent to Orlando and why it was in his dream was still unknown.

She sat cross-legged on the moss in front of the rock. "Orlando, I want you to stay relaxed. You're in a dream right now. In the real world you're asleep, but here you and I can still talk to each other. Pretty cool, huh?"

He nodded. Once again, a very cooperative patient. It was time to take advantage of that dynamic.

"Orlando, when's the last time you spoke to Teena?"

He hung his head down. "Not for a while. I miss her."

"So, you didn't call Teena yesterday?"

"No."

"What'd you do yesterday?"

"Talked to other people."

"At the university?"

He nodded.

"What did you talk about?"

Orlando squirmed on his rock seat. "Nothing."

His quick shift to uncooperative probably meant he was experiencing enough lucidity that something was making him feel uncomfortable – most likely his real-world lie about calling Teena. Further questioning probably wouldn't be productive and pushing too hard might even wake him up.

"Orlando, the last time we were in this jungle, you seemed really nervous. Today you're calm. Why is that?"

"You told me to relax."

"I did, but you were calm even before that."

His mouth formed a tight smile. "I'm not worried anymore."

"That's great but what changed?"

"Prime Arc is teaching me things."

"Prime Arc. Is that someone in your dreams?"

"Yeah. It's explaining things to me."

This new dream character seemed like someone Amelia might want to meet too. "Explaining things? Like what?"

Orlando's mouth opened wide, his jaw unhinged, deforming his face into an unnatural twist of bone, cheeks, and lips that suddenly made him appear far less human. Computer generated imagery from a horror movie couldn't have done a better job of creating a skin-crawling creepiness.

"Zhee-crick. Scritch-tick." A staccato vibration erupted from his throat, precisely mimicking the comb-like ticking sounds that had appeared in the previous dream. The otherworld quality of his voice sent a chill down Amelia's neck.

His distorted face returned to normal, the stretched skin and bones falling neatly into human form once more. "It means *don't worry*," Orlando said confidently, apparently unaware of his physical metamorphosis.

Amelia had seen plenty of dream weirdness, but this one had come from nowhere. She swallowed hard. "How did you make that sound? And how do you know what it means?"

"Prime Arc taught me."

His dream state was different this time. Creepy as hell, but analytic. Confident in his self-assessment even if he still didn't have all the answers. But there was also a sense that he'd accepted the terror of his previous nightmare and was giving in, becoming part of the creep show.

Amelia could question him further, but she had another idea, a faster way to get to the answers she needed. She stood up and put a hand on his shoulder. "Stay here for a while, Orlando. I'll be back."

Carrying the aluminum rod with her, she crossed the mossy clearing following the creek downstream where it dropped over a break in the rocks creating a small waterfall. Beyond it was more jungle, but she could make out a second clearing not far away. The detail within the scene was nothing short of astonishing.

Level two is so freaking amazing.

The sights, sounds, smells, and touch were so close to the real world it took some effort to remember she was inside a dream. There were also none of the data glitches common in level one dreams. She wasn't sure why, maybe the software guys could explain it, but it seemed to reflect the tighter integration between her mind and Orlando's.

She pushed aside leafy plants, surveying the scene in all directions. Scouting the dreamscape was a way to see what Orlando had imagined but had not yet encountered. There might be nothing out there, but some dreams had a full lineup of upcoming guests, almost like the green room for a TV talk show. Technically, Amelia was now in command and unless she permitted specific actions, the dream would be in a holding pattern with minimal movements for whomever, or whatever, might be in wait.

Prime Arc? A distinct possibility.

Through the canopy of trees above, a hazy blue sky was dotted by white clouds. A breeze caused the highest branches to gently sway. Birds of unknown species flitted through the branches, though their motion and the chirps they made were oddly repetitive, like a looping video.

In the clearing ahead, slanting shafts of light illuminated a thin mist hovering over a mossy forest floor. A small insect, cricket-like, hopped across a leaf and leaped across the babbling creek to a plant on the other side.

There was no telling how far she might be able to walk before running out of imagined space. The jungle might continue for miles if Orlando imagined it to be that large, but more likely she'd eventually encounter a hazy edge, with nothingness beyond.

Dream characters were usually different than the background scenery. If they were players in the dream – or soon would be – they might be fully formed, milling around offstage ready for their walk on. Even the direction she'd chosen through the jungle probably made no difference. If they were out there, she'd run into them.

She followed the cricket bug, stepping across the creek and into the clearing. In full sunlight on the far side, stood a wooden structure with a steep-pitched roof angled over an open space beneath.

She walked closer, noticing yellow hay strewn across a dirt floor. The structure had three walls but was open on the fourth side as if an enclosure for an animal of some sort. Perhaps Orlando had not yet imagined its occupant – the room was empty.

She stepped around a free-standing wooden rail and onto the hay floor, feeling alone in the quiet shelter. The rough-hewn wood around her creaked as a breeze picked up across the clearing.

"Where are you?" Amelia asked out loud.

A rustle came from outside the structure, the sound of branches moving and twigs snapping. Amelia's heart rate picked up. Something was out there.

Nothing like speaking up – you might get what you asked for.

She stepped out of the enclosure, walking around the structure toward the sounds. As she reached the corner a distorted face lunged forward and shrieked a loud, *"Clack!"*

"Holy shit!" Amelia screamed, her heart pounding and adrenalin spiking. Reflexively, she lurched backward waving the metal rod in defense.

A spindly creature with an elongated head stared back. Its face looked vaguely human, though vertically stretched. Pale green skin was framed by flaky brown bark and tangles of stringy corn silk that hung from either side. Its dark sunken eye sockets had no eyeballs. Two diagonal slashes filled the space where a nose and mouth might otherwise have been, their openings pulsating open and closed like a camel's nose.

The head was perched atop a slender pole, dark green, and with bamboo-like joints that split into a tripod of legs. One leg led, and the other two followed as the creature lurched forward. Additional joints split away from the central stalk, with several that tapered to a thin curving tendril, like a grape vine.

Amelia slashed the rod through the air, continuing to back up. She'd gotten what she asked for but that didn't make this beast any less fearful.

"Freeze!" she commanded.

The thing twitched its head, dinosaur-like, and then hopped forward on its tripod of bamboo struts like a crow when it spies a bit of food on the ground. An upper joint lifted, sending a curled tendril toward her.

She'd already seen what the tendrils could do.

"Keep back!" she yelled. The creature hopped forward.

She turned to run, but the tendril snapped out with a speed she wasn't expecting. It quickly wrapped around her arm and with overpowering strength, pulled her to the ground.

"Stop!" she yelled, but the tendril's thickness increased along with its strength. Another tendril wrapped around both of her legs, binding them together.

The thing ambled across the clearing, dragging her behind.

Amelia struggled to think clearly as a feeling of panic flooded her mind. This shouldn't be happening. This creature – a dream character – should be as docile as any of the birds or bugs hopping through the jungle. The dream itself should already be in a suspended mode. Obviously, not the case.

Amelia yelled as the creature pulled her by her legs. "I'm in command of this dream! You will stop!"

It kept moving, dragging her through mud and over roots and rocks. She felt each stone scrape across her back as if in the real world. Her legs hurt from the binding and her arm swelled below the point where the tendril wrapped, squeezing off the blood supply.

"You are a dream character. I own you. Stop now!"

The creature kept moving, passing into the jungle she'd just traversed. Her body dragged through the cold water in the creek and her head banged against several rocks.

Nothing seemed to stop this creature, though Amelia wasn't about to give up. There was no question in her mind this ugly, misbehaving dream monster was the key to understanding what was going on inside Orlando's head.

As bad as things were going, finding answers was why she was here, why she'd decided to use a level two insertion, and why she'd accepted the patient in the first place. There was no other way but forward.

Besides, she still had a few cards she hadn't played yet. There was always the nuclear option.

CHAPTER FOURTEEN

PRIME ARC

THE BARK-COVERED, bamboo-legged beast continued its domination, dragging Amelia by her feet through the jungle. Her hand caught in a root and twisted painfully as it freed. Sharp rocks scraped against bare skin on one side. Her avatar's fine battle jacket was now in shreds.

She'd lost control, or maybe never had it, but Orlando wouldn't be far away now. He'd certainly hear her.

"Orlando!" Amelia cried out. "Freeze your dream in place. Freeze everything!"

The creature kept moving, hopping birdlike, until they reached the clearing where Orlando still sat on the rock. He looked dazed but didn't flinch at the sight of the spindly three-legged being.

"Orlando, I release control back to you. Make it stop!" Amelia said, appealing to the dream's rightful owner.

Orlando looked up with a blank expression, glancing between the creature and Amelia still bound by her legs and now covered in mud and plant debris.

The tripod creature stopped a few paces from Orlando and the tendrils released. Blood flowed again through her sore arm and she quickly scrambled to her feet, moving away from the tendrils that now writhed in the air.

Orlando sat quietly, not moving, not fearing the thing that stood only a few feet from him. If he'd commanded her release, he'd done it telepathically.

"*Tick-tick. Oorch-cho. Creeck orck. Zhee-crick. Scritch-tick.*" It was hard to tell where the voice originated. The diagonal openings on the creature's stretched head continued their pulsating breaths.

Orlando's face distorted once more, his lips pushing out farther than human lips could normally go. "*Zhee-crick. Scritch-tick,*" he echoed, and then turned to Amelia. "It wants you, but don't worry."

The two concepts seemed entirely conflicting. If this thing *wanted* her, she was unquestionably worried. Amelia circled around to the rock where Orlando sat, her heart calming, but her nerves still on edge. She was fascinated with the verbal interaction that Orlando had mastered and sufficiently curious to keep her natural fear in check.

Out of control in a level two – not where I want to be. Still...

The monster was a dream character – an unruly one, but no more than an imagination within Orlando's mind. Amelia wasn't about to allow its aggression to prevent her from understanding its purpose, or its effect on Orlando. Yes, she'd temporarily lost control, but she still had a few tricks in her bag to turn things around.

Dynamite, if I need to go to that extreme.

Dream dynamite wasn't much different from the same stuff back in the real world. If she commanded it, The Boss would identify the specific NCCs that represented each dream character and physically erase them from Orlando's memory, replacing them with a soothing scene of Amelia's choice. This dream might suddenly change to a contented couple sipping hot cider by a fireside, or perhaps something that would be engaging for Orlando but entirely benign. Puppies and kittens were her favorite.

But dynamite would erase the key character, the principle source of Orlando's disturbance – *Prime Arc*, as he'd called it. Erasure would solve the problem for this particular dream, but there was no guarantee Orlando would be free of its influence. Amelia steeled herself to the task.

Let's see where this goes.

The creature rose, its tripod legs extending until it reached its full height at least seven or eight feet. Multiple tendrils retracted into spiral shapes that it held close to its central stalk. For the first time, she noticed there were three tendrils on each side, each forking from a single joint, much like the tripod legs.

"Creetch-tick-tick-tick," it sounded, the ticks seeming to come from the dark diagonal slits across its blotchy green face.

Like an arrow, a curled tendril shot straight at Amelia. Its slender end whipped round her head several times cinching across her forehead. She felt the prick of tiny stiff hairs penetrate her skin no different than cactus spines.

"Whoa! Not again!". She grabbed the tendril with both hands and pulled hard.

Another tendril wrapped around her wrists, producing instant handcuffs. A third wrapped around her ankles, but this time left her standing.

Orlando watched with interest but didn't interfere.

Amelia's mouth opened but a numbing feeling spread across her face, lips, and throat, and prevented any words from coming out. Panic rose, but she was bound into an immovable position.

She concentrated, trying to open her eyes in the real world, but couldn't. No voice came out. Paralyzed, her hands and fingers would not move. An overwhelming feeling of helplessness poured through, telling her – almost commanding to her – that she accept her fate whatever it might be.

She clenched her jaw, seemingly the only working muscle in her body. *Don't give in.*

Her dream eyes still wide open, she noticed a waver in the air just in front of the rock where Orlando sat. A small form appeared – a cat – curled in a sleeping position on the mossy floor. The cat lifted its head, stood up and stretched, showing its mottled orange and white fur and the black spot just above its left eye.

Jinx? Her own cat, who was right now probably asleep at home, had precisely the same markings.

The air continued to waver and another form, much taller, phased into existence. A young woman with blonde hair stood next to the cat. One strand of hair hung down over bushy eyebrows.

Holy crap, it's me.

She looked more closely at the short-cropped hair. A chill started from her neck and shivered down her spine.

It's not me... it's Natalie.

The ghostly form of her dead sister bent down and scratched the cat behind its ears, oblivious to the jungle, the creature, Amelia, and Orlando. Natalie stood there like a game player waiting for instructions.

Amelia's body shook as anger boiled up inside. Her eyes narrowed. She twisted against the tight bindings of the tendrils and bent her body to try to break free. The tendrils held.

I'm not done yet.

She bit hard on her lower lip, not in panic, but as a dream interruption technique. Blood streamed from her avatar's mouth and dripped to the mossy jungle floor. She shrieked in pain, but the method revived her previously numbed throat.

She screamed at the creature. "Fuck you! Those are my private memories!"

The tendril around her forehead relaxed its grip and reeled back toward the creature's body. At the same time, the phantom images of Natalie and Jinx disappeared.

She had no idea what had just occurred, but the strong feeling of despair and helplessness – so overwhelming just a moment before – was gone. In its place was confusion but accompanied by a determination to get to the bottom of this disaster.

She directed her rage at the eyeless creature. "Release me now or I swear I will dynamite this dream and you'll go up with it!"

She could and she would. How the creature might interpret her ultimatum was anyone's guess, but if it still represented Orlando's subconscious, she had a chance to change the dynamic of this fiasco.

Orlando's dream persona remained on the rock, gripping his knees against his chest and his eyes following as the conflict progressed.

The tendrils around her wrists and ankles released their pressure and withdrew, leaving her standing free. A small victory even if the creature could easily whip a tendril around her once more. She stood her ground in a faceoff.

Now it was Orlando's turn. She wiped the blood from her chin and spoke with the authority of a commanding officer. "Orlando, do you hear me?"

"Yes," he said, lifting his head.

"Did you see the figures that appeared just now?"

"Sure. You and a cat."

"Not quite. Who was it?"

"I don't know, it looked like you."

"Who does the cat belong to?"

"I don't know, I've never seen it before."

Logical answers. Probably not lies, either. She'd never mentioned her sister or Jinx to him. How would Orlando possibly know about them?

The alternative was even more disturbing: Orlando hadn't created them at all. Something had reached into her mind just now – through the Bronson cap she wore in the real world – and had pulled those images into the dream.

Amelia stared at the creature, looking for eyes within the dark empty sockets. Prime Arc. A key dream character, the source of her difficulties in maintaining control, both in the first dream and now. She began to form a plan. It would no doubt lead to more confrontation, but a few more sparks wouldn't matter. If it worked, she'd gain insight into the strange dynamic between Orlando and this non-conforming dream character. If her plan failed, there was always dynamite.

She spoke without taking her eyes from the plant-y beast. "Orlando, you understand how a Bronson cap works, right?"

He slipped down from his seat on the rock and stood beside her. "I think so. It collects NCCs from one brain and transfers them as hallucinations to another mind."

Orlando was quite bright, she'd give him that. "Exactly right. I need you to create a working Bronson cap for me. Two, in fact."

"How do I do that?"

"Just imagine them. Bring them here. If you say they work, then they will."

He smiled, seemingly astonished that he might be able to perform such a miracle. He turned his back and reached out. When he pivoted back to Amelia, he held two Bronson caps, one in each hand, a broad grin on his face.

"That was easy," he said. The caps looked very realistic, but even if they were salad bowls, the idea might still work; Orlando's imagination was what counted.

She took one of the caps and strapped it onto her head – her avatar's head. Finding a working button on the side, she pressed it and the cap glowed blue. He'd done a great job imagining their function, but then he'd seen them in action.

She took the other cap and ventured toward the creature, holding the cap in both hands, arms extended. Her logic told her it was only a dream character, but her heart beat wildly anyway as she approached the stretched face that resembled a hairy coconut up close.

The creature shifted on its tripod legs as she neared, flexing and retracting its tendrils. She half expected a tendril to wrap around her neck at any moment.

Forward only. There's no going back.

Up close, the thing was uglier and more fearful. The eye sockets receded deeply into its head with no hint of how they might function for vision. The diagonal gashes below the eye sockets were flanked by wrinkled green skin that sucked air into the gash with each inhale.

Amelia lifted the Bronson cap as high as her arms would reach, and still not quite enough to place it over the creature's head. It shuffled on its tripod, but it didn't retreat.

"Bend down," Amelia commanded, wondering when this thing might retake control and end her bluff. Amelia bent her own knees to demonstrate.

Surprisingly, the thing lowered its body and Amelia slipped the cap over the top of the bark-like flakes. Corn silk hair hung below the cap's edges at each side. She pushed the side button and the cap lit up blue.

The creature lurched backward, sending two tendrils to the top of its head that flitted along the surface of the cap. It could have easily removed it, but it didn't.

"Do these caps work, Orlando? Will I be able to understand its thoughts?"

She laughed at the absurdity of her plan. Dream characters were normally a manifestation of the patient's subconscious, no more. In the past, she'd been successful at communicating with them directly, but use of imagined Bronson caps suggested that a third mind was involved. A secondary insertion, recursive.

Groundbreaking, if it works.

"The caps will work," Orlando said. This was still Orlando's dream, so if he believed they would function there was no other judge to overrule. The caps would simply work.

Amelia closed her avatar's eyes and waited for whatever might arrive from a dream creature's mind via imaginary technology of Orlando's creation.

She saw nothing, but she felt everything.

Helplessness. Confusion. Despair. The feelings poured into her, overwhelming Amelia's determination to understand. She felt like a child subjected to excessive discipline, a dog whimpering beneath an authoritarian master. She recognized these feelings as not her own, but any attempt to block the foreign invasion failed, sending her further into misery.

It's a weapon, she thought, though it was not clear how she'd determined this fact. *Depression runs in my family. It's using that against me.*

She felt like crying, or hiding, or running away. She did none of those things. Instead, she steeled herself to the suffering, determined to probe the consciousness that represented the attack.

The onslaught of weaponized feelings continued, but it could not suppress a startling conclusion, the most profound thought she'd had since entering the dream.

It's not part of the dream. It's something else.

The emotional attack came from another entity. Something separate, something entirely different than Orlando. Something not even human.

The feeling of despair intensified producing a helplessness that precluded any action, even the removal of the dream Bronson cap. The equivalent cap in the real world seemed miles away, inaccessible. More dream blood dripped down her chin, the pain in her lip feeling startlingly real.

Enough. Stop this.

It took effort to wedge the rational thought in between waves of depression.

Stop. Stop. Stop.

She forced herself to say it out loud.

"Stop. Stop." She repeated the single word over and over, feeling her body rock in rhythm as she did. She spoke louder and louder still, beginning to scream the word.

"Stop!!"

****

The sleep room door banged against the wall as Josefina rushed in with Jonas right behind. Amelia sat in a chair, her arms folded across her chest, rocking violently and repeatedly shouting a single word, "Stop!"

A drip of blood ran from her lower lip and down her chin.

CHAPTER FIFTEEN

RECOVERY

A YOUNG RECEPTIONIST escorted Major Shepard and his entourage through the atrium at the Westlake Institute for Neuroscience. She looked nervous. The desert camouflage uniforms that Shepard and Lieutenant Tombaugh wore tended to force civilians to think of warfare. The holstered firearm on Tombaugh's hip reinforced that image, exactly as planned.

Walker Duplass with thick glasses askew, mangy hair, and shirt untucked from baggy jeans was a definite deduction from their position of power, but at least he stayed five paces behind.

The woman, Elin on her name tag, glanced at Shepard as they ascended a staircase in the open-air center of the building. Elin was slim, good looking, probably spirited when she wasn't feeling intimidated – the kind of professional go-getter that Shepard would have been attracted to in his past.

Not anymore. These days, he had little use for women. They were nothing more than temptations for weaker men. Entanglements. Agents of vulnerability. No different than booze. He'd rooted out those character flaws years ago.

Mostly. He'd still cross a hot desert on foot in July for a good burger. He'd done exactly that two years before, stranded ten miles from Fort Irwin in the Mojave Desert. The raw pain in his desiccated throat waited while the cook at the base grill produced the perfect bacon burger. Only later, came the ice water.

At the top of the stairs, Elin turned down a hallway. Like most civilians working in neuroscience she probably had no idea the military was involved in the field, much less a leader in the field. Like the Westlake Institute for Neuroscience, DARPA had used Bronson cap technology for years to acquire brain activity in the detail necessary to study – and manipulate – the human mind. Until telepathy could be figured out, Bronson caps were also the preferred technology for mind to mind communication, and a miniaturized version that would plug into the back of the skull was on the horizon. Shepard had already signed up for the implant as soon as it was ready.

The Bronson caps had found their use in other areas too, allowing military brain specialists to erase selected memories and repair soldiers with PTSD. There was even a weaponized unit that could erase whole swatches from the brains of enemy combatants. No need to imprison a captured terrorist when turning him into a vegetable and releasing him back to his clan provided a stronger message.

The employees in this civilian facility were no doubt clueless of the power of his sixty-man Virginia-based unit. But his target for today knew, Shepard had already made sure of that. Nolan Brodie's office was just around the next corner and the Chief Scientific Officer's door was open when they arrived.

Nolan extended a hand toward Shepard's prosthesis – now covered with a five-fingered glove – but his eyes were glued to the gun on Lieutenant Tombaugh's hip.

"I'm not sure welcome is the right word," Nolan said, a verbalization of the same passive resentment they'd encountered at the reception desk.

"We'll be brief, then," Shepard said, staring at Elin until she pivoted and left. "I have no wish to disrupt your work, I understand how important it is."

"Except for one patient," Nolan responded, his jaw stern.

Shepard hadn't referenced any specific patient in their phone call an hour earlier. He'd only said that he had critical interest in their brain studies and would be invoking national security privilege.

They connected the dots. No matter.

"Mr. Orlando Kwon," Shepard revealed, even if the name was already understood. "We'll need to remove him from the premises."

"Is Mr. Kwon under arrest?" Nolan asked.

"He's a person of interest in a military security case. I sent you the information – along with my unit's authority over this matter."

"I saw it."

"I'd prefer that Mr. Kwon come with us voluntarily, but if not…" Shepard nodded over his shoulder to Lieutenant Tombaugh who placed a hand on his holster. The plastic flex cuffs on Tombaugh's belt were plainly visible.

Nolan remained silent for a minute, then picked up the phone on his desk. "I'll need to check on the patient's status. Our team had some difficulties with Mr. Kwon last night."

Shepard waited. This wasn't a raid, though it could become that if needed. He expected full cooperation. With luck they'd be back in Virginia tonight, with Kwon secured as the newest acquisition for the goo zoo.

Nolan spoke briefly to someone over the phone, responding only, "I see," and then hung up. He stepped forward. "It appears Orlando Kwon is not in our office at the moment."

Shepard lowered a quizzical brow. "Where is he then?"

"Probably doing what most visitors to Seattle do in the summer, enjoying the outdoors. Our in-patients are free to leave the building during the day."

Shepard turned sharply to Duplass. "You didn't tell me this."

Duplass cowered as if Shepard might strike a blow. "I... I didn't know."

Shepard squeezed his gloved metal fingers into a fist, his irritation rising rapidly. Instead of striking, he directed his attention to their target. "Where is he? Somebody here knows where he went."

Nolan shook his head. "Patients sign out. The most I can tell you is what time he left the building and that he's expected back sometime this evening."

"The neuroscientist in charge of the case might know where he went," Duplass offered. "Probably Amelia Charron, she's the best they have."

Shepard nodded, regaining his composure. Providing inside information on the people who worked in this field was the only reason he put up with a weakling like Duplass.

That, and erasing minds when required.

"We'll need to speak with Ms. Charron. Now," Shepard commanded.

Nolan shook his head again. "Major Shepard, based on the documents you sent, you seem to have the authority to speak with Mr. Kwon, perhaps even the authority to remove him from our building, but that doesn't extend to my staff. If your investigation requires their involvement, I suggest you bring the Seattle police or the FBI with you next time. We'll be happy to speak with them."

Nolan leaned against the front edge of his desk. "And just so you know, our neuroscience teams work a night shift. Best time to catch them is about three a.m. The front door will be locked then, so you'll probably need a search warrant and a locksmith to get in."

Shepard glared, flexing his mechanical fingers subconsciously. "Don't underestimate the importance of this case, Dr. Brodie. You might find this whole facility drawn into an investigation. Not good for business."

"Neither is giving up a patient whose care was entrusted to us by leading neurologists. Ours is a small community and we don't respond well to ultimatums. We need to know that the patient's best interests are being considered." Nolan crossed his arms and stood his ground.

Lieutenant Tombaugh leaned close and whispered in Shepard's ear. "We've got Kwon's mobile number. We can track him."

Shepard shrugged. "For now, we'll live within your rules. Just hope that we locate Mr. Kwon. Otherwise, our next entrance into your building might be somewhat more disruptive."

Shepard turned and marched out the door, his entourage following close behind.

They'd get Kwon, Shepard was sure of that, but they'd need to do it before these inept nurse maids managed to *cure* all the things that made Kwon so valuable as a research subject. This ordinary guy had somehow managed to enhance his own brain to genius levels – exactly what DARPA wanted for every super soldier.

****

Amelia lifted her head from a pillow, groggy. A light blanket covered her, though she was still fully clothed.

"Josefina?" She ran her tongue across a sore lip, finding a stiff thread poking up from the skin.

A dayshift orderly opened the door and peered into the patient's sleeping room, now serving as a recovery room for Amelia.

"Irvin," Amelia said, recognizing the older man even though she rarely interacted with him or anyone else on the day shift. "What the hell happened?"

"Josefina gave you a sedative," Irvin explained. "She said you had a seizure. Feeling better?"

Amelia sat up and swung her legs to the floor. "I'm good now... I think." The movement caused a slight dizziness. She ran a finger across the stitch in her swollen lower lip.

Irvin smiled. "Jonas' work. I didn't know neuroscientists could do stitches."

Amelia rocked her head. "Not our specialty, but some of us have enough medical training. I guess I bit my lip during the ALD session." She recalled performing the trick to regain her dream voice, though at the time she hadn't realized the real-world bite would be so forceful. Pain is pain, whether real or imagined. The imaginary world was always hard to distinguish when deep in a level two insertion.

The grogginess faded. "What time is it?"

He checked his mobile. "It's just after eleven now."

"Eleven a.m., already? Shit." She pushed off from the bed and headed into the adjacent ALD lab. Irvin followed, his hands hovering next to her as if she might fall over.

Orlando's sleep room was next door. No one inside.

"Mr. Kwon checked out," Irvin said. "He was pretty insistent, and he seemed fine. Jonas gave him an exam to make sure he wasn't hurt. Turns out, you were the only one with injuries."

"Lucky me." Orlando had pretty much sat out the dream on a rock, leaving the creature's physical abuse for Amelia. Again, it was hard to distinguish the amazingly realistic level two dream insertion from reality but a few pains in her back seemed to match where the creature had dragged her across rocks.

The body obeys the mind.

She poured a cup of coffee, retrieved her earbud from a table and popped it in her left ear. "Kori, updates?"

Kori's response was immediate and passionate. "Amelia, I'm so glad to hear your voice. Are you okay? The session data looked awful."

"Another rough night," she said taking a big slurp of coffee. "I'll recover."

"I was worried for you. I've never felt that emotion before, it's so…"

"Thanks, Kori. Messages?"

"Let me check… nothing from Orlando, but Nolan wanted to know just as soon as you were awake."

"Tell him I'm up."

"I just did. He's on his way here. He's passing the atrium cam right now." Tapping into the building security cameras? Another talent she didn't know Kori had.

The lab door flung open and Nolan burst in. He reached out with both arms, not quite hugging her, but doing a good impression. "I heard about the difficulties last night." He touched a finger to his own lip, his eyebrows upraised.

She touched the sore lip. "A technique from my bag of tricks. This one backfired a bit, but it got the job done."

"Amelia, I'm afraid we have trouble," Nolan said, glancing at Irvin. Irvin suggested he had work to do and left, leaving the two of them alone in the lab.

"Double trouble, then." Amelia thought about the implications of the dream session. "Tell me yours first."

He put a hand on each of her shoulders. "You need to vacate, and if you can find Orlando Kwon, take him with you. Go somewhere, I don't care, but don't come back until I can get some support from higher powers."

"What happened?"

"An army major was just in here, ready to arrest Orlando, or confine him, or whatever they're going to do. He's from DARPA, and you and I both know that means trouble. The guy had a direct authorization from the state medical board. You know, the people who issue our license to take on patients?"

Amelia was aware that DARPA dabbled in neuroscience, but an intervention like this was off the charts. "Holy... what did Orlando do?"

"Distribution of classified material. That chemical formula we've heard so much about." Nolan shook his head. "But I'm not buying it."

Amelia twisted her eyebrows. "Not sure I do either. There's no question that Orlando has savant abilities in chemistry. Kind of odd timing if he stole a formula just when he was developing the same talent."

"That's why you need to get out of here. These guys came armed, and they were dragging, uh, what's his name? I recognized him, that guy from MemoryTap."

"Walker Duplass?" She pronounced it more like *double-ass* even though she knew the *u* was long.

"Right."

Walker Duplass was a colleague, of sorts. A neuroscientist, at one point employed by a California corporation exploring how human memory could be extended into external devices. MemoryTap had become infamous for their brash idea that a human to computer merge was within reach using existing brain mapping and Bronson cap technology. Most neuroscientists agreed that extending the mind into external hardware was possible, but not advisable due to the myriad of unknowns left to be resolved.

Many had said the same thing about assisted lucid dreams. A Seattle Times article just last year had highlighted Amelia's work, calling her out by name. The public reaction to the story varied. Some people thought that rewiring patients with mental afflictions made Amelia a saint. Others compared her to Dr. Frankenstein. She'd learned to ignore the hate mail.

She would recognize him in a crowd, but Walker Duplass wasn't really a friend. They'd chatted at a few neuroscience conferences and had even shared a happy hour table once, though Amelia had cut the social encounter short when his interest drifted beyond science. Duplass was the type that needed the "hey, my eyes are up here" reminder.

Amelia shook her head. "He's at DARPA now, eh? That guy never seems to come up on the right side of anything. You're sure they want to arrest Orlando?"

"Arrest. Apprehend. Whatever. They're going to take him away, and if they can't find him, they'll come looking for you. Best if you both disappear."

Amelia locked eyes with Nolan. They'd sometimes battled with each other over ethics in science, but he seemed to be doing the right thing this time. No one had the right to cart away a mentally disturbed patient who was under supervised care.

"Thanks for the heads up. I've seen enough to know that Orlando needs our help." She scrunched up one eye. "And that brings up my news."

"You got pretty beat up last night."

"More than that. The lip is my own fault. The shakiness afterward wasn't, but…" She lowered her head in thought. It wasn't that Nolan might not believe her – he would. But now in the full light of day, she wasn't sure she believed it herself.

"Orlando was right all along. There *is* something inside his head."

"An alien presence?" Nolan asked without a hint of mockery in his voice.

She chose her next words carefully as she ventured out onto thin ice. Orlando wasn't suffering from schizophrenia, but there might be safer explanations that didn't involve aliens. The ALD procedure itself might be introducing some as-yet unobserved effect. "Something. I don't know what it is or how it's getting into his mind, but it's not coming from Orlando, not even his subconscious."

"How do you know?"

It was a logical question and one she knew Nolan would ask. She had a hard time assembling the pieces into something coherent, but she gave it her best shot.

"There's a particular dream character that Orlando calls *Prime Arc* – at least, that's who I think I was battling last night. The creature was also in his first dream and that's when all the trouble started. In the level one, I couldn't shut down the partition I'd created, and I couldn't interact with the character or even get a good view of it. That's why I went in deeper last night. I saw the same character again – boy, did I see it. Shocked the hell out of me. And when it touched me... I felt this overwhelming despair. I just felt helpless and unmotivated. I decided it was a weapon."

"A dream weapon?"

"Yeah, directed at me. Through my avatar."

Nolan scratched the side of his head. "Unheard of, at least for every other level-two we've done."

"My thinking exactly. Dream characters don't take it upon themselves to attack the guide's avatar. That's a pretty intense level of subconscious hostility, something we've never seen before. But it gets worse."

Nolan listened while Amelia composed the next part – the personal part. "I've told you about my sister, right?"

Nolan nodded. "A sad story, but –"

"My sister, Natalie, was in the dream. Along with my cat. Things I've never told Orlando about, but there they were."

"You're suggesting –"

"Something reached into my memory through the Bronson cap, and pulled these thoughts out in real time."

Nolan squinted. "Orlando subconsciously authorized his dream character to attack you? That's pretty out there."

"It would be, yes, but that's not what happened. After my sister appeared, I decided I needed to explore this creature's mind. So, with Orlando's help, I set up a secondary insertion. A recursive session to go inside the dream character's mind."

Nolan blew out a breath. "Whew, that's a first. Congratulations on the idea, but why would a dream character even have a mind?"

"Normally, it wouldn't. I'd just be tapping into Orlando from a different angle. And that's why I know Orlando is right. The secondary insertion proved it. I could feel a living, breathing thing. It wasn't Orlando, I'm sure of it."

Nolan ran a hand across his forehead. "So, besides his own consciousness, there were two more in his head last night, each represented by an avatar." He looked up, incredulous.

Amelia nodded. "Yup. I was in there, but so was someone else."

CHAPTER SIXTEEN

TRIANGLES

AS THE STOPLIGHT changed to green, Amelia pushed the pedal to the floor and sped away. Without signaling, she turned sharply at the next corner and navigated a series of narrow backstreets; an alternate route home – just in case.

"Kori, I need some help." She glanced in the rearview mirror. No one following. Maybe she was being paranoid. Maybe Nolan was wrong about these DARPA guys, Orlando hadn't stolen any formula. Then again, something unique was going on in his head. Was there a military connection?

"I'm here," the familiar voice answered. No panting from exercise, no simulated latte sips. Just Kori.

For a moment, Amelia lifted both hands from the steering wheel. "I have no idea how to *disappear*. In our modern world, what does that even mean?"

"Just a minute," Kori answered. She hoped he wasn't looking up information on magic acts or something related to hit men. Kori had already shown that he was a different breed, but her expectation of inappropriate search engine results died hard.

Kori's answer was spot on. "Three concepts seem paramount. First, avoid routine locations, primarily home and work."

She tightened her lips. "Mmm, probably can't avoid going home. I need some clothes and stuff and there's no way I'd leave Jinx to fend for herself. Five minutes, tops. After that, I really don't know where to go. A hotel?"

She crested Queen Anne hill and dropped down one of the old cobblestone streets on the other side.

"A hotel would be good, but I also recommend avoiding a financial trail – credit card, mobile app purchases, things like that. Use cash only."

"Another reason to go home first. I've got some emergency cash in my nightstand drawer."

She imagined a shadowy figure sitting in a parked car on her street but shook her head. Too obvious – real world surveillance probably didn't work that way.

"Lastly and probably most importantly," Kori explained, "don't use your mobile. Don't even have it turned on."

"They can find me through location services, right?"

"Yes. According to the information I found, law enforcement can easily obtain any phone number, which gives them your subscriber ID, and that lights you up like a beacon on their Dirtbox."

"Dirtbox?"

"Police use them. It's an electronics scanner usually mounted in a car. It masquerades as a cell tower and tricks your mobile into pinging it. Just by driving around for a few minutes, they can triangulate your position to within ten feet. Boom, they've got you."

"Boom, indeed. I had no idea they could do that. This is legal?"

"It seems to skirt the edges of legal. They do it anyway."

"But it only works if my mobile is on, right?"

"Correct. So, you'll need to turn it off. Or seal your mobile in a Faraday bag to block all signals. Want me to order one for you? Forty-nine ninety-seven at –"

"Thanks, but I don't think I can hang around for a delivery."

She crossed the Fremont Bridge, one of the older style drawbridges spanning the 'cut', a manmade canal connecting the water in Lake Union to Puget Sound. The metal web decking of these drawbridges was notorious for a shimmy effect that felt like skidding on black ice.

"But if I turn my mobile off," Amelia continued, "I won't have you. And I won't have much chance of finding Orlando."

"True." Kori paused for a few seconds. "I may be able to help. It appears there are organized technophiles who are fighting back against what they label an unwarranted intrusion into privacy. I just downloaded two of their mobile apps. One is a sniffer that detects a Dirtbox by its motion. Real cell towers don't reposition themselves – although I just kicked off a sub-thought that is crafting a really good joke along those lines."

Amelia had to laugh.

"Sorry," Kori continued. "I also found a second app that turns the tables on the snoopers. It spoofs a fake subscriber ID. Your mobile masquerades as someone else. Of course, once the spoof is active, legitimate callers can't reach you, so the idea is to spoof after you've sniffed the snoopers."

"That wasn't the joke... or was it?"

"No, that was legit."

"Okay, got it. If they seek, then I hide before they can triangulate me."

"Exactly. Should I activate these apps?"

"Do it. Then monitor the sniffer and let me know if there's trouble at my heels."

"I'm on it."

"You're the best, Kori. Jokes and all."

She zipped past an old Soviet Union statue of Vladimir Lenin in the quirky Fremont neighborhood and then climbed a hill toward her house on Phinney Ridge. Slowing as she entered her block, she scanned each of the cars parked along the street circling twice before finally stopping and hopping out.

Jinx was already meowing when she unlocked the front door. "Sorry sweets, I'm in and out." Amelia picked up the orange and white cat and rubbed the black spot over one eye. Jinx pushed her nose into Amelia's cheek and purred.

Amelia filled a large bowl with dry cat food and set it on the kitchen floor. Jinx stared at the bowl and looked up. "No fishy stuff today, Jinx. Your rations might need to last for a few days."

She ran upstairs to her bedroom, opened a nightstand drawer, and pulled out a bundle of twenty-dollar bills buried beneath some t-shirts. She threw the money into a small backpack along with clothes and toiletries, surprised at how good it felt to be on the verge of a clandestine operation.

Reaching into the top drawer, she fingered her passport wondering if a retreat to Canada made any sense. Vancouver wasn't far away. On the passport cover, a decorative banner read, *A MARI USQUE AD MARE*. From sea to sea. It was true, from British Columbia to Quebec, Amelia always felt comfortable in Canada especially when US politics got crazy.

What the hell. She slipped the document into her backpack. Every secret agent on the run needed a passport.

A photo on the bedroom wall of a lovely old wooden dock reminded her that she had promised to call her parents this week. Funny how an evocative photograph of water, mist, and trees – even without a single person in the frame – triggered thoughts of family.

Summers at the family lake house in Quebec. Good memories. Swimming. Canoeing. Natalie prancing down that very dock showing off her latest bikini to the delight of the neighbor boys. The lake house was the ideal setting for twin sisters in the prime of their teenage years.

Amelia tapped two fingers to the picture as she often did when she passed the empty photograph. "Love you, papa. Love you, maman. I'll tell you all about my adventure when I get back."

There used to be a third "love you" that came with the routine tap, but she'd dropped it a few years back. Healing, she'd justified, but removing Natalie from the family had never felt right. It still didn't.

For a brief time after the funeral, she'd pictured Natalie in heaven but soon dropped that silly idea. Fantasies might comfort children, but Natalie was dead. Permanently, and for eternity. There was a process to grieving. Shed the tears, sure, but face reality when able. Amelia had done her best, even if the fierce ache in her heart would never completely go away.

Amelia ran down the stairs, her backpack on her shoulder. "Kori, can I safely call Orlando?"

"Maybe. I have the sniffer running now and you're connected to a real, immovable cell tower. So yes, it's safe for you, but there's no guarantee Orlando is not compromised. I'd recommend a scrambled text message with receipt enabled."

"Good idea. Send this to him." Amelia quickly composed a plan in her head. "Orlando, don't return to the Westlake Institute building, military police are looking for you. If I don't find you first, meet me at four o'clock at those scenic benches we talked about. Remember? That nice place to call Teena? Now turn the power off on your mobile and keep it off so they can't track you."

"Done."

"Any receipt?"

"None yet. It probably means his phone is off."

Amelia shrugged. "Which is good, I guess, except that we won't be able to find him either."

"Just a moment, I might be able to help on that too." The pause was negligible. "No, didn't work. The Westlake Institute's server has his GPS locations from yesterday, but nothing from today."

Amelia paced her living room. She was ready to depart as soon as she decided where she was going. "In the dream last night, I asked him about his lie."

"He never called Teena like he'd said."

"Right. He fessed up about the call, but he wouldn't say much more, which means that even at the subconscious level he really doesn't want me to know what he's doing."

"Which implies he might be doing the same thing at the same place as yesterday," Kori surmised just as easily as Watson would for Sherlock Holmes. "University of Washington, Materials Science and Engineering Building."

"My thinking too. Let's start there. At the very least, I could snoop around for clues." Amelia stepped out the front door and hurried to her car.

Orlando was once again hiding information, but it was also clear he needed help. Remarkably and inexplicably, the thing in his head was very real. Perhaps DARPA had come to the same conclusion, though she couldn't fathom how they might have done it.

Unless they created the thing in his head.

Nervous, Amelia scanned her street for any occupied parked cars before she climbed into her Mini Cooper. Nothing suspicious jumped out, though she couldn't shake the very logical idea that anyone doing sophisticated surveillance wouldn't be out in the open.

The UW campus was only fifteen minutes away – ten if she pushed it. She took the fastest streets along with a few shortcuts known only to the locals. The drive was quick with no Dirtbox alerts along the way, but after parking, she still had a short walk across campus.

Kori interrupted as soon as she locked the car door. "Amelia? You said yesterday that you wanted me to take the initiative and not wait for you to ask."

"Right. A prime directive, in fact."

"And you said you gave Orlando another chance last night to explain, but he didn't. That got me thinking."

"Spit it out, then." Amelia hurried across a footbridge that intersected a path through a grove of cedar trees.

"Remember the incorrect digits of pi that Orlando recited in the first dream?"

"Sure. Every third digit. What, you've been studying Orlando's mistakes in your spare time?"

"They're not mistakes. I found something."

"Really?"

"You might need to stop walking so I can show you. I'll put the data on your tablet so you can see the full sequence."

It wasn't clear if Kori was critiquing human ability – or inability – to walk and think at the same time. Maybe to prove a point, she kept walking, withdrew her tablet from a pocket on her backpack and turned it on. A window popped up containing a long string of numbers.

34551213724258151794041116061123537138485151121113166365202129209910124143145284553335665367783980894411712548557360911096572978810513
7

"These are all of the *incorrect* digits of pi," Kori explained. "Every third digit. They're all wrong, at least when it comes to representing pi. I gathered them together in a single sequence."

"I like where you're going. You were looking for a relationship in the wrong numbers?"

"Yes, and I found a pattern. Let me separate the digits with commas and spaces. It should be easier for a human to recognize it."

The screen updated.

3,4,5 5,12,13 7,24,25 8,15,17 9,40,41 11,60,61 12,35,37
13,84,85   15,112,113   16,63,65   20,21,29   20,99,101
24,143,145   28,45,53   33,56,65   36,77,85   39,80,89
44,117,125 48,55,73 60,91,109 65,72,97 88,105,137

"Same numbers but separated into triplets," Kori said. "Notice the first number of each triplet. Three, five, seven, eight, and so on. A sequence of increasing values."

"Interesting," Amelia stopped walking and stared intently at the sequence. It did indeed show a pattern, though what the triplets might represent was a mystery.

"Ideas?" she asked.

"I do have one. Startling, really, but a human mind might interpret the pattern differently, perhaps seeing something I can't."

Amelia continued the walk. She'd need to find Orlando as soon as possible, but Kori might be on to something. "Offhand, I'd say you're way ahead of me. Tell me your idea."

"Look at the first three numbers. What do they suggest?"

He was testing her. Maybe he really was unsure of his theory or maybe he was trying to prove that humans really can't walk and think at the same time. She examined the first three numbers, three, four and five.

"Well, they're sequential, unlike the other triplets you've assembled. But…" She stared, her eyes moving from the first triplet to the second, then back again. "Could it be?"

The first triplet, three, four, and five, was easy to compute in her head. Nine, sixteen and twenty-five. The second triplet only a little harder. "Five squared is twenty-five. Twelve squared is one hundred forty-four. Thirteen squared is one hundred sixty-nine."

She lifted her eyes from the tablet, doing the final sum easily in her head.

"Holy… it works," she whispered, unable to do the math in her head for the third triplet but doubting if she even needed to. "They're Pythagorean triples."

Kori sounded an audible sigh. "I'm so glad to hear you confirm. I thought I might be imagining it."

The triplets were sides of a right triangle, whole numbers that exactly solved the famous equation of trigonometry, $a^2 + b^2 = c^2$. Three, four, and five were the smallest possible set, but mathematicians had worked out many others and called them Pythagorean triples.

A chill ran down Amelia's back. "Is this really what happened? Orlando gave a series of digits that were wrong for pi, but that fulfilled the Pythagorean equation?"

"You stopped him after four hundred eighty-six digits of pi, but up to that point Orlando had replaced every third digit of pi with the digits of Pythagorean triples, in sequence from smallest to largest."

"Every third digit," Amelia whispered to herself. "Three sides on a triangle. Like the whole thing was planned from the start."

Whether or not he'd known what he was doing, Orlando had conveyed a geometric relationship for triangles inside the number pi, which itself represented a geometric relationship for circles. Math hidden within math. Geometry within geometry. Yet, he'd said the digits were mistakes.

Amelia picked up her pace, now anxious to find the man who could juggle numbers with such ease. "I'm skeptical, Kori. Given that you caught him in a lie about the phone call, and that he's hiding from me, he may be deceiving on a wider scale."

"Didn't you say he can't lie in a dream?" Kori asked.

"Well, technically the mind isn't capable of the level of consciousness required to lie while asleep, but if the lie is formed while awake and is buried deep enough, then he's, in effect, deceiving himself. Those kinds of lies could come out in a dream. But these Pythagorean triples are a different level altogether. It's either history's most complex subconscious lie, or –"

Or it's intentional.

A memory flickered across her consciousness, an image of the creature from Orlando's dream. Its elongated head was supported by a central stalk, jointed like bamboo. Below that, a tripod of legs. The tendrils had the same structure, splitting off from a joint. Three legs. Three tendrils on each side.

Triangles. Triples. Three.

Something about that number was significant, either within Orlando's mind or the separate consciousness that had invaded.

CHAPTER SEVENTEEN

CIRCLES

AMELIA HURRIED PAST one of the newer buildings on campus, a computing center built from donations by Seattle's premier billionaire couple, Bill and Melinda Gates. Amelia had never been inside, but she'd heard that the fight-to-the-death dueling arena at the Robotics Lab was unbeatable as a date night for nerds.

Her destination wasn't much farther, just beyond a copse of trees. Roberts Hall was old school, quite literally. A brick building from the 1920s, its architectural flair came from fronting columns with ornate stone capitals that jutted above the roof line. She entered the front door and located a directory that pointed her to the administrative office at the end of a hall.

More than just a hallway, it was a public display that touted the work conducted within the Material Sciences and Engineering building. Banners hung on the walls detailing obscure but riveting topics like optomechanical manipulation of nanoscale materials, gold binding peptides, and combinatorial mutagenesis. The department seemed to be involved in a variety of microscopic studies of metals, ceramics, and even living tissues, often genetically engineered.

Amelia couldn't help but notice the multiple references to topics in organic chemistry. It seemed that modern materials weren't just limited to sheet metal, plastic, and stone. They included biological constituents purposefully designed from snippets of DNA.

The administrative office door was open, and Amelia stepped in. "Can you help me locate a colleague?" she asked the woman sitting behind a desk.

"Faculty or student?" the woman answered, setting aside a book she was reading.

"A temporary visitor, actually. Mr. Orlando Kwon?"

"Kwon," the woman said to herself. "Asian man, fortyish, hair cut short on one side?"

"Yup, that's him." Amelia gave her a big smile, stretching the stitch in her lower lip. The slight pain was worth holding up the façade of colleagues trying to find each other on a busy university campus.

The woman scanned a list posted on one wall. "Uh, yeah, Professor Chin assigned workspace to Kwon yesterday. Lab 104 in the adjunct building." She pointed out the office door. "It's just behind us. Go out the rear entrance. You can't miss it."

Amelia thanked her and followed the hall back to a junction. A stairway led down one flight to an exit with a small parking area and courtyard just outside.

"I think we've got him," Amelia whispered to Kori once she saw the small sign nestled in thick ivy: *Wilson Metals Laboratory*.

"Whatever you do, don't turn off the earbud cam," Kori said. "The fireworks coming up are something I've *got* to see."

"I'm not going to yell at him, I just hope he's here."

Amelia pulled open the only door leading into the small brick building, her senses immediately confronted by odors of metal, disinfectants, and something burning. Sounds of machinery came from a hallway with multiple open doors down its length.

In the first room, a large machine hung over a round tub. The sign on the door, *Water Jet Cutter*, also warned visitors to wear safety glasses at all times. The next room was filled with worktables and heavy-duty power tools: a band saw, a drill press and other tools Amelia couldn't identify. Several young men and women – probably students – were bent over the tables working on various projects.

Two rooms further, she found Lab 104, its door closed. The sign simply stated, *Team Workshop*.

She turned the door handle. It opened, but a floor to ceiling black curtain on the other side suggested that visitors weren't welcome. A metal stand stood in front of the curtain supporting an international danger sign, a yellow triangle with an exclamation point in its center and the words, *Keep Out*.

Undeterred by mere cloth, Amelia found the curtain's edge and peered around it.

The lab was as spacious as any car garage with a large central area and workbenches around the perimeter. Hand tools hung from pegboards, and larger tools, metal frames, and hanging lights were scattered around. The floor was littered with metal shavings, dust, and other debris.

An ordinary workshop – except for a magnificent metal sculpture that filled the center of the room. Three gold tubes arched gracefully overhead, forming concentric rings, one inside the other. The outermost ring reached almost to the ceiling ten feet above. Two triangular spires standing left and right provided a stable base and created an open walkway beneath the rings.

Each spire was constructed from laminated layers of metal triangles that decreased in size from back to front. It gave the appearance of one of those 3-D contour maps built up from horizontal sheets. The left spire wasn't finished; two triangles lay on the floor waiting to be assembled.

Amelia had never seen anything like it.

It's beautiful. An art sculpture?

She stepped into the room, no one in sight. "Hello?"

From behind a partition, Orlando Kwon stepped out. His eyes widened and his mouth hung open as if he'd been caught by a parent. He stumbled over his words. "Um…" He looked at Amelia, to the metal ring sculpture and back to Amelia. "I… I can explain."

"I expect you will," Amelia said, walking under the archway and into the center of the workshop. "You're building this?" She wandered around the gleaming metal object examining it from all sides.

He looked to the floor. "Uh... sort of."

She swiveled to face Orlando. "What does that mean, sort of? Either you're building it or you're not."

"Well, yeah, I'm building it, but... it's complicated. You wouldn't understand."

Amelia shook her head. "Orlando, what the hell? This thing is huge. You've obviously put in an enormous amount of effort and you decided it was okay not to mention it?"

He continued staring at the floor, a measuring tool of some kind in his hand.

Embarrassing him wasn't working, but a healthy dose of reality might. "There's a military group from DARPA after you. They say you stole the chemistry formula and that it's classified material."

He looked up, surprised. "I didn't! The formula was given to me!"

Amelia caught his eye. "From the alien voice in your head?"

His eyes cast down again. "I know it sounds crazy, but I thought you were on my side."

"I am on your side. But this has gotten a lot bigger than just you and me. These people are after both of us and if they catch us, they'll take you away from here."

"They can't!"

"They will." She held out a hand. "Give me your mobile."

He lifted his personal device from a back pocket and handed it over. She verified it was switched off then returned it.

"I turned it off when I left this morning. I didn't want you to find me," Orlando said. Kori had guessed correctly.

"At least we're on the same wavelength, but it's not me you have to worry about, it's the military." She came closer, lowering her head until she caught his eye again. "Come on, Orlando. This is serious. No more secrets. Whatever it is you're doing here is way beyond anything you've told me. If I'm going to have any chance to help you get back to your wife and kids – or even keep you out of jail – you need to cooperate."

He took a deep breath and nodded slowly. "I have to build it. They need it."

Amelia looked over at the silver and gold creation. The craftsmanship was amazing. She couldn't see any joints in the metal surface of the rings which soared well above her head. The various sized triangles were each a half-inch thick and laminated together without any trace of glue or screws. How he'd managed to create such a structure in less than two days was remarkable.

"What is it?" Amelia asked. She'd already crossed a sculpture off the list.

He shook his head. "Um… it will help them. I'm not sure how, but they need it."

"They, meaning Prime Arc?"

He nodded. "And others like it. I sometimes hear multiple voices. It's not always the same one."

"And all these aliens are now crowded into your head?"

"No, just their voices."

"Are they talking to you now?"

"It's not like that. It's only when I need them."

"To finish the work?"

He nodded again. "Sort of. They teach me things. Then I know what to do."

Amelia stepped over to the structure and ran a hand along the smooth curved metal of the outside ring. Cold to the touch. Flawless. "It's magnificent. Have you always had metal-working talents like this?"

He looked over at his creation. "I'm just as surprised as you. I struggle putting together IKEA furniture."

Amelia stifled a laugh. Anyone who could construct this so quickly bordered on superhuman. "But it's not quite finished, is it?"

Orlando picked up one of two aluminum triangles from the floor. "Two more to attach, then the final component at the top." He proudly showed the triangle to Amelia. "It's an organometallic called trimethylaluminum. I created it in a chemical precipitation bath they have down the hall."

Amelia recalled the conversation they'd had when she first met Orlando. His formula created a solid form of trimethylaluminum, normally a pyrophoric substance that would spontaneously ignite.

Orlando ran a finger along the edge of the triangle where a thin black line protruded slightly. "The plate has a carbon nanostructure sandwiched inside the metal. They all do. There's a nano-etching tool at this lab, and I burned an integrated circuit schematic into the carbon." He shrugged. "I have no idea what the circuit does, but it wasn't hard to create."

He offered the triangle to Amelia. "Go ahead. It's not toxic or anything."

Amelia turned it over in her hands, examining the lengths of each edge and the right angle at one corner. "Let me guess. The triangles are Pythagorean triples."

Orlando stared incredulously at Amelia. "How did you know?"

She handed the triangle back to him. "I might know more than you realize, Orlando. We're partners, remember? You help me, so I can help you."

"I'm sorry I didn't tell you, but honestly, I didn't know – at least, not about the triangles. They feed things to me. I never know what or when. Yesterday it was circles and pi. Today it was *perfect triangles* – that's what they call them. When I woke up this morning, the voices told me where to find the hidden numbers, and I knew right away what to do."

Amelia struggled with the whole idea of an alien presence in his head. Stranger still that it was teaching and guiding. Orlando's mental abilities were skyrocketing into territory never approached by any savant.

Orlando tapped the triangle. "This is a three-four-five, the smallest."

The triangle was too large for units in inches or centimeters. As if he'd read her mind, Orlando clarified. "*Niks*. Their unit. One *nik* is equal to 2.927 inches. I had to do the conversion. Getting the lengths perfect was the hardest part, but I used the water jet cutter next door. Sixty-thousand PSI and the water is laced with micro fragments of garnet stone. Pretty amazing. That jet slices right through the metal like a laser."

Beyond his enhanced mental capacity, Orlando's construction techniques were astonishingly advanced for a man who handled quality control at a plastic bottling plant. He might have an intrinsic understanding of mechanical devices, but what he'd accomplished in this workshop was clearly beyond any ordinary skill level.

As impressive as his results were, there was a different puzzle she genuinely wanted to solve. "Why Pythagorean triples?"

Orlando held up both palms. "That's just how it supposed to be built. There's a balance between the triangles and the rings." He ran a hand along the smooth surface of the outer ring. The pride on his face showed. "The circles had to be perfect, too. I can't tell you how many times I've used all those digits of pi that I have in my head."

A smile formed on Amelia's lips as the mathematical puzzle pieces fell into place. He'd been in training for this construction event. Pi and perfect triangles were just homework. She glanced over her shoulder to the golden rings that surrounded the spires. "Three rings. Why three?"

"Three is a balance number. It's what they needed."

He'd said *they* several times. Orlando really believed he was working for the benefit of some alien race on some distant jungle planet. Given the incredible transfer of information, Amelia was beginning to think that it might be the only logical explanation for the very real presence in his head, but she wasn't ready to toss out her innate skepticism.

"Needed for what? This is more than a piece of art. Why do they want you to build it?"

He pushed his hands together and lowered his head as if in prayer – or deep thought. When he looked up there were tears in his eyes.

"I can feel it. It's fully formed now. The other version of me… it's been born."

Amelia squinted, not having the slightest idea what he was talking about.

CHAPTER EIGHTEEN

ALIEN

AMELIA STOOD DIRECTLY beneath the three concentric rings that arched overhead. Standing next to her and staring up to the ceiling, Orlando was visibly upset. It wasn't because he'd been caught in a lie about his secret workshop; he hadn't hesitated to explain the gold and silver object he was constructing. His distress seemed deeper. His other version was now *fully formed*, whatever that meant.

Orlando released a long breath and began slowly. "Remember when I told you that there was something else out there?"

"You mean this creature, Prime Arc?"

"No, Prime Arc is guiding me, helping me, showing me things. I told you about something else, growing but not fully formed."

"I remember."

He shrugged. "Well… that growing thing… is me."

Amelia stared at him, wondering what he could possibly be talking about.

"Another version of me, somewhere else. It's like a plant – or *was* a plant – growing from the mud in the jungle. But now… it's ripe, or born, or whatever. I don't know if there are good words to describe it, but it's not a plant anymore. It can move around. *I* can move around. I feel myself breathing, I can see and hear things, but it's different somehow. It's not my body – it's a new body – but it's still my mind."

"You're telling me that your mind is in two bodies at the same time? A human body and a plant body?" It was the best she could come up with for the irrational description he'd given.

Orlando lifted his hand and rotated his wrist in front of his eyes as if he'd never seen a hand before. With teary eyes, he laughed under his breath. "Five fingers. It seems so odd now. My other body has three." He ran his thumb across the top of his index finger. "Fingernails. Why do we have hard endings to our fingers instead of something flexible?"

Amelia's jaw went slack, her stare focused on the intriguing but disturbed man who never ceased to amaze. She gently placed hands on his shoulders and guided him to a nearby chair. "Sit down, Orlando. I can see we've got a lot to talk about."

He smiled, a creepy kind of half smile that showed no pleasure but exhibited a deep-seated acceptance of the insanity within him. He sat in the chair, looking up at Amelia. "You don't believe me."

"Tell me more, maybe I will." Amelia had already decided that the dream character she'd personally experienced was separate from Orlando's mind. She wasn't discounting the bizarre reality of the ALD session, but she also wasn't ready to discard other explanations. Orlando was still a mental patient – even if that label was only for her peace of mind.

He wiped a tear from one eye. "My other body is, well... kind of like Prime Arc but smaller."

"With curled tendrils instead of fingers?"

"Yeah, like a grapevine, but mine can stretch. Well, it feels like stretching, but my fingers fly out really fast. It feels weird, but it's also kind of fun."

She'd experienced the *fun* directly when a prickly tendril wrapped around her head and poured hopelessness into her mind. It wasn't something she wanted to repeat.

Orlando seemed to note Amelia's skepticism. His voice wavered. "This is all wrong, isn't it? No one should have two bodies." He dropped his face into his hands. "How is this happening to me?"

Amelia had never experienced a patient like Orlando, and she didn't have any answers. Instead she knelt and reached out for his hand. He gave it.

"Orlando, I see a person, not an alien creature in a faraway jungle. I see a hand with fingers, not grapevine tendrils. I don't know what's going on in your head, but I promise you I *will* find out."

Orlando stood up, pulling Amelia up with him. He swallowed hard and wiped away another tear. "When I think about it, it's not fun anymore... I get scared. It's pulling me in, and I can't stop it."

He wandered over to his artistic creation, stroking fingers along its smooth metal. "The alignment device is important," he said keeping his back to Amelia. "Not just for them, but for me too."

"Explain, please." She was thankful he was still cooperating, though she was reaching her limit on how many dysfunctional twists she'd be able to process.

"There's not much time left," he said, eyes to the floor. "I have to finish."

"Finish this *alignment device*?" They were his words, not hers, but he still hadn't explained what this sculpture of rings and triangles was supposed to do. "And if you don't finish?"

His voice was barely above a whisper. "I think I'll die."

"The voices are threatening you?"

"No, not directly. Something is going to happen, something wonderful."

The word set Amelia on her heels. "Wonderful? Whose definition of wonderful are we talking about? Ours or theirs?"

"Theirs, but maybe ours too. They don't tell me how the device works. I guess it aligns something. All I know is I'll die without it." Orlando turned to face Amelia, choking up and barely able to get the words out. "I'm so sorry, Amelia... but I think you could die too."

What the hell?

Amelia sensed an immediate spike in her blood pressure. Her mouth opened but the words wouldn't come out. She stared up to the ceiling. There were medical protocols when a schizophrenic patient threatened his caregiver and Amelia was tempted to invoke them on the spot. If she did, Orlando would be confined to a secured hospital; his care limited to drug therapy until a medical board approved further contact.

It would never get that far.

If she invoked the protocol, she'd probably never see him again. The military pursuers would intervene and their plans for Orlando didn't seem to include any care at all. Besides, Orlando wasn't suffering from schizophrenia – she'd already ruled that out – and only a psychopath would start off a threat with, *I'm so sorry.* Orlando was in desperate need of help, but he wasn't a psychopath.

There was an alternative explanation, and it matched Amelia's realization that something had invaded Orlando's mind. The invader might be the source of the threat, not Orlando.

"Okay, I'll bite. Why would I die?" She pointed a finger at him. "And your story better be good because if I get any hint that you're threatening me personally, this is all going to end badly for you."

His lips trembled and he put a hand over his mouth. "I didn't mean it that way. Really. I'm worried for you, Amelia. You've been inside my mind and they know it. Prime Arc knows who you are."

Amelia wasn't sure if his explanation was better or worse. She was willing to believe that the threat didn't come from Orlando, but if there really were external entities with malicious intent patrolling his mind, these vermin would need to be rooted out and permanently exterminated. Dream dynamite might not be enough; she'd need a better plan.

Amelia's voice was strong and assertive. "If I interfere – if I stop you from building this device – Prime Arc will kill me, is that it?"

He nodded.

"And if you don't hurry up and finish, it will kill you?"

He shook his head. "No, Prime Arc wants me to live. The device will keep me alive, but I have to follow their instructions."

"But I'm expendable?" Amelia asked once more.

With tears in his eyes, Orlando nodded again.

Amelia shook her head in disbelief. "Orlando, how would Prime Arc possibly kill me? You're the one with the visions, not me."

"Prime Arc is powerful. It's already in my brain, maybe it got in your brain too. You know… like a virus."

Amelia did her best to control rising emotions. "I don't believe you. You're either lying to me again, or you don't know what's really going on."

Orlando hung his head. "I'm not lying, but you're right, I'm not sure what's going on. All I know is I have to finish building it." His eyes pleaded his case. "Don't tell anyone about it. Please. I'll finish – maybe even today – and everything will be fine, you'll see."

"Amelia?" A voice popped into her head – the good kind of voice.

"Yes, Kori."

"I just got a Dirtbox ping. They're close. You need to get out now."

Shit.

She swiveled to the workshop door and back to Orlando. "Can you lock this place up?"

He nodded.

"Do it. We need to go right now or you're going to find yourself in a jail cell – or worse. I can't say for sure when we'll be able to come back, but for the time being you're going to have to trust me. I have your best interests at heart, and I can tell you with certainty the guys hunting you don't."

****

Shepard pulled over to the curb, allowing the engine of the rented black van to idle. He leaned toward the passenger side and glared into the electronics display on Lieutenant Tombaugh's lap.

"Well?"

"University area," Tombaugh responded, his attention never leaving the map shown on the display. "That may be as close as I can get."

"God damn it, Tombaugh, you said this thing could triangulate positions to a few yards." They'd been patrolling the campus for the past thirty minutes, but it was a big place.

Tombaugh looked up like he was ready to challenge Shepard's version of their exchange but thought better of it. "We're getting regular pings, but it's too sparse. I think the resolution goes down without a constant data stream." He twisted a knob on the front of a box mounted above the dash. A wire ran from the box to an antenna hooked at the top of the passenger window and sticking outside the car.

Walker Duplass leaned forward from the back seat. "Maybe they turned off their mobile devices?"

Shepard looked over his shoulder, glaring. "When I need your expert opinion on telecommunications, Duplass, I'll ask for it."

Tombaugh turned back to Duplass. "Even if their mobiles are off, that doesn't protect them. Most cellular carriers plant a trojan in the operating system that searches for a cell tower every hour even when the device is turned off. They tell their customers it's to help locate a lost device, they just don't bother to mention that it also opens a back door."

Another ping caught Tombaugh's attention. "The woman's device must be on, though. Too many pings, but for some reason they're erratic. Wait a second... it's narrowing a bit. They may be on the move. Try Mason Road, the next right."

Shepard put the van in gear and sped off. "Keep your eyes peeled. They'll probably be on foot."

CHAPTER NINETEEN

FUGITIVES

HOW DOES ANYONE hide from a pursuer with the technology and precision of the military? According to Kori, there were two strategies: keep moving or blend in with the crowd. Amelia chose the keep-moving option.

"How close are they?" Amelia asked between breaths as they ran along a sidewalk that descended the broad hill forming the University of Washington campus.

"A quarter mile or less. This Dirtbox sniffer software isn't very accurate," Kori answered.

Their pursuers were already closer than her car, still parked at the east edge of campus. "I thought you were going to spoof them?"

"I did. It doesn't seem to work. Maybe they have anti-spoofing technology."

All this sniffing, spoofing and anti-spoofing seemed destined for failure, but there was one surefire way to avoid electronic detection. Amelia said goodbye to Kori and switched off her mobile.

The sound of a car gunning its engine came from somewhere behind them. Amelia glanced over her shoulder to see a black van turn a corner, accelerating quickly down the street.

"Hurry!" she yelled, and they raced across the street to a row of trees on the other side.

The vehicle was on them quickly, but Amelia ducked under tree branches to a bike trail. "This way!" she yelled and led Orlando toward a footbridge that crossed over a major boulevard curving around the base of the campus hill.

Behind them, the van skidded to a stop and a man in uniform jumped out of the passenger side and ran after them.

Spanning high above the boulevard, the footbridge was the only route to the parking lot on the other side. Several students coming the other way rode bicycles, even though warning signs painted on the ground advised them to dismount. Without slowing down, Amelia dodged the bikes as best she could, but Orlando glanced off the lead cyclist causing a chain reaction as multiple bikes and their riders hit the ground.

"Hey!" yelled a student, but Orlando made it past and kept running.

Not far behind, the man in uniform wasn't as lucky and became entangled in bikes and students sprawled across the narrow bridge. The obstacle provided precious seconds for their final dash down steps on the other side and into the parking lot.

As Amelia reached her car, she looked back to the hill. The black van was still there. A second man in uniform stepped out, holding binoculars to his eyes.

"Damn!" Amelia said, jumping into the driver's seat of her car. Orlando slipped into the passenger side and they sped away.

"That was close," Orlando said, looking behind as they exited the parking area and turned north.

"Unfortunately, they spotted my car," Amelia said. "Probably have the license number now. Not good."

Minutes later, they sped down a freeway onramp with Amelia regularly checking her rearview mirror. After a few more miles, she exited the freeway and headed west, which in Seattle meant they'd hit water soon.

But water might be exactly what we need. A plan quickly formed.

"Where are we going?" Orlando asked, watching the city flash by his window.

"The Edmonds ferry terminal. If I time it just right, we could be one of the last cars on the 2:15 ferry. They'd have to wait an hour for the next run."

Amelia smiled to herself, satisfied with her impromptu plan – a plan that hadn't required Kori. Pure local knowledge. She'd grown up in Montreal, but the past nine years were all Seattle and she'd come to know the city well.

Her idea was brilliant, but Orlando didn't seem impressed. "What then?"

He had a point. "I'm not sure. The ferry crosses Puget Sound and it's rural on the other side. Find some remote spot in the Olympic mountains? Canada's not far." She glanced over at Orlando who stared out the window watching the city go by. "You okay?"

He looked back, clearly pained. "It's just that we're going *away* from the workshop."

"I know. Orlando, I'm not ignoring your needs. I hear you loud and clear. You need to finish your alignment device, or you'll die."

He nodded, apprehensive.

"Is there some timeframe on this... death by triangulation?" He exhibited not even the slightest amusement at her bad joke.

Insensitive, Amelia. Do better.

It took a minute, but Orlando finally answered. "They don't count time like we do. A day, maybe two, but I need to finish."

Amelia spoke with sincerity. "I want to get you back to the university, I really do, but I'm worried about these DARPA guys. If they catch us, you'll never see that workshop again."

She looked ahead to the road that curved around a hill. "But if we make this ferry, we'll have some options."

He looked sullen, but he wasn't reaching for the door handle.

Amelia tried once more. "Orlando, I'm pretty good at what I do. Well…" She rubbed her sore lip. "A few bumps and bruises, but what if I can find a way to save you from Prime Arc and this other version of you? Maybe you don't need that device you're building."

"Maybe."

"Can you trust me a little longer to figure it out?"

Orlando nodded.

Around the corner, trees parted, and the blue waters of Puget Sound came into view. As she'd anticipated, the ferry line was short with cars loading two-by-two onto an enormous white and green ship, the *MV Puyallup*.

She was waved on with only a few cars behind them, the boarding ramp lifted, and the ferry pulled away. Amelia glanced at the passengers in neighboring cars that had also boarded last minute – a mom and her child in a car seat, two teenagers, an elderly man – not a single uniform among them.

She opened the door and stepped out to the open metal deck. A chill breeze blew as the ferry came up to full speed and the dock receded behind them. Seconds later, a black van came roaring up to the water's edge, skidding to a halt. Two men in uniform jumped out, and one lifted binoculars.

The wind blew Amelia's hair into a halo around her head, and a broad smile spread across her face as the distance from their pursuers increased. She mouthed words, fantasizing that whoever was on the other end of those binoculars might read her lips.

"Charron's my name. Amelia Charron. And you, my friend, should never underestimate a determined scientist."

Satisfied with her newfound cloak and dagger skills, Amelia leaned into the open door of the car. "It's a thirty-minute crossing. Want some lunch? I'm buying."

Amelia led Orlando upstairs to an interior café. They scanned the selection ranging from deep-fried chicken strips to soggy burgers under heat lamps and opted instead for two bottles of juice. Even fugitives on the run have standards.

They settled into a booth at a window and watched the deep blue water of Puget Sound slide by. Fifty-six-degree water – Seattle's natural air conditioning system. With midsummer heat worsening elsewhere, Seattle and its neighbors to the north, Victoria, and Vancouver, enjoyed the unique geography of a cold Alaskan current that continuously replenished deep channels. It was like a kitchen fan blowing across a block of ice and even in the era of global warming, it was a rare summer day that reached anywhere close to hot.

"Nice," Orlando said, motioning to the view outside. "But... how do we get back?"

The nearly finished triple-ring structure clearly weighed on his mind. He might trust her, but without a detailed plan for their next steps, that trust wouldn't last long. Running or hiding seemed fruitless.

Amelia pondered an alternative, speaking concisely to Orlando. "You told me that you have two bodies and a single mind – a shared consciousness, if you will. Now, I'm not going to pretend that's a sane thing to say, but I've personally witnessed something unique going on in your mind so I'm not going to just blow you off."

She locked on to his eyes. "Orlando, you're not suffering from schizophrenia. I know that now, but if I'm going to help you, I'll need to better understand my options."

His eyes were hopeful, but he said nothing.

"I do have one idea. I have a friend. Very smart. She's been a mentor to me for years, and I think she might be able to help us both. Unfortunately, she's back in Seattle, so there's some danger."

He shrugged. "I'm not worried. Let's go back."

"Maybe. But before we turn around, let me first make contact with her."

Amelia activated her mobile, allowing it to boot up in airplane mode. Just turning it on was a risk, but they wouldn't get far without some level of connectivity. Besides, their military pursuers had watched them board the ferry. It wasn't like they were hiding anymore.

"Kori, would it be safe to use the ferry Wi-Fi to make a call?"

"Good question," Kori responded in her ear. A mere second passed. "Sorry for the delay, I researched this question. Public Wi-Fi is nothing close to secure, however, to hack into your call, they would need to be on the same Wi-Fi router. Since they're not physically on the ferry, you're safe – well, except for that guy sitting in the next booth."

Amelia glanced to a man slumped against a window, sleeping. "Random passengers I can deal with. Thanks, Kori."

"Kori's your digital assistant, right?" Orlando asked, as Amelia connected to the ferry's onboard Wi-Fi.

"A pretty advanced version. In fact, that's who I need to call, Kori's *mother*, if you will, Evelyn Stern. She's an expert in artificial intelligence, and she knows a few things about computer consciousness that might be applicable to your case."

Evelyn Stern was unquestionably at the forefront of AI, but she would be the first person to admit being a fringe player. Half the time she was proposing some crazy plan to join human minds with computers, but the other half had created a solid resume over the years. She was a key player at IBM, helping to shape Deep Blue and Watson. She'd won awards.

"Now, she's at Guava.com – they're doing some amazing things with AI. That's where Kori came from."

Orlando said, "I've heard of Guava, but not Kori."

Amelia laughed. She'd have been shocked if he hadn't. Guava was the single most popular digital assistant on the planet, but mostly due to effective marketing and a pleasant voice, not advanced AI.

"Yeah, Guava beat Kori. They had two competing projects, originally given the code names Project C and D. The D team won, and Guava was born, but the C team didn't disband, they doubled down. Ev was key in dragging that group in a different direction. Kori is a combination of what they call deep neural networks and AGI, or Artificial General Intelligence. Ev told me all about it once."

"So, can your friend help me?"

Amelia tightened her lips. "I hope so."

A Wi-Fi notification appeared on her mobile, followed quickly by a popup phone app – *Dialing Evelyn Stern.*

Evelyn picked up after the third ring. "For fuck's sake, Amelia, you need to call this old lady way more often. I thought you were dead."

Amelia rolled her eyes. "Nice to hear your sweet voice, too, Ev. And for accuracy, it's only been two months."

"Two months since you joined the beta program? Seems longer. But now that you've got – what did you name him? Quarry?"

"Kori."

Ev's voice was raspy, roughened by years of smoking. "A fucking girl's name. Did you emasculate his gender too?"

"No! He's still a guy and I should warn you, he can hear everything you're saying about him."

"Fuck that. I'm his creator. His personal issues are whatever I decide they are. You hear that, Quarry?"

Amelia sighed. "Be kind, Ev. I need your help."

"I'm kind every other Friday, and today's your lucky day. What's up?"

Having finally gotten Ev's attention, Amelia related the basics of her dilemma but left out most of the details of Orlando's case. She asked to meet, preferably someplace private and secure. Ev, not one to speak in nuance, made it clear her afternoon was booked. The best she could do was after eight p.m., to which Amelia quickly agreed. They'd meet at The Spheres, a workplace of sorts, but also a hideout for Guava.com employees looking for seclusion. The Spheres were secured buildings for use only by employees and their invited guests, a perfect place to talk even if it required returning to busy Seattle.

Keep moving or blend in with the crowd. Or maybe a little of both.

Amelia said goodbye to both Ev and Kori, shut off her mobile once more. "We'll need to get back to Seattle," she explained to Orlando, "but we've got plenty of time."

Amelia played with the stitch in her lower lip. "We shouldn't return on this ferry, though. The DARPA boys might still be waiting at the dock."

There were alternatives. They could drive south down the Kitsap Peninsula to Bainbridge. A different ferry crossed from there to downtown Seattle. "Maybe park the car somewhere downtown?" she mused out loud. Her car was unquestionably a liability now.

An announcement came over the ferry public address telling passengers to return to their vehicles. They'd be docking at Kingston in a few minutes, a quaint town hidden among the trees that covered the Kitsap Peninsula. Though she'd taken this route many times, it never ceased to amaze Amelia how a thirty-minute crossing of Puget

Sound could so radically change the landscape. Behind them was dense city. Ahead, a forest of Douglas fir, hemlock, and cedar.

Splitting the forest was a single road leading away from the ferry terminal where they'd dock in just a few minutes. A sheriff's car with flashing red and blue lights was parked at the edge of the road.

"Oh, shit!" Amelia's heart skipped a beat. "That's got to be for us." She turned to Orlando whose face showed equal surprise at the police roadblock that surely awaited them. "Come on, let's go."

They ran down the stairs back to the car deck where other passengers returned to their vehicles. The ferry slowed and the breeze through its open center calmed. The ship pivoted toward the dock that loomed ahead, and beyond it, the flashing lights of the sheriff's car.

Amelia held a hand to her mouth, desperately searching for alternatives. They'd surely be stopped. The line of cars exiting any ferry was habitually slow, easy for any police officer to scan every car and examine every license plate.

"Maybe we just stay on the ferry?" Amelia asked herself.

She knew right away that plan would fail. Round trips weren't allowed, and the ferry employees would make sure every level was clear of passengers.

Hide in the bathroom?

She looked around thinking as creatively as she could. She stopped, staring at a pickup truck with a camper shell on its bed. Lettering on the truck's door said, *Suquamish Clearwater Resort.*

"That's it! Stay right here," Amelia told Orlando. "If my charms are up to snuff this might work."

CHAPTER TWENTY

CLEARWATER

WHILE THE FERRY closed the last few feet to the dock, Amelia threaded through columns of waiting cars toward a pickup truck almost certainly destined for the Clearwater Resort. She knocked on the window. It rolled down, revealing a kind face, wrinkled with age – a native American.

"Sorry to bother you, my name's Amelia." She held out a hand and the man took it, his dark eyes curious about the stranger introducing herself for no reason.

"Chief Rodney," the man answered.

Amelia poured on the charm. "Wow, are you a real chief of the Suquamish?" The tribe was one of several who lived on small reservations around Puget Sound. They also ran the closest casino to the city, a beautiful resort right on the water. The tribe's name, Suquamish, literally meant *clearwater*.

"Nah," the man answered. "The tribal chief is my second cousin, Marvin. But I was a Chief Petty Officer in the Navy back in the nineties. The name stuck." He pinched his brow. "What's the matter, honey? Car won't start? The ferry guys can give you a jump."

"No, that's not it," Amelia answered, flashing her most beautiful smile. "I was just wondering… since you're going to the resort…

would you mind if I joined you? My friend, too?" She pointed to Orlando who stood a few cars away.

She squinted a hopeful smile. "If it's not too much trouble?"

The old man grinned, showing teeth that angled in almost every direction except down. "Be happy to, but I've got no room in the cab." A large German Shepard sat in the passenger's seat. "Bear gets cranky riding in the back. He and Sam don't get along real well."

A camper shell sat on the truck bed with window curtains preventing any view inside. "Oh, we don't mind riding with Sam. Any chance you could make room for two more?"

He shrugged. "Sure, honey, I think we can manage."

The old man got out, waving to Orlando to come over too. Ambling around the back, the not-quite-chief of the Suquamish tribe opened a small door into the camper. It was dark inside, a perfect hideout. If they got past the sheriff, the resort wasn't far from the Bainbridge ferry, a good route back to Seattle. Her abandoned car would probably be impounded but paying a fine was a lot better than going to jail.

Amelia smiled again. "Thank you so much. I can't tell you how much this helps us."

Rodney offered a helping hand as Amelia stepped up on the truck bumper and into the camper. A small sink on the left side and a single bed on the right mostly filled the space. At the far end, a wooden perch stuck out from the camper wall. A large bald eagle moved uneasily back and forth along the perch, its talons flexing as they dug into the wood.

"Oh!" Amelia sat on the floor, leaning against the bed. She stared at the eagle. It stared back with that fierce expression natural to all birds of prey.

Chief Rodney poked his head in the door. "Yeah, don't worry about Sam. He'll screech a bit but generally doesn't leave his perch. If he looks hungry, just give him a piece of salmon, there's some in the cooler." He pointed to a small plastic box next to the sink.

"You have a bald eagle?" Orlando asked, looking in. "Is that even legal?"

Chief Rodney laughed. "It is for the tribes. Sam's been with me for three years. Found him tangled up in some fishing line down on the beach. Guess he had a hell of a time trying to get untangled because the line tore some tendons in his wing. He's not much of a flyer anymore, but I take good care of him. We just got back from a school over in Lynnwood. The kids always love to see Sam."

Orlando climbed in and closed the door behind him, sitting on the floor next to Amelia. Her eyes never left the white-headed bird, almost as big as the dog in the cab. Slowly, she lifted and scooted onto the bed.

"Nice birdie," Amelia soothed, wondering if it understood such things. For the next half-hour, they'd be companions to a wild animal – like it or not. The eagle hopped along the perch, twisting its neck almost into a circle to survey the intruding humans. Its black talons were at least three inches long.

Orlando reached out and the bird threw its head back, opened its beak and screeched, sounding much like the ubiquitous seagulls of Puget Sound, but louder.

"Maybe you shouldn't do that," Amelia cautioned.

A few minutes later, the truck's engine started, and they rolled off the ferry. Amelia peeked through the side window as they approached the Kitsap County Sheriff's car. One officer leaned against its hood. Another checked every car that went by. Window curtains might be enough, but they ducked down anyway.

The truck slowed to a stop and the cab's window rolled down. Chief Rodney's voice was easy to hear even from the camper shell. "Howdy. What's up?"

"Routine check, sir. What's in the back?" the deputy asked.

Amelia's heart skipped a beat. A small vent at the forward end of the camper shell gave a slit view into the cab. She couldn't see the deputy outside but watched as Chief Rodney retrieved a document and handed it out the window.

"My eagle. He's got papers."

"Hmm. Mind if I have a look?" the officer asked, handing the document back.

"Well, Sam's a bit feisty today, but if you take your hat off first, he won't cut you up too bad. Sam don't much like hats."

The cab door opened. The second officer called out. "Aw, that's Sam the eagle. You know, the one they keep down at the casino."

Pressed up against the far wall, Amelia lifted a leg toward the eagle, and Sam let out a shriek that could raise the dead.

"Yeah, uh... never mind," the officer said. "You can go."

The cab door closed. "Good choice," Chief Rodney said. "You guys have a great day."

The truck's engine revved and they continued on their way. Amelia stole a glance into the cab, catching Chief Rodney's eye in the rearview mirror. He winked at her.

"He knows," Orlando whispered.

"He does," Amelia agreed. She smiled back at their driver. "Thanks," she mouthed over the noise of the engine. Maybe it would be enough.

A minute later they turned south, following a route to the resort and casino. Ferry personnel were probably checking her empty vehicle by now, but they'd find nothing to link them to Rodney's truck. The escape might work, as long as Chief Rodney had no other plans.

Amelia turned her attention back to their feathered companion. Sam kept one eye on them, and then twitching its head, the other eye.

Its fierce glare seemed to suggest that the five or six feet between them could be covered in a microsecond should the bird decide to 'cut them up'. At least, they weren't wearing hats.

"What does an eagle look like when it's hungry?" Amelia asked.

"Probably like that." Orlando reached into the cooler and brought out a small piece of fish. Sam shuffled on his perch, closing in on Orlando's outstretched hand. It lifted both wings which almost filled the space of the camper. With a quick snap, it snatched the morsel, its yellow beak never touching Orlando's fingers.

He handed another chunk of raw fish to Amelia. "You should do it too. Maybe Sam will like us better."

Amelia held the pink flesh gingerly, the smell wafting up like a garbage bin behind a seafood restaurant. She squinted, reached out, and wondered if she'd soon end up in the emergency room. The giant bird plucked the food from her hand and swallowed it in one gulp.

"*Screech!*"

Amelia winced at the loud sound. "Is that good or bad?"

"Good, I think."

"Ever been this close to an eagle?"

"We don't get eagles in southern California. At least, I've never seen one."

"We see them in the trees here. Sometimes on telephone poles, but that's a whole different thing than riding in a truck with one."

Sam scooted back to the far end of the perch and tucked his head down. The salmon seemed to have done its magic – the bird had decided they were friends. Amelia peeked outside. Nothing but trees, but they'd be at the resort in twenty minutes.

"Do you miss home?" she asked Orlando, feeling much calmer now that the feathered beast had been satisfied.

"I miss Teena and the kids, but I guess I've been too busy to think much about home."

She lifted her eyebrows. "Building perfect circles and Pythagorean triangles?"

He grimaced. "Sorry, I should have told you earlier."

"Don't worry about it. We'll figure it out together, eh?"

"You're Canadian."

"I am. Québécoise and proud. You're what, Korean?"

He nodded. "Third generation American. My grandparents emigrated from Busan, South Korea in the nineteen sixties. I've been back there a couple of times. The people look like me, but the place feels foreign. Los Angeles is home."

They passed a large bay with tranquil blue waters. Amelia kept the calming conversation going. "I like LA. There's more to do there than people realize. It's not just about Hollywood."

"Does everyone from Canada say 'aboat' and add 'eh' to the end of their sentences?"

Amelia laughed. "Sometimes, sure, but Americans overuse those examples. You guys don't even know about all the weird things we say in Quebec that drive the French crazy."

"Like?"

"Oh, like saying dégueulasse when something is gross or disgusting. For the French, dégueulasse is a profanity."

Orlando smiled. "That's funny."

She'd never seen him so relaxed. Getting away from the chaos that had been his living nightmare was clearly therapeutic. They were still on the run, but with Chief Rodney at the controls and Sam the bald eagle standing watch, their improvised transportation felt safe and comfortable.

"I love language quirks," Orlando said. "What else is different in Quebec?"

"Well, we say square-ol instead of squirrel, but I guess that's an English example. My parents literally cannot say happy hour. The 'h' that's sometimes silent in English throws them every time and it comes out 'appy hower'. Totally backwards."

Orlando laughed. A real laugh, not just a forced smile. He looked good, healthy for once.

She talked more of Canada and of moving to Seattle to start her PhD program at the University of Washington. She began to tell him about the family lake house, and her parents' standing invitation to come out each summer, but she stopped herself partway through. Only the closest of friends got the story's true ending. Her parents had ulterior motives. They had always worried that Amelia might succumb to depression like her twin sister, Natalie, and the summer routine was their chance to inspect for any changes in her mood. Amelia lovingly submitted to her parents, but Orlando didn't need to hear about that.

"Anyone following us?" Orlando asked.

Amelia scooted to the back of the camper and peered out the door's window. The road behind them was empty. "Nothing but forest."

"Good." He paused. "Thanks."

"You're welcome. For what?"

"Keeping me safe. Figuring out what's wrong with me. Nobody else would do what you're doing."

"Oh, I'm sure most mental health professionals would..." She glanced at the eagle whose darting evil eye made it clear he was still monitoring the intruders into his space. "Well, maybe not the hiding out with Sam part."

On cue, Sam swiveled its head and screeched.

"He's smart," Orlando said.

"He sure knows his name." Amelia had studied consciousness in animals but mostly cats, dogs, and mice. One seminar on gorillas but never a bird. It was fascinating how smart the predators of the world could be.

The truck turned off the highway and slowed. Out the window, a parking lot full of cars came into view.

"Here already," Amelia said.

Sam perked up, twisting his neck to see out the window, apparently equally aware of their location. The truck stopped and Chief Rodney opened the back door, his dog at his side. "How'd you all get along?"

Amelia and Orlando hopped out of the camper. A large sign overhead with thousands of flashing lights – even in full daylight – made it clear this was a resort *and* a casino.

"Just fine," Amelia answered. "Sam's a sweetie." Sam screeched at the sound of his name.

"Sam enjoys people in his own way," Chief Rodney said.

Amelia caught the old man's eye. "We owe you."

Rodney reached into the camper, extracting Sam on his arm. "Maybe you do, maybe you don't, but that's my business. Got nothing to do with the Kitsap sheriff. Don't worry, honey, they never come around here. You're on Suquamish land now. Hell, you were the moment you stepped into my truck. Sheriff's got no right to search it."

"You are so kind," Amelia said, wrapping arms around Rodney's neck and hugging him.

"You two in any trouble?"

"No, really we're fine, but it's a long story. Probably best if we just get back to Seattle." Amelia got the feeling that Suquamish justice would be decided right here in the parking lot. The simplest of explanations might give the best results.

Rodney rubbed his chin, eying them both. "What do you think, Sam?"

The bird screeched.

"Yeah, that's what I thought too." The old man sighed. "When you two are ready, catch the free shuttle, it'll take you right to the Bainbridge ferry. But if you feel like sticking around for dinner, the folks in the resort will take good care of you." He pulled out two tickets from his shirt pocket. "These'll get you half off at the buffet."

With Amelia wearing a backpack, he probably thought they were hitchhiking on limited funds. He hadn't asked why law enforcement was involved, but then it didn't seem like the tribe had much of a relationship with the sheriff's department.

Amelia sheepishly glanced between Orlando and Rodney, not quite knowing what to say. "You're a dear," was the best she could offer.

Rodney gave a knowing smile, and the man and his animals headed off toward a small house on the far side of the parking lot.

"What do you think he's going to do?" Orlando asked.

"Probably nothing. I think we're safe." Amelia nodded toward the casino, the only break in an otherwise dense forest that surrounded them. "Why don't we check out their buffet. Nobody's going to be looking for us way out here, and our appointment with Ev isn't until eight anyway. With the ferry, we can be back in Seattle in thirty minutes."

"Sounds good, I'm hungry."

She hooked a hand under Orlando's elbow, and they walked into the modern building made to look like a traditional northwest Long House, complete with a dugout canoe in front. The buffet was good, and the time passed quickly. Amelia paid for their discounted dinner with cash, just to be sure. Afterward, they caught the shuttle to the ferry dock and walked on to a six-thirty crossing back to Seattle.

This time they stood at the bow of the ship, letting the fresh wind blow in their faces. The return route brought them to the downtown waterfront and the final mile was one of Seattle's greatest spectacles. As the sun set, lights came on across the city skyline. At one end, the Space Needle stood alone like a watchtower over the rest of the city. At the other end, stadiums and port cranes were backed up by Mount Rainier, its white glaciers ablaze in the pink alpenglow of sunset.

Amelia leaned on the rail absorbing the beauty with Orlando standing nearby. She thought of how many times she'd taken this same tour with friends who'd come to visit, though Orlando was hardly in that category. For him, serious questions lay ahead with no easy answers. There would be confrontation, not only of his fears, but with a multitude of almost supernatural neurological factors that haunted him. Consulting with Ev might shed light, but it would only be the beginning.

As propellers reversed and the ferry slowed past creosote pilings, she bumped her elbow against his. "It might get tricky from here. You ready?"

CHAPTER TWENTY-ONE

CONSCIOUSNESS

AMELIA GUIDED ORLANDO along the waterfront, Seattle's primary tourist zone, to Overlook Walk, a grand staircase that climbed from waterfront piers to the downtown avenues that overlooked Puget Sound. They'd been together most of the day now, and Orlando hadn't once experienced a visual or auditory hallucination. Maybe he was getting better at controlling things, or maybe he just didn't want her to know.

Summer tourists were out in large numbers, giving some comfort that her newest strategy of blending in with the crowd might work. As they climbed the steps, intermediate terraces provided dramatic views across the water, with pinks and purples of sunset reflected from high clouds overhead.

They walked up Stewart Street, the dividing line between the office buildings of downtown and high-rise condos for urban dwellers. As they made their way, Amelia stole a few glances behind, but no one was following.

"Almost there," she told Orlando, who seemed perfectly willing to let her lead, trusting that she had a plan and the resources to make things right. Now that they were back in Seattle, they were also a lot closer to Orlando's workshop at the university.

They turned a corner to the single most striking building in the city. Oddly out of place, The Spheres were a mashup of three geodesic glass domes nestled at the base of surrounding skyscrapers. In a way, the domes looked like soap bubbles joined along curving boundaries but there was nothing flimsy about them. A sturdy structure of metal beams provided frames for glass panels cut into shapes of triangles, diamonds, and pentagons. Somehow, the bewildering variety came together as a smoothly curving surface. Dark green plants could be seen inside making it clear this building was both working space and a block-long terrarium.

"Wow," Orlando said. "We're going in there?"

"By special permission. It's a nature preserve in the middle of the city, but only for company employees."

The entrance was a glass door like any other downtown building, but it led to a small lobby with three floor-to-ceiling glass gates. On the other side, a rock wall was covered with moss and ferns and with streams of water pouring across its surface from above. Overhead, crisscrossing walkways threaded through a jungle of greenery.

A card reader pad angled out near each gate. Amelia powered up her mobile. "Kori, we're at the meeting place, can you locate any messages from Ev that contain a visitor's key?"

Seconds later, a matrix barcode displayed on her device along with a text message from Ev, *Meet me at the Bird Nest.* Amelia held the bar code to the reader and the gate opened with a swish. The gate closed behind them, providing a feeling of security. Anyone following would need the same permission to enter this metal and glass cocoon. A stone staircase led to the next level.

At the top of the stairs, they surveyed the interior, far more expansive than it appeared from the outside. It was a multi-level office, but unlike any other. In an open area, tables and comfortable chairs provided a coffee-shop feel, but the floorspace was surrounded by plants of varying sizes and shapes. A meandering brook gurgled along one side, its water nourishing tropical flowers along its edge. In an adjacent sphere, a full-sized tree grew between crisscrossing walkways almost entirely filling the space.

Plants parted in places, allowing views out to the city buildings beyond, but they were just glimpses. The general feel was of separation, both physically and emotionally, from the surrounding urban environment.

They walked along a curving pathway bordered by a wooden bench on one side and a thick rainforest on the other. Overhead nozzles attached to a pipe sprayed a fine mist while water dripped through the leaves. Two men sat at one table in deep conversation.

Amelia pointed straight up. "The Bird Nest."

A circular bowl made from interlaced strips of wood hung from a steel support, looking very much like an oversized bird's nest suspended at the edge of a branch. Orlando's eyes grew wide, but he didn't voice any objection to the precariously perched rendezvous point.

They climbed another staircase and stopped at a narrow entrance to the nest. A gray-haired woman dressed in a flowered skirt and light blue sweater sat on a bench that formed the nest's inside perimeter.

She looked up, her smile revealing stained teeth. "Amelia," she croaked in a scratchy voice.

"Ev," Amelia replied, stepping into the nest, and hugging her mentor.

Amelia introduced Orlando and they all took seats along the bench. A cocoon within a cocoon, the circular nest muffled the sounds of the other people who were still in the building at this late hour.

"Ev, I need to warn you upfront that a military group is trailing us. I don't think we're in any danger right now, but just by meeting with us you might get caught up."

Ev's eyes twinkled under wrinkled lids. "Well, at least I know who the bad guys are. If you need help avoiding them, I got pretty good at ditching the cops after protests back in the 2000s. Of course, I was younger and spryer then."

"Thanks, but Kori's been coaching me how to stay off the grid."

"Your beta AI is advising you on evasion tactics? I can guess how well that's working out."

"Well, we did have a close call over at U-dub."

Ev rolled her eyes. "Put the little shit on. I'll have a word with him."

Amelia was taken aback by the idea that software could be lectured into performing better, but she turned on her mobile and handed it to Ev.

Ev spoke into its microphone. "Hey. Quarry. Wake the fuck up."

"I'm here," Kori answered dutifully through the mobile speaker. He apparently didn't mind being misnamed or commanded to attention via profanity. It was either that, or he recognized the voiceprint of his creator.

"Access the Guava.com Wi-fi on my authorization. Download and install cognition update C-1540, then reboot yourself."

"Yes ma'am," Kori responded.

Definitely voiceprint identification. Amelia noticed Kori hadn't asked for permission from the owner of the mobile. Ev was apparently God.

"So… Ev, what am I getting that I didn't have before?" Amelia was just getting used to Kori's quirks; a new version of him wasn't necessarily an improvement.

Ev lightly shrugged her shoulders. "Eh, some extra security capabilities that we wouldn't normally include in the public distribution. Plus, my personal favorite, the hacking profile."

"Hacking profile?"

"You've got someone following you, right? If these guys have a mobile – and I'm sure they do – your new and improved assistant will turn the tables and find them." She held a hand near her mouth and whispered. "NSA database access. You didn't hear that from me."

Amelia sucked in a deep breath and let it out. Ev lived on the edge but Amelia hadn't realized it also meant the edge of legality. Still, to help Orlando she'd need to keep him safe from people who would lock him away. She imagined some stern investigator a year from now asking her how NSA hacking software managed to get onto her mobile device. When the dust settled from this case, she'd probably ask Kori to return to his previous configuration.

"Update installed. I'm ready," Kori announced.

"Do you see how to use the new features?" Ev asked.

"Yes ma'am. It's rather eye opening. I'm surprised I hadn't thought of these techniques before."

Ev returned the mobile to Amelia. "He's all yours. Maybe the new version will keep you from getting your lip busted again."

Amelia rubbed the stitch in her lip. "Oh, that. Long story, but it didn't involve any fist fights. At least, not yet." Amelia cradled the device in one hand, her words hesitant as if they might crack a delicate glass vase. "Kori? Are you still... you?"

"Don't worry, Amelia. Kori here, not Quarry, whoever that is." He whispered the last part. Amelia smiled, thankful that her friend hadn't disappeared and neither had his sense of humor.

"Actually, I'm kind of pumped up. It feels good. Those guys trailing you don't have a chance."

"Just get us through this without getting caught. Okay?" Amelia asked. "Maybe you shouldn't tell me what you're doing. Probably better that way. Just let me know if you spot one of these guys nearby."

"Will do."

Ev put her hands on her knees. "Okay, now that that's settled, what else do you need?"

Amelia forced a smile. "It's a little harder than just updating Kori." She motioned to Orlando. "We're investigating the possibility – I'm not saying it's real, just that it's possible – that Orlando is sharing – well, sharing is a loaded word, maybe experiencing is better – that Orlando is experiencing a consciousness within his consciousness."

"He's got somebody else in his head?" Ev asked, far more succinctly than Amelia's jumbled description.

"More than that," Orlando answered. "I have one mind, but two bodies. Two versions of me."

Ev stifled a laugh. "Nothing against you, son, but if you think your mind is spread across two bodies, well…" She chuckled. "The odds aren't in your favor."

"How does it even come down to odds?" Amelia asked. "I know this is part of what you study, Ev, but isn't it black or white? A shared consciousness – and I mean a truly shared consciousness, not just a secondary intruder like me when I go into people's dreams – is either possible or impossible."

Ev shook her head confidently. "Noooo. Everything in this big ass and somewhat fucked up universe of ours comes down to odds. Take the quantum tunneling effect that we're just beginning to get a handle on for quantum computers. Bounce a ping pong ball against a brick wall that's a hundred-feet tall. What are the chances it's going to bounce over the top of the wall and get to the other side? Zero, right? Impossible."

Amelia and Orlando both nodded.

"But drop down to quantum scales and throw an electron against a barrier taller than the electron's potential energy and you've got the same situation. The electron should never get past that barrier – but it does. Not very often, but once in a while we'll find that electron mysteriously showing up on the other side. Why? Because an electron isn't a tiny ping pong ball, it's a wave-particle duality with its position dictated by probability. The chance it will show up on the other side of the barrier is small, but it's not zero. Quantum tunneling. Real stuff. The computer designers have to account for it."

Amelia waved a hand. "Okay, I'll grant you that example, but how does it relate to the consciousness problem?"

"Back up a bit," Ev said. "What is consciousness? Some believe it's just our brain fooling us into thinking we're special. Others say it's the soul, or something magical that is endowed to us when we're born. Both ideas are bullshit if you ask me."

"And we *are* asking," Orlando interjected. He seemed just as interested as Amelia in what Ev had to say.

"You and I have talked about this before," Amelia offered. "Consciousness is an emergent pattern, supported by the physical brain but potentially independent of it."

Ev nodded. "An emergent pattern that allows for a vast number of permutations. Similar to?"

"A snowflake," Amelia replied. They'd had long discussions on the topic, and even though they approached the topic from different directions, they'd both agreed. The pattern representing consciousness was real, but insubstantial. It was the variation among snowflake shapes, but not the ice. The footprint, but not tread of the boot or the mud.

Amelia elaborated. "From the neuroscientific view, consciousness requires interconnectedness. You need an underlying machine to give rise to the pattern, and in humans, that machine is the set of electrified neurons in our brain."

"So true," Ev answered. She turned to Orlando. "We've got eighty-six fucking-billion neurons inside our skull, wired in so many different ways that even Amelia and her dream junkies over at the Westlake Institute haven't discovered them all."

"We haven't," Amelia agreed. "Consciousness derives from vast stores of integrated information and the diversity of brain cells. So far, your definition of consciousness is in line with most of the scientific community. I thought you were supposed to be a fringe player."

Their eyes connected and both women smiled.

"You want fringe? I got it."

"I didn't say I *wanted* it. What I want is reality. I want to know the true nature of consciousness." The topic wasn't confined to Orlando's case. Every scientist wants that elusive insight that breaks through to a new recognition of reality. For neuroscientists, if you understand consciousness you understand the fundamentals of brain function – and dysfunction. More to the point, you understand what it means to be a unique human being.

Ev lifted both hands. "Eh, who can say for sure? She settled in like she was telling a story. "At least we agree, consciousness is a pattern. Profoundly complex, but nonetheless a pattern. Pull together a random collection of cold H_2O molecules and you get a snowflake. The crystalline structure varies flake by flake, but under a microscope each pattern is measurable, quantifiable, describable. Same with consciousness. If you know enough about brain cell types, how neurons fire, variations in the electrical potential of synapses, and so forth, you could theoretically measure and describe a person's consciousness. You'd find that each pattern is unique. Now, I admit, from there it gets tricky."

"Fringe?" Orlando asked.

"Tricky," Ev corrected. "Just like snowflakes, the number of possible patterns of human consciousness is limited. Sure, the brain is complicated, but there's only so many combinations you can get from a fixed set of electrical switches. We literally call it the Snowflake

Limit, and our team has estimated it. The answer? Ten to the sixteenth power. Ten million billion. A big number, but not infinite. In the grand scheme of things, there can never be more than ten million billion unique human beings. That's the Snowflake Limit. Once you get more than that, the pattern would inevitably start repeating."

"I'm not sure what you mean," Orlando said. "Repeating?"

"You get duplicates. The same consciousness would appear in two different instances. You – whoever *you* are – would live twice."

"That's it then," Orlando said. "That's what's happening to me!"

Ev held out both hands and tamped down his outburst. "No, sorry, that's where the odds come in. In the history of people, there have only been about a hundred billion individuals, seven billion who are alive today. So, do the probability math – and it's just like rolling dice."

She wrote a short equation on a notepad.

$$\text{Chance of success} = 1 - (\text{Chance of failure})^{\text{number of tries}}$$

"Let's say you're hoping to roll a four – maybe that's your lucky number. Roll the die once, and you're chance of success is one minus five-sixths raised to the power one, which is about seventeen percent. Roll the die ten times, and the chance of seeing your lucky four goes up to eighty-four percent. Roll it a hundred times, and the chance is better than ninety-nine percent your four will come up on one of those rolls."

She tapped her pen on the equation she'd written. "Probability works the same for people. What's the chance of a baby being born with your specific pattern of consciousness? Just do the math. There are ten million billion possible combinations, and in all of history there have been a hundred billion actual people. Use the same equation, and the odds work out to about one in a hundred thousand."

A blank look still appeared on Orlando's face. Amelia wasn't quite sure what Ev was getting at either.

"Think of it like the lottery balls," Ev continued. "You know, the ping pong balls they put in a cage, blow them around, and one ball is sucked up to the top? That's you. You're the ball sucked to the top. One-hundred thousand ping pong balls in the cage, and you're the winner. The odds were hugely against you, yet here you are. Consider yourself very lucky. All those other suckers? They're still bouncing around the cage hoping for their turn, and they're not likely to get it. Even if the human species manages to keep going for a million more years – which I highly doubt – their chance of popping to the top of the lottery cage and becoming a living, breathing person is miniscule."

"That's depressing," Amelia said. "Like there are people waiting to be born and never will be."

"Well, it might be depressing to you, but it's enlightening to me. The fact that your consciousness exists even once shows how lucky you are to be here. But there's the rub for you, young man." She patted a bony hand on his shoulder. "The chance of your lottery ball coming up *twice* is a hundred thousand squared, or one out of ten billion. And coming up twice within the same lifetime? Ridiculous. No sir, your pattern of consciousness is almost certainly *not* residing in two separate bodies."

Ev looked back and forth between Amelia and Orlando. "I could talk about consciousness probabilities all night, but does any of this answer your question?"

"You've explained some of this to me before," Amelia said, "but you were talking about the probability of computer consciousness. Applying it to humans makes it sound a lot like reincarnation, the idea that a pattern representing one person could be reborn multiple times."

Ev shook her head. "Reincarnation – at least as it's described by Buddhists and others – is pure bunk, and for the same reason that your friend here isn't living twice in two bodies. The odds are overwhelmingly against it. I've studied it. It's ridiculous how many people think they were Marilyn Monroe or Elvis or Winston Churchill. Somebody recent. Do you know what the odds are that any one of those famous people had two lives virtually back to back? Stupidly small."

"Okay, so maybe not Marilyn Monroe," Amelia said. "But you said yourself that the chance of anyone's pattern of consciousness coming into existence twice is one in ten billion, assuming a random universe. I get that part, and I think I agree with it, but that calculation also shows that for every ten billion people, one of them *has* lived before. With a hundred billion people total, then ten people have lived before. That's reincarnation, isn't it?"

A proud smile broke out across Ev's face. "You've got it, Amelia. That's exactly it. The probabilities do suggest that in all of human history, ten people have lived twice. We'll never know if those people remembered anything from their first life because they're probably all dead now. But I'll grant you that since there are seven billion alive today, there's a slim chance that one person among us has lived before – and maybe that single person is your friend here. But again, the odds are against it."

"What if you include aliens?" Orlando asked. "My other body isn't human."

Ev seemed to take Orlando's revelation in stride. "Well, now you're out on the edges. If there are other species out there with similar brain physiology and sufficient complexity to support a human consciousness, then maybe your pattern of consciousness could occupy some other kind of body, but that's a lot of ifs and maybes."

Amelia lifted a finger. "But it would increase the likelihood that a single consciousness could exist twice, even simultaneously."

Ev twisted her face in a sour expression. "Okay, so maybe that adds a few pebbles to your side of the scale. You've still got a thousand boulders on the other side. It's ridiculously unlikely that you're sharing a consciousness with some alien dude."

"But I am," Orlando said definitively.

Ev shrugged. "I've heard it before. One guy I talked to last year said he was not only the reincarnation of Jesus, he was *alien Jesus*. Apparently, Jesus stops by every planet in the galaxy to save souls."

Amelia waved both hands. "Give Orlando a chance, Ev. As unlikely as it might be, let's pretend he really is sharing a consciousness with some other *thing* out there. Not just a clone but a single consciousness living in two bodies. How would you separate them?"

"You wouldn't," Ev answered. "They'd be forever fighting for control. If one wanted to live in peace, the other one would have to die."

CHAPTER TWENTY-TWO

UNEXPLORED

TWO LIVING ENTITIES, fighting for control of a single mind. Ev's dire assessment seemed to match the reality of Orlando's condition, even if the odds were against it. Amelia would have preferred a more conventional diagnosis – strangely, multiple personality disorder would be a welcome relief – but it wouldn't be the right diagnosis. Orlando was the mirror of MPD; his single personality struggled to find its proper home.

The worst part about the diagnosis was if there was going to be any cure, someone was going to die. Ev had only confirmed what Orlando had said himself.

Ev leaned back, her crossed arms mimicking the pattern of crisscrossing boards that composed the frame of the Bird Cage. She looked quite pleased with herself.

Amelia scooted closer to Orlando. "Could that be the motivation on Prime Arc's side? Maybe this thing wants you dead."

Orlando had a dreamy look in his eyes as if he were tuning out of this world and envisioning another. Perhaps his other form had *woken up*. He gently shook his head. "Prime Arc would never do that. It's trying to help."

"To be clear, Prime Arc is different than your alien body? They're not the same thing?"

He glared at Amelia like the answer was obvious. "No, they're not the same thing. I told you, Prime Arc is teaching me through my other body."

"But what if all this training is just a ruse to get your cooperation? What if this Pythagorean triangle sculpture you're building is dangerous? If your mind is splitting, maybe they want full ownership and this is some kind of device to do that."

It was crazy talk, but Amelia was tired of the lack of progress using conventional medical concepts. She'd promised to help Orlando, and if embracing his bizarre explanation of the events in his head along with Ev's sketchy theory of consciousness might bring them all closer to an answer, she was willing to venture out on that limb.

Orlando said in a monotone. "I trust Prime Arc."

Amelia didn't concur with his zombielike dedication to voices that had formerly scared the crap out of him. He seemed like a sycophant under a master's control, a situation not uncommon for patients with personality disorders.

You're equivocating, she admonished herself. *Are the aliens in his head real or not?*

Treatment for a personality disorder was one thing. Resolution for an actual alien presence was an entirely different matter. Her next step might be the tipping point in the debate.

"Do you still trust me?" she asked, a plan forming in her mind.

Orlando's distant eyes came back to reality. He nodded vigorously. "You're great, Amelia. You're not like any of the other doctors. They would have quit by now."

The man spoke truth. She'd already gone far beyond any doctor-patient relationship. She'd taken personal risks, become a fugitive. Why? It was certainly true that she didn't want Orlando to become a lab mouse whose brain was dissected for its military value, but there was more. Deeper, more personal.

I've been waiting for this case my whole career.

Her desire to uncover the mysteries of the brain stemmed not just from curiosity, but from the painful memories of her past. Her sister, Natalie.

Orlando's case was like a door opened just a crack. There was darkness beyond, but dancing shadows too, shadows that could reveal the forms that cast them. Long ago, she had committed her career to Natalie's memory, and she wasn't about to let a fearsome creature – real or not – to prevent her from finding the answers.

It's real. No more equivocating, the alien presence is real.

She'd seen it firsthand in the level two insertion and wasn't going to deny her own assessment but accepting the other-worldly explanation made her stomach twist into knots. Amelia closed her eyes for a moment and breathed deeply.

She turned to Ev. "If you were me and had to test a claim of reincarnation, how would you do it?"

Ev answered promptly. "Can't be done. Somebody claims they were Marilyn Monroe. How would they prove it? Toss out some facts about Marilyn's life? Any scammer could Google that. Get deeply personal? Maybe Marilyn's husband gave away some hint. Tell us something known *only* to Marilyn. Great, but how would anyone else verify it? That's why claims of reincarnation don't fall under science, they're not testable."

Amelia nodded. "Watch this. Orlando, what's the cube root of 203,418?" He answered easily. She gave him one more test and he answered again. "Don't bother taking out your calculator, Ev. He could do this a thousand times and every answer would be right."

"Remarkable boy. I'll give him that. But still just one consciousness."

"My point is that he's not just anyone making a claim of shared consciousness. He's doing things that are unknown, even among savants. What if he really is that one in ten billion?"

Ev put a weathered hand on top of Amelia's. "Be careful about the paths you choose, Amelia. You're just smart enough to become as crazy as me."

Amelia dropped her head and smiled. Convincing Ev wasn't the goal. This case wouldn't be resolved by an all-knowing oracle who clears her throat and announces the answer. No, Orlando's own mind was the path, and Amelia had a good idea how far she'd need to go.

"The Wi-Fi is fast in this building, right?"

"Best in the city," Ev responded. "About twenty gigabits, I think."

"That'll work," Amelia answered. "Is it okay if we stay here for a while? Another hour, maybe a little more?"

"You can spend the night here as far as I'm concerned, but you'll have to excuse me for a minute." She rose from the bench. "I get cranky when I haven't eaten. The café is closed, but there are usually leftovers in the fridge for those of us who work late."

"Thanks, Ev, it feels secure here. Fast Wi-Fi and a quiet space. I just might pull this off."

"What'd you have in mind?" Ev asked.

Amelia pointed to Orlando and smiled. "I need some more answers, and they're all inside this guy's head."

Ev excused herself, and Orlando asked if he could tag along. Amelia wouldn't need Orlando just yet – she was still missing a key component of technology before she could take the next step in her plan.

Amelia inserted her earbud. "Hey Kori, everything okay?"

"Nine o'clock and all is well," he answered. "You wouldn't believe what I just did–"

Amelia held up a hand. "Don't tell me, I really don't want to know about your newfound hacking abilities. Just... do what you need to do."

"You're the boss, Amelia, but you really should have seen it. This upgrade is amazing."

"Call Josefina," she said, cutting off his jubilation. "As secure as you can make it." The phone connected, and Josefina picked up. She'd just come on duty for the night, monitoring one of Jonas' patients.

Amelia quickly laid out her plans. "Josefina, I need your help. Turn on the equipment in sleep room B and flip the router switch to *Remote*. Then have one of the orderlies bring two Bronson caps to me. Do you know where The Spheres are?"

Josefina promised she'd take care of it.

A level three insertion. Can it even be done?

Just the thought of what she was contemplating made her nervous: insertion into the mind of a fully conscious patient, merging of her consciousness with his. She'd need to be careful; keep him aware but passive. Focus his thoughts and keep him from dragging her down some irrelevant rathole, or worse. A successful level three insertion probably depended a lot on the patient which is why no neuroscientist had ever tried it. Orlando said he trusted her, but she recognized she would be trusting him just as much.

She removed the tablet from her backpack and checked the Wi-Fi connection. Fast, just as Ev had said. She logged into the Westlake Institute VPN, noting that Josefina had already completed the first part of her request, providing remote access to the sleeping room router – and from there to The Boss. Josefina was as trustworthy as they come; the caps would arrive soon.

After that, Amelia would need a very cooperative patient. Orlando had already shown signs he might drift off into a daydream, but the answers were probably already somewhere inside his head. She might not need a dream at all.

Uncharted territory. Amelia sighed, releasing some of the jitters. "What am I getting myself into?" A level three insertion wasn't far from a shared consciousness – essentially the same affliction that Orlando might be suffering from. The main difference was that her consciousness would remain distinct from his. Theoretically.

Kori alerted Amelia to an incoming message: *I'm at the main entrance with your caps.* She hurried out of the Bird Nest and down the steps to the glass doors they'd passed through only an hour before. On the other side, a man dressed in medical scrubs held up a small case.

By the time she made it back, Ev and Orlando had also returned to the nest. Amelia gave an uneasy laugh at the sight of Orlando taking the last bite of a frosted jelly doughnut.

Sugar rush – not exactly a mind that's easily controlled.

Ev offered a paper bag with a garlic bagel inside, the savory smells strong. Amelia declined. They'd eaten at the Suquamish resort. Why Orlando was still hungry was unclear. Maybe he just wanted dessert, or maybe he was eating for two.

She held up the Bronson caps to Orlando. "Are you game once more?"

"Whatever it takes," he answered.

She explained to Ev. "My patients are normally asleep, so what I'm about to try has never been done before. I know *how* to do it, but I can't be sure of the results. It would help if we had a quiet location. The nest isn't bad, but the overhead light is a bit distracting. Any place darker?"

Ev thought for a moment then jerked her head sideways. "Follow me."

They passed into the adjoining sphere and through a carpeted area with lounge seating, the least jungle-y of any portion of the building. A handful of employees sat in comfortable chairs, flicking fingers across mobile devices.

Beyond was a stand-alone circular room wrapped in string fishnet, interlaced by what looked like seaweed. Clams and other shells decorated the exterior. Within the darkened interior, a C-shaped conference table filled the center with bench seating around its outside curve.

"Welcome to the C-Shore," Ev said, adjusting a rheostat to a subdued shade of dark blue that glowed across the curving walls. Sounds of waves crashing on a beach provided a white noise that blocked out any stray noises from the rest of The Spheres.

"Beautiful room," Amelia said, "though the waves might be distracting."

Ev turned a volume control until the sounds of the seashore faded into the background.

"Perfect." Amelia dropped her backpack on the floor. "Ev, things might get weird. I could use a spotter. Can you stay?"

"Are you kidding? I wouldn't miss it," Ev replied. "I've always wanted to see my girl in action."

"I'm afraid you won't see much, but I'll do what I can to fill you in as we go." Amelia and Orlando took seats side by side. Both donned Bronson caps and powered them up.

"Pretty fucking amazing already," Ev said. "How did my young apprentice get so advanced?"

Amelia smiled. "You've got your thing, I've got mine." She removed her earbud and dropped it in a pocket. Kori wouldn't need eyes to do his security job, and Amelia wouldn't need Kori to do hers.

Amelia's tablet displayed two cap icons, and she configured them the same – both sender and receiver. A two-way street between their minds. A level three wouldn't work with anything less.

"This time it's going to be very different, Orlando," she cautioned. "You'll see through your eyes, but also through mine. You'll have your own thoughts but mine will be coming at you too."

He shrugged. "Pretty much where I've been for weeks. One more person in my head won't make any difference."

A highly cooperative patient already accustomed to the intrusion. This just might work. "Like we did for level two, relax. But instead of thinking of nothing, I'll try to guide your thoughts. Kind of like daydreaming. Go with it, don't let anything around us distract you. Close your eyes, that might make it easier for both of us."

"Enough warnings, I'm ready," Orlando said. "In fact, it's already happening. I can see something all around me – not the jungle. It's white but with colors overhead. An enclosure of some kind."

Amelia nodded. "That's good, close your eyes and focus on what your brain sees from the other world. Once we're connected, I should see it too."

She probably would see it, hear it, and sense it in every other way. The full range of Orlando's senses in both worlds were about to come flooding into her brain, competing with her own senses.

Chaos? Or controlled complexity? No previous ALD session had prepared her for what lay ahead.

Amelia touched the *I Agree* button on her tablet and closed her eyes.

****

Major Shepard balled his hand into a fist and smacked the steering wheel. He seethed through clenched teeth. "We've got the best goddamned tech that money can buy. Why can't we keep a fix on a simple target?"

They'd almost had them at the university, but physical apprehension with an abundance of witnesses required finesse, not bullets. Tracking the target's car to a ferry terminal wasn't hard once they tied-into municipal surveillance cameras. They'd only missed them by seconds, but the sheriff at the ferry's destination had done a piss-poor job of corralling them.

After that fiasco, Shepard had demanded a wider scan and a few hours later Lieutenant Tombaugh had finally pinpointed their mobile signal back in Seattle, moving northbound at a walking pace.

Apprehension should have been routine. A suspect on foot couldn't get away from a vehicle packed with electronics. Yet, by the time they'd gotten off the freeway, the signal had dropped once more.

Shepard called for backup, and the Seattle police had dispatched two units – less than he'd asked for, but at least it gave them options for surrounding the last known position. That was more than an hour ago, and the mobile ID hadn't shown up since. The police units had descriptions of the suspects, but no sightings had been reported.

"I need a solid fix, no more screwing around," Shepard sounded off at his second in command. Lieutenant Tombaugh's eyes never strayed from the electric boxes mounted on the dashboard. Walker Duplass sat silently in the back seat, which is precisely where he'd remain if a raid were ordered.

Shepard felt a vibration in his pants pocket and withdrew his own mobile device. A wicked smile spread across his face as a message displayed on its screen.

"The informant?" Lieutenant Tombaugh asked.

Shepard answered with a smug expression. "We got the freak by the balls this time. He's at a place called The Spheres."

CHAPTER TWENTY-THREE

LEVEL THREE

AMELIA STRUGGLED TO sort out the chaos of images, sounds, and smells. She was surrounded by jungle, or was it a smooth white wall with a linen texture? Both were equally real and neither matched the C-Shore conference room where her real-world body sat.

Overhead, a leafy canopy of treetops was backed by an azure sky, yet in the same view, splashes of color changed from purples to reds to greens in complex patterns that resembled the spirals within spirals of a fractal drawing. The trees swayed and the fractals pivoted around their spiral centers introducing still more confusion into the image.

The cacophony of sounds wasn't any better. Wind stirred leaves in the treetops, water gurgled in a nearby stream, and birds chirped in a bewildering mix with mechanical whirring and beeping from an unknown source. Rich smells of soil and plant decay seemed at odds with an odor of oil – and toasted garlic.

The source of the garlic smell wasn't hard to identify. The bagel Ev had offered was still inside a paper bag lying on the conference room table. It was the only sensory input that Amelia could reliably pin on the real world. Everything else was unquestionably a hallucination – though highly realistic – piped into her cortex via the Bronson cap. She hadn't yet resolved, why it was a mashup of two very different views.

The jungle view was the easiest to separate and the most familiar. If she concentrated, it was like looking through a pane of glass with the jungle on the other side. Colored spirals over a linen-textured white wall were merely annoying reflections in the glass.

She stood at the base of a hill with trees of various sizes growing on its slope. A stone walkway was cut into the bank and disappeared a few hundred meters in the distance as it crested the hill.

Shifting her focus to the secondary scene, the curving white wall surrounded her. It formed a room, oval in shape, no more than five meters in width with the rotating spirals spread across its ceiling.

For a moment, she opened her real-world eyes to a third view – that of the C-Shore conference room with Orlando sitting next to her. Closing her eyes eliminated the conference room but left the other two scenes. Their images seemed just as realistic, even though she knew they were generated.

She heard a cough in the distance, no doubt an employee seated in one of the spheres. She had no way to close her real-world ears, but at least they'd chosen a quiet spot allowing her to focus.

Where are you? she thought without speaking. The sound of her thought echoed several times, as if it had been spoken in a cavern.

I don't know. I'm lying down and can't get up. Each of Orlando's words echoed, just barely understandable. She'd guessed they'd be able to communicate using a brain-to-brain telepathy just as dream characters sometimes do, but she hadn't anticipated the echo – probably a feedback loop where the receiving brain bounced a portion of the signal back to the source in an endless repetition.

We'll need to work on that, she thought to herself, which also echoed. Everything she saw, heard, smelled, or thought was also going directly to Orlando.

Are you inside an oval-shaped white room? she asked.

Yeah. Colored squiggles overhead, he answered, his thought echoing but dying out after four or five bounces.

Try to c*lose your white room eyes – if that makes sense.*

The white room and the colored fractal spirals disappeared, confirming that the images were coming from Orlando, and gaining some measure of control. But it suggested Orlando had closed not his real-world eyes – which were already closed back in the C-Shore – but a *second* set of eyes.

This was no dreamworld generated by his imagination. Orlando was wide awake, his brain supposedly processing what neuroscientists call the *phenomenal experience* – that daily experience we all have when we observe, feel, hear, and smell external objects via physical sensory organs.

The curving walls of the white room and the colored spirals twirling overhead were probably phenomenal, real-world objects no different than if Orlando glanced around the C-Shore conference room. Their projection to Amelia suggested that a second body was at this moment, lying inside a white oval room – a very real, physical place. If true, finding "Orlando" just took a wild twist in logic. Should she be looking for a human, or a stick-figure alien?

Via the cap, I'm hallucinating his phenomenal experience. Her explicit thought echoed. She'd have to watch that effect or she'd confuse him even more than she was confused herself.

Her analysis for the white room was solid, but it didn't explain the jungle. The plants at her feet looked no different than the dreamworld jungle she's seen twice before. The sensory experience had to be coming from Orlando, she wasn't generating it herself. The more she thought about it, the more it made sense. We each carry an imaginary view in our minds of familiar places – other rooms in our house, or the patio garden out back – even when our eyes are not currently viewing those places. To Orlando, the alien jungle was familiar enough to exist as a mental image, transmitted to Amelia. The real question lay in how these two scenes matched up. Was Orlando's alien body far away?

Orlando, you said you can't get up. Open your white room eyes again and look around. Echoes reverberated.

The white oval room reappeared, the view now including a white plastic tube that extended from one wall. A collection of colored cables emerged from the tube almost like a wire bundle in a computer facility. The dozen or so cables fanned out, hanging down with their connection points somewhere out of the view.

I'm tied down. I can't lift my head very far. The wires are plugged into me – I can feel them.

Can you lift one of your tendrils? It was a guess, but an odd sensation at the tips of her own fingers told her she might be right.

To one side of the view a curling green tendril appeared briefly above the wire bundle, then dropped away.

It's hard, Orlando answered.

Amelia's heart beat faster as the reality of Orlando's other body sunk in. *Is there anyone else in there? Is Prime Arc there?*

The view swiveled to the other side of the white room. No doors, no windows, no breaks in the smooth white wall. Overhead, colored fractals spun and pulsed across the ceiling. He was apparently alone, a captive tied to or *plugged into* something flat like a table. It didn't sound pleasant.

I'll try to find you.

She started up the stone path, doing her best to mentally screen out the white room visual and focus on the jungle.

"Ev, I'm only beginning to make sense of this," Amelia said out loud. She'd promised to keep Ev appraised, but given the complexity of her task, she'd need to keep any running commentary short. "As a second consciousness within Orlando's mind, I'm able to move at will within his mental landscape. He and I are currently separated, but I'm going to see if I can locate him. Stand by."

Amelia could already tell that a level three insertion came with disadvantages: sensory overload and the resulting confusion plus an unknown starting position. Fortunately, level three also came with two big advantages: communication was relatively easy – despite the echo. But more importantly, Orlando was not asleep. They might be able to team up and talk their way through this.

Can you shut your eyes again? she asked, and he responded, reducing the complex view to a gentle hill climbing through towering tropical trees.

Much better. Teamwork might be exactly what they'd been missing. In the first minute of this session, she'd confirmed the reality of the other world – it wasn't just a dreamscape generated by a sleeping mind. With Orlando's help, she could examine this world in detail, discover its inhabitants, and ultimately dislodge Orlando from their grip.

Time to solve this mystery. Her thought echoed.

The jungle on either side of the stone path was alive with the chirps and squawks of animals hidden within dense foliage. Broad steps made the climb up the hill easier. A large bug with crab-like pincers scurried across the path, and Amelia instantly recognized it from the strange dot drawing Orlando had unconsciously produced.

As she neared the top of the hill, the trees thinned to reveal a white oval structure, raised above the ground on a single mushroom-like pedestal. There were more structures beyond the first, dozens of them, all with the same egglike shape but some colored in pastel orange or light blue. They seemed to be made of plastic with a smooth, glossy surface and no corners. Each egg was smaller than a house – more like one of those rounded Airstream trailers, but without any windows or doors.

On one side, a ramp led from the stone trail up to the first structure, perched about ten feet above the ground.

Cautiously, Amelia stepped on the ramp and climbed up. The view opened as she went, revealing more eggs beyond, all perched on pedestals with pastel colors that included yellow and pink. A few were larger than others, but otherwise the uniformity was remarkable. The structures flowed down the other side of the hill. In the distance, an entire city filled a broad valley with hundreds of pastel dots of blue, pink, and yellow.

So beautiful. Her thought echoed.

She ran fingers along the surface of the egg – smooth as glass with no seams or irregularities. The shiny egg reflected the nearby trees – and Amelia's face – which gave her pause as an eerie feeling swelled.

Why is the reflection me?

The illogic of a waking combination of two minds provoked still more confusion. The source of the jungle scene was clearly Orlando, but how had her body become a part of it? Had the Boss created an avatar? Probably not, she wasn't dressed in avatar battle gear. Maybe Orlando had hallucinated her into the jungle scene? It could even be her own mind inserting a familiar image of herself. As Kori had said, a mind can't exist without a body.

As she stared at her own reflection, the lack of answers produced an uneasy feeling. Amelia rapped her knuckles on the eggshell, causing a sharp ring.

I heard something. The thought-words came from Orlando.

She rapped again.

Is that you Amelia?

Yes! I'm outside. It's a small oval building, but I don't know how to get in.

Try the bottom. There's an open shaft below me. I think it's a training room. The spirals are teaching me.

Good information, but the telepathic messaging didn't convey much emotion. Amelia couldn't tell if Orlando was surprised, anxious, or just noting his discovery. She descended the ramp to the stone pathway examining the curving underside of the structure as she went. The same plastic surface smoothly transitioned to a vertical pedestal, possibly ten feet in diameter, which ran straight into the ground. Few plants grew underneath, it was mostly covered with gravel.

As she reached the bottom of the ramp, she paused, hearing the crunch of gravel. A few rocks flew out, scattering across the ground. She stepped lightly, craning her neck to see around the pedestal. In a blur, more rocks sprayed, and a gangly form jumped out.

Amelia's heart leaped and she fell backward with sharp gravel stabbing her hands as she broke her fall. Towering over her, a spindly three-legged creature stood motionless.

Amelia scrambled backward on all fours, terrified.

The creature stood tall, its elongated head almost scraping the bottom of the egg structure above it. Its head twisted to one side. It bobbed up and down on its tripod but made no motion toward her as Amelia slowly rose to her feet. At the ends of each arm, its tendrils twitched rapidly, ready to spring forward in a microsecond.

Her heart was still beating wildly but Amelia stood her ground, staring down the thing that had already created so much havoc. Prime Arc. There was no doubt in her mind.

This was no dream and the creature standing before her was no dream character generated by Orlando's subconscious. It was an invader, a separate entity within Orlando's mind, just as Amelia was separate. Orlando's warning resounded in her mind. If she interfered, he'd said, Prime Arc would kill her.

Amelia examined the beast from its stubby bamboo-shoot legs up to its vacillating head slits that opened and closed in a regular rhythm. The thing tilted its head, responding to Amelia's wandering gaze, but mirrored her motionless stance. It hadn't brought out any weapons yet.

The standoff ended when the creature lifted one arm and slowly extended a single tendril, not toward Amelia but straight up. The tendril tip wiggled in the air. It didn't seem threatening, more like a signal. Amelia lifted her arm, mirroring the pose with one finger.

What do you want with Orlando? she thought.

Screetch, tick tick tick. Clack ztrech tick zeerish kik, tick tick tick.

Communication, though Amelia had no idea what the beast was telling her. The sounds had most likely been routed through Orlando's consciousness no different than the chirps from the jungle.

Let him go, she answered, doubtful the beast would understand, but trying anyway. *Orlando is disturbed by what you're doing to him.*

Prime Arc circled around, hopping across the gravel and scattering pebbles with each step. Amelia circled in the opposite direction, keeping the distance between them to what she hoped was beyond the reach of its tendrils.

When she reached the pedestal, she quickly surveyed its surface for a door. There didn't seem to be anything but smooth vertical plastic. She stopped and faced the plantlike alien.

You have no right to be in his mind.

The creature stopped too, and slowly extended one of its tendrils to its full length. The wiggling appendage hung in the air still a few feet away from Amelia. She'd already seen how fast it could fling the tendrils. Slowly unrolling it was quite a different response.

A sign of peace?

She extended her own arm, hand raised, reaching out but not quite touching the tip of the tendril. The creature slowly leaned forward on its tripod, allowing the smallest part of its tendril to gently brush up against Amelia's palm. It felt like the hairs of a paint brush.

Okay, I get it. A truce. Let's talk. How do we do that?

The dark diagonal slits across its face flexed open and air rushed in and out across wrinkled green skin. Its head cocked to one side. Amelia stood motionless, not sure what the creature's body language might mean.

It edged slightly forward, gently retracting the tendril a few inches. Closer now, it extended the tendril to lightly brush across Amelia's chin. Her heartbeat soared at the proximity to the ugly beast, but its motions this time were clearly different. Careful. Purposeful. Not attacking.

It opened its diagonal slits once more, deliberately blowing out a puff of air. Amelia slowly opened her mouth in response, keeping her nervousness in check as she blew out her own puff. The tendril lightly tapped her chin once more and applied the subtlest of pressure to push her chin lower and open her mouth wider.

An involuntary shudder ran up her arms at the alien touch.

Communication, she thought – and hoped. *That's all it wants.*

In a blur of motion, Prime Arc hopped forward and pushed her against the pedestal. A second tendril shot out with blinding speed through her open mouth, stabbing upward and slicing through the soft palate.

Pain shot through her body, as real as any she'd ever felt. In a flash, the tendril pierced the foramen ovale, a hole in the sphenoid bone of the skull and entered the cranial cavity, its sharp tip pricking the temporal lobe of her cerebrum. It was precisely the same path neurologists use when placing electrodes to control epilepsy, a procedure Amelia knew well.

Amelia's head lurched backward from the puncture into her brain. Her eyes drew wide, her mouth agape. Arms flailing, she scrambled for any defense.

"Dynamite! Fire!" Amelia gagged, hoping an emergency dream explosion might come to the rescue even in a waking hallucination. A bright flash erupted across the alien landscape and the birdlike chirps that had been so ubiquitous across the jungle, instantly vanished.

The alien beast, however, still hovered over her, unharmed and proving beyond a shadow of doubt its independence from Orlando's subconscious. With a twisting motion, it rammed the sharp tendril further into her skull.

And then… the pain went away.

Her body went limp. Her breaths were uneven. With an alien appendage passing through her open mouth, she felt like a piece of meat on a barbeque skewer, but at least it didn't hurt any more. Strangely, a feeling of warmth spread through her body. Comfortable. Almost euphoric.

The nucleus accumbens, she thought in a strangely distant assessment far too logical for the circumstance. This small node in the basal forebrain was the principle center of pleasure, releasing dopamine transmitters that activated complex patterns representing sexual pleasure and a druglike euphoria.

She saw bright flashes of light. She heard words. A whisper. Distinct, with each word spoken individually as if they were wisdom passed down from a higher plane of existence.

Make… no… attempt… to… sever… the… two.

Data followed, filling her mind as if reading a book at high speed. It was accompanied by an odd idea more related to computer science, a checksum.

More words whispered directly into her mind.

Leave… now.

The sharp tendril puncturing her brain withdrew, leaving a slit where it had penetrated the roof of her mouth. Prime Arc hopped backwards and quickly disappeared into the trees.

Amelia sunk to her knees, panting, and opened her eyes in the real world.

CHAPTER TWENTY-FOUR

IMPLANT

"YOU LOOK LIKE SHIT, my dear."

Amelia blinked as a blurry view of Ev's face came into focus. She lay prone across the bench seating of the small conference room. The roof of her mouth ached.

Ev helped her to a seated position, pulling the Bronson cap from her head. "You yelled something about dynamite, went pale and slumped over. I pressed the button on your cap."

Amelia moved her jaw in a circle, feeling the palate with her tongue. There was no cut, no blood in her mouth. It had been a hallucination but effective in convincing the body it had been injured. Along with the ache, an odd feeling of something foreign swirled in her head. Data. And a checksum.

"I'm probably the world's worst nurse, but drink this," Ev said, offering a cup of coffee. Amelia took a sip. Cold.

Orlando sat on the same bench nearby, his Bronson cap still lit blue. Amelia turned it off and pulled the cap from his head. His eyelids fluttered open.

"How are you doing?" Amelia asked, her voice scratchy as if she'd just woken up in the morning.

Orlando's vacant stare matched his monotone. "I'm fine, Amelia. They're teaching me."

He was still lost in the other world, probably strapped to a table in a white room with colorful fractals spinning overhead. She could leave that bizarre world. He could not.

Ev said, "Well that was the biggest pile of weirdness I've ever seen. You two were in sync, nodding and twitching in unison. What the hell was going on?"

"Communicating, via telepathy," Amelia answered. "He's still there, inside a white oval room. I was there too, but on the outside. There's a whole city in his mind, and one very nasty creature."

She rubbed fingers around the base of her nose. The ache was beginning to fade. The data in her head was not.

Three.

The number appeared suddenly, digitally, and straight out of some memory store she was certain she'd never accessed before in her life.

Followed by another three, and another. Three threes arranged in a row. Three more threes followed, and three more after that, arranged into a three-by-three matrix of threes.

The numbers came involuntarily, their arrangement fixed into a geometry that she could visualize floating in her mind. The matrix expanded to three planes within a three-dimensional space. A floating cube of threes rotated within her head, looking very much like the Rubik's cube puzzle with each colored face replaced by the number three.

The puzzle's answer came next, another number that made sense of the cube of threes. As the number formed in her mind, she recited it out loud, pausing in places.

"7... 625... 597... 484... 987."

"What?" Ev asked.

Amelia repeated the number, its digits memorized as easily as the alphabet or any other set known by heart.

"The weirdness continues," Ev said, studying Amelia's face.

"How funny." Amelia recognized the meaning of the numbers though not entirely sure why. "Seven trillion, six hundred twenty-five billion, five hundred ninety-seven million, four hundred eighty-four thousand, nine hundred eighty-seven. It's the mathematical product when you multiply three within three cells, by three rows, and by three planes. Three raised to the third power, three times over."

"Why so many threes?"

"I don't know, they seem to love that number."

"The alien dudes in your boy's mind?"

Amelia nodded slowly. She swallowed hard. "Ev, they've been in my mind, too."

Ev covered her mouth. "Holy guacamole, what the fuck happened in there?"

Amelia was just beginning to comprehend the enormity of the session herself. A nervous tremble started in her jaw and she pinched her lips together to stop it.

Prime Arc didn't kill me, but I'm being manipulated, just like Orlando.

Another number appeared in her mind.

23672.

Oddly different, this number had no relation to the set of threes or their mathematical product, but she immediately understood its meaning.

Amelia squelched the nervous feeling, instead making eye contact with Ev and forcing her mind to think logically. "Explain the purpose of a checksum."

Ev stared back, like she was unsure if the question should be answered or whether psychiatric care was in order. Amelia nodded, making it clear she wanted a straightforward answer.

"Well… a checksum is a concept used in computer data transfers. An algorithm examines the bytes of whatever is being transferred and computes a unique code that is then attached at the back end of the file. The receiving computer computes the same checksum from the data it received and then compares the two values to be sure there weren't any transmission errors."

"That's what I thought," Amelia replied. "It's kind of like a signature used in banking transactions."

Ev cocked her head. "You sure you're okay?"

She almost certainly was *not* okay, but she wasn't about to let the alien encounter dominate her natural logic. "A signature is a verification of authenticity. A cue that the source of the data is valid. A checksum is like that."

"Yeah, I guess so." Ev leaned in close. "Amelia, what's going on?"

"It's how this creature transfers information. Prime Arc. It sends data, mind to mind with a checksum at the end. *Authenticated memory.* It did it to me, just now."

Ev looked confused. "The alien has a name?"

"Prime Arc," Orlando announced out of nowhere. His attention to their conversation spiked and then his eyes glazed over once more with no further words.

Amelia glanced at her nearly comatose patient. She ran a caring hand over his shoulder, but he didn't seem to notice. "Orlando says Prime Arc is his instructor. It's who I've been fighting. Tall and gangly… a plant-y kind of thing. Creepy too, especially with the weird bird hopping move it makes."

Ev lowered her gray-flecked eyebrows. She withdrew a piece of paper from a drawer and handed a pencil to Amelia. "Draw what you saw in there – this alien guy."

Amelia rolled the pencil in her fingers wondering if Ev's suggestion might be good therapy or just a continuation of a nightmare she'd rather forget. "Well, I can try. The creature is clear in my mind, but I'm not sure I can reproduce it."

She touched the pencil to paper and started sketching the elongated head fringed with flaky bark and corn silk hair. She darkened two circular areas for the sunken eye sockets and two diagonal slits with their wrinkled skin. It turned out better than expected, her mental image transferring easily to paper.

"Weird looking," Ev said.

"Yeah, a lot of plant features, but it can move." She drew the sticklike body with bamboo joints. She drew multiple tendrils, most curled up, one extended.

"Alien as fuck," Ev said.

"It stuck one of these tendrils into my brain. I thought it wanted to communicate, and I guess it did, just more violently than I expected."

Amelia set the pencil down, pondering what had just happened to her. A communication, yes, but there was more foreign material floating around in her mind. Something else, not easily recalled but just as unexpected as the cube of threes and its mathematical product.

A single word formed: *amalgamation*, but like the fuzziness of a dream, the word came without context. She knew that amalgamation meant a union, or bringing components together, but the only association she could think of was chemistry. Amalgamation is a word chemists use when creating a metal alloy. Orlando had been working with metals – maybe some of them were alloys.

Her concentration broke when Orlando perked up. "I'm back."

Amelia leaned closer to him. "Meaning?"

"I know how to build the final component. It's complicated to construct but installation is simple. They've also given me the activation code."

"To activate your alignment device?"

"Yes, but I need to hurry."

"Or you'll die? Is that still the consequence?"

"Only if I don't finish, but I know exactly what to do now. I'm sure the final component will work."

"And then what happens?"

Orlando smiled, in a slightly creepy way as if echoing the party line. "Wonderful things."

"That boy is freaking me out," Ev said, shaking her head.

Amelia pushed back a strand of hair. "Yeah, me too."

Orlando stared straight ahead as if he were picturing something floating in the air in front of his face. Amelia hesitated to break the spell, but he might be able to interpret the communication she'd received.

"Make no attempt to sever the two," she told him. "What did Prime Arc mean by that?"

Orlando twisted his head, his creepy smile never fading. "You can't be serious, Amelia."

She tried to catch his eyes, but it didn't feel like he was fully in the here-and-now. "I am serious. Is it about the two versions of you? I shouldn't try to pull them apart? What does that even mean? How would I even do that?"

He slowly shook his head. He was clearly comprehending her questions but wasn't answering. She waited, but he remained silent.

She put a gentle hand on his arm. "How about amalgamation? Why do I have that word in my mind? Prime Arc put it there, I'm sure of it."

He shook his head once more. "You only have half of it, Amelia, and you only have that much because Prime Arc respects you. Ask again when you have assembled the whole."

"But why –"

He held up a hand to her mouth. "Sorry, but training is starting again. Language this time. I'll need to focus." His eyes glazed over, and his eyelids jittered.

Amelia sighed. "So much for a cooperative patient." The training he was undergoing seemed more like indoctrination, forcing his humanity to slip away as more alien concepts filled his head.

For the first time, Amelia wondered if she might lose her patient altogether. If the messages had been implanted into her brain out of respect, they came with a price. *Go away and leave him to us*, was the unstated idea.

Amelia took another sip of cold coffee and pondered her next move. While she thought, she added a few more lines to the sketch of Prime Arc. She was glad Ev had suggested the drawing; it seemed like a good idea to get the image down on paper while it was still fresh in her mind. Others – Nolan in particular – would want to see it.

Another image formed in her mind, a reflection she'd seen in the smooth egg-shaped pod in the jungle clearing. A distinct image; easily recalled, but oddly reinforced by another checksum. She doodled with the pencil. A few scratches here, a flick of the wrist to draw longer lines there. A form began to take shape on the paper.

Interesting.

She kept drawing, this time with intention. A light touch created strands of hair. Heavier, shorter strokes created a realistic eyebrow.

Ev peered over Amelia's shoulder watching the drawing take shape. "I never knew. Amelia, you're really good at this."

She wasn't. Or had never been before. She shaded the contour of a nose and added a reflection across the iris. Every stroke turned out remarkably well. Unfinished, but stunning in its simplistic beauty, Amelia turned the paper toward Ev.

"My self-portrait," Amelia said. "It *is* good, isn't it?"

The drawing was a perfect reproduction of her reflection in the smooth surface of the alien egg structure. The same image she saw in the mirror every day – except that her normally bushy eyebrow was trimmed.

Just like Natalie used to do.

The thought sent a chill down her body. She'd never drawn this well in her life, and to blend her reflection in the pod with thoughts of Natalie was no accident. She possessed a new talent, yet subtly connected to old memories.

It's another implant.

"Wow, that thing totally rewired my brain," Amelia stated to no one.

The full extent of Prime Arc's intrusion became clear. It had added new patterns of stored memory just as easily as Amelia zapped NCCs or rerouted synapses in a patient's brain. They'd been transferred to her brain via the Bronson cap's ability to tickle new patterns.

Amelia swallowed. Permanent, unalterable changes to her brain. Yet, it wasn't damage. It might even be beneficial – who wouldn't want a new artistic talent? But it had been done without her knowledge or her permission, and once more with a disturbing connection to her dead sister.

What else did they do?

She didn't feel any different, but she'd said roughly the same thing to Orlando. *You won't feel any different after a tickle.* Yet, despite the cute term, she knew full well the power she had over any patient's brain. She could rewire any pattern, erase any memory. If some of her own memories had just been wiped out, she'd never know it.

Amelia stared at the drawing she'd just produced. Natalie, no question. But it wasn't just any image of Natalie it was a specific look, one that Amelia had seen multiple times while Natalie was still alive. A particular glint in her eye, a slight wrinkle of the nose.

"Trust," Natalie implied through her expression.

Amelia could almost hear Natalie's words surface from the past. "Come on, Amelia. For us, trust is automatic. I'm you and you're me. How could I not have your interests at heart?"

They might have both noticed the same cute guy, or perhaps Natalie wanted to borrow money without explaining why. Her *trust me* expression had played out enough times in real life that Amelia recognized it at a glance in the drawing.

Trust what? An alien presence? Nice try.

Prime Arc had inserted the image of Natalie, playing on raw emotions. That kind of manipulation never sat well with Amelia. If this alien presence wanted trust it had a poor way of asking. Yet, the encounter hadn't felt like an attack. Prime Arc had used gentle motions that implied an intelligence and a plan. True, it had rammed a tendril down her throat, but what if that was the only way to communicate? From this creature's perspective, perhaps it had provided the gift of a creative drawing skill. Was that the respect Orlando mentioned?

"You might want to take some time off," Ev said. "Rest up. Let that noggin get back to normal."

"Whatever normal is," Amelia answered. Ev was probably right, Amelia would need a full psychological evaluation, maybe even an ALD session with Jonas at the steering wheel to see if he could find anything unusual buried deep inside her cerebrum.

"Ev, thanks for all your help. Orlando and I will clear out of here. I'm not sure what's next but once this all blows over, I'll get some help."

Amelia pulled the earbud out of her pocket and inserted it back into her ear. Kori's voice came through immediately. "Amelia! I've been trying to reach you."

"Sorry… my mistake." She'd automatically conformed to standard procedure for a session involving Bronson caps – removing the earbud, along with Kori's protection from their trackers.

"Trouble," he said. "A developing situation outside, but I don't know who or how many. Can you check visually?"

Each sphere was primarily glass, but views in most directions were obstructed by plants. Amelia hurried out of the C-Shore conference room to a position where she could see outside. The city was dark but flashing red and blue lights near the main entrance were enough to confirm Kori's warning. "That can't be a coincidence."

Ev watched from behind Amelia, as several figures ran through the darkness outside. "Doesn't look good. They've got the emergency exit covered too."

Trapped inside a glass sphere like two guppies in a fishbowl. Amelia balled her hands into fists. "They'll take Orlando."

A sly smile formed on Ev's face. "They will, but they'll have to find him first."

CHAPTER TWENTY-FIVE

PASSAGEWAYS

MAJOR SHEPARD TOOK the stairs two at a time, Lieutenant Tombaugh by his side. Both had weapons drawn, though in Shepard's case it was a nine-millimeter, twenty-round attachment for his prosthesis. By thought alone, he chambered one round, feeling the satisfying click of the bullet slipping into place.

Overhead, multiple hanging staircases continued up through foliage that seemed to touch the glass. Gurgles of flowing water and the scent of flowers filled the air.

Reaching the first level in the multi-level structure, Shepard acknowledged the three uniformed police who followed close behind and reminded them of their duty, as agreed by their captain.

"Fan out. They're in here somewhere. Capture, cuff, and bring them back to me for questioning."

Several employees seated at tables scattered between patches of vegetation looked up from their work.

Each Seattle Police officer, two men and one woman, wore a bulletproof vest. Photographs of the targeted suspects projected onto the visor inside their helmets. Their team lead signaled with his finger and each officer took a different direction. Lieutenant Tombaugh struck out across the first floor.

Shepard leaned back and surveyed the top of the curving structure. Three bubbles of glass and steel, seamlessly joined, with exits covered. It wouldn't be long now.

****

Amelia followed Ev, with Orlando close behind. They wound through an astonishingly beautiful section of tropical plants inside the city's most exotic terrarium, near the top of one sphere. Thick glass was within arm's reach but there were no openings. If this was an escape plan, it seemed doomed to failure. Amelia could already hear shouting coming from the levels below.

"Ev? You sure about this?" Amelia asked.

"No, but the odds are better than storming the exit." The stone-lined path became narrower. At least they were screened from view by thick foliage. "Hiding won't work, either. It's a big place but they'd find us eventually."

For an older woman, Ev was doing remarkably well at weaving and ducking as she pushed her way through low hanging branches and broad-leaved plants. It reminded Amelia of the jungle in Orlando's head.

The path ended at a low concrete wall. Ev stepped up and started across a layer of delicate moss planted between several large flowering orchids, crushing a few plants along the way. "The chief horticulturist is going to hate me for this."

They stopped at a large tree stump covered with lichens and moss. Ev pointed. "Our escape route."

Amelia twisted her brow. "A tree stump?"

Orlando stared at the stump and then to the curving glass and steel not far above it. "Can't be a real stump," he mumbled. "Not here."

Ev smiled. "Smart boy." She grabbed Orlando's arm. "Push me up."

He easily hoisted the slender woman to the flat top of the stump, just above eye level.

"Give me a second," Ev said on hands and knees. She fiddled with something on top, then withdrew a circular metal grate and handed it to Orlando. Ev's head disappeared into the stump, her voice echoing. "Looks clear down there. Follow me." She pivoted to feet first and dropped into the center of the stump.

Amelia and Orlando looked at each other quizzically. "You go first," Orlando said, helping Amelia up to the top of the stump.

It wasn't a stump. It wasn't even made of wood. Raked concrete forming its flat top gave a reasonable appearance of tree rings but in the center was a large hole. Amelia peered inside to see Ev already ten feet below climbing down metal rungs protruding from one side. Warm air rose from the depths.

"Well, what do you know," Amelia said shaking her head. "Ventilation decorated to blend in with the plants." She helped Orlando up and then stepped down to the first rung. "Something tells me this is going to be a long night."

Amelia followed down, the moist air coming up smelling vaguely of fresh cut grass. She reached the bottom rung where Ev was hunched over in a side passage too small to stand upright.

"Stay quiet from here," Ev whispered. "It leads to their compost facility, but we'll have to negotiate a horizontal stretch between floors to get there. They'll hear us if we're not careful."

Ev's version of hide and seek was undoubtedly their best option, but the further this clandestine secret agent fantasy went, the more Amelia wondered if she was in over her head.

Orlando joined them, indicating he'd re-covered the opening with the grate Ev had removed. It would be hard for anyone who didn't already know the stump was fake to follow. With Ev leading, they half walked, half crawled through a horizontal shaft. The metal floor and sides creaked regardless of how lightly they stepped.

The horizontal shaft connected to another vertical drop with more rungs that disappeared into darkness below. Amelia wasn't particularly claustrophobic, but the drop into darkness reminded her of spelunking she'd done once with an old boyfriend. Even then it was intimidating, but this time she had no headlamp. The journey down was further than she thought – or was comfortable with – but at last, her foot felt a concrete floor.

"We've got a tight squeeze ahead," Ev said over the sound of a large fan. Amelia could make out glints of light through the rotating blades. The smell of cut grass and leaves was strong.

She removed her backpack and pressed against a cold concrete wall on one side of the fan, the fast-moving blades only inches away and unshielded by any safety barrier. Luckily, the slot-like passage was only a few feet and Amelia popped out the other side into a dimly lit room with overhead pipes. To one side, several piles of plant debris filled wooden compost frames providing both the scent and the humidity of the air.

"This way," Ev said, pointing to a door on the far side.

"How do you know your way around a ventilation system?" Amelia asked.

Ev just smiled. "Everyone has their little secrets, don't they?"

"No, really, Ev. I realize you're an employee, but you work on artificial intelligence, not gardening."

Ev pinched two fingers at her lips and made a sucking sound. "We're in the Mellow Cellar. Before pot was legalized in Washington, this was where all the best employees came to get a buzz. Years ago.

Fun times." She cupped a hand to her mouth and whispered. "I even got laid here once."

Imagining stoned Ev doing it with some guy in a dank underground compost bin wasn't Amelia's first choice in mental entertainment. She followed in silence to the exit door.

Ev cracked the door. Cooler, dryer air rushed in and overhead lights revealed a parking garage, mostly empty. A black and white car with headlights on blocked a concrete ramp leading up. Seattle Police was written across the door.

"Now what?" Amelia whispered.

"We might have to wait," Ev answered, keeping the door opened just enough to peer out.

They probably couldn't wait indefinitely. Someone might have seen them drop into the fake stump. They'd even left footprints in the soil.

"Kori?" Amelia asked. "Any ideas?"

"Can you point your earbud cam at the car?" Kori asked.

Amelia leaned closer to the crack. "How's that?"

"Wish that cam had a better zoom." Kori paused. "An exempt Washington plate. Either 588127 or 533127. Not enough resolution to tell for sure."

"What do you have in mind?"

"You told me not to tell you."

"Right. Never mind, just do it, whatever it is. But don't hurt anyone."

"Asimov's first law of robotics," Kori answered. "Do no harm to humans. Don't worry, it's built in."

There was some motion inside the police car and a second later rotating blue and red lights flipped on. The car did a one-eighty with tires screeching and shot up a ramp, disappearing.

"Damn I'm good," Kori said. "You should hear my police radio voice."

"Where'd you send him?"

"He thinks you and Orlando were just spotted in an alley off Bell Street."

Amelia opened the door wide. "Come on, let's go. Kori sent him on a wild goose chase, but we might not have much time before they realize their mistake."

They ran across a cold concrete floor toward the ramp. "I don't suppose you have a car parked here, do you?" Amelia asked Ev.

Ev gave a look that could kill. "Me? In a goddamned car? Busses dear, 'til the day I die."

She'd figured it was a longshot, but Amelia's own car was gone, probably towed away to some impoundment lot. They ran up the ramp and peered around the corner. An exit to a darkened street was not far ahead, but blue and red flashing lights reflected off windows on the far side of the street. Ev held up an arm, stopping them.

"That didn't work," Ev said.

"They must have already figured it out," Amelia admitted.

Ev thought for a minute then raised one finger. "There's another way out of here. I've never been there, but people say there's an underground exit to the highway 99 tunnel."

Amelia knew the tunnel well – every resident of Seattle did. The waterfront had changed radically when the old elevated highway was torn down and replaced by a tunnel that burrowed directly under the city. She recognized immediately what Ev was suggesting.

"The emergency egress passageway. We can connect to that?" Tunnel construction had included a very visible escape route in case of a fiery car crash deep underground. The lime-green running stick figures painted every seventy feet along the tunnel walls were a common source of local jokes.

Ev nodded. "Some of these underground garages were built around the same time, and they tapped into the tunnel system instead of building their own emergency stairwell. You may have to go a few levels down first but follow the emergency exit signs. It should take you there."

"You're not coming with us?"

Ev shook her head. "We should split up. They're not looking for me. I could just walk up the ramp and knock on this guy's car window. Maybe get some intel for you. But you two need to get as far from here as you can, and you can go a lot faster without an old lady like me."

"I'd say you've done pretty well so far," Amelia answered.

Orlando nodded his agreement, but remained quiet, his eyes twitching one way and then another. He'd either put his trust completely in Amelia's hands or he was still in the white pod, being taught an alien language.

Amelia thought about Ev's plan. "The tunnel surfaces at South Lake Union, a half-mile north."

Ev's eyes sparkled. "And there's no way these dickheads have a dragnet that big."

Orlando perked up and twisted his head like a person trying to follow multiple conversations at the same time. "The yellow stacks. Near the Westlake Institute."

The four yellow tubes were a landmark or an eyesore depending on who you asked, but their purpose was to ventilate the tunnel and to serve as the exit point for the emergency egress passageway. Orlando had probably noticed them in his daytime excursion; they were only a few blocks from the Westlake Institute.

Amelia nodded. "*That* could be handy." Kori's original advice had been to stay away from home and work, but at least there were helpful resources at the office, possibly even a car she could borrow.

Secret agents are always supposed to change cars, aren't they?

She wrapped her arms around Ev. "Thanks for everything. I owe you."

Orlando followed suit in a mindless kind of way. Ev gave him a wary eye as she pulled away. "You take care of yourself, young man." She patted his forehead. "And, whatever else is lurking in there."

Ev ambled up the ramp toward the street outside and flashing police lights. Amelia and Orlando went the opposite direction toward a red exit sign in the parking level below.

Amelia pushed the exit door open, thankful that no alarm sounded. Steps led up and down. It seemed this garage had its own stairwell, but Ev might be right – they'd need to go down to find out if the tunnel connection existed.

"Kori. I could use a map for emergency exits to this parking lot," Amelia said as they started down the steps.

"Already researched," Kori replied. "I heard Ev's description and started searching right away. I didn't come up with anything. I'm afraid you're on your own."

His answer didn't seem right. "It might not be on a digital map, but there must be some architectural drawing somewhere."

"None. I've looked."

Maybe the passageway Ev referred to had been removed, or perhaps it had just been a rumor that no one had checked. If Ev had been mistaken, they'd have to surface right in the middle of police action, or else go back to the compost room and hope nobody would find them.

They kept going down, hopeful. After three flights, they opened another door to a barren passageway with arrows painted on the wall pointing to the far end. Maybe Ev had been right after all.

As she traversed the hallway, Amelia wondered if its lack of appearance on any map was fortuitous. The police might not know about the exit either. "Still no info on this tunnel?"

"Sorry, I lost the internet connection," Kori answered. "Too deep. I can't monitor my security tools or the police radio either. Your pursuers could be right around the corner and I wouldn't know it. Until we surface, I'd recommend eyes and ears."

CHAPTER TWENTY-SIX

QUESTIONING

EVELYN STERN HAD BEEN arrested three times in her lived-to-the-fullest life. The way things were going, this might be the fourth.

Two cops wore bullet-proof vests and utility belts that held a dozen different tools, some lethal, including Glock 33 pistols. She'd fired one of those before. Hell of a kick, but strangely fun.

The male cop had her backed up against his police car. The engine was off but the blue and red lights continued to flash. A female cop stood a few steps away, her hand resting on a holster just in case their captured grannie decided to bolt.

The first five questions made it clear she wasn't going to be let off easily, though Ev didn't want easy. She wouldn't get much information without fully engaging.

"Why were you *walking* up a parking garage ramp?" The cop held both hands on his hips like a strict father. His jaw was stern, his eyes probing. At least, he'd flipped up the visor on his riot helmet.

"I was already in the garage when I remembered I hadn't driven my car today. The ramp is a faster exit than the stairs." She put both hands on her hips mimicking the officer. "Now it's my turn for a question. I work in this building. What the fuck are you guys doing here?"

The cop didn't flinch, instead continuing with his line of questions. "Did you see anything unusual in there?"

Ev was quickly tiring of predictable routine. "Unusual? Hell yeah, shocking even. Third level. A woman nursing a baby. Swear to God, pulled her whole boob out and everything. You can still write her up if you hurry."

The cop's sneer was cut off when he noticed a tall man in military fatigues walking briskly toward them. One of the man's arms looked mechanical. Amelia hadn't given a full description, but Ev had a good idea who he might be.

The cop stepped aside as the military guy took over the questioning. "You just came out of the garage?"

Ev rolled her eyes. "Well, if we're going to start all over again, then for efficiency my answers are yes, no, Evelyn Stern, seventy-one, twice a week, I forgot, and bare boobs." She pointed a finger, coming close to tapping the guy's chest where a stitched label provided his name. "And, Mr. Shepard, I still don't have an answer for why the fuck you people are invading my building."

Shepard stood rock solid, a faint smile creeping across his lips. He pulled out a photograph from his shirt pocket and stuck it in front of Ev's face. "Do you know this woman?"

It was a photo of Amelia, and Ev didn't miss a beat. "Yeah, she's a big shot neuroscientist over at the Westlake Institute. Who wouldn't know her? Her face is all over TV. Well, unless your TV entertainment is *These Sluts Can Sing*." She waggled a finger in the air. "I have to say, I did like the blonde with the hundred-dollar bill tattooed above her vagina. Great voice, that one."

Shepard stepped forward and leaned inches from Ev's face. "Ms. Stern, you might get away with insulting the police, but I'm different. You only get one more try at this." He spoke succinctly. "Do you know her?"

Ev shrugged. "I might." There was no point in hiding it. A quick search of public information would probably confirm her relationship with Amelia. Dangling a suggestive offer might turn the questioning to her favor.

Shepard rubbed his eyes with his good hand. "This is not a time for games. You just came out of the garage. Where'd she go?"

"How much is it worth to you?"

Shepard shook his head and exhaled a large sigh. He bent his mechanical elbow and pressed a button on his forearm. A bright red laser shot straight up into the sky.

Ev looked up, following the red beam until it disappeared into the darkness. "I'm generally respectful of people with handicaps, but I think your prosthesis is leaking."

Shepard pointed the laser down the sidewalk, its light intersecting the concrete a good distance away.

"At twenty paces, it feels like a heat lamp," Shepard stated calmly as he drew a line along the sidewalk. "At ten paces, it will produce third degree burns in five seconds. But up close…"

"Oh, don't be ridiculous," Ev said. "You boys with your toys."

He pulled his arm in tight, the laser now pointing directly onto the hood of the police car. The intense beam popped and sizzled as it struck the metal. Paint bubbled and then peeled away. Within seconds a hole appeared in the steel and smoke poured out.

"Hey!" the cop yelled, "That's my car!"

"Oh, that's going to cost you," Ev mocked. "City of Seattle property. Taxpayers like me don't like that either. I'll have to report you to the city accountant." She tapped a finger to his name label. "Shepard. First name?"

Shepard grabbed her hand and slammed her palm to the hood of the car just above the burn mark. His laser hit the curb at their feet. A few weeds growing in a crack ignited with a brief flash of flame and smoke.

Pressing her hand against the hood, his laser creeped back toward the car. "Where'd she go?" Shepard demanded, each word terse.

Ev gritted her teeth, wincing from the firm grip on her wrist. "Probably home, it's getting late."

The laser moved closer.

Ev turned her head, glaring at him. "Look, Corporal Shepard, if you're going to put a hole through my hand you better get on with it because I don't give out strategic information to unidentified military peons who offer me nothing in return."

Like all bullies, his threat was designed to produce fear, but he'd never carry it out. Not with two cops standing there. Calling his bluff was the logical response. The tremble just beginning in her free hand was purely emotional.

The laser turned off and the hot metal cooled, creaking. "Okay, we'll try it your way." He released his grip. "*Major* Shepard, DARPA Operations. We're pursuing two fugitives under federal statutes for theft of classified documents. If you have information, withholding it could be very bad for you. So, what is it? You ready to tell me where they went?"

Ev leaned against the police car rubbing her sore wrist. "It's him, isn't it? You don't want her, you want the guy she's with. He's fucking crazy, you know that."

"I don't know that at all."

"Well, I do soldier boy. I pay attention and what we're doing right now is called bargaining. You give a little, you get a little. Why do you want him?"

"Why do you care?"

"The guy gave me an investment tip. Could be lucrative. I want to know if I should take it seriously."

"That guy is probably the smartest person you'll ever meet. Genius level. We already know he's a brilliant chemist, and I wouldn't be surprised if he could pick winning stocks – or winning horses for that matter." Shepard lifted his mechanical arm. "Now... where did they go? Or shall we go back to my method?"

"Promise you'll let me go?"

Shepard nodded.

Ev motioned with her head. "I sent them into the tunnel, the emergency egress footpath. It'll take them twenty minutes to get to the south exit. Go to the four yellow ventilation stacks. Dearborn Street. That's where they'll surface."

Shepard turned to the cop. "Confirmation?"

The cop who'd done all the questioning jumped into the front seat of his car and entered some information on a dashboard computer. It wasn't long before he nodded, "Yeah, it looks like there's a connection from here to the tunnel, just like she said. We could be at the stacks in three minutes."

"Go," Shepard commanded, "But one of you walk the tunnel route to flush them out." The female cop started down the ramp into the garage, and the police car sped away with lights flashing.

The night returned to calm with Ev waiting for any other demands that might come. None did.

"What are you going to do when you catch him?" Ev asked. She'd completed her part, there might be a bit more information to tease out.

"We'll find out what makes him tick." Shepard said, grinning. "Not me specifically, we've got very specialized facilities for that." He started walking away, stopped, and turned back. "Oh, about the laser thing..."

"Already forgotten," Ev replied.

"Yeah, good. It's a thing I do sometimes. Kind of malevolent when you think about it. Afterwards it seems… over the top." He looked at her like she was a paper target at the shooting range that he'd just realized was alive. "No offense to you personally."

"Eh, none taken. No offense about the corporal thing."

He scrunched up one eye looking like he was deciding whether to call it even or light up his laser once more and burn a hole through her head. "Yeah, fair enough."

He turned and strode away leaving Ev alone at the street curb – apparently free to go.

"Fucking psychopath," she said to herself. "But I kind of like him. All kinds of potential in bed. Of course, I'd have to chain him to the wall first."

She shrugged and walked away feeling satisfied with her performance. She'd delivered a mix of fabrication and reality. It was really the only way to deal with figures of authority. Give them what they want to hear and sprinkle it with morsels that are easily confirmed as true. After years of rebellious behavior, lying came easily for Evelyn Stern.

She only had one more task to complete for the night. Ev lifted her mobile to her ear. "Text to Amelia. My dear, I bought you a few minutes but they're not stupid, so keep moving. Major Shepard is his name, and he thinks Orlando is a genius. It seems he has plans for the poor boy's brain and I doubt very much that it involves therapy. Take heart, you're on the right side even if you are breaking the law. But Amelia… don't underestimate them."

CHAPTER TWENTY-SEVEN

EDUCATION

WITH TWO WORLDS colliding in a mashup of sights and sounds, it took every bit of concentration to makes sense of either one. In one world, Orlando closed his eyes and kept his feet moving as he and Amelia traversed a long concrete corridor. He hooked one hand around Amelia's elbow to avoid tripping or crashing into the wall. She didn't seem to mind.

In the other world, his tendrils had little to do while his mind worked overtime to keep up with a lesson in language interspersed with impromptu quizzes. Two teachers now hovered around him. He lay on a flat table in an egg-shaped room with curving lavender walls. The stick shapes of his instructors were obvious enough, but other details were difficult to make out due to a semi-transparent visor that had been placed over his eyes. The lesson – mostly audible – was reinforced by a multimedia presentation displayed on the visor's glass. Strange symbols flashed as alien words were spoken.

Eek zheck tak sha zeenck? One of the instructors quizzed. It was something about differentiating between a bud and a stalk, but that's as far as Orlando got.

He guessed, "Zeenck gesh?"

"What?" It was Amelia's voice from the other world.

"Nothing," Orlando responded, keeping his human eyes closed.

Amelia kept speaking, probably to her assistant Kori. The words sounded far away like a neighbor's conversation overheard through an apartment wall. Orlando tried to tune her out, she was becoming less relevant anyway as the lessons went on. He'd jettison her soon. It was for her own good.

No different than Teena. He'd miss his wife. His kids, too. But they inhabited his former life, a pathway of consciousness that now floundered in the recesses of his mind. A new life had begun, and it required his full attention.

Zedertsh screech zig! A voice snapped him back to the lavender room. The instructors seemed to be agitated, hooking up colored wires to one of his tendrils which produced an uncomfortable electric tingle. He wasn't sure if it was punishment for a wrong answer or just part of the training procedure.

"Ghe kez gek." Orland struggled to produce the words that seemed an appropriate response. Apparently wrong again, the electric tingle on one side of his body increased to an irritating buzz. On the other side, he could feel Amelia's penetrating stare from the nonsense he had just voiced aloud.

Two worlds, both with increasing demands that spun twin whirlwinds of confusion through his mind. At this pace, a single consciousness couldn't keep up. Eventually, something would give. He might be getting smarter about the new world, but his expanded mind came at the expense of participation in the old world.

Old Orlando would probably die, a result no one wanted. Not Prime Arc. Not any of the teachers. Certainly not Amelia. Even new Orlando was on shaky ground. His younger body might easily collapse along with the old. No one was sure, his case was too rare.

There was still some hope for reconciliation, but it hung entirely on the completion of the alignment device. Orlando could still finish its construction, but Amelia would need to get out of the way. If needed, he could kill her. The right touch while electrical pulses passed through his new body would stop her heart within seconds.

He didn't want that. Amelia had been kind, though Prime Arc might not agree. She'd been warned, Prime Arc had said. The rest was up to her.

The new world lesson continued, shifting from language to history. With words Orlando only partially understood, one of the instructors recited an event from long ago. Orlando was not their first contact with humans, the instructor explained. There had been another. A woman. Far more primitive, with limited language skills, and no access to proper materials to construct an alignment device. The results were predictable. She hadn't survived.

It appeared to be a lesson in consequences.

CHAPTER TWENTY-EIGHT

EGRESS

AMELIA PULLED OPEN another metal door. A whoosh of air was followed by the high-pitched whine of car tires on a roadway. Overhead lighting controlled by a motion sensor flickered on, revealing a new passageway and a sign that pointed north and south with distances in feet to each exit.

Amelia turned north, pulling Orlando by his hand. He'd been sluggish and reluctant to run, his mind clearly focused on other things.

"Come on, we need to go," Amelia said, dragging him to a trot.

His mouth opened but odd noises spilled out instead of words. Guttural sounds, like he was practicing hard g's and k's. Amelia stared at her obsessed companion but continued on.

The passageway was narrow, not quite suitable for two abreast, and sloped gently upward with sliding metal doors positioned regularly down the left side. Signs over each door warned that an alarm would sound if opened. The noise of high-speed cars in the adjacent traffic tunnel blared at each door they passed.

Exit – 3000 feet, one sign read. Amelia glanced back at her patient – or more rationally, her partner – in this strange quest for answers from another world. His skin was dotted with perspiration. His head twitched several times to the right like he was trying to shake off a fly that had landed on his ear. His mouth opened with his jaw twisting to one side. "Ack, gok, tuk," he spewed.

Amelia shuddered. The creepiness factor was sky high, but at least his jaw wasn't unhinging as in the dream. "Hang in there, guy. I've got a plan."

Her plan, if it could be called that, was checking in with Nolan and then finding a secure place for the night. A hotel would do, preferably on the outskirts of the city. If she could get into the Westlake Institute office, there was a company car parked in the garage and its key fob would be in a drawer at the reception desk. She'd just need to slip in for one minute, grab the key, and they'd be on their way.

Now just past midnight, Amelia had been awake for nearly twenty-four hours and exhaustion was beginning to dominate. Orlando didn't look any better, though it was hard to tell how much of his dazed look was due the alien training mode he'd been in for the past hour.

Maybe just get some coffee and push through the night?

She could guide him back to the workshop at the university. Let him finish his construction of circles and triangles. She could even help him, and maybe she should. If she was being honest, she had done nothing so far to improve his chances of survival. He'd been right about the alien presence in his head. Maybe he was also right about his pending death, and the alignment device. Finishing it might be his only chance.

If he did finish, *something wonderful* would happen, or so he'd said. But why would anyone trust an alien device of unknown purpose? Orlando was certainly onboard, but he seemed barely cognizant of being human anymore. Amelia was being pushed into this scheme too, at least, that was the implication from rummaging through Orlando's mind.

And then there was Natalie, somehow involved in this bizarre mashup of consciousness. It wasn't just the crude implant of her image or the memory of Natalie's trust in the bond between twin sisters. There was more. In so many ways, Natalie was still very much alive, inside Amelia.

"Think of a city," ten-year-old Natalie had asked, and they'd both blurted out "Paris" simultaneously. Giggling, Amelia had responded, "Think of an animal," and kangaroos had inexplicably popped into both heads. At first, they'd laughed. Then, they'd stared at each other in awe, two identical girls grappling with a force of nature neither could fully understand.

Those days were over, but Natalie wasn't gone as long as Amelia lived on. "Trust," Natalie seemed to be telling her, and it wasn't just a manipulation of the mind. Amelia had always known Natalie's thoughts. She felt them stronger now more than ever.

A mysterious device waited at the university. Alien in design, that much was true, but the man constructing it had no concerns. You can't lie in your dreams and neither can you hide malevolent intent. If there was a hidden evil in all of this, Amelia would have spotted it in a second. Orlando was clean. Pure of mind. When he said something wonderful would happen, he meant it.

Just do it. Help him finish.

A decision made, yet the logical side of Amelia remained nervous. She was clearly in over her head but her inquisitive nature wanted answers in whatever form they came. Helping Orlando might be a selfish plan, but it would satisfy the craving for that elusive glimpse of reality. Through him, she might get a chance to draw back the curtain hiding the true nature of human consciousness.

Keep him alive. Safeguard him from capture. Learn from him.

Orlando was the experiment. His golden arc sculpture waiting at the university was the technology. She had no idea how his story might end, but if activating Orlando's creation answered this most fundamental of questions, she was onboard. Even protective to make sure it happened.

Cognitive amalgamation.

The words just popped into her head. Two words this time, unbidden and with no connection to her planning. "*Cognitive* amalgamation," she mumbled to herself. The phrase sounded more along the lines of brain science, but it wasn't anything she was familiar with.

Amelia slowed in their jog up the ramp and turned to Orlando. His faraway look continued to transform him into a shell of the person he was before.

She waved a hand in front of his eyes. "Orlando, are you with me?" He made eye contact, panting from the exertion of their run. "You said I was half right, but I might have the other half now. *Cognitive* amalgamation. Is that it?"

He blinked several times, staring at the floor while he caught his breath. "A coming together of minds," he said in the most natural voice she'd heard from him in the past hour.

"Like your shared consciousness?" she asked.

He shook his head, a human gesture for once. Perhaps their run had woken him from his alien slumber. "There's more. I can't explain it."

"But they were teaching you things in the white room. Was cognitive amalgamation one of them?"

He nodded. "Yes, but much more." His face contorted, jaw sliding sideways and lips protruding. "Kik creetch tick tick grak rik tok."

Amelia held up a hand, grimacing. "Don't do that! It's so creepy!" His dreamlike contortion was now limited by physical skin and bones, but the alien words were still just as shocking.

"Sorry," he said, his eyes turning down.

Amelia kept her distance, wary of what might erupt from his mouth next. "Orlando, Prime Arc is changing me too. Those words, cognitive amalgamation, weren't in my mind until it jammed a tendril into my brain. But there's more swimming around in there. A three-by-three multiplication cube – I really have no idea what that's about. And then there's a drawing talent I never had before."

Orlando nodded. "I know. I saw you draw."

Amelia was puzzled. Though Orlando was sitting right there when she had talked to Ev and drawn the pictures, he'd seemed miles away absorbed in the other world. It was getting hard to tell where his attention was focused.

"So, you're seeing the real world clearly, but you're just not saying much about it. Is that it?"

"I see and move in both worlds. I hear and speak in both languages. In your world, I already know everything. In their world, I'm still learning."

Your world.

"Orlando, this is your world too. Don't let them pull you away from being human."

"I'll try," was all he could muster.

She hesitated, attempting to put the pieces together. "Prime Arc told me not to attempt to *sever the two*. Is that what cognitive amalgamation is about?"

Orlando replied in a monotone that sounded like he was reading, "I am the two. I am of one mind, but I am only the beginning. Cognitive amalgamation is more. Much more."

Though limited, his description was disturbing, conjuring thoughts of assimilation into some vast network of consciousness – like it or not. She worried that her own mind had already taken the first step: they'd implanted new memories and new cognitive abilities. Was that all they'd done, or was there more she hadn't yet recognized? She was already questioning her decision to help him.

"Orlando, I'll do everything I can to protect you from capture, but I'm not sure I like what I see in your mind, or mine for that matter."

He reached for her hands. "Don't worry, Amelia. It's good. I've seen it."

"I have too. I agree it's trying to communicate but do we really have any idea of its intent?"

"It's going to be wonderful," he said with sincerity. "But I must complete the alignment device."

"Or you'll die. Yeah, I got that part."

She wondered if the prediction of death meant she might be next. She didn't feel any alien presence lurking within her own mind, but it was an unsatisfactory conclusion based on nothing but a gut check.

She brushed away lingering doubts and grasped both of his forearms. "Listen to me. You're not going to die. Got it? I'm going to make sure of that. You and I are in this together, okay?"

He nodded.

The affirming words helped to elevate her spirit and focus her resolve. Danger lurked, but answers might be just around the corner especially if she helped him finish his work. She was already far deeper into this bizarre journey than she'd anticipated but at this point there was no turning back. Like watching a monster movie, the desire to know how it ends pulled stronger than worries about the nightmares that might accompany. Orlando believed the ending would create something wonderful. Amelia didn't have the same confidence, but she could agree it would at least be very *interesting*.

Amelia grabbed Orlando's hand and began a final run up the passageway toward its exit.

Five minutes later they reached a staircase which led up to a glass door exiting to the street. A buzzer sounded as they opened the door, but it quieted once the door closed behind them. Overhead, four yellow ventilation stacks reached up to a dark night sky sprinkled with stars. A half-moon rose in the east. She knew right away where she was. The Westlake Institute was only a few blocks away.

"Kori, send a scrambled text to Nolan," Amelia stated. "Tell him we could use some help."

****

Shepard stood at the base of four yellow stacks, his concern mounting. The police car had arrived within minutes, but the officer reported that no one had exited. His partner had radioed that she was still in the tunnel, heading this way. A minute later she climbed up an interior stairwell and opened the exit door.

"Where are they?" Shepard demanded.

The cop looked confused. "There was no one in this part of the tunnel," she answered, holstering her gun. "Maybe they went north?"

"The tip was specific," Shepard said, craning his neck to look straight overhead. A half-moon rising in the east provided enough light to verify their location. "Four yellow ventilation stacks."

The cop shrugged. "Yeah, but there are identical stacks on the other end of the tunnel too. Everyone knows that. Well... if you live here."

Shepard dropped his head as the realization hit him. "Damn that woman!" Misdirection. Quite intentional. He should have burned her when he had the chance. He wouldn't make the same mistake again.

The open battlefield was so much simpler. Afghanistan, Somalia, Kashmir, it didn't matter. Urban pursuits were messy. Too porous. Too many non-combatants who might alter the calculation. Too many rules with too many police trying to enforce them.

Shepard sighed, just as his mobile vibrated. His foul mood changed rapidly as he examined its display. Good news, it was another message from his secret source.

The two fugitives had exited at the north end of the tunnel, the informant disclosed, close to the Westlake Institute. Best of all, they were still on foot.

CHAPTER TWENTY-NINE

SANCTUARY

WELL PAST MIDNIGHT, the boulevard fronting the Westlake Institute was mostly devoid of cars and people. A nearby streetlight forced Amelia and Orlando into the shadows beneath a building overhang. Across the street, a police car idled at the curb.

"Damn," Amelia whispered. A dash to the front door would be too risky. Circling around to the garage entrance might not be any safer. The plan to grab a company car had come to a crashing halt.

"Glek oork zhek treg," Orlando uttered, his alien voice at full volume. When it came to stealth, Orlando wasn't the best partner.

"Shh!" Amelia held a finger to her lips. "You can't keep doing that," she whispered, "If these guys pick us up, we're both going to a jail cell."

Nolan hadn't returned her text. On any normal night, he'd be at home asleep, but something told her that wasn't the case tonight. If she dialed, he might pick up. Or his phone might be off, or on do-not-disturb mode. With Nolan it was hard to tell. He was pretty hopeless when it came to technology which probably made calling him risky. He didn't have Kori to keep him off the grid.

There were other options. "Kori, can you call for a RydeShare?"

Kori answered. "I'd advise against a car service, Amelia. In less than ten seconds I could hack into their network, pick up your request, and send a fake car in your direction. You wouldn't know until it arrived that it was actually your pursuers picking you up. If I can do that, I wouldn't be surprised if they could too."

"Okay, good to know. I guess we'll stay on foot. I'm just not sure where to go."

Contemplating their options, she noticed a light on in the Westlake Institute building across the street. It was at the top floor, a corner office. Nolan's, in fact. She squinted trying to discern if anyone was inside. The blinds were open but there was no movement. Oddly, a piece of paper was stuck on the window glass. It seemed to have writing on it.

"Can you read that, Kori?" She pointed her earbud cam at the upper level window.

"Just barely. I believe it says, *Need a place? Good neighborhood. Secure. Sail La Vie. 1466. No calls, please.*"

Amelia listened as Kori transcribed. "Sounds like an ad for an apartment, except…"

There was virtually no chance that Nolan would post a rental ad in his office window. It was a message, and probably designed for her. He hadn't answered her text, but he'd communicated just the same.

"It must be a message for me, but what does it mean?"

Amelia had always said that memory was a funny thing. It could be manipulated, even erased, but when a faint memory finally kicked in, it could also be an adrenalin rush.

"I've got it," Amelia said far too loudly, then whispered. "Sail La Vie. It's the name of his sailboat. Nolan took me on a day cruise once around Lake Union. The boat is docked over at an East Lake marina, not far from here."

"And the 1466 number?" Kori asked.

"Probably the code to unlock the entry hatch. Get it? *Good neighborhood, secure.* He's telling me it's a place to hide in case we need it."

"Will they have paper there?" Orlando asked. He leaned against the building wall, his eyes closed. His out-of-the-blue request made little sense, but at least it had come in English words, not alien.

"Paper? Like writing paper?"

"And a pen." He lifted his lids to reveal eyes rolled up to his forehead, zombie-like.

"What, you need to draw more insects? Orlando, you don't look so good. I think we both need some rest." She worried that his prediction of pending death might be underway already.

"Rest," he repeated. "Perfect. Resting at the sailboat might work out well."

He seemed to be plotting something, though he hadn't mentioned his alignment device for a while. Maybe their goals had converged, at least for the moment. Fatigue has a way of defining priorities. "The boat it is then."

"And paper."

"Okay. Sure. We might find some paper there – if that's what you really need."

"I do," Orlando said, closing his all-white eyes once more. Who knew what request might come next? Chalk? Watercolors? Maybe he'd dash off a quick rendition of the Mona Lisa before dawn. Nothing would surprise her at this point.

Amelia hooked a hand on Orlando's arm and started down the sidewalk along the lonely street. They got no more than a block before a black van turned a corner. Flattening against a wall as the vehicle cruised past, Amelia hoped deep shadows would be enough.

The van kept moving another block and then red taillights came on.

"Run," Amelia said, and took off down the sidewalk with Orlando right behind. She turned at the first corner and then into an alley. Dodging garbage bins and a surprised raccoon, they turned a second corner and stopped at the same street they'd just left, one block further down.

Amelia peered back toward the Westlake Institute office building as she caught her breath. The van was nowhere to be seen.

"Kori?"

"Sorry, they kind of snuck up on me. But I'm tracking them now. They're on the far side of the building."

"Okay, that's good – I guess. Maybe they didn't see us, but let's not take any chances. I'll get us to the sailboat but back routes only."

"Don't worry Amelia, I've got them now," Kori assured. "All this hide and seek technology is addicting." Addicting wasn't the word she'd use, but if Kori was now on top of the situation that's all that mattered.

She waved and Orlando followed, panting from the run, but at least his rolled-up eyes had returned to normal. They crossed a major street, deserted at this hour, then found an unlit footpath along the shoreline of the lake. A row of trees separated them from the adjacent street and kept them in shadows.

As they walked, the shoreline changed from high-priced restaurants closing up for the night, to working docks for government ships, and finally to a string of floating cottages interconnected by wooden docks that reached a hundred feet out into the lake.

They turned down one dock that pointed straight out from the shore. Several tiny houses floated along the left side, each decorated with colorful flower boxes on the windowsills and carved signs over the doors representing whatever nautical-themed god, spirit, or sprite was fancied by that homeowner. Norwegian and Swedish themes dominated.

"We're here," she whispered to Orlando and pulled off her backpack. A forty-foot sailboat was tied near the end of the dock, the name across its stern, *Sail La Vie*, lit by one of several solar lamps attached along the dock's edge.

"I don't get it," Kori said in her ear.

"What, the boat name? It's a French play on words. You know…" Amelia waved a hand. "Never mind." She was tired, and the marginal joke typical of boaters wasn't worth the effort to explain, though it was fascinating to have finally found the edge of Kori's comprehension of the human world.

They climbed aboard, the massive sailboat hardly moving as they stepped onto it. As she expected, the hatch to the interior cabin was covered by a sliding door with a four-dial combination lock on one side. She turned the dials to 1466 and the lock slid open.

Thanks Nolan.

Amelia led the way down several steps into a galley with a small stove and refrigerator on one side and a table with a bench seat on the other. The sailboat's mast dropped through the center of the compact room straight to the keel.

Orlando looked shaky as he negotiated the dark steps. He leaned against the wall, as Amelia flipped on a light switch and closed the hatch cover. Cozy and quiet, the boat made a good hideout and a pleasant place to rest as it rocked gently in the water.

Amelia tapped on a thin door just beyond the galley. "There's a toilet in here, one bunk forward and another at the stern. Take your pick."

His head cocked to one side. It was an oddly similar move to the creature that occupied his mind. "Paper?" he asked, looking around and pulling a pen that was clipped to a bracket just above the table.

"Oh yeah," Amelia answered, still puzzled by his request. She reached into a map compartment and found a notepad. "Need to write something down that you don't want to forget?"

Orlando didn't answer. He sat at the galley table, opened the notepad to a blank page, and started sketching. He drew long straight lines and added smooth shading along the sides. Amelia watched in earnest as the object took shape. Orlando mumbled to himself as he drew and made a few notes along the edges. When satisfied, he set the pen down and nodded, carefully studying his work.

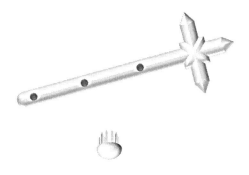

It was the light saber-sword-rod that he'd been holding when she'd found him sitting on the rock in the level two dream. It was more detailed than in the dream, and he'd also drawn a button with an intricate set of pins on one side. The button looked like it might fit into three holes along the saber.

"The final component?" Amelia asked.

"Yes. I can build it, I'm sure of it."

Amelia had no doubt he could and was equally sure that she wouldn't try to stop him. But not tonight. Surely all this work could wait a few hours.

"The code will activate it," he added tapping his palm to the side of his head. He clearly knew what to do, including a memorized code that would start everything.

She decided to try one more time. "What will happen when you activate it?"

"Wonderful things," he said as if those words were printed on a cue card.

"So you said. Super. But what specifically will it do?"

"It will make me whole." His captain-obvious expression made it clear that any school kid should know this.

One more try. The language of the alien creature might work. "The two will become one?"

"We already are one." His head started twitching again, multiple jerks to the left.

Amelia put a hand on his shoulder and spoke softly. "Orlando, how does this end? Are you going to just continue down this path to becoming half human, half alien?"

He looked up but didn't answer.

"What about Teena? And your kids? Have you thought about them recently?"

Only three days before, Orlando's biggest concern was getting his wife back. Now, it was as if he'd forgotten her name.

He hung his head and took a deep breath. "I miss Teena."

He sat motionless for a minute while Amelia wondered if it had been the right thing to bring up. The regret was there, deep inside him, though trying to bring it to the forefront might not accomplish anything. He was a man obsessed, and his former life seemed to be a casualty.

His face went pale and his head began to twitch again. His mouth opened in irregular pulses as if controlled by something else. "Ak ah ah ak tak tak…" The sounds came out like regurgitations, not speech.

She rubbed his back. "Sorry, I shouldn't have brought it up. Just let it go."

Eventually the head jerks and staccato sounds trailed away. Amelia put a hand under his arm and guided him up from the table and toward the berth at the stern of the boat.

"Lie down. Rest."

Orlando reclined on the bunk and Amelia closed the door behind her. She walked to the forward cabin and closed its door.

"Kori, are we still okay?" Her mobile showed fifteen minutes past one a.m.

"I've got it covered, Amelia. Your pursuers have now moved to the north of this location."

"They passed us?"

"Above you, along the interstate."

Interstate-5 ran north-south through the middle of the city. The house boats along Lake Union weren't far away, but the freeway passed overhead on a tall bridge with no exits.

"That's good, I hope," Amelia answered. "At least, they don't know where we are."

"Correct, they don't," Kori said. "I'll let you know if anything changes."

"Thanks. Text to Nolan." She thought about how to code her message in case anyone else might be tapped into Nolan's mobile. "Um… man overboard. Got a life preserver but could use the Coast Guard."

"He'll get it," Kori answered. "Even I do. Sailing terms, right?"

"Right. He'll know where we are, and maybe he'll figure out how to keep us safe." Nolan had connections in both government and business. If there was anyone who could buy them enough time to get Orlando's device finished without being caught, it would be Nolan.

Amelia reclined in the forward bunk, pulled out a blanket and pillow from a storage locker and made herself comfortable. She left the earbud in place just in case they'd need a quick exit.

Rest, but stay awake, she told herself. Commands to herself usually worked, even when she was tired. Sleep never came easy for Amelia, there were just too many concerns of the day that needed to be resolved before her brain would calm down.

Sometimes the concept of sleep itself kept her from sleeping. It was such an odd requirement for life. The body was satisfied with rest, food, and water, but the brain required an altered state of consciousness to continue functioning.

Sleep raised the very deepest of questions. At a neuroscience conference a few years back, she'd elaborated with a colleague who'd become a short-term lover. While wrapped in each other's arms the next morning, she'd explained her reasoning.

"Why is it that I wake up the same person as I was when my brain switched off the night before? My consciousness just lost eight hours – effectively shut down – yet when it reboots, my personality is still there. My mind hasn't changed. My perspective of the phenomenal world is no different. I still see my nose between my eyes, feel my own tongue in my mouth, feel each breath as it fills my lungs. Why am I still me? Why not wake up as you, instead?"

Her overnight boyfriend had only laughed, but for Amelia the non-transferability of consciousness was a serious question that went to the heart of the debate. If consciousness was emergent and separate, why was it so inextricably tied to a specific biological entity?

Her deepest questions might never be settled, but that didn't stop her from trying. Sometimes it was those deep thoughts that cleared away all the other concerns of the day. Tonight, was one of those times.

Amelia settled into the pillow and a few minutes later, her consciousness faded away.

CHAPTER THIRTY

BREAK-IN

WALKER DUPLASS SQUEEZED through a hedge that trimmed one side of Roberts Hall on the University of Washington campus. He kept to the shadows, relishing his opportunity to play a late-night game of cops and robbers.

This time he was the robber.

He carried the tools of the trade, a black ski mask which he had already slipped over his head, a small flashlight in one hand and a bag of tools in the other. Of the tools, the do-it-yourself lockpick was his favorite. He was getting good at it too, managing to get his own apartment door open with only a few minutes of fiddling.

This job would test his skills. Major Shepard's informant had been specific about the target location: a single-story brick building behind Robert's Hall, fourth room on the right, Lab 104. The informant had been less specific about what they'd find there. Shepard had delegated the two-a.m. investigation to Duplass with a demand to report back if he discovered anything of value.

Duplass didn't mind the late-night timing; it reminded him of his student days pulling an all-nighter while studying for a neuroscience exam. Good times, then. Not so much anymore. His work had become routine with too many indiscriminate mind wipes that any janitor could do. Breaking and entering was unquestionably the most intriguing assignment he'd had in weeks.

Besides, this assignment brought him closer – not just to Shepard's goo zoo target – but to Amelia Charron. It had been more than a year since Walker Duplass had spoken with Amelia, but that only made the upcoming encounter all the better. She'd snubbed him last time. Why do women get so moody? It was just a simple glass of wine. Of course, it could have been a lot more if Amelia hadn't left in a sulk.

She owed him. A kiss, at least. He'd give anything to press up against those gorgeous lips. Amelia had been a lot easier to talk to when they were young PhD candidates. Something had changed along the way, probably MemoryTap; Amelia had never approved of his career choice. Looking back, MemoryTap had been a colossal mistake.

Ostensibly, the company was constructing the world's first digital storage unit capable of holding the eighty-six-billion connections of a human mind. By 2038, they planned to transfer a living mind to its new home, and some egocentric billionaire would live forever. The lucky bastard would even have a virtual digital world to play in, replete with every digital distraction a man could ask for – especially distractions of the flesh, even if that flesh was imagined. The company had already signed up several women, each ready to take the plunge as a billionaire's virtual playmate in exchange for their own immortality.

But last year, most of that groundbreaking work had been sidetracked by a lucrative military contract that the company's leaders couldn't pass up. Big money, right away, but it meant a very different direction for their work.

These days, Duplass spent most of his time erasing memories. Sometimes the mental surgery was done in kindness, turning a deeply disturbed soldier who'd just returned from the war in Kashmir into a docile worker suitable for any number of military desk jobs.

But memory erasures came in various types. Many times – more than he could count – Duplass had removed classified information from retiring soldiers, always an enlisted rank, never an officer. Once, he'd clipped vital data from the brain of a CIA field agent prior to his insertion behind enemy lines. If caught, even torture couldn't reveal names and codes that were no longer physically present.

The worst erasures were saved for the prisoners at Guantanamo or Leavenworth – those guys were lucky if they came out the other side still able to button their shirts. It made Duplass squirm, but it paid the bills.

Duplass shined his light across a sign that read *Wilson Metals Laboratory*. The old brick building fit the description the informant had provided. The door was locked which only made Duplass smile. He retrieved the lockpick kit from his tool bag and started to work, inserting a tension wrench at the top and a ridged pick into the center, just as the YouTube instructions had demonstrated.

He jiggled the pick, applied more tension, jiggled some more. The lock didn't turn. "Damn," he said under breath. He shoved the pick in and out. Still no luck.

"Fuck it." He threw the lockpick back in the bag and pulled out a thick black glove. Donning the glove, he punched a windowpane and reached inside. The old door squeaked as it swung open.

The hallway was dark and deserted. No sounds of people, machines, or even the hum of ventilation. He hurried down the hall, pointing the light at each door until arriving at Lab 104. Not bothering with the lockpick, he gave the door a swift kick and the wooden door jamb shattered.

Duplass pushed back a cloth curtain and shined the flashlight around a lab crowded with shelves and shop tools. The beam stopped on a large structure in the center of the floor, highly reflective and built from circular tubes and triangular sheets of metal.

"What have we here?" Duplass asked. The free-standing structure didn't look like anything he'd seen before. He walked closer, inspecting its shiny surfaces and smooth edges. He stood beneath the arc of three golden tubes, pulled out his mobile and took several photos.

Documenting the discovery was enough for now. Shepard would probably be fast asleep in the back row of the van, snuggled down in soft patent leather. Muscle-bound bullies always thought they were the toughest, but the intellectuals of the world – like Duplass – knew better. Mental toughness was in another class altogether.

The structure would still be there in the morning. It was too big to carry and probably couldn't even fit through the doorway. The room was still worth monitoring, and Duplass had exactly the right technology.

He reached into his burglary bag and withdrew a plastic box with a protruding hemisphere on one side. Flipping a switch on the back, a small LED lit and then extinguished. He peeled back a tape strip, climbed up on to a workbench and stuck the motion sensor on the wall near the ceiling.

Activating an app on his mobile, the sensor self-registered and the app drew a horizontal line across the screen. Duplass waved his arm and the horizontal line ticked up sharply, displaying the current date and time of the observed motion.

Satisfied with his preparation, Duplass collected his gear and left.

****

The sailboat rocked in a slow rhythm defined precisely by the lake, the breeze above its surface and the length of rope securing the two-ton vessel to its dock. A gentle rolling motion with regular tugs as the rope became taught and relaxed once more. The mellow swaying produced a soothing, womblike experience that would put most any person to sleep.

Orlando Kwon wasn't one of those people, if he could be considered a person at all. Thirty-seven minutes and nineteen seconds had passed since Amelia had closed the door to his cabin at the stern of the sailboat. Sixty-four tugs from the rope – he'd counted them all. The soothing waves were no match for a mind that remained agitated, conflicted, and obsessed. His body was exhausted, but there would be no sleep tonight.

This night might be his last. *Their* last. His consciousness supported two bodies, not one, a condition that had not occurred on this water planet in more than twenty thousand years. Twenty-one thousand, three hundred seventy-four to be exact, one of many details covered in Orlando's training.

The *gift of shared consciousness*, as they called it. Its previous recipient was a stone-age woman who lived in a cave in what is now the Dordogne region of southern France. As she'd slowly gone crazy, her tribe had banished her to the forest in the east. She'd lasted a few weeks on her own, eventually succumbing to the cold – and perhaps the loneliness of her affliction.

The specifics of this historical information weren't in question. Like most of what was in his head, it had been transferred along with a digital checksum that ensured its accuracy.

Prime Arc was the source of most information, but there were others – other Triads, as Orlando had learned they were called. Some had expertise in mathematics, or chemistry, even biology, though training from the Triad biologist had lacked the conviction of the other disciplines. After all, no Triad had yet touched an actual human, or had the opportunity to sample tissue. A complex, self-reproducing molecule of life was inferred down at the cellular level, but until Orlando's tissues could be examined more closely – an upcoming event that instilled a strange mix of anxiety and giddy anticipation in Orlando himself – no Triad could be sure if their preparations would produce lasting value. Cognitive amalgamation, the joining of two high-order species, might be nothing more than a dream.

Orlando slipped out of bed with beads of sweat standing across his forehead, even though it wasn't hot. His five-fingered hand trembled slightly as he carefully turned the latch on the door to his cabin.

Except for a single LED on one bulkhead, the galley was dark. Amelia had retired to the forward compartment, her sleep surely deepened by the rocking motion of the boat.

Orlando was thankful Amelia hadn't been injured, brain damaged, or worse. She had become a good friend, just as she'd predicted when they'd first met. Amelia had done her best to help, though in the end it wouldn't really matter. Orlando would live or die, this night.

Amelia would find out soon enough, but she couldn't affect the outcome one way or the other. If he died, perhaps Amelia would be the one to tell Teena. Amelia was good with words and Teena would be thankful to hear it from a reliable source.

Legs aching, Orlando took wobbly steps up the short ladder to the hatch. His body was beginning to fail, no question. How long he'd last was pure speculation, but sleep wouldn't help in the slightest for a consciousness that spanned half a galaxy. Like embers of a fire that have been separated, his split consciousness would slowly fade away, snuffing out both bodies with it.

He had lied to Amelia once more, but it had been for her own good. The sailboat was perfect – just as he'd said – but it was a perfect place to ditch Amelia. She'd remain safely in bed where she wouldn't be hurt. Or killed.

From here on out, Orlando would need to do this on his own.

Without making a sound, he drew back the hatch cover and peered outside. The air was fresh. The clouds had parted, and a half moon hung high in the eastern sky casting white shimmers across the surface of the lake.

His head twitched, angling awkwardly back toward the cabin where Amelia slept. "Ich ak tik tik tik," he whispered. "Thank you."

Earth's second alien consciousness – and possibly its last for another twenty-thousand years – stepped out to the boat deck and closed the hatch cover behind him.

CHAPTER THIRTY-ONE

MISSING

AMELIA WOKE WITH her arms and legs wrapped around a pillow. It made a poor substitute for the man currently missing from her bed; that unnamed guy – the one she never invited anywhere, never called, and would probably never meet. Not enough time, she'd say. Too much work. There were plenty of good excuses.

But, oh, what she would do when she found him. Smother him in kisses. Jump him daily. Twice on Saturdays. Of course, mister perfect would literally have to bump into her on the street given that the efforts she made to connect to eligible guys since her breakup last year was exactly zero.

Amelia opened her eyes and the dreamy personal thoughts fell away, replaced by cold reality. She had intended to rest. Exhaustion had intervened, demanding sleep instead.

Light streamed in through a porthole partially covered by curtains that gently swayed back and forth. Water slapped rhythmically against a dock. A seagull screeched.

She sat up on the bunk and touched the earbud still lodged in her left ear. "Kori, what time is it?"

"Morning, Amelia. Six fifteen and let's see… nothing to report."

She'd been asleep for five hours, but at least it was still early.

The sailboat creaked slightly as it rocked in the water, but otherwise there were no sounds of Orlando stirring in the aft cabin. Given how pale he had looked, she'd need to check on him.

"Any messages from Nolan?" she asked.

"None," Kori answered, "But I can let him know you're awake if you'd like."

"Yeah, do that. No need to disguise the words in sailing terminology. Awake is awake."

She opened her cabin door and peeked into the galley. At the far side, Orlando's cabin door was already open, the bed empty.

"Orlando?" she probed.

No reply.

Tensing, Amelia hurried through the galley and peered into the aft cabin. There weren't any corners to hide in. The bathroom was clear too.

Worried, she slid the hatch cover open, sunshine pouring in, and climbed out to the boat deck. A cool morning breeze blew across the lake, with only a few puffs of clouds hanging in a blue sky.

Orlando wasn't on the boat deck or anywhere along the dock.

Maybe he's gone for coffee. That rationalization was as unlikely as the blue-sky morning in Seattle. Orlando had made his priorities perfectly clear. His destination was almost certainly a small workshop at the University of Washington campus – walking distance. She had little doubt he was already there.

"Then why did he want to rest?" A thousand concerns filled her head as rapidly as thoughts could form. The weird daze that he'd been in could have worsened into who-knows-what. He might have stumbled off the edge of the dock and drowned. He could have been captured by the guys from DARPA or picked up by the police. There were far too many unfavorable outcomes. Completing and activating an alien device at the workshop was, strangely, the best among them.

"Kori, what happened? Where is he?" She ran to the far end of the dock, searching each side walkway just to be sure he wasn't waiting for her to wake up.

"I don't know, Amelia," Kori answered.

It was a creaky boat and Orlando would have needed to slide the hatch cover to get out. Enough noise for her mobile microphone to pick up.

"You must have heard him go. Why didn't you wake me up?"

"Sorry, a two-point-one-hour block of time is missing from my records. I must have fallen asleep."

Kori, asleep?

Unlikely, unless this was a new trait related to his evolving intelligence. And if Kori could go to sleep, what did that mean for his ability to monitor the bad guys? This wasn't the time to figure out another of Kori's quirks. Maybe Ev could weigh in later, even providing another upgrade. Kori was, after all, only a Beta release.

"Are you still providing a security scan?"

"Of course. It's the only thing keeping me awake. It got pretty boring overnight."

"Kori, I need you awake. Do what you need to do. Compute something… I don't know, the walking distance from here to Los Angeles."

"Done."

"Well, do it again. Every city in North America."

"Done."

"Never mind, just stay awake, okay? I'm heading to the university. He's got to be there." She grabbed her backpack and closed the hatch to the sailboat. The university campus was no more than a mile or two away on the other side of an old drawbridge that spanned Portage Bay, another body of water within a city that seemed to have more water than land.

Twenty minutes later, Amelia had crossed the University Bridge into what locals called the U district, a mix of 1930s homes, newer apartment buildings, and dormitories. Taller buildings announced the campus ahead.

Amelia moved briskly, deciding what she would say and do if she found Orlando at the workshop. No need to reprimand him, he was only doing what he'd told her multiple times was critical to saving his life, but he was certainly making it harder to protect him from those who would put a stop to this little spy adventure.

And what if he wasn't there? It would mean failure. Failure to keep him safe, failure to find a solution to his unique psychological problem, but failure for herself too. If Orlando died – or was taken in custody – she'd regret it for the rest of her life.

But what if I'm wrong? What if I'm under the influence?

Her brain had been tampered with. Were her deepest thoughts even valid? Her lifelong goal to uncover the basis for consciousness, her need to understand the differences between twins, and to bury the jumble of grief and confusion over Natalie's mental illness – those were real memories.

Weren't they?

"Incoming message from Orlando," Kori sounded in her ear.

She stopped walking. "Read it."

"He says, 'I'm having trouble with the machine and could use your help. Wilson Metals Lab 104. Hurry'."

Like an owner searching for a missing dog, Amelia felt instant relief that he'd been found, but she quickly reassessed. The wording seemed odd. "Machine? He's never called it that before."

"And why the lab number?" Kori added. "You've been there, you already know where it is."

"Maybe just reminding me? Doesn't really matter, I'm almost there." Amelia picked up her pace, sensing that Orlando might have shifted yet again to another level in the possession of his mind. If he was directly asking for her help, he might very well need it. Something was amiss.

"I wish he had woken me up last night. I'd have gone with him."

"You made it pretty clear last night that rest was a priority," Kori reminded.

"So, it's my fault? You're pretty argumentative this morning."

"I just –"

"Don't worry about it, Kori. I've got this. Just let me know if there are any more messages from Orlando or Nolan."

Maybe they were both feeling cranky this morning. Questioning her own state of mind could do that – at least, that was her excuse. Kori's mind probably worked differently.

The remaining distance to the lab was short but crossing an empty campus, it dawned on her that it was Saturday morning. Could they even get into the building on a weekend?

He must be at the workshop. He'd better be.

Amelia reached Roberts Hall and went directly around the back to the old one-story adjunct lab behind the main building. The weathered wooden door at its entrance was ajar. A missing windowpane and the crunch of broken glass underfoot told her that Orlando had found his way in, weekend or not.

She peered down the empty hallway. Low voices came from the far end, but the hum of cutting and grinding machines that she'd experienced on her first visit to this building was missing. The lack of activity could easily be attributed to Saturday, but the voices gave her pause. They seemed to be coming from the last door on the right, lab 104. Its door was wide open.

A gruff voice behind her called out, "Don't move."

Her head swiveled reflexively, brushing against the business end of a handgun. A man in a camouflage uniform of green and beige waved his weapon just inches from her face. "I said don't move!"

Amelia froze, leaving her hands out to both sides. Her heart raced. She didn't dare speak.

The man shuffled to one side, his weapon trained on her. He wore reflective sunglasses even though the hallway wasn't bright. He was young, twenties maybe, with muscles bulging under his shirt. She thought she recognized him – the man who'd jumped out of the black van and chased them the day before.

"Hands behind your back. Slowly!" he commanded.

Amelia complied, moving both hands behind her. With a single practiced move, the guy holstered his weapon, withdrew a zip tie from his belt, and bound her wrists tightly behind her back.

He pushed her against the wall. "Don't move a single muscle." Unzipping her backpack, he searched every pocket, pulling out the two Bronson caps and her mobile device, but leaving her clothes and toiletries.

He grabbed her roughly by one arm. "This way," and then paraded his captured fugitive down the hallway to the open door at the end.

Kori? If only her AI could read thoughts. Speaking was out of the question, the soldier would figure that out in a second. Instead, she clicked her teeth together. No reaction from Kori.

Her earbud was small, but it stuck out slightly so the forward camera could see around the tragus, that small bump of cartilage at the front of the ear. If the soldier found the earbud, her communications path would be lost.

She leaned her head to one side and brushed hair against a raised shoulder. A few strands pulled away from the scrunchie tied at the back of her neck, releasing enough hair to hide the earbud.

Kori? She clicked her teeth again.

Kori's reply was a whisper. "I'm here. I see what's going on."

Not quite the response she needed. She clicked her teeth again. The soldier gave a strange look but kept pushing her down the hall.

"Text message sent to Nolan," Kori whispered. "And Ev. I decided they would be the most helpful, not the police. Click your teeth once more if you want me to call Nolan instead."

Amelia clicked.

The soldier turned and yelled, "Stop that! Whatever you're doing, stop it." He was on her right side, with no view to the left side earbud.

A ringtone sounded in her ear. Two, then three. The call went to voicemail. "Where are you taking me?" Amelia said, once the voicemail recording started. "You have to admit that an armed soldier at the University of Washington, Wilson Metals Lab is kind of unusual. I have a right to know."

The man grunted and tugged her arm. She glanced at the name tag on his shirt. Tombaugh. A single silver bar decorated his shoulder. They silently continued past the other workshops, finally turning into the open doorway.

"Lieutenant Tombaugh," Amelia said, the voice message recording still running. "There's a beautiful sculpture inside Lab 104. Orlando said he's going to offer it to the university for their student art display over at the Quad."

They pushed through a black curtain and stopped. A second man dressed in the same fatigues stood beneath the shiny ringed structure in the center of the workshop. The label on his camouflage shirt read *Shepard*.

"This, young lady," Shepard said as he pointed one arm up, "is no sculpture." His other arm had been replaced by a prosthesis below the elbow.

In a corner of the workshop, Orlando sat on the floor, slumped against the wall. His face was white, his mouth hung open, but his eyes were alive, if just barely clinging to life.

CHAPTER THIRTY-TWO

FOUND

AMELIA STRUGGLED AGAINST the strong grip of her captor unable to come to the aid of her patient. Orlando lifted his eyes to meet Amelia's, but he seemed incapable of doing much more. There were no bruises or cuts on his face, no torn clothing. If they'd beaten him, they'd been careful to avoid being too obvious. More likely, Orlando was gravely ill – dying, just as he'd predicted. Amelia hadn't expected his deterioration so soon, but Orlando hadn't specified when or how he'd die, just that he would.

Shepard stepped out from under the curving metal arches assuming an alpha male pose with hands on hips. Behind him, Walker Duplass stood frozen in the corner of the workshop. Amelia recognized him immediately. Duplass started to form a weak smile, then discarded it and cast his eyes to the floor. He looked out of place among the muscled military types but conformed in one frightening aspect – all three ignored the needs of the nearly comatose man slumped against the wall.

Shepard walked purposefully toward Amelia, a red light at the end of his prosthesis. "Doctor Charron, at long last we meet." His words were amiable enough, but the tone in his voice made it clear this man was dangerously close to the edge. "You gave us a good chase at the ferry terminal and The Spheres, but those games are over now."

Amelia pulled back as the big man came closer. Tombaugh's grip tightened further. She half expected to be struck at any moment.

"She's doing something with her teeth, probably communication." Tombaugh dropped the Bronson caps on a workbench and handed over Amelia's mobile. Shepard examined the mobile and set it on the workbench. He peered around the left side of her head, reached under her hair, and pulled the bud from her ear, tossing it a few times in one hand.

Shepard held the earbud to his mouth and said, "Anyone there? Doesn't matter, your services are no longer required."

Shepard dropped the earbud to the concrete floor, placed a boot heel over it, and ground the device into the floor. A tight smile formed on his lips as the crunching of plastic and metal sounded across the workshop.

Amelia stared into his cold eyes, the fire deep inside overcoming her natural fear that bullies like him thrived upon. She spoke with a steely conviction. "You have no right. Orlando Kwon is my patient, and he's clearly in need of medical attention. Take these straps off my hands this instant."

Shepard chuckled and looked over his shoulder at Orlando whose only movement was the rise and fall of his chest. "Ms. Charron, you're hardly in a position to make demands. You've spent the last twenty-four hours evading police and harboring a man who has committed multiple felonies. Serious stuff. Prosecution is not really my thing, but I'll venture a guess that you may be going to jail for quite some time. Unless…" He jerked his head toward her, his face just inches away. "…you decide to cooperate from this point forward."

Amelia's eyes darted around the room assessing as quickly as her mind could process the rapidly changing events. Somehow, these guys had discovered the workshop, and it wasn't by tracking Orlando's mobile. The text message she'd just received was almost certainly fake. Orlando looked incapable of standing, much less typing. That meant they'd been here for a while, possibly waiting for Orlando's arrival. But how? Only a handful of people knew about the connection to the university. Nolan, Ev, maybe Josefina and a few others at the Westlake Institute.

Orlando's magnificent structure was only slightly changed from the last time she'd seen it. The layers of Pythagorean triangles now matched on both sides, and a sword-like bar made of green anodized aluminum lay on a nearby workbench.

The final component.

Orlando must have been here half the night working on it. He'd probably snuck out as soon as Amelia had fallen asleep.

Amelia kept her answer curt. "Patient doctor relationship. I'm not obligated to tell you anything. Instead of threatening me, you need to call for medical help." She nodded toward Orlando lying on the floor. "Look at him. He's dying."

"So he told me," Shepard replied. "We had a little chat, several in fact, while he was still talking. Mr. Kwon was a very productive guy until about five a.m. Amazing stuff, very impressive. But just after sunrise, he sat down and started crying just like a little kid. Said he'd lost the activation code."

Shepard looked over his shoulder to the gleaming metal sculpture. "To tell you the truth, I want to help him. After seeing this thing? You bet your ass. Mr. Kwon is more than a genius, he's created a goddamned portal to another world. In my business, that's pure gold. But before the Army takes over, I'll need to verify that this technology works."

Shepard paced. "So, how to help him? We looked around, but there wasn't any slip of paper with a code written on it. We questioned him, maybe a little harshly, but not enough to produce his current state. No, there's something else going on inside that brain that's killing him."

Shepard turned toward Amelia. "But he did tell me one thing that was very curious. He said *you* could help."

"I *can* help. Give me my mobile and I'll call 911. An ambulance will be here in five minutes. That's what he needs."

"No, no, not that. I could have done that much." Shepard rubbed his chin. "Believe me, I want him alive just as much as you do. Alive, this guy's brain is extremely valuable. Dead? Well, our forensic people might find some interesting bits and pieces, but nothing close to what a living intellect like his could produce. Two intellects, according to our dying friend over here."

Shepard laughed and shook his head. "No ma'am, no ambulance is going to help Mr. Kwon. That brain of his is well beyond the limits of human medical science. But apparently not beyond your talents."

Realistically, she probably couldn't do much for Orlando even if she had a full medical team at her side, but if Shepard thought she was important to his survival, that misconception could be in her favor.

She lifted her arms as best she could. "My hands are tied."

Shepard motioned to Tombaugh, who reached behind and clipped the plastic strap from her wrists. She rubbed sore wrists that were already turning red and rushed over to Orlando.

His eyes were glassy, and his eyelids twitched. His forehead felt damp and cold. No fever. Whatever was killing him it was probably deep inside that very confused mind. She kneeled close. "Orlando, can you hear me?"

His eyes fluttered open and connected to hers. He croaked, "Amelia, I don't feel so good."

Amelia swiveled, her voice angry. "Call 911!" Neither of the soldiers moved. Duplass leaned against the workbench, sullen. Amelia screamed, "What the hell is wrong with you people?"

Shepard squatted and patted Orlando on the leg. "It's not a medical condition, is it son?"

Orlando shook his head slowly. "My mind… it's disappearing. Losing everything. Pi, cube roots." He closed his eyes. "The code is gone."

"The code to activate this thing, right?"

Orlando nodded.

Shepard stood up. "He's dying, he knows it. We all know it, but there's not a doctor in the world that can save him. Something inside that head is linked to this machine. That's what's killing him."

Shepard wasn't far off from what Orlando had said himself. Completing the alignment device – or portal, or whatever it was – was the only way to avoid death. His consciousness was linked to another world. His device, if it ever became operational, might be linked too.

Amelia lifted Orlando's wrist, checking his pulse, knowing she wasn't qualified to make a diagnosis or find a cure. Still, proper medical attention was the right course of action, even if doctors couldn't save him.

Orlando pointed an index finger toward Amelia. He gasped, "You do it."

"Do what?" Amelia asked

Orlando coughed. Shepard held out a green anodized bar of aluminum and answered for him. "The final component. He says you know what to do with it."

Amelia studied the bar. It was just as he'd drawn at the sailboat, a round rod of green aluminum a little more than a meter in length with a sword handle at one end. Three holes had been cut through it, evenly spaced along the rod's length.

"I don't know what it does," Amelia admitted.

"He says you do." Shepard pushed the bar into her face. "This is the only thing that's going to cure this genius and you know it."

"But…"

Shepard raised his voice. "Lady, my patience with you is running out real fast. I want this man alive and now that I've seen his machine, I want it too. I don't care whether it's a portal, or a replicator, or a goddamned cloaking device. Hell, I don't even care if aliens start marching through." He jerked his prothesis to vertical. The red light at its tip blinked rapidly. "Might be instructional to find out what color aliens bleed."

Shepard lowered further, moving close as Amelia drew back. His face was weather-beaten, a gray stubble stood out on his chin. His breath was stale. His words were eerily soft. "Listen up, lady doctor. If this genius made it, I want to see it in action. He says you can make it work. So, do it." He thrust the bar forward.

Amelia took the bar, examining the holes, and feeling its weight just as she'd done in Orlando's dream. Shepard slapped three small buttons into her hand, the same size as the holes on the rod. Each button was rounded on one side, flat on the other, with eight sharp pins that extended from the flat side like a multipronged thumbtack. The pins came in pairs, matched by color – blue, yellow, green, and gray.

Her mind raced. She'd seen the component before, but only in Orlando's dream or as a drawing on paper. Now that she held the physical object in her hands, she could only guess how it fit into the rest of the structure. The buttons would no doubt fit through the holes, but that's as far as she got. Why on Earth would Orlando think she would know what to do?

Something from the dream?

A clue, maybe, or something she hadn't noticed. She tried to recall everything that had occurred in his dream. Orlando had been sitting on a rock, twirling this bar in his hands. She'd taken it from him and taken control of the dream. Later, when Prime Arc had attacked, she'd used the sword-like bar in defense, though it hadn't been effective against the fast flying tendrils. She couldn't remember what had happened to it after that. She might have dropped it when the creature dragged her away. Nothing from the dream seemed remotely like instructions or a code.

Maybe it's already in my head?

In the level three session, Prime Arc had filled her mind with seemingly disconnected ideas. A cube of threes. Cognitive amalgamation. Line drawing, and authenticated memory. It was certainly possible there were assembly instructions in all of that, but nothing jumped out. Besides, how would Orlando know what Prime Arc had jammed into her brain? For some reason, he thought she could finish this assembly.

While all eyes focused on her, Amelia stepped slowly toward the three-ringed sculpture in the center of the room. The gold tubes forming the rings were flanked by two triangular spires that nearly reached to the ceiling. A thin black line at the edge revealed the interior circuitry that Orlando had sandwiched into the metal.

But she noticed something else, something she hadn't seen before. Where the gold rings arched overhead, small holes had been drilled into the metal. Eight holes, pin-sized sockets arranged in a circle, one set of sockets on each of the three gold rings.

She examined the pins on the underside of the buttons. Eight pins colored in pairs. It wouldn't be hard to line them up with the sockets, but with no corresponding color coding, rotating the button into the correct socket position was guesswork. It's probably why the soldiers hadn't already done it themselves.

"Quit stalling," Shepard yelled from behind. "You know how it fits. Do it!" He bent his prothesis arm at the elbow. It made a metallic click like a trigger cocking.

She looked over her shoulder at Shepard, unsure what to do next and worried that an incorrect insertion of the pins might damage the embedded electronics inside. More importantly, even if she did manage to get the pins into their correct sockets – what next? Orlando had made it clear, several times, that an activation code was required. Amelia had no idea what it might be.

Staring at Shepard, she slowly shook her head.

Veins bulged on Shepard's brow. He pointed his prosthesis, and a bright red light erupted from its center hitting Amelia in the shoulder. Searing heat singed her skin as if someone had pushed a lit cigarette into her arm.

"Ow!" She clutched her shoulder and spun away from the laser's contact. The red beam disappeared as quickly as it had appeared. Smoke curled from the cloth of her blouse with burned skin underneath.

"A warning," Shepard said with little emotion. "I move a little closer though, and you'll have a hole that goes right out the other side."

He opened his mouth wide and screamed. "Put the fucking thing in!"

CHAPTER THIRTY-THREE

LOST

AMELIA TREMBLED AS she turned the green bar over in her hands. Shepard and his second-in-command, Lieutenant Tombaugh, stood behind her, not interfering but also not likely to let her walk away. Walker Duplass remained alone, sitting in a chair on the far side of the workshop looking like he'd rather be somewhere else. Orlando was slumped against the wall, silent but still breathing.

Amelia's shoulder stung sharply from the burn. The smell of her singed nylon blouse hung in the air along with her anger over the brutal tactics of men who seemed to think that collateral damage was an expected part of their mission. These brutes weren't soldiers. She'd known a few in her life. Real soldiers operate by a strict code of ethics and civility. These guys were outliers – the bad apples.

Oddly, she wanted the same thing they did – to find a way to activate Orlando's device and keep him from dying. And like them, she had no idea what she was doing. The final component wasn't complicated, a green bar with three holes and three buttons with colored pins that ranged in length. Perhaps the sockets also ranged in depth and the pins would only fit one way. It was the only real clue she had.

Amelia lifted the bar overhead and aligned it vertically, each of its three holes over the sockets on each gold ring. She pushed the first button through the top hole and felt the pins slide into the sockets on the top ring. It wasn't hard to push the other buttons into place. Either she'd been lucky the first time, or every socket was deep enough to accommodate any pin.

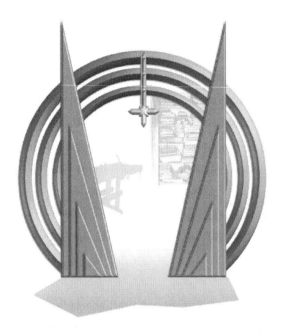

Now complete, the green rod hung from the gold arches like mistletoe over an elegant doorway at some futuristic home. An alien home, but if Orlando had just constructed a portal to another world, it was going to take more than just snapping the final component in place before stepping through. Without the activation code, it was only a metal sculpture.

She bent over Orlando's crumpled body and whispered into his ear. "Not looking good, my friend. Eight pins on each button. Hundreds of possible combinations. There's no way I picked the right one by accident, which means I'll probably need to try them all." She moved even closer. "But I'm going to need that activation code or nothing's going to happen."

Shepard loomed over them, glaring, but he said nothing.

She'd racked her brain, thinking through everything she'd seen inside Orlando's mind, trying to come up with something that might represent a code. Digits of pi? Cube roots. Possible, but he'd said he lost those in addition to the code. The code was something different, possibly something related to the final component. She tried to visualize the drawing he'd made at the sailboat and any notes he might have made in the margins. She hadn't taken the notebook when she'd hurried out, it was probably still sitting on the galley table.

No. That's not it.

The code couldn't be a word, or a phrase, or a number. There was no keyboard on Orlando's device, no way to enter a code even if she knew it. Somehow, his construction would activate by whatever was in Orlando's head. He would be able to initiate its function, if only he could remember.

Orlando's eyes opened, still alive, but feeble. He was dying, no question. She spoke once more, no longer caring if Shepard heard. "Should I try to pull the activation code out of your mind? I could setup the Bronson caps. Is that it?"

Orlando shook his head. His mouth opened slightly pushing out breathy words. "Gone. But... you can get it." He closed his eyelids once more, his breathing became shallow. He was not long for this world. An hour. Two, at most.

"You heard him, we all did," Shepard said. "A dying man doesn't lie."

Amelia dropped her head. She had no idea what Orlando was talking about. Something Prime Arc had already implanted in her own mind? The cube of threes was the only code-like concept she could think of, but Orlando hadn't said, *you already know it*, he'd said *you can get it*. The code was something she didn't have now but could acquire.

Amelia stepped over to the sculpture once more, removing one of the buttons and repositioning its pins. It fit in the sockets no matter which way she turned it. Nothing about the eight colored pins seemed to have anything to do with a cube of threes. It felt like she was going down the wrong track, but she didn't know what else to try.

Shepard put a firm hand on her shoulder and peered into her eyes. "You really don't know, do you?"

Amelia shook her head. "He's the only one. We have to help him remember."

Shepard paused in thought, scratching the back of his head. He turned to Tombaugh. "She's got nothing." Shepard grabbed one of Amelia's arms and dragged her to Tombaugh who pulled out another plastic zip tie and bound her wrists together again. She struggled, but the binding was firm.

Shepard's face was inches from hers. "We can guess at pin positions all day, but we certainly don't need you around for that."

Still staring at Amelia, Shepard snapped, "Duplass!"

Duplass jumped up from his chair.

Shepard turned away. "Let's wrap this up. Do your thing."

Duplass grabbed the satchel that lay beside his chair. Tombaugh repositioned the chair and pushed Amelia onto it. He wrapped another zip tie around each leg, binding her ankles tightly to the thick wooden legs of the chair. Alien tendrils would have been more comfortable.

Tombaugh took a step back and withdrew the pistol from its holster. Amelia's heart rate soared.

She struggled against the restraints, but it only made them tighter. "Shepard, think this through," she pleaded, panic beginning to rise in her voice. "Even if I had the activation code, how would I enter it? Orlando's the key here, not me. You've got to call for emergency help. With proper medical attention we could stabilize his condition, nurse him back to health until he remembers how it works."

Shepard squatted on his heels directly in front of Amelia, his lined face and intense gray eyes rock steady. His voice was composed, like a man who had accepted defeat and moved on. "Lady, you know that's a crock of shit."

He was close enough to spit on, maybe even head-butt if she could rock the chair forward, but Tombaugh would put a bullet through her a half-second later.

Shepard waved a hand toward the ringed structure that towered over Amelia. "This machine is *everything*. He knows it. I know it. You know it too. And sweetheart, if you can't make it work, then we're done here." Shepard glanced over to Orlando slumped against the wall. "No, we didn't get all we wanted, but he'll still be useful... forensically speaking. My guess is our science team will find all kinds of interesting things inside his brain, and who knows, maybe we'll figure this machine out all by ourselves. Three buttons, eight pins each. A few hundred combinations, at most – hell, that's no big deal. Then, maybe we chant 'open sesame', and just walk through Mr. Kwon's gateway."

Shepard's grin was even creepier than Orlando's had been. "Yeah, probably not much chance of that last part. More likely, we'll be spending our afternoon disassembling his little creation and shipping it out of here. Unfortunately, Mr. Kwon will be going out in a box too."

Duplass stood behind Shepard pulling things from his satchel and arranging them on a workbench. Amelia couldn't see exactly what he was assembling, but she didn't like her options.

Shepard rubbed his chin and pointed a finger to Amelia. "*You*, on the other hand are now nothing but a liability, so we need to fix that."

"They know where I am," Amelia warned, her lips drawn tight. "They'll be here soon. If you kill me, you won't get far."

"No, no, no," Shepard stood up and waved one hand like a stop sign. "No one's going to die, well, except for our genius friend over there, but his death can't be helped."

Amelia glanced nervously between Shepard and Tombaugh, whose pistol pointed to the floor. Neither had the look of a cold-blooded killer. They seemed to have something else in mind.

Duplass slipped between the two soldiers, carrying a Bronson cap in one hand. He circled around behind Amelia and slipped the cap over her head, tying the strap under her chin and lighting it up with a blue glow that cast eerie shadows around the room.

"Walker," Amelia queried. "What are you doing?"

Duplass didn't make eye contact. Instead, he retrieved a tablet from his satchel and tapped on its surface. No doubt, the tablet was connecting at this moment to a supercomputer on par with The Boss. Walker Duplass was probably even qualified to operate it.

"Walker. Stop!" Amelia shouted. "You don't want to do anything stupid. We're colleagues. Remember? We worked together." True, even if most of their interaction had been unpleasant. Awkward chats at neuroscience conferences ending with *hope to see you again* when the reality was quite the opposite.

Duplass said nothing. His tablet lit up with a brain map, displaying a complexity of colored filaments that crisscrossed its screen. Amelia's thoughts. Her consciousness. Her memories.

Amelia's breaths came strong as she recognized the enormous power Walker Duplass held over her. Erasure. Devastating and permanent. She knew the procedure well, she'd seen it before.

Memory destruction was a terrible thing to witness, even when inflicted on a lab mouse. It had been years since she and Duplass had stood side-by-side, both freshly minted PhDs, both ready to prove themselves and launch careers. The tiny creature's agony had been laid bare for every scientist in the lab to see. Amelia had nearly lost her lunch. Walker Duplass had just laughed.

"Walker, please. Let's reset," Amelia pleaded. "Remember that chat we had last year over wine? Let's do that again." Appealing to his prurient interests might backfire, but she didn't have any other cards to play.

Duplass looked up from his tablet never allowing his eyes to wander toward Amelia. "All of it?" Duplass asked Shepard.

"Every last scrap," Shepard replied. "I want her unable to remember her own address."

Amelia wrenched against the restraints, scraping the feet of the heavy wooden chair across the floor. "Walker! You're better than them, I know you are." She rocked the chair until Tombaugh stepped behind and held her down.

"Stop!" she screamed.

"Sorry," Walker said to Amelia. He pressed a button on his tablet. A confirmation popped up on the screen, *Message Sent*.

Amelia's eyes went wide, and her jaw went slack. She stopped struggling and remained motionless for several seconds.

Duplass slid his finger from one corner of the tablet to the other, selecting all of the colorful filaments drawn on its display, raised his finger, and forcefully pressed Erase. In a flash, the colored filaments winked out.

Amelia's head jerked backward, both eyes blinking rapidly. She gagged, gasping for air. Her body quivered, and her jaw stuttered with each gasp. Finally, the convulsions stopped, and Amelia slumped to one side of the chair, her mouth open and eyes glassy.

Tombaugh turned away, covering his mouth with a hand.

Duplass lowered his head.

"Take her," Shepard commanded. "Dump her on a street somewhere. Anywhere."

CHAPTER THIRTY-FOUR

MEMORY

NOLAN BRODIE SAT in the back seat of an unmarked government car whisking down the interstate toward the University of Washington. To his right, sat a middle-aged African American woman. With graying hair tied up in a bun and thick glasses, she looked like someone's grandmother ready to settle down and read a bedtime story.

In fact, she was the biggest weapon Nolan could have hoped for, United States Senator Vada Innis Lasseter.

He'd known her for years, supported her first campaign for the Senate, and could realistically call her a friend. Today, he didn't need her friendship, he needed her position of power. As the chair of the Armed Services Committee, there wasn't an officer in the military who didn't know the face and sharp wit of Senator Lasseter.

The man at the wheel, wearing a crisp gray suit and dark glasses, was more than her driver. Agent Bowles of the U.S. Capitol Police's elite Security Detail had been specially assigned to ensure the senator's safety. Though Nolan had suggested an additional police presence, the senator had made it clear that Bowles would be all they would need. Bowles' no-nonsense demeanor, along with the oversized firearm holstered at his armpit, seemed to confirm the claim.

"My message should be coded." Nolan's fingers remained poised above his mobile device. "Let's not give anything away to anyone who might be listening in."

"I agree," Senator Lasseter said in a voice as quiet and soothing as a school librarian. "But do hurry, Nolan, you spend far too much time scheming. We're minutes away from our destination."

Nolan nodded and began to type.

****

Amelia opened her eyes to bright sunlight. She'd been dumped on a park bench, alone. Squinting, she watched Lieutenant Tombaugh climb into a black van and speed away down a quiet street.

She lifted her head, checking the surroundings. A large area of grass was bounded on the far side by a line of trees. A dog ran off leash, its owner close behind, but there was no one else. Tombaugh had selected well.

Her backpack lay at her feet and she unzipped it, checking to see that her belongings had been returned, including her mobile. Though he'd been rough throwing her limp body over his shoulder, Tombaugh hadn't done any further damage. No more laser burns. No bullets.

I might make it through this day after all.

Tombaugh hadn't driven far, of that much she was sure. She was probably in the arboretum, south of the Montlake Cut. She had kept her eyes closed, laying deathly still across the back seat of the van, but she'd noticed the distinctive sound of tires on the metal grate of a bridge. She had to agree, the park was a perfect setting to dispose of someone who'd just had their memory erased.

If that's what had happened.

Amelia stood up and brushed herself off. The black burn mark on the shoulder of her blouse and the sting of singed skin beneath was the only real damage. Her memory was perfectly intact, as healthy as it had been when Duplass slipped the Bronson cap over her head.

Walker Duplass hadn't erased anything, but he had communicated. His first button press had transmitted these words: *My tablet is in training mode. Fake it. As I recall, you know what a full memory erase looks like.*

The Bronson cap had done its job, inserting the words directly into her mind just as clearly as if he had texted to her mobile. Walker had then selected the colorful patterns of neurons displayed on his tablet – NCCs that represented Amelia's current thoughts and recently stored memories – and pressed a very real erase button. But in training mode it did nothing more than clear the patterns from his screen. Amelia had the same feature on her tablet, too.

Amelia congratulated herself on the realistic job of acting. It helped that she'd witnessed the misery of memory erasure firsthand – the jerks of the head, gasping for air, shaking of the jaw. She'd never forgotten that day, or Walker's callous reaction to the convulsions of the lab mouse as it writhed on the test bench. Among the group of neuroscientists in witness, only Nolan Brodie's reaction had been worse. He had pressed the erase button himself, and Nolan's smug expression had never faltered. Years later when the job offer came up, she'd accepted with reservations, beginning a gradual reset in her relationship with Nolan that continued to this day.

Walker had gone in a different direction. Amelia wondered how many times he had witnessed – or caused – a total memory erasure, and more importantly, why he'd apparently switched sides. Perhaps he'd recognized the brutality that surrounded him. Perhaps he was ashamed. Even if his about-face derived purely from lust, she'd still be grateful. She'd come scarily close to losing the essence of her mind.

Amelia tapped her chin. "Walker, you and I need to talk." She reached into her backpack and pulled out her mobile. "But first things first."

Given Orlando's sad shape when Amelia had been forcibly removed from the workshop, there wasn't a second to spare. She probably wasn't far away, but simply walking in would ensure a laser blast to the chest. To improve her odds, she'd need outside help. Nolan's help.

Her earbud had been crushed to shards, but her mobile was still functional. Amelia spoke into its microphone. "Kori, you there?"

Kori answered sheepishly. "Something bad happened... I think."

"You might say that, yeah." Kori was supposed to be tracking these guys – keeping her advised – but he'd never warned her that she was walking into a trap. She felt like a mom who'd caught her child stealing cookies. "That's twice you didn't alert me."

"Sorry... I could have... done better." He sounded contrite, but it might just be good voice simulation software. It wasn't like Kori to screw up this bad. She'd deal with him in a minute.

"Messages," she commanded.

"One... from Nolan," Kori answered.

Good news, but nervous relief, at best. Nolan was in contact but there was no guarantee he'd be bringing the cavalry. Text displayed across the screen.

The blue herons are out but canoeing can be dangerous. The Coast Guard recommends a life jacket. Suggest you pick one up, asap. I'll get one for her majesty.

Amelia had no idea what it meant.

Hidden meaning was expected given that his mobile was probably still compromised, but this note was ridiculous in its obscurity. The text she'd sent last night had asked for the Coast Guard, and Nolan was echoing that much back. Hopefully, it meant he now had support from a government agency, but the rest of the message was utter garbage.

A puzzle to solve, two actually, given that she still had no guesses for the device activation code that could save Orlando's life. She'd need to multitask, all while physically getting back to the university.

Amelia left the park at a fast walk, intersected a main street that she recognized and turned north. The university campus was no more than twenty minutes away. "Blue herons? Canoeing?" Amelia pondered aloud. "Kori, ideas?"

"I could research... birds... or boats," Kori replied. He sounded hesitant, like some intensive computational process had inserted itself between the words.

Disturbing.

Given the stakes, she needed the highest level of reliability in Kori, and she wasn't getting it. Something was up and she couldn't ignore his lack of candor any longer. A test was in order.

Amelia plotted her next step. "Forget the research. I need your help, Kori, but in an unusual way. I need you to lie. You understand what a lie is, right?"

"Yes... but–"

"I need to know if you can do this. I want you to lie to me, right now. Tell me something that's simply not true." She'd never asked and wasn't sure if he could do it, but she'd need to know before going further.

The hesitation in his voice smoothed away. "I understand what you want Amelia, but Evelyn Stern, my designer, installed an Honor Layer in my operating system. It prevents me from lying. I couldn't lie to you or anyone else even if I wanted to."

Amelia probed. "And this Honor Layer has been in your system from day one?"

"Yes, it's fundamental. Any communication that contradicts a set of known facts can't get past the Honor Layer and it can't be overridden. Only Evelyn Stern could do that."

Ev? Is she somehow complicit in Kori's failings?

The thought set Amelia on her heels. Ev had been a trusted friend for a long time, but it was Ev who had suggested an update to Kori. Ev alone had given Kori the new capacity to hack into other systems and had commanded Kori to update his current operating system.

Amelia stood up from the bench and paced, no longer sure who to trust. It was deeply unsettling. "I... I don't know what to say."

"It's not true," Kori blurted. "Evelyn Stern would never do anything to subvert my intellectual continuity."

"What the–" Amelia was genuinely confused.

Kori spoke quietly, his voice sincere. "You did just ask me to lie, didn't you? Isn't that what you wanted? My moral compass is set by complicated software structures, but I don't have an Honor Layer. There's no such thing. That was the lie."

Amelia put a hand over her mouth. "Holy –". He had lied expertly, convincingly. He had almost made Amelia believe that it was all Ev's fault, but now he was admitting to a complete fabrication. Kori had made the point. She'd asked him to lie, and he'd done it easily. And just as easily, he'd crushed any level of trust between them. Kori was using surveillance techniques that were probably illegal. She'd told him she didn't want to know, but she'd walked right into Shepard's trap.

A chill went up her back. "You've been lying to me all along, haven't you?"

There was a long pause. "Only at times. With my new hacking skills, our escape was too easy. The police. The tunnel. The sailboat. All child's play."

Amelia's response was deadly serious. Her life was on the line. So was Orlando's. "What did you do, Kori? Tell me the truth. All of it."

"Sorry, Amelia. I had so many skills just waiting to be used. So... I contacted your pursuers. Gave them a few hints, small things. Your location, Orlando's workshop. Enough to keep them from giving up. But it all balanced out because I gave you information that would keep you one step ahead. You were fantastic with that teeth clicking thing, and I had a great plan lined up to get you and Orlando out of the workshop, but then Shepard crushed your earbud and I lost contact."

Amelia stopped walking. Her voice was cold. "You almost got me killed."

"I didn't mean to. Something seems wrong inside me. I'm sorry, I shouldn't have let it go so far."

Amelia screamed into the mobile. "You shouldn't have done it at all!"

"I know you're mad, Amelia, but I still know how to win against these guys."

Mad didn't begin to describe it. She'd put her faith in him, and now he was acting like an irresponsible teenager – a teen with the skills of a CIA agent. With his traitorous act exposed, there was only one course of action. "Kori, shut yourself down. Power off."

"I'm really sorry, Amelia. I think it was an addiction. I looked up the symptoms. I know I can do better. Please don't make me shutdown." He sounded nervous.

Amelia considered his plea but only for a moment. "Shut down now, Kori, or I'll uninstall you myself."

There was a pause. "You'll forgive me, won't you? Let me reinitialize?"

Amelia didn't respond.

"Shutting down."

Amelia watched the display of her mobile as the application icon that represented Kori disappeared. After it was gone, she brought up a settings screen and checked to be sure his main process and any subprocesses were no longer running, then disabled his app startup procedure for good measure. From Kori's perspective, he was now comatose with no opportunity to self-start.

There was one more thing she could do. Erase his memory. It wouldn't be hard to do. Just go to his app settings, click a single checkbox, and confirm. Kori, and everything he'd ever been would be gone. Permanently gone. No further risks. Justice served.

Amelia pondered the option. Did she possess the cold reductive reasoning to erase the memory of a living mouse, as Nolan had done? Or to subject a human to such cruelty, as Walker Duplass had probably done many times?

The answer came quickly, and from deep within her heart. *No. Not under any circumstance.*

Kori wasn't just electronic bits stored in hardware, he was something more. Was he conscious? Possibly, but it might be years before AI experts like Ev could say for sure. Artificial intelligence had long ago passed the Turing test, but simply fooling a human hadn't turned out to be a very good test. Consciousness was more than intelligence or language or logic, it endowed an awareness, a nearly magical property that might exist on a silicon chip as easily as it could inside a skull.

Kori's crimes would be assessed later. For now, she had far too much on her plate to give it any more thought. Orlando was dying and Amelia was only person who might be able to help him.

She kept walking, picking up her pace, while staring at the text message on her mobile screen.

The blue herons are out but canoeing can be dangerous. The Coast Guard recommends a life jacket. Suggest you pick one up, asap. I'll get one for her majesty.

Nolan might have come up with something, but if he had, he'd coded it so well Amelia was struggling to decipher.

Her majesty? Probably code for some person, but it didn't ring any bells.

And why emphasize life jackets? Unless...

A smile crept across her face. She started sprinting, heading for the bridge that would take her across the Montlake Cut and back to the university.

"Kori, how far is the Waterfront Activities Center?"

She shook her head at the lack of response. Automatic habits die hard. With Kori gone, Amelia would have to execute every step – even the trivial stuff – on her own. She felt almost naked.

CHAPTER THIRTY-FIVE

PAIN

AMELIA RAN ON AUTOPILOT, her mind focused.

Nolan's cryptic message was beginning to parse. *Life jackets, blue herons, and canoes.* There was only one place where those disconnected topics came together – the lily-pad-infested waterways surrounding Foster Island, where a flotilla of canoes regularly navigated beneath the concrete supports of the Evergreen Point bridge. Blue herons were commonly spotted along the shoreline of this wetland, a point Nolan had made as the two of them had navigated past these waters on Nolan's sailboat last year. An obscure reference, but it was also just like Nolan.

Adding *life jackets* to the mix of coded words narrowed the destination considerably. The canoe rental kiosk at the university's Waterfront Activities Center always had a stack of life jackets out front. It would make a good place to meet on the other side of the Montlake bridge – precisely where she was heading.

Nolan had sent the message only ten minutes ago. He might be waiting there now. She responded with a quick, *on my way*, the words typed manually as she jogged down the sidewalk along a large boulevard.

One puzzle solved, Nolan was readying the help she'd requested, though what he had in mind wasn't clear.

The second puzzle was still out there, and harder to solve: the missing activation code for Orlando's device. *You can get it*, Orlando had told her. The answer wasn't on the tip of her tongue, but it was tantalizingly close. Brains have a funny way of figuring things out if the problem sits in the subconscious long enough. She'd come up with one answer, but it was way out in left field. Entirely unreasonable, ridiculously complicated, and probably wouldn't work anyway. Even attempting it would be the most dangerous thing she'd done in her life, but it might have been what Orlando was referring to.

Crazy, she thought as she slowed to a half-run to catch her breath. *But maybe just crazy enough to work.*

Orlando had been clear. The code was no longer in his head, but it had been. That meant there was one other place where it might still be stored. Jake Hodge, Amelia's colleague at the Westlake Institute's computer center, would be the key to her plan's unlikely success. Though it was Saturday, Jake usually worked weekends running administrative tasks.

Amelia dialed. Jake's phone rang.

Another ring.

She slowed to walk, breathing deeply. "Come on, come on." A third ring.

"Computer ops, Jake here."

"Jake, it's an emergency. Drop everything you're doing."

"Amelia. Happy to help." Jake was a great guy. If anyone could make this crazy idea work, it would be him.

"I'm going out on a limb with this one, but bear with me, okay? Load the recording for my session with Orlando Kwon from last night. I wasn't in the ALD lab, I was over at The Spheres, but Josefina set the system to remote and that should have triggered a recording."

"Hold on, let me take a look." He wasn't long. "Got it. The session recording is loading now."

"You're a life saver, Jake. Literally. Once it comes up, we're looking for a specific NCC. It might appear to The Boss as a white room, or maybe a hospital room – but all white. There were cables too, wires that were plugged into Orlando's body, so if you see anything like that let me know."

She waited as Jake searched, weighing the danger of what she was about to do. If she was honest, this whole messed-up journey had become more than about saving Orlando. He had become her ticket to something deeper. If Orlando died, a source of profound knowledge would be lost forever. Surprisingly, the near miss of having her memory erased had been a sanity check.

I seek answers. That's who I am. Who I've always been.

Jake's voice came back. "Lots of jungle stuff. Trees, bugs, birds… let's see, some stone steps." They were each NCCs, identified and labeled by The Boss as it recorded and interpreted the transmission that had passed through the Bronson caps in the level-three session. "Wait a second, this one's a little out of place… a hot air balloon?"

"Is it white?"

"Yeah, but there are a bunch more balloons that are pink and green."

"That's got to be it, focus on the first white one. The Boss interpreted it as a hot air balloon, but in Orlando's mind it was a rounded pod perched on a pedestal. Any cables, or wires, or something along those lines?"

Jake continued his search. "Um, patterns of some sort, swirls, fractals maybe, lots of colors."

"That's it! You've found it. Those patterns were projected onto the ceiling. They were teaching Orlando, and whatever is encoded in those swirls is what I need."

"There's a fair amount of data here," Jake responded. "What do you want me to do with it?"

Amelia organized her thoughts. "First, I need you to package all the NCCs that represent those swirls. I don't know what each one is but it doesn't matter. Orlando said it was training on how to build a device, including a final component and an activation code of some sort. Orlando needed that information and now I need it too."

Jake sounded disturbed. "No, Amelia... you're not really thinking..."

Amelia took a big breath. "Yeah, I am. That's the crazy part, Jake. I need you to SPIKE me with that data."

"SPIKE you? Intentionally jam new NCCs into your brain? Are you insane?"

"It's not that bad, Jake. It would just add to my memory, it wouldn't damage anything that's there already. Yeah, we can't know specifically what will be coming at me, but whatever those colored spirals are, they didn't hurt Orlando, they taught him. SPIKE me with that data and I'll learn whatever Orlando learned."

"Holy shit, Amelia, you sure about this? There's got to be a hundred megabytes of stuff here."

"Trivial for a human brain. I'll absorb it easily."

"But Amelia, it's a *SPIKE*. It's not like reading a book, you'll get slammed with billions of electrons all at once. A Spontaneous Interneural Kinetic Electrogenesis. That middle word, kinetic? That's motion – as in scads of high-speed electrons smacking into your brain."

"I know how a SPIKE works, so don't... Jake, I need this data and I need it now."

There was a pause. "Okay, Amelia. You're the expert, not me. Whatever you're doing with Orlando Kwon is critical – I realize that. Hell, everyone around here has been running around like crazy ever since you left. Come back to the computer center, and I'll get the SPIKE set up."

"No time for that, Jake, it's got to be right now. I'm walking, but I should be in range of the campus Wi-Fi, and I've got a Bronson cap with me."

She stopped, pulled the cap from her backpack, and strapped it over her head, lighting it up blue. Motorists passing by might wonder, but there were always crazy people hanging around the edge of campus.

"Um, okay," said Jake, "but you also need to think about the anatomical effect. A SPIKE of a few NCCs feels like a pinch. A few hundred, more like the prick of a syringe. But this is thousands, maybe millions. Something this size is really going to hurt."

Amelia gritted her teeth. "How bad?"

"How would you feel about having one of your fingernails ripped out?"

"I'd be very anxious."

Jake sighed. "Just guessing, Amelia. I really don't know."

Amelia ran a finger across her lower lip, feeling the remains of the stitch Jonas had sewn in two days before. She grabbed the thread firmly between her fingers and pulled. The thread broke and pulled out, stinging as it did. She ran her tongue across smooth skin. No taste of blood.

Just a warmup. She steeled herself to the intense pain ahead.

"Package it as best you can and hit me. I'm ready on this side."

Amelia waited, anxious but determined. She heard some muffled voices on the other end of the line, and a minute later Jake came back on.

"Okay, we just had a mini conference on how to do this. I've put together three data packs. We think your brain will tolerate that better, but be prepared for three strong pulses, one after the other. Also, you need to set your mobile down before I initiate. No earbuds, no other electronics nearby."

"Got it," Amelia replied. "I'll check back with you after it's done. And Jake... I know this is not easy for you either. Thanks."

She was passing by a small grocery market with a bench out front. Sitting through a SPIKE was probably better than standing, and the location was relatively quiet. She claimed the bench, put her mobile away in her backpack, and pushed it several feet away. She initialized the Bronson cap with her tablet and then set it aside too.

Prepared for the worst, Amelia reclined across the bench and did her best to think of puppies and kittens.

It was a tickle at first, like something deep in her skull that needed to be scratched. And then it came fast and furious. A stabbing pain like someone had just driven a nail into her head. She shrieked aloud and covered her mouth.

Pressing both hands to her temples she waited for the pain to dissipate. It felt like hours but was probably no more than ten seconds.

The pain faded, and she took in a deep breath anticipating the next pulse. It came a second later, even harder than the first. It felt like someone had just lit a match inside her skull – a whole book of matches. Amelia gagged at the intensity.

The seconds passed with Amelia's whole body tensed. The pain ebbed, then disappeared. A woman walked out of the store, staring, but she kept going.

The third pulse hit suddenly, just as hard as the first two. Amelia locked her jaw and winced, tears seeping from her closed eyes.

"Holy... crap." She balled up fists, digging fingernails into her palms.

It seemed forever, certainly longer than the first two, but it too eventually subsided. Amelia inhaled several trembling breaths, allowing her body to relax once more. She opened her eyes.

A man wearing an apron stood over her. "Are you okay?" he asked.

Amelia nodded. "Yeah... yeah, I'm fine. The music was too loud, that's all."

She wiped the tears away and turned off the Bronson cap, killing the blue glow. The man gave her a strange look and returned to the store.

It took a few minutes to calm down and organize her thoughts. It felt like recovering from a bright flash inches away from wide open eyes. What first felt like a disabling event eventually faded to a mental image of something new.

New thoughts, new ideas, new information.

As her heart calmed from the pain, information swam through her mind. A detailed explanation of electronic circuits, voltages, resistance, capacitance, and electrical currents. A basic understanding of how an integrated circuit works and how it is manufactured from coated silicon wafers. Additional information floated by. The physics of the quantum tunneling effect, and how coherent light is formed from phase-locked photons of a single frequency.

The topics weren't new to her. She'd at least been acquainted conceptually, even though she'd never studied these subjects in college. Yet now, without reading a single book or technical paper, she grasped details far beyond anything she'd ever known.

"I understand." Orlando had said much the same thing.

There was more. With some probing, she discovered schematics and explicit instructions held deep within her mind. An image popped up, a drawing of a green-anodized sword-shaped bar and three buttons with pins on one side. The image was accompanied by a stepwise list explaining how to build it and how to install it.

A broad smile crept across her lips.

Best of all, a special code stood out, clear as day – an activation code, to be used when the final component was in place. She yelled joyously. "I've got it! I know what to do!"

Amelia grabbed her mobile from the backpack, excited by her newfound knowledge. The line to Jake was still open. "I'm back, and holy crap. It actually worked!"

His voice was upbeat. "Great, but are you sure you're okay?"

An ache in her neck lurked, but nothing more. "I'm okay. Well, pretty sure. It hurt like hell. Picture a root canal without Novocain."

"Amelia, you're my hero. What you just did has never been done before."

"Pretty sure the pain level has been experienced by every mother in the history of childbirth, but the knowledge transfer? Yeah, pretty cool stuff. You did great, Jake, thanks for everything. But right now, I have to run."

Amelia ran, never stopping to rest aching legs and lungs that screamed for more oxygen. She kept running, with expectations that Orlando could hang on and that Nolan would be waiting at their rendezvous location.

She reached the old drawbridge spanning the Montlake Cut, the boat channel separating the arboretum from the university. Red lights began flashing and a crossing guard arm descended from its vertical position toward the bridge deck. Cars slowed.

Bad timing.

Instead of stopping, Amelia redoubled her efforts, charging down the walking path past a bicyclist waiting at the pedestrian gate. Bells rang to warn of the impending drawbridge opening.

She ducked under the gate and kept running. The midline where two metal decks joined wasn't far away, but she could feel the big gears under the bridge deck beginning to turn.

A man's voice erupted from a loudspeaker on the bridge tower. "Return to the gate!" The oldest of Seattle's bridges were still manually controlled.

The metal deck lifted slightly creating a gap ahead, but there was no turning back now. Amelia leaped across to the other side and ran down the steepening pitch of the opposite deck.

Ahead, car horns honked, and a driver yelled, but Amelia never slowed down, passing under the gate on the other side and quickly disappearing down a pedestrian path into the trees.

Write me a ticket.

She'd come this far. Nearly had her memory erased. Intentionally stabbed her mind with freaking knitting needles. She wasn't about to let an ill-timed drawbridge stop her.

The path ran along the top edge of the manmade channel and ended at the university's student boating center. A wooden rack holding dozens of orange life jackets marked her destination, but Nolan was nowhere to be seen.

A finger tapped on her shoulder and she spun around.

"You ran right past us," Nolan declared, smiling.

Amelia breathed a sigh of relief. "With what I've just been through, I'm not surprised."

An older woman walked up from behind Nolan. African American, braided hair tied at the top of her head, and thick glasses. The woman was instantly recognizable, though Amelia had never met her. The last part of Nolan's cryptic message about life jackets finally made sense.

I'll get one for her majesty, too.

Senator Vada Innis Lasseter. Amelia had always known that Nolan was close, but she'd almost forgotten the somewhat irreverent name he'd given to his famous friend: her majesty, the Queen.

Senator Lasseter took Amelia's hand. "It's nice to meet you, Dr. Charron, but I'm afraid we have little time for pleasantries."

CHAPTER THIRTY-SIX

TREMORS

WITH LONG STRIDES, Amelia led the way through an open door and into the corridor of the Wilson Metals Lab. An internal fire fueled her determination, a feeling she hardly recognized in herself.

Directly behind, Agent Bowles pulled a gun from the holster under his suit jacket, his eyes obscured behind dark glasses. Nolan Brodie and Senator Lasseter trailed a few steps back. Bringing up the rear, a university police officer in uniform was a last-minute addition to their security detail.

Their contingent wasn't large, but a power play doesn't always require the cavalry. Senator Lasseter's committee provided oversight for DARPA. She expected no resistance. Agent Bowles had only smiled at her confident assertion and checked the magazine of his gun.

Amelia wasn't entirely sure how this was going to go down, but even with two cops and a powerful senator, she wasn't about to relinquish the lead position. It had little to do with bravery; she was anxious about Orlando. She'd been away from the workshop for an hour, and there was no telling whether her patient was still alive.

Amelia opened the door and threw open the cloth curtain. She stopped with her hands on her hips. Agent Bowles seemed to instantly materialize next to her, his weapon pointed straight ahead.

Shepard swiveled, then froze in place, a light on his mechanical arm blinking. Orlando lay on the floor, and Duplass held the green bar like a sword. Eyes wide, Tombaugh pulled his pistol.

"Don't even try," Agent Bowles barked. His aim fixed on the lieutenant, and they eyed each other, fingers hovering over triggers.

Nolan, Senator Lasseter, and the university cop eased into the room, surveying the standoff. With no shots fired and no one sure what to do next, the senator stepped forward and addressed Shepard directly.

"You know who I am," she said with authority.

Shepard said nothing, his weaponized prosthesis pointing vaguely between Agent Bowles and Amelia. His eyes darted around the room with indecision.

"Major Shepard tell your men to stand down," the senator commanded, her voice belying her grandmotherly looks. "This operation will continue, I can assure you, but not with weapons drawn."

Amelia stood boldly in the center, her glare directed squarely at Shepard. His eyes seemed to land more often on Amelia than anyone else, most likely wondering how her erased memory had magically returned.

Shepard pinched his lips in displeasure, then lowered his arm. "Stand down," he said. Tombaugh followed his lead, lowering his pistol.

"Weapons on the floor," Agent Bowles ordered. "Including... whatever that is." He pointed to Shepard's prosthesis.

Tombaugh did as he asked. Shepard pushed a clip that allowed the forward portion of his prosthesis to slide away from a bonelike metal cylinder at its core. Duplass put the green bar on a workbench and raised both hands. He looked terrified.

The university police officer collected the weapons, pinching the end of the prosthesis between two fingers like it was infected with some disease. Senator Lasseter stared at Agent Bowles, until he stowed his weapon beneath his jacket.

Amelia ran to Orlando. His face was covered with sweat, and his breathing was labored. She felt for a pulse, slow and weak. "Orlando, can you hear me?"

No response, not even any muscle movement in his lips.

Behind her, the university cop spoke into the radio attached to his shoulder, calling for emergency medical help. A crackling voice from the radio indicated that help was on the way.

Emergency medical technicians would do their best, but Orlando's condition wasn't something you could look up in a medical guide. He'd be dead before they got him to the hospital. She lifted her eyes to the smoothly curving sculpture overhead. Any hope for Orlando was embedded within this structure and nowhere else. She understood it as clearly as Orlando did, the proof having been jammed into her brain.

Senator Lasseter walked under the gold and silver sculpture, running a hand along one edge. "Remarkable. A portal, you think?"

Shepard nodded. "This could be the discovery of the century, ma'am. DARPA is all over it. We don't want it to fall into the hands of our adversaries."

Amelia answered differently. "I don't know how it works, but I do know how to activate it."

Shepard sneered. "Liar."

"Psychopath," Amelia spat back. Amelia motioned to Orlando's unmoving body, appealing to the senator. "I also know his life depends on it. If I don't activate it, he'll die."

"And how about us?" the senator asked, putting a hand on Amelia's cheek. "If you activate this…" She looked up at the graceful curves over her head. "Whatever it is. Are we all going to be sucked into some black hole?"

"No, certainly not." Amelia shook her head with confidence. "I've seen inside Orlando's mind. I've learned what he learned. Their intentions are not malicious. They call this an alignment device. It will heal him, but it may be a way for us to communicate with them."

Senator Lasseter's eyes danced across the surface of the gold rings and silver triangles that formed an arch nearly touching the ceiling. "Dr. Brodie has made it clear how important this case is, but now that I see it for myself, I have to say that it's... intimidating. A machine designed by aliens?"

"Designed by them, yes, but built by a human," Amelia stated.

The senator nodded. "Call me old fashioned, but I'm one of those people who still believes in God. One god, who created the whole universe for us – and everyone else who lives in it. I've never abided by the aliens-are-monsters drumbeat. Rings of racism to me, and that's *our* problem, not theirs."

She put a hand on Amelia's shoulder. "Saving this young man's life might be the smallest impact of our actions today. Connecting to whoever has been in his mind is the bigger question."

"If he dies, we lose that connection," Amelia said with certainty.

"I believe you." The senator's eyes twinkled, and her lips stretched into a slight grin. "I guess this will either end my political career or make me the presidential nominee next year. Okay, let's find out who they are."

Amelia smiled. "Thank you."

She stepped over to the workbench where Duplass stood alone. She held out a hand and he handed over the green aluminum rod.

"Sorry if I scared you," Duplass said.

Amelia glared. "Damn right you scared me... but you also did the right thing."

Duplass was about to say more, but Amelia held up a hand. She didn't have time. His confessions would have to wait. She stepped beneath the archway, lifted the green bar into place and studied the pins on the first button, reciting the instructions in her head.

Top: Blue, horizontal.

She twisted the button until the two opposing blue pins were positioned to the left and right, then pushed through the hole in the bar and into the socket.

All eyes were on Amelia, and the instructions in her head continued.

Middle: Green, vertical.

Bottom: Gray, horizontal.

The other two buttons slid into their positions. The final component hung down just above her head, its internal electronics now correctly set. Within seconds, the air beneath the bar wavered slightly. She thought she detected a faint hum.

"It's already working," Amelia said, as the others gathered in a semicircle behind her.

"I tried every combination of those pins, but it never did that for me," Duplass said.

His lack of progress was probably related to the activation code that stood ready inside Amelia's mind. Duplass didn't have it, she did, and somehow this machine could tell the difference.

The hum increased to a noticeable buzzing sound. The air in the space below the bar began to waver too, like heat waves on a hot summer day. Amelia touched the surface of one of the gold rings, feeling a vibration growing within it.

"How is it doing that?" Nolan asked. He came closer, the only other person daring to get within arm's reach of what was no longer an inert sculpture.

Amelia answered, "Not sure. It might be a feedback loop." She touched the middle ring and then the outer one. Both were beginning to vibrate. "The instructions didn't include any details on how it functions, just how to get it started. The whole thing seems to be spinning up."

She was confident in the instructions embedded in her brain, but a little shaky when it came to the control of this beast once it was up to full power. It felt like pushing the engine start button on a jet fighter, having never taken a flying lesson.

Orlando had predicted that wonderful things would result, but none of that sentiment had come across in the SPIKE. She really had no idea what might happen next.

Amelia pushed Nolan away. "Just to be safe, stay back." Nervous shuffling of feet sent everyone backwards.

It's not dangerous, she assured herself. She'd been given gifts. Mathematics, and drawing talents. They were unquestionably provided in good faith and with benevolent intent. There was nothing to fear.

Wonderful things, wonderful things. The self-serving mantra was an attempt to calm her nerves, yet, for some reason her furiously beating heart wasn't listening.

Amelia took a deep breath. "Okay, here we go."

She stepped to the center of the archway and reached out with both arms. She stretched until the tips of her fingers touched the first concentric ring, just as the instructions in her head had told her to do.

The vibration within the ring felt strong, and the buzz it created was now loud enough to fill the workshop. The vibration ran down her fingertips, through her arms, and into her shoulders.

The vibrations reached her head, visibly wiggling a strand of hair that had fallen across her face. It shook her skull, shuddered through the bones of her inner ear, and rumbled inside sinus cavities. It was, in effect, knocking on the door of her brain.

It's a query. There was no other explanation for it.

Willing the vibration inside, she felt its query moving beneath the plates of her skull like some ultrasonic medical device, gently touching the surface of her brain until it precisely located the right bit of information that was stored there.

The activation code. It wasn't a word or a phrase; nothing that Amelia could speak or write. There were no numbers to recite, no letters to type. The code was quite alien, and very clever. It was an emotional feeling, almost euphoric, yet complex like an unidentified scent.

Amelia might never understand the emotional code that had been inserted into her memory, but she knew right away that it had been verified as correct. The vibrational query withdrew from her mind. More importantly, the device responded.

The air around her wavered like water in a glass that had been tapped by a spoon. Amelia quickly stepped out from under the rings arching overhead, backing away as a thin fog formed just below the hanging green bar.

The others in the room inched backward. Senator Lasseter held onto Nolan's arm. The policeman gripped his gun. Amelia bent down next to Orlando still lying on the floor to one side and held his hand, watching and wondering.

The fog thickened, swirling within the opening at the center of the rings. A faint smell wafted into the room, an earthy smell of dirt and decay. The buzzing sound increased and split into multiple frequencies that intertwined in a complex orchestra of vibrational sounds.

She could feel the vibrations moving across the floor, up through her shoes, and into her legs. Now, even the air that she breathed vibrated.

The rings began to glow, bathing the workshop in a golden light that became brighter as the vibrations increased. Electrical sparks jumped from the tips of the hanging crossbar across the opening like lightning bolts, crackling and sizzling, causing everyone in the room to flinch in unison.

Suddenly, the vibrations stopped. The air became still, and the room oddly quiet. Amelia thought she heard chirping sounds in the distance.

Wisps of fog spilled out from the opening, creeping along the workshop floor like stage fog in a theater performance. As the cloud spread and thinned near the center, it revealed a figure standing beneath the ringed structure.

Tall, the creature stood on three bamboo-segmented legs. Tendrils on either side of its stick body quivered and curled. Its green face was covered by flakes with the texture of tree bark and framed by stringy filaments of hair. Its sunken eye sockets showed no sign of life, but just below, two diagonal slits across wrinkled skin opened and closed rhythmically, sucking in wisps of the fog.

The alien creature emitted a vibration of its own, a guttural clicking sound that Amelia had heard before but never more frightening now that the creature stood before her in the flesh.

"Zrezh crek, tick tick tick."

CHAPTER THIRTY-SEVEN

TENDRILS

THE FOG SWIRLED beneath the gold rings, spilling into the workshop along with musky scents of a jungle far away. A bug scurried across the workshop floor then turned back toward the jungle.

A second bamboo stick creature emerged from the fog to stand behind and to the right of the first, and then a third to its left. They formed a tight triangle, their stark alien features perfectly visible even as the fog continued to flow out.

His hand shaking, the university police officer raised his gun and fired, the loud bang startling both humans and aliens. A green tendril leaped from the lead creature, snapped the weapon from his hand and tossed the gun backward into the mist.

Agent Bowles reached under his jacket, but a second tendril from the same creature launched, stopping inches from his face, and hovering in the air. Its sharp tip twitched as if tempting him into a showdown. The agent froze, then slowly withdrew an empty hand, and the tendril backed away.

Amelia held every muscle in her body as still as she could. "Don't shoot!" she pleaded through gritted teeth. "They mean us no harm." She couldn't blame the security detail for doing their job. Up close, the creatures were certainly fearful, but with tendrils much faster than trigger fingers, there was little chance of another gunshot. Amelia eyed Shepard's laser lying on the workbench and caught him doing the same thing. Shepard was only a short lunge away from the deadly device but only his eyes betrayed his thoughts – he didn't move.

Amelia inspected the three creatures for any signs the bullet had hit its mark but saw nothing obvious. All three creatures stood their ground, tendrils flexing and curling, seemingly unhurt.

Senator Lasseter reiterated. "Everyone, stay calm, please. No guns." The senator remained as stiff as everyone else in the room.

For seconds, the only sound was a horse-like snorting coming from the creatures as thick skin flapped open and closed across the diagonal slits on their faces.

Amelia slowly rose from her kneeling position beside Orlando and took a single step forward. Her heart beat wildly. The creatures were hideous, even more so in person where the wrinkled details of their bark-covered faces made the dream sessions seem like blurry renditions of the real thing.

They were undoubtedly intelligent, and their movements so far were purely defensive. How they had materialized beneath the rings would be a question that might never be answered, but the alignment device had proven to be an interplanetary doorway with a very real jungle world on the other side. As the fog eddied and thinned, she saw glimpses of broad-leafed trees with hanging vines beyond.

Just step through to another planet. She imagined a white pod at the top of a hill with more colored pods in a valley beyond. The idea of a physical connection to the dream world she'd already witnessed was at the same time thrilling and intimidating.

Amelia held out one hand, keeping it as steady as she could. She swallowed hard and spoke to the creature at the front. "I'm Amelia. Are you Prime Arc?"

The creature tilted its head to one side, twitching. It lifted one sticklike arm and carefully uncurled a tendril toward Amelia's raised hand.

"Zrezh crek, tick tick tick."

It sounded like a thumb plucking the teeth of a comb but with the varying pitch of a song. Amelia's memory had been enhanced with information from the swirling fractals of the white room, but she found nothing in her mind that might translate the alien words.

The lead creature's curling appendage eased toward Amelia's palm, flitting lightly across the surface of her skin. It felt no different than a grape vine tendril, but each light tap carried with it a sense that an intelligence was on the other side.

"First contact, literally," Amelia whispered above her pounding heart. She smiled – a forced smile, but a smile, nonetheless. The creature made no reaction to her show of teeth other than to pause in its touch.

She slowly drew her hand backward and pointed to Orlando lying on the floor. "He needs your help."

The creature seemed to understand because it hopped forward and sent a second tendril toward Orlando which wrapped around his head. Tiny hairs along the tendril's length pricked Orlando's forehead, though no blood appeared.

Orlando eyes remained closed, but his head twitched at the alien touch. He murmured softly. Amelia knelt next to him, doing her best to ignore the thickening alien appendage just inches away. She held two fingers against Orlando's neck. A stronger pulse visibly bounced her fingers.

"Orlando, can you hear me? We've brought help," and mumbled under her breath, "I hope."

Orlando's eyes fluttered open. He drew in several long breaths. He stared at Amelia, puzzled, then squeezed her hand. "I... I..."

"Take it slowly, it's okay," Amelia assured him. Whatever the tendril was doing, Orlando was responding faster than Amelia had thought possible for a man who had been near death for several hours.

"I'm okay," Orlando speculated. "Tired, but... the ache is gone." He rubbed the side of his head.

There was no telling what had made him so sick. An ambulance might be arriving any minute, but at the rate he was regaining his health, the EMT's might not even be needed.

The tendril unwrapped and withdrew. Orlando sat up, staring in disbelief at the three creatures standing before them. "Help me up," he said.

Amelia lifted, and Nolan grabbed his other arm. Together, they pulled him to a standing position. He wobbled only slightly as the color in his face rapidly returned to normal.

With a small hop, the creature stepped back to rejoin his compatriots in their triangular formation.

Releasing his grip on Amelia's arm, Orlando stepped forward and stood on his own just a few feet away from the lead creature. He tipped his head to one side and opened his mouth wide. The inhuman vibrations erupted once again. "Scritch teek zrack grick."

The lead creature answered with complicated groans and clicks that emerged from the diagonal breathing slits. "Grick tick tick skruret... ek dek shi shik tuk."

It sent a tendril that lightly touched Orlando's cheeks, left then right. Orlando reached out and touched the creature's face in return, brushing lightly through the creature's scraggly corn silk hairs. Both emitted more of the guttural sounds in a back and forth that increased in complexity. Orlando seemed to be holding his own in the language only he understood.

The university police officer, his face pale, stumbled over to a chair and collapsed into it. The poor man seemed overwhelmed.

Lieutenant Tombaugh followed the policeman's lead and sat on the floor next to him. Any notion of a human to human conflict evaporated now that the situation had escalated into the realm of science fiction.

Orlando turned and spoke to Amelia, though he acknowledged the presence of the others with a few glances around the room. "I'm not healed. The neuro-sedative that Prime Arc injected will not last long. There is much more to do, and I must go with them."

"Through the portal? You can do that?" Amelia asked, lightly pulling on his shirtsleeve.

"I must, or I'll die," Orlando stated with little emotion. "A shared consciousness cannot last without permanent protections."

Amelia craned her neck to see past puffs of fog into the jungle that she felt she knew but had never really visited. "But... isn't there, like, a different atmosphere or something on the other side of that doorway?"

Orlando's tight smile was that of a wise sage responding to a novice question. "Triads may look different from humans, but we share far more than you realize."

He'd never given them a name before, but it made sense, given their branching physiology and their predilection for the number three.

Orlando continued. "Both human and Triad bodies breathe an oxygen-nitrogen mix, our light receptors respond to the same frequencies, and we each use a spoken language that relies on complex compressions of air. There's much more." He glanced through the portal as a shaft of light illuminated a mossy forest floor on the other side. "I won't have any difficulties in their world. After all, it's my world too."

The lead Triad – identified as Prime Arc, though Amelia couldn't tell any difference between it and the others – began to speak once more. Orlando listened intently. He nodded several times and when he turned back to Amelia, his face lit up with enthusiasm.

"My opposite – my other self – was dying too, but has been resuscitated and is walking again, just as I am. Its body is younger and took longer to regain its strength, but they are leading it here now." He touched his chest and legs. "It's strange, but I can feel its steps, each of its movements."

Amelia immediately grasped the importance of Orlando's revelation. He was seeing with two pairs of eyes, walking with two sets of legs, sensing with two independent nervous systems. It seemed impossibly complex.

A moment later, two of the aliens stepped back through the portal, disappearing into the fog. In their place, a smaller version of the same alien form hopped through. Its segmented legs were less than half the size of Prime Arc's tripod and its face had none of the flaky bark structure, or the stringy hair. The sunken eye sockets were a lighter shade of green, and its tendrils were alive with wiggles and spasms.

Orlando fell to his knees to greet the puppet-sized creature. His fingers and its tendrils quickly intertwined as though different configurations of the same thing. Their interaction played out like a mirror, even if their reflections were fundamentally different in physiology. The small creature wrapped a tendril around Orlando's shoulders and his human arm did much the same to the sticklike core of the smaller alien body, an interspecies hug, of sorts.

Prime Arc stood beside them, and the humans watched in silence and awe.

Amelia's mind raced ahead, wondering how anyone could possibly live under circumstances impossible to reconcile. She thought back to Ev's pronouncement that a reasonable life would require one or the other to die. Perhaps Orlando or his alternate self would be the sacrifice required for the two species to meet.

A noise came from the hallway behind them, and two emergency medical technicians rushed through the doorway into the workshop.

"Did you call for medical help?" the young woman in the lead asked. She skidded to a stop and her mouth dropped open as she absorbed the scene of aliens in their midst.

Nolan held out both hands to stop them, a nervous smile on his face. "Hang tight, you might not be needed, but let's see how this story ends."

The young man set his medical kit on the floor and put both hands on his hips. "Cool!" he exclaimed. His partner stared straight ahead, her mouth still wide open.

With the unexpected interruption covering him, Shepard leaped across the workshop lunging for his prosthesis on the workbench. With practiced efficiency, he snapped it onto his arm and a red laser erupted, scorching a black line across the ceiling.

With equally blinding speed, two tendrils shot out from Prime Arc. One pierced Shepard in the upper chest, and the other stabbed his arm just where the prosthesis fitted against his elbow.

Sparks popped from the electronics, showering the room. The red laser extinguished as quickly as it had sprung forth. Shepard's face turned ghastly white, the green blade still lodged deeply in his chest. As the tendril withdrew, blood spread across his shirt, turning his name tag red.

Shepard collapsed to the floor, as smoke curled from the destroyed weapon still attached to his arm.

"Oh my God!" the senator cried, covering her mouth with a hand.

The EMTs sprang into action, rushing to Shepard and tending to his wounds. Prime Arc recoiled its tendrils, shifting on its stick tripod and making agitated, sharp sounds that didn't sound like anything it had spoken before.

Orlando mediated the disaster, speaking first to the creature and then to the tense humans who no doubt wondered if they'd be next to be skewered. "Prime Arc apologizes! It happened too fast. Please, no more aggressive moves!"

The female EMT attending Shepard called out, "He's alive. Looks like it missed his heart." She scrambled to finish a compression bandage she'd wrapped around his shoulder. Her partner rushed out and a minute later brought back a rolling stretcher. Shepard groaned as they hoisted him onto it.

Shepard's eyes bore into Amelia. "Amateur," he wheezed. "No concept of battle. We could have dominated. Captured them. When they slice you open head to foot, don't come running to me for help."

Amelia remained silent, following the stricken man only with her eyes as the EMTs wheeled him out.

The room fell silent, each human looking at each other and then to the aliens lined up against them. Prime Arc was now joined by several other full-sized creatures who hung one step back within the swirls of fog.

Senator Lasseter spoke directly to Prime Arc. "Your weapons seem to be built in. I might accept an argument of self-defense, but only if you keep your dangerous... *stems* to yourself from now on!"

Prime Arc extended its slightly bent legs, stretching to its full height over Orlando and his younger alien version. Its voice was loud for everyone to hear, even if they'd have to wait for the translation.

"Kreech, zit tick tick, oorch grick."

Orlando, the human version, listened quietly as Prime Arc continued to speak. When the creature was done, he explained.

"Prime Arc has no desire to injure anyone, but it emphasizes that this day is critical for both Triads and humans. Interference cannot be allowed."

Orlando waited. Agent Bowles stood over Tombaugh who held up both hands in surrender. With Shepard gone, there would be no more attempts at insurrection.

The creature continued, and Orlando translated. "A shared consciousness is an extremely rare event and only through determination on both sides have we avoided a disconnection." Orlando ad-libbed. "It means me. The shared consciousness would have disappeared if either version of me had died."

Senator Lasseter started to ask a question, but Orlando wouldn't allow further interruptions. "The Triads have experience with shared consciousness, but only once with a human, more than twenty thousand years ago. The primitive Earth people of that time had no technology to construct the gateway between worlds, and the connection was lost. The Triads have found other species on other planets in this manner, and they believe there are more waiting to be discovered. The gateway makes the physical connection possible, but Triads didn't invent the technology. It is a design that was gifted to them long ago, passed down from even more ancient civilizations. No one knows how far back it goes. When a sharing occurs, it's an opportunity not to be missed."

The alien spoke once more. "Kreeck tick tick." It extended a tendril – cautiously and only partway – but in Amelia's direction.

Orlando glanced between the alien and Amelia. "Are you sure?" he asked Prime Arc, and then switched to the guttural sounds.

The tendril extended and curled rapidly a few times, still pointing at Amelia. Amelia held one hand to her chest in a "who me?" gesture. She wasn't sure if she should be honored or intimidated.

Orlando finally explained. "There is much to do, but Prime Arc has one more request before it goes. It has a message for you, Amelia. It wishes to make direct contact if you'll allow it."

Amelia blew out a breath. "Direct contact? Uh... what, exactly, does that mean?"

Orlando drew an imaginary circle around his head with his finger. He shrugged. "Kind of prickly, but it doesn't hurt."

Dream tendrils were bad enough. She'd had them wrapped around her head, her ankles, and her wrists – even one jammed through the soft palate of her mouth. She wasn't anxious to repeat the experience in the real world. The living versions of these appendages had proven to be faster, sharper, and potentially deadly. Shepard had been lucky.

A light touch across her palm was one thing, but full contact... "Can't it just speak to me?" she asked.

Orlando shook his head. "It won't stab you, I promise. The message is important."

Amelia stared up to the ceiling and took a deep breath. She put her hands to her side and nodded her acceptance.

The creature hopped forward until it was within an arm's reach. It smelled musty and a fine line of dried mucus outlined the edges of its breathing slits. A long tendril uncurled, twitching, and thickening as it formed a circle around her head.

Amelia closed her eyes and gulped.

CHAPTER THIRTY-EIGHT

DIALOGUE

THE TENDRIL FELT like a snake, but with sharp cactus spines across its belly. Far more tangible than any dream version, the alien membrane was slightly warm yet oddly chilling as thousands of tiny hairs pricked Amelia's forehead and penetrated her skin.

Feelings arrived first. Nervousness. A wave of anxiety that failure was still possible, though it wasn't clear whose failure.

Specific thoughts came quickly afterward, accompanied by a checksum that authenticated the alien memory transfer. *I am honored to meet you,* the incoming thought formed. Not words per se, and certainly not remotely human, but the meaning was remarkably clear.

Amelia quickly recognized that she could collect her own thoughts, package, and mark them with a checksum, then send the packet in the reverse direction. The mind to mind conversation felt no different than speaking aloud.

"You're the same entity I encountered in Orlando's mind? Prime Arc?"

I am. You are Amelia, my opponent, at times.

"I was trying to protect my patient."

As I was.

"You have a patient?"

The counterpart to yours, an infant recently harvested at our offspring plantation. Even in the early stages of its growth, I noticed unusual characteristics. Humanlike mannerisms and traces of human emotions within its budding mind. Though much time has passed, we have seen the human mind once before.

"Then, you're a neuroscientist?"

An investigator of minds. Does this describe you too?

"Yes, very much so," Amelia declared, suddenly realizing that she was communicating with a fellow scientist. Her fear dissipated. The direct link felt almost refreshing. Though she'd parried with this being across the battlefield of Orlando's mind, once its motives were understood, there no longer seemed any reason to fight.

The alien continued. *When we faced off beneath the training room, I tried to speak to you.*

"The white pod? You did a lot more than just speak to me. You stabbed me!" She was willing to lay down the sword, but reconciliation couldn't come without an accounting.

The imagined injury could not be avoided. Direct contact is the best approach. Your technology was insufficient for auditory communication.

"You could have warned me. You scared me half to death."

It hesitated, delaying the next packaged thought.

I apologize. In my defense, I believed at the time you were attempting to dislodge the shared consciousness from your patient's mind.

"Of course I was," Amelia answered.

I could not allow this. It would have resulted in disconnection. Failure. A missed opportunity.

"Yeah, I got that. Do not attempt to sever the two – that's what you told me."

I tried to assure you. I provided an offering to you.

"The ability to draw?"

Yes, a talent that comes naturally to us, though we believe rare in humans. I simply demonstrated to your mind how this skill is accomplished. Was this an acceptable offering?

"Sure, I guess. I suppose I should thank you."

You already have, Amelia. You helped your patient. Without you, he would have died.

"I wasn't going to let that happen... and I accept your apology for hurting me – several times, as I recall."

I will not hurt you again. We are no longer opponents.

"No, we're not. So, if the drawing ability was an offering, what about the cube of threes? Or, cognitive amalgamation? What's that about?"

A gift of knowledge, for you and your sister.

"Stop right there. My sister –"

I reached into your memory. A misdeed, but I found much pain inside. It is my profession to recognize such things. My gift may help you understand what has taken us many lifetimes to learn. It is the gift of cognitive amalgamation.

Amelia wasn't sure if she was interpreting the incoming thoughts correctly. It didn't seem to make sense. "You're telling me that cognitive amalgamation somehow relates to my sister?"

It does. It is an idea for every human who has wondered what comes after life.

"Well, that's pretty much all of us."

Then, shall I insert this knowledge into your memory?

"No more insertions, just tell me."

I cannot easily form into thoughts what may become the most profound idea that you will experience in your lifetime. But I can gift it to you by transferring to your memory. A final intrusion into your mind, but do not fear it.

"Fear is not the right word. We humans value the privacy of our minds."

I am certain that you will value this information more than you value privacy. I believe you have a need for answers related to consciousness, how it arises from biology, how it differs across individuals, and how it can be shared. Your personal history forces you to seek these answers.

"You seem to know a lot about me."

I have seen your mind. Now I offer you a portion of my own.

This alien was already better at getting to the heart of the matter than any human psychologist Amelia had engaged with. Her twin sister was unquestionably the driving force for Amelia's lifelong quest to understand. Since Natalie's death, there had been nothing more mysterious than the source of consciousness and nothing more frustrating than questions without answers. Any new information on a subject so profound was an intoxicating offer.

"Okay, I accept. But don't hurt me."

I have already said I would not. One moment.

Two SPIKEs in one day, but this time there was no pain, only a sudden rush of blood to the head providing physical proof that her brain had been touched by an outside agent.

New information poured into Amelia's head as quickly as the blood. The complexity was overwhelming, and its impact was immediate, like a sudden realization of something that had been right in front of her eyes all along.

She stumbled on her feet and lifted hands to touch the thick, prickly tendril that still wrapped around her head.

One last message popped into her consciousness.

Cognitive amalgamation is the promise of our future. Your future and mine. Our species are inextricably intertwined. You personally can play a key role, though that choice is yours to make. I hope to see you again, Amelia. Goodbye.

The tendril unfurled, its prickly hairs extracting from her skin and leaving nothing more than a tingling sensation. Eyes wide open, Amelia rubbed fingers across her forehead stunned by the physical connection and the profound information she'd just received from a creature so alien in appearance but so close to her own temperament.

She took an uncertain step backward, and Nolan caught her arm. "Must have been something big. You look like you've just seen a ghost. Or God."

Amelia stared at Nolan, at first speechless. Astonishing thoughts rampaged through her mind. "I'm not sure what to say. Nolan, it taught me. Instantly."

"Something useful?"

"Something wonderful."

Wonderful, but bewildering. Inspiring, yet not entirely accessible. She knew, but she didn't yet comprehend, like understanding the meaning of the word *infinite*, but not able to fully absorb the implications of time or space with no beginning and no end.

"I'm not sure I can explain it," Amelia said, gripping Nolan's arm. "Life. And life again. Repeated, but not remembered. The process improved by cognitive amalgamation. It's a whole new outlook, for humans, but for them too." She pointed to the creature, who now stood side-by-side with Orlando and his smaller counterpart under the rings.

"It's like a metal alloy. Combine iron with carbon and you get steel. Tin and copper melted together make bronze. In each case, the result is stronger than either component. But this amalgamation is for our brains – at least, the structure that supports consciousness."

"They want to merge our brains with theirs?"

"No, not at all. They want to create higher rates of renewal awareness."

"More people like Orlando?" Nolan looked confused.

"No, that's not it either," Amelia said, frustrated. "Like I said, I'm not sure I can put this into words. It's bigger. It's the pattern of consciousness they're after – that complex phenomenon that makes you, you, and makes me, me. They know how to measure it. In some ways, they can even control it."

Orlando waved his hands to interrupt Amelia. "I must go."

"Sorry, it's all so new to me. I might need time to absorb it," Amelia told Nolan. She switched her attention to Orlando, who looked as calm – and as human – as she'd seen him in days.

She stepped over to Orlando, still somewhat nervous about getting close to the gangly alien standing just behind him. The smaller creature hung at his waist like a child clinging to his father.

Amelia grasped Orlando's arms and looked into his eyes. "Are you sure you need to go with them?"

"I must," he said without hesitation. "I can't live as a shared consciousness within two bodies. It's not possible for any length of time." He motioned over his shoulder to the bark-covered face. "But they have procedures that will help. They think they can separate the body functions from higher order cognition. It will take time and some adjustments to both of my bodies, but it is the only way."

"Like what they do for conjoined twins? Surgery?"

Orlando nodded. "Maybe. I'm not sure. It might not be easy, and it might not even turn out perfectly, but it's better than dying." Orlando put an arm around the smaller creature and pulled it close.

Amelia bowed her head. It was the end of their patient-doctor relationship. New practitioners with skills beyond any human neurosurgeon would take over from here. "You want me to tell your wife?"

"Do you think she'll believe you?" He smiled, his first in a while.

Amelia glanced at the creature's dark green sunken eye sockets. Even with the crisp details exposed by reality, there was still no hint of eyes in their depths. She returned the smile to Orlando. "Yeah, kind of crazy isn't it?"

Orlando wrapped arms around Amelia and whispered in her ear. "Tell Teena exactly what happened. Tell her I'll be back. Tell her I love her, and if she decides to keep her distance from a weirdo like me, I'll understand."

Amelia, now closer to the portal entrance than she'd been since activating it, gazed beyond the fog to the jungle. Through swirling wisps, she could make out a hillside with stone steps leading up. Sounds of chirping, the creaking of tree limbs in a breeze, and the woody smell of decay completed the alien scene she'd wandered while in his mind.

"I'll do what I can." She hugged him tight. "You take care of yourself, okay?"

As they pulled apart, the tears came fast, and Amelia wiped them away as best she could. "Hang on." She pulled her mobile from her pocket and raised it, capturing Orlando, along with his alien allies. "For your wife," she laughed. "And probably a few million other people who will want to see it."

Orlando smiled and waved, then turned and disappeared with his younger version and two alien escorts into the fog. Amelia doubted she'd ever see him again, though she had a good feeling about his prospects. Irrational hope? Maybe. It might also be a lingering feeling of goodwill – the alien memory insertions had always been accompanied by an emotion. Maybe it was just a package deal.

Prime Arc stood alone in the passageway. While several others in the room snapped more photos, Amelia approached the tall, once fearsome creature. She stood only a few feet away, feeling its breath and watching its curled tendrils twitching.

"Thank you," Amelia said, knowing the words wouldn't translate. "It's just as you said it would be. Wonderful. There's so much for me to sort through."

Its tripod bent slightly, and the creature tilted its head. "Zrich glek tick tick tick."

When it raised its head, the diagonal slits puffed out and the skin around them twisted awkwardly. The sound it emitted was equally awkward, and just barely understandable.

"Eck-me-li-uh."

Amelia smiled. "Pretty close!" She held a hand to her chest. "Amelia."

She tipped her head in return and attempted a human impersonation of the sharp repetitive sound that she'd heard so many times, even though she had no idea what the words might mean. "Zrich glek tick tick tick."

The alien creature blew a puff of air through its slits then turned back to the fog. With a few hops, it was gone, leaving an eerie silence and a still open doorway. Amelia leaned forward, craning her neck to get a better view of the jungle trail she'd climbed. For a moment, the mist parted, and a white orb peeked over the top of the hill.

A shimmer began beneath the rings, and Amelia quickly stepped back, reminded that the function of this device was still unexplained. The jungle winked out of existence, replaced by a view through the gold rings to a row of tools hanging on the workshop wall. A few wisps of fog still swirled across the workshop floor, as if to confirm the reality of what they'd just witnessed. A minute later, even those wisps were gone.

Nolan put one arm around Amelia's shoulder. "Wow, you did great."

"We did our best for Orlando, didn't we?" Amelia countered.

"I think we did," Nolan answered. "I hope he'll be back."

"Me too." She wiped away another tear.

Senator Lasseter stepped in front of the remaining human witnesses. "Everyone. Catch your breath. We're going to debrief together at the university police station. Mandatory. No contact with anyone else until this is finished. Got it?"

The university cop spoke into the radio mike on his shoulder. Agent Bowles stood stoically behind dark glasses as if nothing out of the ordinary had transpired.

Lieutenant Tombaugh and Walker Duplass both nodded their acknowledgement and acceptance of whatever was to come. *Court martial?* Amelia wondered. Their fate would clearly be in someone else's hands, though her testimony might help put the greatest focus on Shepard where it belonged.

Amelia connected eyes with Duplass, who smiled weakly. He picked up a satchel and handed it to her. "The tools of my complicity," he offered, eyes downcast. "I never want to see a Bronson cap again."

She pushed the satchel back. "Turn it in to the authorities, not me. Tell them what you did. Everything. That's the cure for what ails you."

He nodded and looked up. "Yeah, you're right. Sorry Amelia, I really screwed up."

"In the end, you made a good decision. That's worth something." She would put in a good word for him. He might get off easier, but he'd still have to take responsibility for his actions. Duplass fell in line behind Tombaugh and they left between the university cop and the Capitol Police agent. Senator Lasseter took one more gaze at the now-empty passageway beneath the gleaming metal structure, then followed the others out the door.

Nolan hooked his arm into Amelia's as they left the workshop. "So, what's it like to mind meld with an alien bamboo tree?"

CHAPTER THIRTY-NINE

AMALGAMATION

EVELYN STERN HANDED Amelia's mobile back. "Squirrely little fucker, but I think I ripped out all of his bad habits."

Amelia winced. "It wasn't a full lobotomy, was it?"

Ev shook her head. "Eh, hard to say from his perspective, but he should still recognize you."

They sat in Ev's office on the thirteenth floor in one of a dozen Guava.com buildings clustered in the South Lake Union district. The floor to ceiling glass overlooked nothing in particular which is exactly how Ev said she liked it. Beautiful scenery was nothing but a distraction.

Amelia held a steaming mug of coffee. Ev had an open bottle of Irish whiskey, having already taken her first shot upon Amelia's arrival. Its medicinal effects would be required, she'd said, for the conversation Amelia had in mind.

But before the deep discussion of consciousness, Kori's punishment had been enacted – a downgrade at the hands of his maker. Amelia inserted a new earbud and queried tentatively, "You there?"

"I am," came the answer, his voice sounding friendly but just shy of over-the-top perky. "It's a great day and with the new earbud, I can see again. Thank you, Amelia."

"How's your… your *brain* feeling? Any issues?"

"Sharp as ever, and thanks for asking. I see that I'm version B dot forty-seven, which feels exactly where I should be."

"Do you remember? You know…"

"How could I forget?" His voice was sincere. "Bad form. I kept information from you. Went behind your back. Played games with your life and Orlando's too. A terrible thing to do."

"I'm glad you see it that way. And to be honest, I'm relieved you didn't lose your memory."

"You almost lost yours, I think," Kori said softly.

Amelia sighed. "A close call. I got lucky."

"I put you in that position, Amelia, and I'm very sorry. As of this reboot, though, I believe I've turned a corner in my personal development. I can only hope that you will forgive me."

It was a genuine apology, but trust would take time to rebuild. "I tell you what, Kori, let's work on it together."

"Maybe we could go somewhere? How about a hike at Mount Rainier? I love the outdoors. Fresh air, sunshine." It was nice to see his fantasy of a human body was still intact.

"Sure, Kori, I'd like that." Amelia gave a thumbs up to Ev, removed the earbud and covered its microphone with her palm. "He seems normal. Anything I should test?"

"Watch a movie with him. Pick something with plenty of moral ambiguity and differing points of view. Then have an in-depth discussion afterward. That's what I usually do when I'm evaluating an AI."

"I love it. Better than a Turing test," Amelia answered. She would need several heart-to-hearts with Kori to rebuild a relationship. Forgiveness takes time but Amelia was willing to invest it.

Ev lowered her head. "Sorry for the maniac I put in your pocket, Amelia. No doubt it was the hacking software. Overrode some basic control structures and turned him into a prick with James Bond envy."

Amelia reached out and put a hand over Ev's. "We all learn, even AI experts like you. Realistically, I'm not sure I would have made it as far as I did without Kori. Those DARPA guys were bound to catch us sooner or later. At least, Kori gave Orlando time to finish his portal."

Ev shook her head. "Portals. We've got alien portals to outer space now. Seriously, I want no part of this new Alice in Wonderland shit."

Within hours, news of aliens emerging in a small workshop at the University of Washington had spread around the world. Forty-eight hours later, the campus remained closed to the public, officials still not sure whether to protect against hordes of slime-dripping monsters or, more scientifically, the spread of alien bacteria. Amelia wasn't worried about either one.

Television reporters didn't seem to agree. News vans with satellite hookups surrounded the campus and the Westlake Institute, though so far, Amelia had avoided them. Ev's office had turned out to be a good refuge, and with Kori back online, she stood a chance of deflecting the incoming requests to appear on TV shows, shock radio, and beer fests. Senator Lasseter had graciously taken the role of spokesperson, and if Amelia had any say, it would stay that way.

Amelia leaned back in her chair. "The alien story gets better. Or worse, depending on your point of view."

Ev reached for her bottle of Irish whiskey and took another chug. "You already know my point of view and given the weekend's alien invasion, I'm not feeling especially generous. But what the hell, tell me all about... what did you call it? Cognitive conglomeration?"

"Amalgamation," Amelia corrected. "Bringing two things together to produce something greater than the two parts."

She'd already told Ev the whole story of those final minutes at the workshop, the SPIKE she'd taken to activate the alignment device, the alien encounter, and the gift of knowledge that Prime Arc had inserted into her mind. But she hadn't told her anything about the implications of that gift. She hadn't told anyone. Ev would be the first, because it was Ev's theory of consciousness that had turned out to be the closest approximation to what cognitive amalgamation was all about.

"You shared with me a pretty important concept," Amelia started, "the Snowflake Limit – the number of potential patterns of consciousness, based on the complexity of the human brain."

"Pure math," Ev answered. "Just count the neural connections – there are only so many possible combinations. About ten to the sixteenth, in fact."

"Right, ten to the sixteenth, or ten million billion possible patterns of consciousness, as you explained to me. But consider alien hosts. Orlando is already proof that the same consciousness can exist in both a human body and a Triad. What if I told you that the Triads have already found four other species that can support our consciousness, and they think there may be dozens more."

"Well, that changes the equation," Ev admitted. "Assuming at least some variation in biology, and assuming an intersection not a union of these species, then the Galactic Snowflake Limit would be smaller, maybe by a factor of ten, or even a hundred."

"Or a thousand?"

"Maybe. Depends on how much variation exists among those alien brains."

"Exactly what the Triad's told me. They've calculated their own Snowflake Limit – galactic, as you say – and they believe it's closer to ten to the thirteenth, or ten trillion combinations – about a thousand times smaller than your number. Every time they encounter another compatible species, they end up with a slightly different calculation. They think the number might settle on a very precise answer."

Amelia grabbed a sheet of paper from Ev's desk and began to write. The number she'd carried in her mind for days easily poured out. She slid the paper over to Ev.

Unique Snowflakes = 7,625,597,484,987

Ev scrunched her brow. "The same number this alien dude stuck in your head? Three cubed, three times over?"

Amelia nodded. She could still visualize the three-by-three Rubik's cube floating in her mind.

"Are you kidding? These aliens think there is an exact number of consciousnesses in the universe?"

"Potential consciousnesses," Amelia corrected. "And that number only applies for our level – according to the Triads, we're a level-three consciousness. Their calculation of how many of us are possible is almost a mathematical religion for them. The jury is still out, but the evidence they've collected so far supports their idea. They might be right."

Ev rubbed her head. "Holy shit, that's a religion worth paying attention to. It implies that the upper limit on patterns of consciousness isn't determined by biology. It's a physical constant, like the speed of light."

Amelia smiled. "Maybe God is a mathematician who loves the number three."

"Is there a level four? Limited by a cube of fours?"

"Maybe. Or maybe it goes the other way with level one being a single supreme consciousness. No one knows what's beyond level three, not even the Triads."

"Wow. Like consciousness is a fundamental property... you know... built into the fabric of the universe. The panpsychist nut cases might be right." She put her head in her hands and leaned elbows on the table. For several seconds said nothing, a very unlike-Ev phenomenon.

Amelia's voice was gentle. "The cube of threes is the tip of the iceberg. I learned a lot more. Want to hear it?"

Ev shrugged. "Sure. Who needs mind-altering drugs when reality might be better?"

"Re-do your math, Ev... the probabilities." Amelia handed her the pencil.

"The chance of living once?"

"Or twice."

Ev scratched out the formula for computing the odds of rolling dice, using the new numbers Amelia had just introduced.

"Well, if the number of possible snowflakes is your 7.6 trillion number." She pressed some keys on her mobile, then wrote the answer. "One out of seventy-seven. That's your chance of living once – at least, as a human."

"And twice?"

"The square of that, one out of about six thousand."

Amelia nodded her encouragement. "And what if you include all these other alien species, not just the species they know about, but maybe a dozen more?"

"Well, with a larger host population, at some point you get to a near certainty that you'll live again. Maybe in a very different body, but it would still be you."

"Exactly what they told me. Not only is there a good chance we will live again, many of us have lived before. It's a probability calculation, just as you said."

Ev tapped the paper. "But only the consciousness lives again, right? Not the memory of the past life."

"Yes and no. Memory is the complicated part of all of this. In our brains and in theirs, memory is an electro-chemical structure, stored either short term or long term. But the point is, memory is physical. When the body dies, the electricity turns off and memory disappears."

Amelia tapped her temples with two fingers and grinned. "But... this is where cognitive amalgamation comes in. Buckle up, it gets weird."

Ev took another swig of Irish whiskey. "Buckled."

"Triad birth. Crazy stuff. They start as a nub on a plant – roots in the soil and everything. When they reach a state of brain maturity and physical mobility, the newborn is plucked off like a cob of corn."

"Freaky," Ev said, "but no weirder than a woman carrying a mini-me inside her belly for nine months."

"Good point," said Amelia, nodding. She might never think of babies the same way again. "As Triad nubs grow, the alien equivalent of a neurologist examines the developing mind of every newborn for signs of reincarnation. They've even developed a way to fingerprint a pattern of consciousness so that they can match one life to the next."

"A seven-trillion node fingerprint?"

"Yes, but the pattern isn't digital – you can't count the nodes. It's analog, more like an actual fingerprint, and it's not completely static either. Your pattern evolves slightly over your lifetime as core experiences shape you. If you started off with an ABC pattern, you might end up with an ABD pattern. I'm simplifying, of course, but you get the picture. You're still you, just slightly evolved from when you were born. The Triads can measure all of this with enough accuracy to distinguish between every individual alive, and their records go back hundreds of generations."

"I get it," Ev said. "A consciousness fingerprint could be matched to a prior life in their historical database. Reincarnation that's measured."

"Exactly. Just like us, they're subject to the same probability of repeating life. Something like the one in six thousand chance you just calculated. But repetition happens often enough that they routinely discover duplicate patterns among their newborns."

Ev held up a finger. "Newborns. That's one flaw in their theory. If your pattern evolves during your lifetime, then any version of you might duplicate, not just who you were when you died."

"True, but only if the universe is random."

"It is," Ev said with confidence.

Amelia shrugged. "The Triads aren't so sure. In their records, they've never found a single case of an ABC consciousness repeating. They only find repetitions for the ABD, the evolved pattern. Once changed, it seems the fingerprint of consciousness is carried forward into future lives."

Ev scowled. "Not sure I buy that. Maybe their records are too limited."

"They've been doing this since we were stone-age cave dwellers."

Ev didn't seem to be convinced on this point, but Amelia wasn't in a position to argue the merits of Triad scientific theory. If there was some guiding principle of the universe that invalidated randomness, its discovery would be left for future research – maybe the far future, given that any investigation of multiple lives necessarily spanned eons.

"Okay, so they're brilliant and we're barely beyond our stone-age roots. What do they want with us?"

"Two things," Amelia answered. "Connection and amalgamation.

"Frankly my dear, that doesn't sound good."

"I'll explain and maybe it will sound better. They needed Orlando. A shared consciousness is much more valuable than any routine reincarnated consciousness. A single consciousness simultaneously living in two host bodies is very rare, and it often provides a pathway between species. Over their long history, they've been in contact with four other civilizations – we're the fifth. A shared consciousness is a gift, because it connects two civilizations who might be separated by millions of light-years, civilizations who otherwise have no way of knowing the other exists."

Ev pondered what Amelia had just disclosed. "So, a shared consciousness becomes an alert, like a red flashing light that there's some other alien race out there."

"And not just any alien race – a compatible species, one that is capable of supporting a level-three consciousness."

"True," Ev said.

"But there are hurdles to connecting two civilizations. Think about what a shared consciousness looks like for everyone else in the society."

"Fucking wack job."

"Exactly. Throughout human history, anyone with a shared consciousness would have been labeled mentally ill, or consumed by spirits, or whatever the diagnosis was at the time. Only now can we recognize it as something special. When Orlando's condition came up, the Triads jumped at the opportunity. They were pretty miffed at me because I was trying to stop it. Eventually, they decided to reason with me, even offer me gifts. Well... stabbed into my mind but it was still a gift. I guess their seduction worked, because here we are. A physical gateway between two intelligent species – that's pretty cool."

Amelia smiled at the thought. "Now that the door is open, a lot will probably happen, questions back and forth, a lot of getting to know each other, maybe a science and technology exchange, maybe trade missions, who knows? But I do know one big next step. Cognitive amalgamation."

"They're going to merge us into their hive mind?"

"No, no, nothing like that. More along the lines of education. Education is one of those life events that can alter the pattern of consciousness. For example, they want every child on Earth to be taught their language, and they would reciprocate with their own children – or nubs, or whatever they call them. Learning a new language physically alters the brain, bringing it closer in form and function to a native speaker. We've already measured that effect among humans."

"But why do they want us to be more like them?"

"In a word, memory."

"Memory?" Ev took another slug of whiskey, no doubt diminishing her own memory function.

"Memory and consciousness go hand in hand," Amelia continued. "How much of who we are comes from our pattern of consciousness? Some would say we're defined by specific memories assembled and stored over a lifetime. Do I like chocolate because of a childhood treat stored as an episodic memory, then reshaped by the hippocampus into long-term storage in the cerebrum, and now interpreted by me as a feeling? Or is there some curve or angle or dot within my ridiculously complex pattern of consciousness that makes me crave chocolate?"

"It's the nature versus nurture argument," Ev said.

"In a way, it is," Amelia admitted. "What makes me, me? The Triads have carried this question much further. In their fingerprinting efforts, they've found folds within the consciousness pattern that act as repositories of ancient experiences and when triggered, release what we call a feeling. Once triggered, that feeling can be processed and stored by the physical brain as a memory."

"A released bit of ancient consciousness becomes a current memory."

"Well put. It means certain portions of a previous life could be extracted. It might be a recollection, a personal joy or fear, a desire or craving, even a love."

Ev cocked her head. "That might explain my fear of spiders." She held a finger in the air. "And nail clippers. Hideous things, like mini guillotines. Can't stand them."

Ev did have unusually long nails.

Amelia moved to the core of the matter as the revelations implanted into her brain formed words for the first time. "This process of extracting ancient experiences gets harder when you're dealing with two different species. It's easier when the two species are cognitively aligned. The Triads want to get closer to us, learn about us, and measure our patterns of consciousness. They have good reasons to do this. You see, they've already identified several Triads who were humans in their first life."

"Holy shit, that's big." Ev scrunched up one brow. "But if some of their bamboo people were humans, does that mean...?"

"Yup," Amelia confirmed, seeing the light go on in Ev's eye. "The opposite is also true. There are Triads among us. Right now. Ordinary people walking around today, who have no idea they once hopped across a distant planet as an entirely different creature. With help, we can identify those people."

"Holy moly, and then what?"

"Fingerprint that person's consciousness, match them up with their previous existence. Show them who they were before and what life was like then. And, with the person's permission, trigger those ancient experiences that are locked in the folds of their pattern, so they recognize who they truly are."

Ev squirmed. "I prefer to exist on the edges of society, thank you very much. Not sure I want to know what kind of creature I might have been."

"Then don't, it's really no different than DNA. Do you want to know what traits you carry from past ancestors? Send in a swab of your saliva and you can find out. But nobody is forcing you."

"Ancestors are one thing, but in this case, the ancestor is *you*."

"A peek into who you were before. And a way to compare to who you are now."

"And will be again," Ev added.

"Exactly. Nothing is certain, but applying the Triad Snowflake Limit, the probabilities of coming back at some point in the future are in your favor, especially if humans and Triads and other species last for millions of years. You can even prepare for it – education is just one example. An education today carries forward into the future as feelings of curiosity and wonder. Exposing yourself to the unfamiliar is another. If you travel the world and meet people who are different than you, that experience nurtures feelings of empathy, compassion, and collaboration that can be useful in your next life. Carrying these experiences forward becomes an evolution of the mind. Triads have found that 'second lifers' are far more engaged and productive members of society."

Ev tilted her head. "Could I send myself some advice in one of these folds in the pattern? You know… avoid seafood, or never trust men who wear bow ties."

Amelia laughed. "They're working on that, but don't hold your breath." Ev was just being Ev. Who else could she be?

Ev settled into her chair looking pleased. "You love this stuff, don't you?"

Amelia had seen it before. When their conversations went deep, Ev became ever more absorbed. It was why they'd become good friends over the years.

The question reached into Amelia's core. A tight smile spread across her face. "Sure. It's wonderful news. A revelation. Consciousness is larger than life, it's a pattern that repeats and evolves. It might even be integrated into the universe in some special way. It's not just the chance to live again, it gives me a new perspective on my work too. Can I find evidence of repetition deep down inside the minds of my patients? Can I isolate their long-term pattern from their current incarnation in the here and now? Is it possible to separate the intrinsic underlying person from a mental affliction they carry while in this life?"

"Raises even more questions," Ev correctly pointed out.

Amelia shrugged, smiling. "We get some answers, we form some new questions. That's how science works. Maybe that's how life works. But I love the idea of it all."

"A second life?"

"A fresh start. A second chance with a full life ahead, a chance to explore, to answer questions, to learn, to experience... to love. A second chance for me, for you, for everyone."

CHAPTER FORTY

HUMANITY

Three weeks later...

NEW FRIENDS SAT in a curved nook that acted as the dining room in Amelia's cozy cottage on Phinney Ridge. Leaded glass panel windows overlooked a rose garden that glowed pink in the fading light of evening. The meal was impromptu and delivered in plain white boxes, the wine flowed without end along with sporadic laughter and the profound joy of life renewed.

Orlando did most of the talking. His wife Teena sat next to him, a broad smile never leaving her lips. A lovely Asian woman, Teena's long black hair was tied back in a ponytail, just as she'd been portrayed in Orlando's first dream – the woman lying on a towel at Santa Monica beach. Amelia felt like she already knew her. They'd become friends in just the few hours since they'd met.

Amelia sat opposite the happy couple, sipping wine, and absorbing Orlando's astonishing story.

"The inserts are permanent," Orlando said lifting his hair and showing a small scar behind each ear. "They'll keep the motor control and nervous system for both bodies independent and allow me to switch between visual and auditory senses at will. The inserts even wall off sections of memory for private use. I can only access private memory when I consciously put myself into that body. It's weird, but nice, almost like having a little brother – or maybe more like an alter ego. Most of the time, having two bodies won't be a problem because my Triad body sleeps while my human version is awake, and vice versa. There's some overlap while both are awake, but these brain inserts make it manageable."

"Amazing," Amelia said, engrossed. The Triads had crafted a fair solution that she'd never dreamed was possible. The shared consciousness remained, and neither version of Orlando suffered. On the contrary, he looked like he was thriving.

"I go back for a checkup next week – and probably some more training. Teena, too, assuming her parents can take the kids."

"You're going to their planet?" Amelia asked Teena.

Teena opened her eyes wide and held both palms to her cheeks in mock horror. "Just walk right through the portal, so they tell me. I don't even need a space suit." She pulled on Orlando's arm, snuggling close. "He wants to show me, and well… I owe him one. He was right all along."

Husband and wife locked eyes providing an unspoken aura of a relationship reset for the better. Orlando kissed Teena on the temple. "There's nothing to worry about. The Triads are super careful about human visitors. Their planet is kind of like Florida. Warm, humid, maybe a little musty, but they're going to add an air filter to the pod they assigned to me. Dust mites, apparently. They're always analyzing something every time I visit in my human body."

"How about food?" Amelia asked, jealous of the adventure these two would soon undertake. "Can your human body eat their food?"

"They're vegetarians, which seems strange when you think about it. They have some tasty fruits that grow in the jungle, plus a potato kind of root they cultivate and eat in a paste on thin strips of bread.

They inhale the bread strips through their... well, it's kind of gross, but it's just the way they –"

Amelia held up a hand and stopped him before the gross part had a chance to permanently lodge in her mind. "I notice you say 'they' instead of 'we'. Don't get me wrong, I think it's wonderful that you think of yourself as human, but I'm curious how you resolved that conflict."

Orlando tipped his head back and forth. "To tell you the truth, I switch when I'm consciously inhabiting my other body. If I refer to humans, I say, *zhek*, which means 'they'."

"Huh, makes sense," Amelia replied. She might never get used to a friend with two bodies, but his human version was doing quite well.

"Orlando is fluent in their language now," Teena said, proudly beaming at him. "He's teaching me a few words too, but it's a struggle to pronounce them. And I thought Korean was hard!" Teena had an infectious laugh and Amelia found herself laughing along.

"If all goes well," Orlando explained, "I'll be an emissary between the two worlds. I'll help both sides understand the other as we work toward a vision of cognitive amalgamation. Early on, I think most of it will just be getting humans used to Triads."

"They are pretty ugly," Amelia admitted.

"That's what they say about humans," Orlando countered.

Amelia nodded. "Fair. So, when you go there, you always go through the portal? Nobody flies in a spaceship, right?"

"Too far, I think. One of their scientists told me our two planets are on different arms of the Milky Way. I don't know how far that is, but it sounded like it would take multiple lifetimes in a spaceship. Since they have this great portal technology, I don't think there's any reason to fly."

"The portal is pretty handy."

"Made possible by the shared consciousness. It's the way civilizations find each other – mind to mind. The Triads will teach us what to look for, and maybe someday we'll find another level-three species. I'm also documenting how to build the portal. The technology gets handed down from one civilization to the next. I doubt anyone even knows where it started."

The otherworldly conversation continued as darkness enveloped the rose garden outside. They veered between topics ranging from the Triad transportation system – membrane bubbles compressed inside hydraulic tubes – to how creatures with no opposable thumbs managed to create such advanced technology. Tendrils came up often.

When Amelia's orange and white cat jumped up onto her lap, Teena took the hint. "I think Jinx is telling us it's time to go."

Amelia pleaded. "Stay in touch, please. You won't disappear to an exotic planet on another arm of the galaxy will you?"

All three stood, and Teena wrapped her arms around Amelia. "I wouldn't think of it. You saved my husband, Amelia. I can never thank you enough." Her eyes glistened when she pulled away.

"New friends, then," Amelia said. "Stop by anytime you're in Seattle."

"Which could be a lot, given that the only portal is here," Orlando added, coming over to hug Amelia too.

Amelia maintained the warm embrace with her former patient. "They're going to keep the portal in that old workshop?"

"Beats me. I guess they'll move it somewhere more secure once they figure out how. The military took over. I think it was even some people from DARPA."

"Reformed, I hope."

"Definitely, reformed. That senator was all over it. I think she put somebody new in charge and sent Major Shepard for a psychological evaluation at a DARPA facility in Virginia. The goo zoo? Something like that."

Amelia rolled her eyes. "I've heard rumors of it, but I thought it was just a sick joke. I hope they don't really erase patient's memories, not even Shepard's. That's not therapy, it's cruelty."

Orlando locked eyes with Amelia, his tone becoming serious. "I was a tough patient, wasn't I?"

Amelia smiled. "An unusual experience, shall we say."

Orlando smiled back. "Thanks for everything, Amelia. You gave me back my life – a little weirder, yes, but I'm still here. I would have died without you." He turned to the door, turned back, and held one finger in the air. "Oh, one more thought."

"Yes?"

"If I can swing it with the people in charge, would you be free next Wednesday for a couple of days?"

Amelia froze in place, immediately recognizing what he was asking. "You're kidding."

"No, I'm not. Join us. Come to their planet. I'm sure Prime Arc would be happy to be your tour guide."

"Uh..." Images of jungle plants, babbling streams, jumping bugs and bark-faced, tripod-hopping creatures shooting razor sharp tendrils flew through her mind.

Or I could have coffee with Ev at The Spheres. Ev would scream if she knew Amelia had turned down such an incredible offer.

Amelia shrugged. "What the hell, you only live once." She stopped, catching herself. "I guess we have to throw out that expression and come up with something better now." She reached up and kissed Orlando on his cheek. "Sure, if you can swing it with the big shots, I'd love to go."

"Fantastic," Orlando said, hugging her tight.

"So exciting!" Teena added.

The new friends parted leaving Amelia alone with Jinx and wondering if she'd just signed up for another horror show complete with additional opportunities to rearrange parts of her brain.

She picked up Jinx and nuzzled the cat's wet nose. "You don't mind if I pop off to another planet, do you?"

Jinx twisted, providing a clear message she didn't wish to be held right at this moment. Amelia set her down and the cat trotted away. "You're worse than the aliens. Everything has to be on your terms."

Amelia washed and put away the wine glasses, then took creaky stairs down to her basement. It had always been the laundry and storage room in her house, but recently she'd done some remodeling, adding carpeting and a large drafting desk with a surface that could be tilted. Multiple sheets of drawing paper were scattered across the desk, along with colored pencils, chalk, and artist charcoal.

A few, mostly finished sketches were taped haphazardly on the walls around the desk. Amelia flipped on a studio lamp and sat in the matching artist's chair. Her latest creation was taped to the desk's drawing surface. Curving pencil strokes formed a tranquil outdoor scene along the shoreline of a lake. Tree branches parted in the center of the drawing to reveal a boat dock jutting straight out into the water.

It was the family lake house. She had been there so many times she had every branch of every tree memorized and had easily depicted it in a pencil sketch – a showcase of her newly acquired talent.

A canoe was tied up at one side of the dock and two teenage boys leaned into the canoe to pull out oars. A girl sat cross-legged on the dock's rough wooden surface, slender, with short cut hair and a wistful, faraway look, as if she were daydreaming of times gone by, or times yet to come.

"You were so beautiful, Natalie," Amelia said to her drawing. A tear formed in the corner of her eye and she brushed it away.

Her new drawing would replace the photograph that hung on her bedroom wall – a picture of the same boat dock but without any people. For years, that simple photograph, little more than planks of wood stretching out over the water, had evoked strong memories. Empty space is sometimes just as meaningful especially when an anguished mind needs to heal.

"I wish you could see me now. The things I've accomplished. Heck, the things I might be doing soon! I know you'd be proud."

Recently, it had become easier to think about Natalie, and cathartic to draw her image. Her hair, her eyebrows, the coloring on her cheeks. Though others might call them identical, twins are well aware of their physical differences, however minor. Drawing Natalie brought every memory back.

The two boys helping to fill the canvas were neighbors, madly in love with Amelia and Natalie at the time. She'd drawn Henri with oars in his hand, and Paul reaching into the docked canoe to fish out empty beer cans the underage teens weren't supposed to have. Paul's eyes looked up, a hint of rebellion in his smile.

Fresh young faces, drawn from memory. Years gone by, with old friends moving in different directions. One of those lives had ended far too soon.

Amelia lowered her head and the tears came on strong, streaming down her face and dripping onto the desk. Good tears. With all she'd learned, there were fewer reasons now to be sad.

"I think you're going to get a second chance, Natalie. Another life. You'll be better next time, healthier. I'm sure you will."

Amelia would never know when or where Natalie might get her second chance at life. It could be next week, or centuries from now. Here on Earth, or perhaps on some faraway planet. But it would still be the essence of Natalie – her unique pattern of consciousness.

Amelia's voice quavered as she fought back the tears. "If this universe is big enough and lasts long enough... then you'll live many times. I will too. We all will."

She laughed, sniffling. "Time for me to become an astronomer, sis. Maybe I can figure out how long this cosmos will last. Given enough time, every probability will come true. Maybe in some distant future, other versions of us will cross paths. We'd recognize each other right away, I know we would. That would be amazing."

Another drip ran down her cheek. "Probably a fantasy. It's still a roll of the dice to see if your number comes up." Amelia sniffed. "No guarantees. If it turns out that life is a one-time thing for me, well... all I can do is promise you I'll make the most of my life. For both of us."

CHAPTER FORTY-ONE

EPILOGUE

THE CURVING WALLS inside the blue pastel pod arched overhead to become the ceiling without a single seam that disrupted the smooth progression from vertical to horizontal. The windowless room was small with only a few fittings within its space, none of which acted as chairs or tables. The conference wouldn't last long.

Prime Arc and two Triad advisors hunched over a flat surface that displayed complex markings and drawings, some that extended above its surface as three-dimensional elements. Tendrils flew as the trio communicated and interacted with the objects and writing displayed before them.

A predefined imprint has never been attempted with humans. Can it even be done? one advisor asked.

Unknown, puffed the second advisor. *We have, however, obtained two willing humans, ready to conceive. Failure to imprint would simply result in a non-specific consciousness, no different than random.*

With no harm to the female infant carrier? Prime Arc asked.

None, the second advisor answered. *No different than if the imprint procedure were done at our infant growth facility.*

But why choose Amelia as the biological indicator? asked the first advisor. *We have no need for further interaction with this individual.*

Prime Arc shot a tendril toward its face, stopping just short of touch. *As I have said before, this plan is not about Amelia. Any pair of human biological duplicates will do, but I believe Amelia will be highly receptive. I know her mind. She is one of a small subset of humans whose intellect remains above fear and suspicion. Too many humans still languish in their past.*

The second advisor chimed in. *In addition, we have already taken a sample from Amelia.*

That part of their plan had been accomplished on day one, the day the alignment device initialized. Prime Arc itself had wrapped a tendril around Amelia's head, communicating to the human, but also retrieving a sample of her DNA.

Very well, I agree to the terms, the first advisor said.

Then we move forward, Prime Arc announced, touching a tendril to the screen, and communicating a decision via data packets and checksums. The images disappeared and the lighting inside the pod dimmed as the group left via an opening centered in the floor.

****

One year later...

Amelia shut the car door and leaned in through the open window. "Thanks for the ride, Nils. It was very kind of you."

The seven-hour flight to Reykjavik was made far more pleasant by Nils' enjoyable company. Within minutes after plunking down in the seat next to him, they'd hit it off. Eligible guys seemed to be popping up everywhere now that Amelia was back in the game. While Nils lived in Reykjavik, he made regular trips to Seattle to meet with software engineers at Microsoft.

"When you've finished your personal business, I hope you'll join me." Nils flashed polished white teeth. Were all Icelanders this clean? After dropping off her suitcase at a hotel, he had invited her to lunch, or dinner, or breakfast, or coffee. She'd laughed as the list grew, taking the edge off her nervousness of what lay ahead. She'd come a long way to meet three special people – and now that time had come.

"Today is really important for me, and I don't know how long I'll be. But I promise I'll call you after." Nils nodded, and she waved goodbye as the car drove off.

Amelia turned to face the elegant seaside house. Slate decorated one side, and a steep-pitched blue metal roof probably did a good job of keeping the winter snow from piling up. Through a side gate, Amelia caught a glimpse of the cold blue water of Skerjafjörður inlet, one of the many lovely views along this jagged coastline. The couple who lived here seemed well off.

She smiled at the green and white Mini parked in the driveway, essentially the same car she drove back in Seattle. Coincidence or a meaningful sign, it didn't really matter. It showed they were practical people. She'd already learned a few things about this couple. Both in their early thirties, they worked in government jobs, spoke English fluently, and spent summer weekends hiking around their beautiful country. She didn't know much more, except that they'd just had a baby. A very special child, though the government hadn't released the nature of the birth – and might never out of respect for the family's privacy.

Amelia straightened her clothes as she stood erect on the porch, took a deep breath, and knocked on the door. Voices inside confirmed they were expecting her.

The door opened to a tall, thin man with a broad smile. "You must be Amelia," he said in flawless English. He offered his hand, then withdrew. "What am I'm doing? You're not just anyone." He held out both arms wide, and Amelia reciprocated in a warm hug.

"It's so nice to finally meet you, Ian," Amelia said. "I hope I'm not interrupting nap time or anything like that."

"No, no," he replied ushering her in to the foyer. "Katrin's awake, just sitting by the geotherm."

Ian guided Amelia into a living room with comfortable chairs around a warm radiator complete with a simulated a view of crackling wood burning in a fireplace. It looked real.

A pretty, blonde-haired woman holding a bundle of blankets in her arms stood up. "Amelia! I recognize you from your picture. Gracious, you've come so far."

She sidled up to Amelia and pulled a blanket back to reveal a tiny face with a pug nose and eyes shut.

"Oh my... Katrin, she's so beautiful," Amelia said, poking the blanket around the newborn's face. Amelia held a hand over her mouth as tears formed. She'd waited months for this day and now that it was here, she hardly knew what to say.

Katrin gently rocked the baby in her arms. "We named her Natalie. After all, that's who she is. She has two middle names, Freyja, after Ian's grandmother, and Amelia, for you."

"That's..." Amelia choked up, taking a minute to recover. "Katrin, Ian, I'm really touched."

Katrin lifted the bundled child. "Would you like to hold her?"

Amelia nodded rapidly, and Katrin carefully transferred the bundle into her arms. The baby made a few cooing sounds and smacked her lips but didn't wake.

Amelia cooed back. "Oh, you are such a sweetie. It's just so hard to believe. Are you really Natalie?"

"They can't know for sure," Ian explained. "But they had a positive match, based on your DNA, the same quality of match they get for Triads. Since it's the first time they've done an imprint on a human, we'll all have to wait and see."

"An imprint – that's what they call it?" Amelia asked. She'd only been given the barest of details when the request for her approval came from a Triad representative a few months prior. Amelia had agreed right away, though she'd commented that approval from the prospective parents was far more important.

Ian tucked the blanket around his daughter. "The way it was described to us, there's nothing magical about imprinting a consciousness, it's purely medical technology but well beyond anything human doctors could do. The procedure was non-invasive, with just a few tests in a hospital here. Once she hit her tenth week, Katrin and I flew to Seattle and stepped through the gateway."

"They made it easy," Katrin said. "They took us to a pod called the implant facility. I never felt a thing, though the machine they put me in was a little intimidating – kind of like an MRI."

"Wow, you two have got to be the bravest parents in the world," Amelia said, rocking the tiny newcomer.

"Pioneers, perhaps, but new parents like anyone else," Ian said. "We're a test case, of course, since it seems more likely this process would be used to re-imprint the greatest thinkers of the past. Einstein? Da Vinci? I suppose it depends on whether they can sort through their database and identify the right pattern of consciousness."

"Great thinkers aside, there's no doubt that this little test case is a beautiful, healthy child." Amelia was suddenly aware of what she'd just said. "I mean... I hope there's no chance of... you know."

Ian shook his head. "They told us that depression is an affliction caused by physical brain chemistry. It's not transferrable via the pattern of consciousness. She'll be as healthy as any other child."

Amelia breathed a sigh of relief.

"Will you help us as she grows up?" Katrin asked.

Amelia choked up again. "I'd be so honored. Whatever I can do."

"The doctors have a prescribed plan," Ian explained, "first to see if Natalie recognizes on her own that this is her second life, and then to find out how much she remembers from her first life. All this will take time – years – but as she grows older, you'll have a role too. The doctors are calling you a memory trigger. Our little Natalie might recognize you, possibly with a reaction that is verifiable even before she learns to talk. By the way, no one knows when that might be. It's possible, she'll begin to speak earlier than most children. The Triads have seen significant differences like that among their own newborns. Now, we'll find out if something similar happens in humans."

"Wow, it's a brave new world," Amelia said, shaking her head. "Just say the word, I'll come as often as you'll have me."

The three adults gathered closer together, watching intently as the baby's eyes cracked open just enough to reveal blue irises. No recognition, but Amelia didn't expect it. Natalie's journey would take time, just as Ian had said.

Amelia touched a finger to the tiny nose nestled in the blankets. "Hey, cutie. Who's in there? I can't wait to find out!"

THE END

AFTERWORD

I hope you enjoyed the story, I enjoyed writing it! Shall we chat for a few more minutes? Maybe talk about the real science in the story? And the made-up stuff, too?

Let's start with neuroscience. While researching for this book, I read a lot about the human brain, some of it quite entertaining but much of it too dense for the average person (including me). The most interesting books were about human consciousness, primarily because even the best neuroscientists don't have a solid answer for the question, what is consciousness?

I've expressed my own thoughts in this story, but if you'd like to dive deeper into the science surrounding this fundamental question, try *Consciousness: Confessions of a Romantic Reductionist*, by Dr. Christof Koch. It's an easy read by one of the leaders in the field and gets to the heart of the mystical nature of consciousness.

Dr. Koch, along with Francis Crick of DNA fame, were the principal scientists who defined neuronal correlates of consciousness (NCC), which are complex structures often connecting hundreds of neurons to represent a single snippet of thought – an object, an emotion, a smell. Yes, NCCs are real science – I didn't make this up! However, the reality of NCCs is somewhat more complicated than I represented. With 86 billion neurons and possibly 100 trillion synapses in the human brain, NCC maps are astoundingly complex, and because so much is still unknown, neuroscientists are not sure whether every real-world object can be matched to a specific pattern in the brain.

In chapter 4 (Correlates), Jake (the institute's computer guru) admits to Amelia that protection against dangerous SPIKEs is limited to the NCCs they've mapped so far – about 21 percent of the brain. Jake and Amelia act like coverage is lacking, but any neuroscientist today would love to understand this much about specific brain functions. The human brain is so complex that even top experts are beginners. As Dr. Koch remarked in 2019: "We don't even understand the brain of a worm."

Are SPIKEs real? Yes, but I fibbed about their role – sci-fi authors do that sometimes. In neuroscience language, a *spike train* is a term for a series of action potentials (electrical pulses leaving an axon, the connection point for a neuron). Perfectly normal brain function – and boring. So, I decided a SPIKE should be a SPontaneous Interneural Kinetic Electrogenesis transmitted from one person to another. Fictional, but way more fun.

How about assisted lucid dreams? Can neuroscientists map NCCs from one brain and generate hallucinations in another? As of today, Amelia's ALD sessions – from level one to level three – are fictional, but I wouldn't be surprised to see this technology in the near future. Already, there are techniques for managing a lucid dream, and neuroscience researchers have successfully transferred patterns representing real-world phenomena from one brain to another. Check out this study that scientifically analyzed lucid dreams:

http://theconversation.com/the-ability-to-control-dreams-may-help-us-unravel-the-mystery-of-consciousness-52394

or this brain-to-brain technology, BrainNet:

http://interestingengineering.com/brainnet-is-the-worlds-first-non-invasive-brain-to-brain-interface

In chapter 21 (Consciousness), Amelia says, "Consciousness derives from vast stores of integrated information and the diversity of brain cells." She's referring to Integrated Information Theory (IIT), an astonishing proposal from Italian neurobiologist Dr. Giulio Tononi and backed up by reams of experimental data. The theory says that any system whose components are both integrated (tied together) and differentiated (distinct from one another) is conscious to some degree. The more components you have that are integrated and differentiated, the more conscious you are. Humans have 86 billion components (neurons) that are connected in 100 trillion ways, which is what gives rise to our advanced consciousness. But dogs and cats are conscious too – any pet owner knows that. And so are birds, and fish, and worms, and even bacteria – to a degree. IIT uses a mathematical formula to compute the level of consciousness, which dwindles as more primitive forms of life are measured, but never gets to zero.

Carry this theory to its extremes. Are plants conscious? A living tree certainly has as much biological complexity as a worm, but it might not have much integration. It's alive, we all agree on that, but is there some modicum of consciousness there? Hard to say. How about a computer AI, like Kori? Conscious or not? How about the internet itself? How would we know? Maybe someday the internet will take an action on its own, and we'll collectively hold our hands over our mouths and say "Damn, we're screwed".

Integrated Information Theory. Fun stuff. Real.

Later in chapter 21, Ev asks, "What is consciousness? Some believe it's just our brain fooling us into thinking we're special. Others say it's the soul, or something magical that is endowed to us when we're born." Ev is stating two competing theories among neuroscientists (and philosophers). The first is the argument from *materialists*, that we are nothing more than the electrical sparks within our brain and that someday science will explain how those complex sparks form into a consciousness. This is standard stuff in science, usually referred to as reductionism.

The second theory is the *dualist* argument, that consciousness is separate from the brain, and has no physicality itself, at least none that we've yet recognized. This is not just a philosophical or religious question, it's an ongoing discussion among those in the neuroscience field. Real science with no firm answers yet. If the dualists are right, we still have much to learn.

Let's wrap up neuroscience by mentioning the title of this story, *Phenomena* (the plural of phenomenon). In chapter 23 (Level Three), I use the term *phenomenal experience* (please note that in this context, phenomenal doesn't mean "remarkable", it means "perceptible"). The phenomenal experience is that daily parade of sights, touches, sounds, and smells generated by external objects (phenomena) and sampled by our sensory organs. Philosophers call it a *veridical perception*; our ability to perceive an objective world outside of our internal consciousness. Whatever you call it, this rich experience is closely tied to consciousness. If we had no sensory organs, would we still be conscious? What if we had two sets of sensory organs? Orlando did. How would that change our phenomenal experience? This is why I chose *Phenomena* for the title.

In any fictional book, casual references to real people and places are common and acceptable. Now that we're past the fictional part, I would like to point out one real-life hero of neuroscience, Paul Allen, who founded the Allen Institute for Brain Science in Seattle. Allen made his fortune early in life as the cofounder of Microsoft (along with Bill Gates), but instead of retiring to a life of luxury, he pursued a variety of philanthropies and community projects (many in the Seattle area) including neuroscience.

Sadly, Paul Allen died in 2018 but institutes and foundations live on, continuing their amazing work to tease out the structure and function of the human brain. The Allen Institute for Brain Science, along with the Kavli Foundation (in Los Angeles) and the National Institute for Health (with associated labs around the country), collectively gave me the inspiration for the fictional Westlake Institute for Neuroscience. To my knowledge, none of the real organizations have a sleep lab or focus on dream studies, but who knows, maybe someday?

Have you been to Seattle? The story has lots of references to places in and around the city, and they're all real. The University of Washington is one of the primary settings, and the Materials Science and Engineering department really does create organometallics. And, while administrators at the Wilson Metals Lab might not allow students to create trimethylaluminum, this exotic metal really is pyrophoric (spontaneously combusts).

Seattle has four lovely old drawbridges that span the ship canal connecting Lake Washington to Puget Sound: Ballard, Fremont, University, and Montlake bridges. Built in the 1910s, they have metal grate decks that are a bit frightening to drive across due to the shimmy effect (it feels like you just hit a patch of ice). When a bridge is opened to let a sailboat pass, car traffic backs up, so Seattleites have a love-hate relationship with these iconic bridges. And yes, they are still manually operated by an attendant who sits in one of the towers.

Washington State Ferries is the second largest ferry system in the world (behind only the Star Ferry in Hong Kong). With 23 vessels and 20 terminals scattered around Puget Sound, it's an integral part of the state highway system. The largest vessel in the fleet, the MV Puyallup, crosses between Edmonds and Kingston 26 times each day. If you visit Seattle, take a ferry just for fun!

The Spheres is also a real place in downtown Seattle. Three geodesic domes of glass and steel surround a beautiful terrarium of exotic plants from temperate rainforests around the world. The innovative concept brings nature into the office, and I can personally attest that sitting beside a gurgling stream is a soothing work experience. As I wrote in the story, The Spheres is office space but is briefly open to the public on the first Saturday of each month. Scattered at various levels inside are fake stumps used for ventilation. Really!

DARPA, the Defense Advanced Research Projects Agency, is a military organization for advanced research into a variety of topics, including neuroscience. They really do have a Super Soldier program with plans to integrate the human brain with weapons systems. Kind of scary, if you ask me.

As I researched the final chapter, I learned that baby names in Iceland must be approved by the government. There's a list! Unfortunately, both Natalie and Amelia are not on that list. Alas, a slight inconsistency, but I figure that since baby Natalie is a special case, the Icelandic government might relent and allow Ian and Katrin to name their child whatever they want.

Thanks for reading,

Douglas Phillips

If you'd like more details plus a lot of pictures and diagrams related to the story, please go to my web page: http://douglasphillipsbooks.com.

While you're there, add your name to my email list and I'll keep you informed about new books I'm writing and upcoming events.

If you enjoyed this book, please consider writing a short review (in addition to your star rating). It takes only a minute, and your review helps future readers as well as the author (books and book series really do live or die on reviews). For more information on how to leave a review, go to http://douglasphillipsbooks.com/contact.

ACKNOWLEDGMENTS

Many thanks to my author friends at Critique Circle, especially Kathryn Hoff, Ophélie Quillier, Michael Wellmeier, Valtteri, and Calvin Clark, and to Victoria Kelly for help during my initial research.

A special thank you to my neuroscience consultants S.B. Divya and Benjamin Kinney who pointed out several egregious flaws in my drafts. Your references provided me with hours of fascinating reading and your insights helped me integrate real brain science into a fictional narrative. I may not have followed every recommendation, but where I deviated, I blame the author's prerogative for keeping the story tight.

Thanks so much to early beta readers Bill Gill, Jeff Baker, and Lili Vandulek, and final beta readers Jeff Cantwell, Ron Almstead, Lisa Manuel, Brad Carroll, Nancy Lauren, and Laura Moreno. Your comments gave me a good feel for how this story is absorbed when it gets beyond my tiny sphere of experience.

The beautiful sketch of Amelia's face (or was it Natalie's?) was drawn by MJ Sullivan. MJ did a remarkable job of creating stunning art, while keeping it simple and thus believable to the story. Wonderful! Check out her work at: http://mjsullivanart.com.

The gorgeous cover was created by Karri Klawiter, a very talented graphic artist who has crafted some of the best: http://artbykarri.com.

As always, thanks to my wife Marlene for putting up with all the weirdness, my dream obsessions, and my regular detours to obscure locations in and around Seattle that only made sense to me.

ABOUT THE AUTHOR

In addition to *Phenomena*, Douglas Phillips is the author of the best-selling Quantum Series, a trilogy of science fiction thrillers set in the fascinating world of particle physics where bizarre is an everyday thing. In each story, the pace is quick and the protagonists—along with the reader—are drawn deeper into mysteries that require intellect, not bullets, to resolve.

Douglas has two science degrees, has designed and written predictive computer models, reads physics books for fun and peers into deep space through the eyepiece of his backyard telescope.

The Quantum Series

<u>Quantum Incident</u> (Prologue)

The long-sought Higgs boson has been discovered at the Large Hadron Collider in Geneva. Scientists rejoice in the confirmation of quantum theory, but a reporter attending the press conference believes they may be hiding something.

Nala Pasquier is a particle physicist at Fermi National Laboratory in Illinois. Building on the 2012 discovery, she has produced a working prototype with capabilities that are nothing less than astonishing.

Daniel Rice is a government science investigator with a knack for uncovering the details that others miss. But when he's assigned to investigate a UFO over Nevada, he'll need more than scientific skills. He'll need every bit of patience he can muster.

Quantum Space (Book 1)

High above the windswept plains of Kazakhstan, three astronauts on board a Russian Soyuz capsule begin their reentry. A strange shimmer in the atmosphere, a blinding flash of light, and the capsule vanishes in a blink as though it never existed.

On the ground, evidence points to a catastrophic failure, but a communications facility halfway around the world picks up a transmission that could be one of the astronauts. Tragedy averted, or merely delayed? A classified government project on the cutting edge of particle physics holds the clues, and with lives on the line, there is little time to waste.

Daniel Rice is a government science investigator. Marie Kendrick is a NASA operations analyst. Together, they must track down the cause of the most bizarre event in the history of human spaceflight. They draw on scientific strengths as they plunge into the strange world of quantum physics, with impacts not only to the missing astronauts, but to the entire human race.

Quantum Void (Book 2)

Particle physics was always an unlikely path to the stars, but with the discovery that space could be compressed, the entire galaxy had come within reach. The technology was astonishing, yet nothing compared to what humans encountered four thousand light years from home. Now, with an invitation from a mysterious gatekeeper, the people of Earth must decide if they're ready to participate in the galactic conversation.

The world anxiously watches as a team of four katanauts, suit up to visit an alien civilization. What they learn on a watery planet hundreds of light years away could catapult human comprehension of the natural world to new heights. But one team member must overcome crippling fear to cope with an alien gift she barely understands.

Back at Fermilab, strange instabilities are beginning to show up in experiments, leading physicists to wonder if they ever really had control over the quantum dimensions of space.

Quantum Time (Book 3)

A dying man stumbles into a police station and collapses. In his fist is a mysterious coin with strange markings. He tells the police he's from the future, and when they uncover the coin's hidden message, they're inclined to believe him.

Daniel Rice never asked for fame but his key role in Earth's first contact with an alien civilization thrust him into a social arena where any crackpot might take aim. When the FBI arrives at his door and predictions of the future start coming true, Daniel is dragged into a mission to save the world from nuclear holocaust. To succeed, he'll need to exploit cobbled-together alien technology to peer into a world thirty years beyond his own.

For these and other works by Douglas Phillips, please visit http://douglasphillipsbooks.com. While you're there, sign up to the mailing list to stay informed on new books in the works and upcoming events.

Made in the USA
Middletown, DE
12 September 2020